Broken Bars

Chris Allred

Published in 2009 by New Generation Publishing
c/o Legend Press, 2 London Wall Buildings,
London EC2M 5UU
www.newgenerationpublishing.info

Broken Bars

Chris Allred

Cover design by

Chris Rizzo Design

To Kari

For all of her love and support

My Love

My Life

My Wife

Habeas Corpus was nationally revoked when President *Abraham Lincoln* declared Martial Law on Tuesday, September 15, 1863…one hundred and fifty-six years later; it happened again.

PROLOGUE

The look of surprise as the unknown screamed by, and the brief sound of panic and confusion as the weapon detonated upon impact. Buildings crumbled in an instant, and flesh burned from its victim's skin before the light devoured them.

"Please," a young man watched as the missile struck its target. "Why? I have a wife and child on the…" The young man was gone along with everyone around him.

Ground Zero left no evidence except ash and debris. Separating who from who would be impossible, and once again America felt vulnerable to a mass assassination of life.

The war that crushed the belief that America was the foremost super power of the world started on Wednesday, March 23, 2016. Moments after the United States government received Russia's Declaration of War, a PT-2УТТХ Тополь-М nuclear missile struck America's most populous city. Millions of innocent American citizens were killed, and millions of others hopelessly watched as the Statue of

Liberty, freedom, and the American way of life fell for the first time in its history as a unified country.

"Mr. President, Russia hit New York City. It's a total disaster, 9/11 had nothing on this," John Andrews sputtered as he ran into the Oval Office without a knock on the door.

"How many dead?" The overwhelmed President asked as reports from the attack came over every radio and television station across the U.S.

"It's too early to tell sir, and the demographics don't give an accurate estimate either, because most of the causalities probably lived outside of the blast zone. It happened in the middle of the freaking workday. For God sakes we had children and families outside enjoying the uncommonly warm weather. Did you know that the cherry blossoms in New York were already in bloom? Funny…I saw something on the news last night about this warm streak…or Global Warming…or something, and how people are bringing their families to the city to enjoy the weather. Sad…because either way, they're probably all dead." Andrews shook his head with remorse of what the people of such a young country have been through.

"Andrews, do we have any Intel of what hit us, or what we can do to keep it from happening again? I don't want to be a sitting duck," the worried faced U.S. President stated as he put his elbows on his desk, and his face in his unshakeable hands.

"At this time Mr. President we have an unconfirmed report from an inside source that stated Russia fired a RT-2UTT Topol-M intercontinental ballistic missile which was modified before deployment to carry six nuclear warheads. Again, that was an unconfirmed report..." The leader of the free world cut Andrews' words short.

"Unconfirmed or not...NYC was pummeled by a nuclear blast of some sort," President Mason replied as he stood up from his thoughts to face the Secretary of Defense.

"Yes, Mr. President...and the people are scared." The Secretary of Defense turned his head towards the opened door to try and hear the news report from the television in the other room.

"John...we need to evacuate the Northern part of the Eastern seaboard. Do we have any idea on what we are looking at for immediate and future effects from a nuclear blast?" The President's words snapped Andrews' attention back to their present situation.

"We have a team of top scientists and military personnel working on what we should immediately expect from a nuclear detonation in an area like New York City, and the delayed effects in all the outlaying fallout areas." John turned back towards President Mason.

The President walked over to Secretary of Defense Andrews and put his right hand on the back of Andrews' shoulder. "Do we have an ETA?"

"No sir…they're working as fast and as diligently as they can. The truth is…that we weren't prepared. We knew that we were not prepared after the September 11 attacks of 2001, but we did not do enough to keep it from happening again; and this time we're looking at millions dead." The Secretary of Defense took his own words to heart as he spoke them.

"No one knew, John. We could not have stopped this." President Mason faced John Andrews as a friend, "This was not our fault. 9/11 was a terrorist attack that showed the world that they could find a so-called chink in our armor; and they did, and it hurt for a long time…it still does. This was an all out attack of aggression in the form of a nuclear weapon being fired into the heart of our country. This isn't a terrorist attack…this is war. A war that will be fought on our soil if need be. The terrorists may have exposed a weakness, but the Russians exploited it. They knew what made us tick, and they attacked without any remorse for human life." The thought of the entire notion enraged the U.S. leader.

Nobody knew that the Russian Federation was capable of such a feat. In the early twenty first century Russia became increasingly upset with the U.S. and the United Nations for questioning them on their missing nuclear missiles, and the Unified Korea's sudden leap as a nuclear threat to the free world. Russia eventually removed themselves as permanent members of the United Nations, and closed their boarders to all outside influences. Russia remained a partial democracy with high communistic tendencies. President Ubiikobyla was elected by his people, and soon thereafter made it clear that General Rachlav would be his successor, which gave the General total control over the massive Russian military. General Rachlav ran his country with complete and absolute military control, and to many he was the true and actual ruler of Russia despite Ubiikobyla in the role of presidency.

CHAPTER 1

Rachlav was a boy, twelve or thirteen years of age, when the Communist USSR fell with the help of two unlikely allies, Russia's *Mikhail Gorbachev* and the United States' *Ronald Reagan*; even though they were not the only people that changed the face of Communism in the Soviet Union, nor was this change done overnight. In Rachlav's opinion, however, they were the two individuals that elevated themselves to celebrity status over Russia's embarrassing downfall. Even in Rachlav's village, he heard the immortal words as they eerily echoed from the wall in Germany spoken by the United States' President *Reagan*.

"General Secretary Gorbachev, if you seek peace, if you seek prosperity for the Soviet Union and Eastern Europe, if you seek liberalization: Come here to this gate! Mr. Gorbachev, open this gate! Mr. Gorbachev, tear down this wall!"

Rachlav was old enough to see what those new Democratic ways of thinking did to his father, and fathers of his friends in the small village that he grew up in. Times had always been hard, but then they became almost unbearable with the so-called help of the Americans.

"Father, why don't we fight the Americans?" Young Rachlav questioned as he slammed the blade of his axe into the piece of timber from the pile of wood he and his father had been chopping.

The elder Rachlav looked deep into his boy's eyes and said, "Fighting is not always the answer my son."

"But Father, we were at the brink of war with the Americans even before I was born, and now we call them allies. War creates opportunities; war creates men. Let us fight for our own freedoms, not the American's. Why is their way right, and ours wrong? Father can't you see, the Americans are destroying us; they're winning the war." The teary eyed boy ran off before his father thought him weak.

Rachlav's father tried hard to embrace a new way of thinking, but his forty plus years of life under Communist control was a hard thing to forget. Besides Democracy did not work in a land that did not know change. They were not in the city. They were not in Moscow, a place where laws are changed, and people accepted them. Laws were for the rich and the powerful. Laws were in place to protect the haves and destroy the have-nots. Democracy demoralized Rachlav's father, and Rachlav knew it, even though his father never willing showed it.

"Our son is embarrassed of our life, and of me." The elder man shamefully expressed to his wife as he looked towards his filthy rough hands.

Marina Rachlav took her husband's hands in hers and kissed them one at a time with her gentle lips. "Our son respects you for providing for your family in such hard conditions. Every Russian is facing bad times. Do not fear about your son's love for you." Marina softly ran her hand over her husband's weather beaten cheek.

The young Rachlav was fresh into his adult years when he proudly joined the Russian army. Soon his father passed away from years of undiagnosed heart trouble, and it was he, the only son, who now took his fathers place at the head of the Rachlav family. The young man swore that the American way of life would not break him the way that it broke his father. He would not beg for meaningless work as his child lies at home dying because there was no money for medicine, and not enough food to feed his entire family. Rachlav vowed on his father's grave that he would avenge the life the Americans took from him. He vowed to make them pay. Rachlav would work long and hard, until one day he would be in a position were he could make a difference; a difference to his family, Mother Russia, and to his father's memory.

"How do I fill your shoes?" Rachlav spoke to his father's grave maker. "I am unable to raise your family the way that you did. I want more than a worn out back for all of my years of service to my duty. I want more from life."

Rachlav grew through the ranks of the military rather quickly. He was a self-educated man with a goal in life that drove his very existence. It is said that Rachlav became one of the youngest, and fiercest generals in Russian history. That sort of thing impressed a lot of the right kind of people; people like a man named Ubiikobyla, who was on the right track to become the president of Russia one day. Ubiikobyla liked Rachlav, and in so took Rachlav into his political circle of contacts. There within that political circle, were a lot of different charismatic type characters, some with political pull, and some with street pull. Never the less they were all impressed with Rachlav, just as Ubiikobyla was. Rachlav used this to his advantage; making Ubiikobyla's friends his friends, and making Ubiikobyla's associates his associates.

"So this is the famous General that we have all been hearing about," one of Moscow's more well established aristocrats grinned as he stood and put out his right hand for Rachlav to take.

"I don't think that I am that famous. I just enjoy what I do for my country," Rachlav countered as he accepted the large bellied wealthy gentleman's hand as they shook on the thought of a promising future.

"Rachlav my boy, there are more ways to serve your country than by military means. There are politics! Now please sit and eat. Being famous is not something that one can do on an empty stomach. You look as though you are wasting away."

General Rachlav looked down at the massive amounts of food and Vodka on the table before he sat down to join the conversation. "Ubiikobyla, my friend, I will leave the politics up to you. I feel as though the country would be in much better hands with you, than with me. I may shoot a foreign political power when peace talks break down."

"Ha! Ha! Didn't I tell you guys that the General here was the real thing? Barbaric, and on our side," Ubiikobyla whole heartily laughed.

The thing that Rachlav probably liked most about Ubiikobyla was that he was easily swayed by a kind, yet demanding tone. Rachlav became Ubiikobyla sole confidant, and in return Ubiikobyla unwittingly became Rachlav's political puppet. With Rachlav's help, Ubiikobyla easily won the president ship in a history-making landslide.

As he was sworn in, Ubiikobyla repeated the Russian Presidential Oath, *"I vow, in the performance of my powers as the President of the Russian Federation to respect and protect the rights and freedoms of man and citizen, to observe and protect the Constitution of the Russian Federation, to protect the sovereignty and independence, security and integrity of the state and to serve the people faithfully."*

"Congratulation my friend, or shall I say Mr. President?" Rachlav shook his friend's hand.

"Thank you General Rachlav, I could not have done it without you. I know, I hear things. You are the reason that I won. There was no opponent that could touch me. Tell me how did you do it?" Ubiikobyla questioned Russia's most powerful military leader.

"Mr. President, you don't want to hear the details, you want to celebrate."

"Yes of course, but tell me what can I do to show the respect and gratitude that you deserve?"

"Make me general of all the armies, and maybe one day your successor."

"Rachlav, Rachlav that is a lot to ask, even from me."

"Is it...Mr. President?"

"No...no it's not. Not for you my friend, my confidant, my successor." Ubiikobyla shook his head up and down in an almost fear like agreement.

In a press conference later that day, Russian President Ubiikobyla announced to the people of Russia of Rachlav's new position within the ranks of the Russian military and his role within the folds of the government.

"He will rule as my right hand," Ubiikobyla stated. "General Rachlav will lead our military into the new and exciting future. He will have rewritten history for Mother Russia. No more will the world view us as a potentially fatal third world country that cannot keep track of their own weapons. General Rachlav will succeed my reign as President of our stand alone country, and continue our vision of turning Mother Russia into an empire that surpasses even the United States as leaders of this world."

Rachlav quickly took on his new role and the rather large monetary gain that came with it. He was a tyrant of sorts; he ran his country with an iron fist, but he also had deep feelings for the lower class, at least the ones who tried to make a living...the ones who tried to make a difference, just as his father tried to do his entire and pitiful life.

"I will make you proud Father," Rachlav spoke to the cloud covered sky. "I know what to do for our family."

Rachlav did not have the biggest house in Russia, but he lived richly. For his mother and sisters, Rachlav built them a historic castle on a hill about a mile from his new city home.

"Mother I know life has been hard on you since father's death. Even before his death you have struggled. This family has struggled, but struggle no more." Rachlav held his mother's hand tenderly between his as he kneeled in front of seated body.

"Your father is proud of you my son. He looks down on you now smiling on what you have become, and what you have done. You are a man, and I am proud of you, but do not become a man of hate because of what has come down upon you. Become a man of vision who has learned from a troubled path, but remember that it was a path that was also filled with love from his family, not just trouble alone." Marina kissed the top of her son's left hand, and then briefly held it to her war cheek.

From that day forward Rachlav made good on his promise to take care of his family. Never again would his mother and sisters scrub the floors of some silver spooned politician for crumbs, or leftover meat scraps.

It was General Rachlav himself who went to his old village to personally oversee the move of his mother and sisters to their new home that he had built for them. It was there that Rachlav's heart eased the raged grip of his iron fist. For he saw Nikolaevna, his first and only love. He had wished on many lonely nights that he would one day have the courage to ask for her hand in marriage. He could not, however, put her through what his father put his mother through. He would not marry solely out of love. Then, as he saw her again and knew that he was wrong; you should always marry for love, and the rest would fall into place.

"Nika?" Rachlav asked with an embarrassed blush to his chiseled face.

"General," she quietly said as her blushed face looked towards the semi-frozen ground unaware of her dream man's similar expression.

"Nika…it has been years…I'm sorry…please forgive me, I've been…"

"Shh! Speak no more…you…you are here now." Nika put her hand to Rachlav's mouth, and allowed her fingers fall over his lower lip.

"Nika, my love…I was wrong. I love you. I have always loved you, but I was stupid letting wealth and pride get in the way of my future with you." The mighty Russian General looked helpless in front of the petite young woman.

Rachlav properly proposed to Nikolaevna in front of the entire village after he passed the traditional and trying task of speaking with Nikolaevna's father. Nikolaevna's parents were pleased to have their daughter married to a most powerful and wealthy man.

"Please join our new family in the city?" General Rachlav asked his new in-laws for the second time.

"Our life is here," Nika's father expressed to his new son. "We would be miserable to fit the confines of the city. We need our freedoms for a healthy life."

Rachlav knew what Nika's parents had meant, and so he left it at that. "My offer will always remain open to all of my family, both new and old."

Nikolaevna's parents, although worn and tired, refused to leave their home, because of who they were and where they belonged.

Rachlav learned a lot from Nika's parents and the village that he had grown to manhood in. He should not be ashamed of where and how he grew up, his father was not, and he would not be from that day forward. The Russian General got their point, and so if Nikolaevna's parents did not want to move to a big house in the city, he would bring the city to them. In fact he rebuilt the entire village from the ground up, giving everyone new homes, and creating jobs for the hundreds of people who lived there. To most Rachlav became a good man, and to others he was a ruthless killer.

CHAPTER 2

No matter how many medals Braden received, or how many battles he had seen; nothing compared him for the brutal Russian assignation that murdered millions of American people on March 23, 2016. Russia did that to his people. Russia did that to his home. Russia was the enemy. Russia needed to pay.

Unlike General Rachlav, Jack Braden grew up in a nice upper class home outside of Seattle, Washington. Jack had always felt that school was kind of an annoyance. In his teenage mindset, Jack felt that he always had rude teachers interrupting good conversations between himself and his friends, who most of the time where across the classroom from him. To Jack Braden, the fall of the Iron Curtain meant a Friday morning history test. In all actuality, Jack, like most Americans, had no idea what really went on outside the confines of their homes; and outside the confines of the United States of America. Watching the news was a lot different than living the story.

"Mr. Brown, why do we have to learn about things that will never apply to real life?" Jack asked as he raised his hand from his back corner school desk.

"History is real life Mr. Braden, it is who we are and where we came from. We learn from the people before us, and we learn from our own mistakes. Just like I hope that some of the students in here have grown from their own mistakes and have learned to study. And don't laugh! I know your parents won't after looking at your last test scores. But back to the point Mr. Braden, history is life. There is more to life than living in the Emerald City, it's about finding who you are. Once you know that, then you can find a place for you," Mr. Brown pointed at Jack, "in this world. Once you have made your stand, then you have just written a beautiful piece of your own history. If that piece is big enough Mr. Braden…class…then others will also know your story. And that, my knowledge thirsty students, is history." Mr. Brown smiled when he saw that a few students understood his message; which in turn helped the History professor remember why he became a teacher.

Braden did all the things he needed to do to make his father and the college recruits happy; like becoming the head quarterback and captain of the high school football team. He also won state four years in a row in wrestling, which was a huge feat in a world of talented athletes. He built his first car, a black 69 *Camaro*, with his dad in their garage the year prior to turning sixteen; a car in fact that he was never without.

"Dad, did you ever have a dream car?" Jack asked his father while under the hood of his classic muscle car.

"You are looking at it son," Jack's dad stepped back and spread his arms out to showcase his son's automobile.

"What? But this is my car old man," Jack openly teased.

"I guess that you can say that I'm one of those parents who live through their children. I do love this car though. I had a 69 just like this when I was your age."

"What ever happened to it?" Jack looked impressed by his dad's sometimes-lapsed memory.

Jack's father opened the driver's side door and sat down in the front seat and gripped the steering wheel loosely. "I flipped it in a race around Dead Man's Point by Junction 6."

"What?" Jack was in total shock. "You never told me that. What happened?"

"As you can see I walked away from the scene, but not without loss. You know that your Grandma and Grandpa Braden didn't have a lot of money, and so I worked for our neighbor Mr. Jacobs. I did odd jobs here and there, but it was mostly taking care of his Quarter Horses."

"Did you ride them and stuff?" Jack asked in awe as he listened intensely to a part of his father's past that he knew nothing about. Jack had always lived in the Seattle metro area and never had been around animals except for a visit or two to the *Point Defiance Zoo*, and so the thought of growing up around horses interested him immensely.

"It wasn't like that," his dad answered back. "It was more like the behind the scenes job. I mended fences that the horses destroyed, I cleaned stalls, dug ditches, and things like that."

"I thought that you always lived in Seattle…or assumed? Wasn't Grandpa born here?"

"Your Grandfather, my Dad, was born here in Seattle, but moved to the other side of the mountain when he was in the military. I believe that he was stationed in Yakima, and met your Grandma one night at the local movie theater. Her parent's had a small farm in the Lower Yakima Valley in the country outside of this small one horse town called Wapato. And when my Dad got out of the military he moved from the big city to take up rural living. Your Grandparents got married, had us kids, and took over the farm. That was life until they finally lost the farm to bad crops and taxes. My Dad moved us back to Seattle when I was in high school, and took a job for the City of Seattle, and eventually retired from there. And that my son is my family's history in sixty seconds or less." Mr. Braden spoke without taking a breath as to get it all out before he was interrupted.

"Yeah Dad…like you ever talked for less than a minute. What happened to the car?" Jack asked excitedly.

"Well with the money I saved from working at our neighbors, I bought the 69 *Camaro*. I spent a lot of time under the hood like we've been on your car, except that I was self-taught. I spent every possible moment of my waking day with that car. When I was done I could whip anything out there. Man…was that car fast. When we moved to Seattle I took the Westside by storm. I swear that none of those yuppie wannabes ever seen anything like me. That's when I met your Mother. She was so beautiful, and she loved me so very much. She hated the fact that I liked to race. This one night, I was racing this guy down Dead Man's Point. Your Mom was there for moral support, even though she hated to see me race. I somehow lost control of the car and flipped it head over heel twenty-seven times until both the car and I landed in the bottom of the ravine. I still don't know how I walked away from the crash, but I did." Jack's dad leaned back in his son's driver's seat as he recalled the accident in his mind.

"Holly crap dad…are you serious?" Jack who was squatting on the driveway pavement jumped up to his feet in a leap of excitement.

"What happened next? I can't believe that you kept this from me my entire life."

"After the crash I didn't have any money to rebuild the car." Bill Braden patted the black steering wheel.

"Was there any car left?" Jack asked.

"There was that too. I couldn't do it. I mean that I could of…it would just have taken a long time. However, I chose at that moment to give up that life for a life with your Mother."

"Did people think that you were scared? I mean that you just walked away from a crash, and never go back to it?" Jack questioned from the squatted position that he had retaken.

"Yeah maybe, but it was okay. Me and your Mom got married, and the rest is history. We never told you because your Mom thought that it would glorify that life style, and we didn't want anything to ever happen to you." Bill pointed at his son as he spoke.

"Did Mom flip when I bought the same car that you had?" The thought amused young Braden.

"That would be an understatement, but we talked about it, and we both agreed that you were a responsible enough young man to make your own choices. The car wasn't given to you. You worked hard for it, and with that comes a little bit of self worth. The car means more to you because of that sweat equity you put into it. We trust you, and my story shouldn't make you change who you really are." Bill winked at his son.

"Got it Pops. So…is that a big no on telling Mom that you told me your Camaro saga?" Jack lightly punched his Dad in the shoulder.

"That's a big ten-four, unless you want to see someone sleeping on the couch." Bill playfully punched his son back as he sarcastically joked.

"And how is that my concern?" Jack laughed.

"Because it won't be me on the couch. I'll take your room, and make your butt sleep downstairs. Capeesh?" Bill pulled himself out of the classic automobile, and pretended to push his squatted son backwards; which caused Jack to briefly flinch.

Jack Braden did it all through high school. On top of sports, he held a job at the local movie theater, maintained a 4.0 grade point average, and even kept his room clean. To most people Jack was a walking contradiction; a nerd, a jock, popular, and a world traveler to some extent. The summer between his junior and senior year of high school, Jack joined a summer student exchange program where he lived with an honorary host family in Frankfurt, Germany for the entire summer vacation. Back home in Seattle, Washington Jack Braden was very popular, especially with the girls; most importantly one girl, Beth Anderson.

Jack loved Beth ever since the first time he laid eyes on her. It was the first day of Eighth Grade, and Jack was the self-proclaimed big man on campus. As Jack walked down the student-cramped hall to his first class he saw a pretty new girl who was having trouble with her top tiered locker.

"Need help?" Jack smoothly asked as he leaned his back against the lockers that connected to Beth's.

"This locker is stupid!" Beth said to herself as she slapped the palm of her hand against the green painted metal of the locker door.

"Do you need help or what?" Jack's wink went unnoticed by the new female student.

"I don't know…yeah…sure…whatever. It's unlocked, but it is jammed or something." Beth looked and sounded frustrated.

Jack put his stuff down and tried his luck at the locker door. He pulled and pulled, but with no luck.

"I can almost get my fingers in…" Jack started to say with a soft grunt.

The locker door flew open from one last big tug, hitting Jack in the face, and breaking his nose.

"Oh my...um...are you alright?" Beth bent over as she tried to look the hunched over boy in the face.

Not wanting to cry in front of a girl, or the entire school, Jack cupped his hands over his nose to catch the blood, stood up straight, and choked out, "Yeah...I think so."

A couple of teachers, who had been walking down the hall, saw what had happened and took Jack to the school nurse. The school called Jack's mother, and told her what had happened, and that they took her son to the Minor Emergency Clinic two blocks from the school on Division, and that they needed her to meet them there. A couple of painful days later, Jack unwillingly went back to school to face the crowd of questioners and gawkers. One of the first people he saw that Monday morning was that new girl having trouble with her locker.

"Need help?" Jack jokingly asked as he once again leaned against Beth's neighboring lockers.

"I'm so sorry," Beth smiled as she looked away from her locker combination that she had scribbled in the inside flap of a red notebook that she used for English assignments. "I can never remember this dang thing," as she turned the dial on her locker. "Is there anything I can do? I am so sorry." Beth looked at the injured young man.

"You can keep that locker away from me," Jack joked.

"Done! By the way my name is Beth," as she held out her right hand with enthusiasm.

"Jack…"

"Yeah I know. I asked around after the accident. We have the same homeroom!" Beth looked uneasily at Jack's nose, but never the less she smiled a warm friendly grin.

"Cool!" Jack said in a voice that was way too loud, which only embarrassed him even more in front of the girl that he liked.

Jack and Beth became very good close friends, and it lasted. They did everything together, and as time went by their feelings grew for one another, and soon they were officially a couple. Jack and Beth were perfect for each other, and it showed. Their love for each other radiated in everything that they did, even when they were apart, their loved never wavered. Beth and Jack were the stereotypical fairy tale sweethearts that graduated high school together, and were destined to live out their lives as man and wife. During summer vacation from their freshman year in college Jack proposed marriage on a romantic weekend at a secluded mountain getaway.

"Beth, would you like to go down to the lake? I know that it's getting dark, but the moon's light is at full force, and it looks like a perfect time for a little moonlit stroll." Jack looked up at the night sky.

"What about a moonlit…"

"Skinny dip?" Jack interrupted Beth's question with what he felt was a little too much excitement.

"No silly…a moonlit picnic," Beth played off Jack's outburst with a slap to his left muscular shoulder.

"That's what I love about you Beth…we're always thinking alike. I already have the stuff set up down by that crooked tree. It was going to be a surprise, but oh well." Jack put his arm over Beth's slender shoulders and pulled her close to him.

When the loved filled couple arrived at the spot on the lake for dinner, Jack set the mood with soft piano instrumental music from a small portable radio that he had brought along in the picnic supplies. As they ate, Jack could not stop looking at his girlfriend.

"What is it Jack? You've been starring at me all night." Beth looked away shyly.

"Well I have that right…you're beautiful." Jack slid closer to his girlfriend so that he could see her face.

"Right?" Beth blushed, even though she did not know why.

"No really…I have a question for you, and I was waiting to see if you got that little sparkle in your eye like you do on Christmas morning." Jack put his warm fingers on Beth's chin and pulled her face up so that he could see her clearly in the moonlight.

Beth shuttered. "Well what is it?" Beth asked with anticipation.

Beth, with all honesty, said yes before Jack even finished asking the question.

"Yes! Yes a million times…yes…of course I'll marry you." Beth cried from the overflow of love that she had for Jack.

A couple hours away, both sets of parents waited somewhat patiently for their return, and of course Beth's answer. Jack had prearranged the entire weekend, and had not only Beth's father's blessing, but the blessing and support of the entire Braden and Anderson families.

Unfortunately, Beth never actually got to see her own wedding. She died about a year after the proposal from a rare form of Cancer.

"Doctor Morrow what is it?" Beth's voice trembled as she sat across from her doctor behind the closed doors of his office.

"Sorry Beth…I don't know how to tell you this without being blunt and just coming out with it, but you have a rare form of Breast Cancer called IBC. I would like to try an aggressive form of therapy…but the truth is I don't know how well it will do, or how long it will give you." The doctor did not hold anything back from his patient.

"Wow! You are blunt," Beth sighed. "What is IBC?" Beth asked dumbfounded and scared.

"It stands for Inflammatory Breast Cancer. It's a lesser-seen form than you hear about on the nightly news. It usually attacks younger people, but I have never seen it in someone your age." Doctor Morrow looked concerned.

"I didn't feel a lump! I wasn't really looking or anything, but I would know right?" Beth asked if she had hoped that her doctor had been mistaken about his diagnosis.

"Not always...IBC doesn't always have a palpable mass associated with it," the doctor answered his patient with his most caring tone as if to tell her that it was not her fault.

"There had to signs of it, right...please? Doctor tell me something. I don't want to die...Jack...what about Jack? We're to be married." Beth pleaded with Morrow.

"I know Beth, and I'm sorry. You may have had swelling or redness..."

"I did! I play on a girl's Rugby team, and I took a hard hit to the chest. The doctor that checked me out said that the redness, tenderness, and swelling would go away in a week or two. I was just bruised from taking such a hard hit, and that I should wear protective gear. I didn't really get better, and so I went back. The doctor checked me out and asked if I started my period yet, and I told her that it usually hits within a few days. She told me that some women have swollen breasts during their time of the month, and that if the problem persists to come back." Beth Anderson felt that her trusted doctor was wrong based on a previous diagnosis by another physician.

"And did you?" Morrow asked.

"No, it wasn't that bad. Plus I still play Rugby, and I can't go to the doctor every time I fall down." Beth shook her head with disbelief.

"I see! Anything else that I can tell you?" The doctor's face showed his deep concern for his young patient.

"How long do me and Jack have…honestly?" Beth asked as she started to cry as the thoughts of her fleeing mortality sunk in as to what Dr. Morrow tried to calmly explain.

"I really don't know Beth…three years, three months; I can't say. Honestly the survival rate is a lot lower than other forms of Breast Cancer…I just don't know, but we'll try everything that we can to beat the odds. We will beat this Beth…you, me, and Jack." Dr. Morrow stood up and came around his desk. He took Beth's trembling hands in his as he sat down next to the girl that he had helped deliver years before.

Jack instinctively moved the wedding date up so that Beth could still have her wedding, but it wasn't soon enough. In the end it was just the two of them in a sterile hospital room with two off duty nurses and a doctor witnessing the reverend's words. Beth Anderson died before she could utter her last breath of, "I do."

Beth was buried on a Saturday with Braden on the headstone; a sincere tribute to what Beth would have wanted; both the Braden and the Anderson families mutually agreed.

"If anyone would like to come up and say a few words about young Beth Braden; to help others remember the good times. Beth enjoyed life. In fact, she loved life. So please, come up and help us rejoice the life of this incredible young woman who gave so much to the church and to others that she met along her journey."

As the Pastor of the church finished his heart filled plea for support; others in the church turned their attention to Jack, who had his head down to hide his face and tear soaked eyes. Jack could feel the eyes of the his family and friends, who had come to morn and pay tribute to Beth. He knew that they wanted him to stand up and take the stand. He knew that they wanted him to talk in detail about the good times that he had with the woman that he vowed to wed. He knew what they wanted, but did they care about what he wanted? He wanted things to be okay. He did not want to see Beth lose a fight to the Cancer that eventually took her precious life. He did not want to remember her pain…his pain. He knew that he loved Beth, and Jack knew that they shared a lifetime of wonderful memories together, but he could not separate the good memories from the bad. Pain was bad, and Jack wanted to stop feeling the pain. Jack looked for an escape from his thoughts.

Jack thought to himself, "If I could only erase my memories of Beth? What if I could erase my memories of love? Love only brings pain to the one who survives it. If I never would have met Beth, then I would never have known love…known death…known pain. I never would have felt how I feel right now. Would it have been better to never have loved than to survive it?" Jack cried silently to himself, but he never looked up at the crowd mourners around him.

Jack Braden joined the military to stop the pain. He felt as though if he could just run away and stop thinking for himself, that he would forget love and the pain it brought with it. Braden did his duty one hundred and ten percent of the time. He was smart, worked hard, knew the angles, and it did not hurt that he knew how to correctly read people.

Braden made the rank of Colonel as quickly as any soldier out there. It was not the fact that he could have advanced any faster, he chose not to. Braden took on roles that allowed him to go to war, or at least overseas; anything that would have kept him from going home, and kept him from Beth's lonely grave.

Every holiday, every one of Beth's birthdays, and every one of their wedding anniversaries that passed; Jack wrote a letter to Beth, which he never mailed.

Dear Beth,

I'm still away from home, and I can't see you. I'm lost, and I don't know how to live without you. I can't find my way home Beth. It's always dark here, even in the daylight. My thoughts haunt me, and I don't know if I can face them alone.

I need you. I'm sorry that I left you alone,
but I couldn't cope. I know that it sounds like an
excuse, but the nightmares over took me. I had to
run. Please forgive me Beth. I love you.

Yours forever,

Jack

Jack continued to do the duty that his country asked of him, and after Braden made Colonel; John Andrews approached him.

"Mr. Secretary of Defense…it's an honor sir." Jack stood erect and saluted proudly.

"At ease Colonel," Secretary of Defense Andrews stuck out his right hand to shake the hand of the man that he had heard so much about. "I hear that you're in the military for life. Is that a correct understanding?"

"Yes sir it is. I am proud to serve my country," Jack followed suit and excepted John Andrews' hand in a traditional firm but brief handshake.

"And we are proud to have you son. And please call me John…we can speak freely here." Secretary of Defense Andrews motioned for Colonel Braden to take a seat on the long black leather sofa that sat along the far wall.

"Yes sir…John…why have you asked me here?" Braden respectively asked as he took the seat that was offered to him on the firm new couch.

"I need a man of your…unique abilities to oversee some special projects of mine." John Andrews answered his guest as he also took a seat on the same piece of furniture. "You would report directly to me, and only me. No one else will have access to your files, and in return your compensation would be whatever you demanded."

"What kind of projects?" Jack countered, even though he felt that he might have overstepped his boundaries with his sarcastic tone.

"Ones of a delicate nature that need to be dealt with, but can't because of political bullshit. You've seen it…you know that there are people in power that shouldn't be. Besides you would just be following orders Jack." Andrews leaned back and adjusted his suit jacket.

"Orders that don't exist?" Jack again answered sarcastically, but with less care for his host's feelings. If he wanted answers, then Jack needed to get things into the open.

"I like you Jack…I like the way that you present yourself, and how you get to the point. At no time should you feel remorse about what is said between us," John Andrews sternly spoke as he pointed his right index finger in the direction of Jack Braden's face. "If you are honest with me, and honest with yourself...then we will have a great relationship. Is that fair?"

"Yes sir it is." Jack could feel the intense energy as John Andrews spoke.

Secretary of Defense Andrews eased his look and let his hand fall back into his lap. "Good! Back to the point of you being here. There are people who need to be dealt with a degree of caution...per say. There are people that we can't touch because of laws, somewhat gray areas, and things of that nature. Don't worry Jack; you'll be taken care of. You'll be amazed how many doors will open up for you. Nobody could touch you, and they wouldn't even know why. Of course, it would be better if you kept a low profile and didn't get into situations that would require my help."

"And why me again?" Jack asked in a lower and lot less sarcastic tone.

"Jack, I've seen your file. You walked out of an unknown P.O.W. camp in North Korea after three weeks. You left no survivors. You've also talked your way out of a firing squad in South America. You went from being blind folded in front of a wall of armed gunmen to having drinks with your captive's General. All this before you blew his brains out all over his new dining room table, and then you walked out of camp like you were going home after a night out with the boys. Hell Jack…nobody does that." Andrews knew Jack Braden inside and out.

"And that makes me perfect for this job…a killer who can entice his victims? Why don't you get Charlie Manson…I think he's still alive." Jack did not like the fact that the Government probably knew all of his deepest darkest secrets. They must have known about Beth.

"Jack! Come on Jack, you would be working undercover. CIA, the military…whatever you need Jack; it's yours. You would be in complete control of the situation. Rank, jurisdiction; they wouldn't be a problem. Your in charge…you have my word. Whatever it takes to get the job done." John slapped Jack's knee and then stood up.

"Okay then. When do I start?" Jack followed suit as he also stood up.

"What are you talking about Jack," Andrews looked down at his Swiss made watch, "you've been on the clock all morning."

CHAPTER 3

After the attack on New York City, the U.S. struck back so quickly that Russia did not have enough time to gather all of it's forces, thus leading to the war being fought on Russian soil. Moscow was taken within the first year; which forced President Ubiikobyla and his family to relocate to a fortified bunker far away from the capital and closer into the frigid wastelands of Siberia.

"Tell me General Rachlav...why must I flee my home for a war being fought over a women?" The Russian President asked as he carried a small personal bag down the hall towards the front door of his house.

"Mr. President, you and your family must temporarily relocate outside of the city for the time being for your own safety...nothing more," the General answered as he took the President's bag from him and opened the Ubiikobyla family's front door. "I will fight the war with the Americans over a woman...my Nika will have her revenge against the American scum and their families."

"General...I misspoke...Nika...she was a lovely woman. And I am sorry for talking ill about the deceased...especially Nikolaevna. Her death was misfortunate to say the least."

"Mr. President, you and your family must go. There is a car waiting outside for you now. Your furnishing and personal items will be set up and waiting for you in a secured location. It won't be home, but you'll be alive." Rachlav looked cautiously up and down the driveway that led up to the house.

"Thank you my friend, and my children thank you." Ubiikobyla truly trusted his friend and advisor.

"Go!" General Rachlav demanded as he opened the back passenger side door of the black Presidential limousine so that President Ubiikobyla could slide in next to his wife and children as they set off for their new life of hiding.

General Rachlav was a brilliant leader, who knew that the Americans would retaliate against his country. He wanted the Americans to take the Russian capital within the time frame that he had predicted, even though the United States took Moscow a little sooner than Rachlav had first anticipated, it did not matter; the Russian General had set the U.S. up to fail in front of the entire world. Rachlav knew from his secretive studies that the Americans would pride themselves on the prize of Moscow, and let their egos get in the way of strategic planning. It were times like those that Rachlav missed Nika most; it was she that had first taught him of the American ways and lies long ago.

"I will avenge our love, Nika," General Rachlav mumbled to himself as he watched the President's car pull away. "They will pay for the place that they put you in. Nobody deserves to die the way that you did. I know how the Americans killed you slowly over a long grueling time until you could take it no longer, and finally you gave into the deep sleep of death. I am sorry for your pain. I am sorry for your loss. I am sorry for my loss. I swear to avenge you in life and death, Nika!" The Russian General slammed the front door to Ubiikobyla's house shut.

Rachlav's plan was to increase his forces by three fold, and he did that by forcefully recruiting civilians and soldiers alike from his populated homeland of Russia, and by reaching deep into the Siberian region for strong men spread out through the small-desolated villages.

"WE NEED MORE FORCES," Rachlav screamed at his men. "We need the combined forces of the former Eastern Europe alliance that was under our grip when I growing up as a child. We were fools to let those countries go, and now we need them to help us fight this war with the Americans. However, we cannot do this. We do not have the time or the resources to take these other countries under our wings."

Rachlav gave a powerful speech in front of his men.

"What do we do General, sir?" Asked one of Rachlav's Colonels.

"We use our other options. We do not target the armies of our neighbors...we attack their leaders. War is a political game, and that is how we are going to play it." Rachlav had learned the political game from his country's leaders.

Neighboring countries joined Russia's fight, and within months their governments fell into Rachlav's rule. Most of the governments collapsed by mere words, mostly former Soviet countries that broke off when the USSR let the reigns of Communism fall in the late Twentieth Century. However, there were the occasional political leaders that needed to be sent into the working Gulag system to get Rachlav's point a cross.

"Poland surrenders our lands. Our armies are your armies...General Rachlav," Polish President Olszewski unwillingly agreed to Russia's terms after he witnessed first hand the life that the labor camps provided, and the lives it took from his political leaders.

After President Olszewski's surrender of Poland, other political leaders that were taken into the Gulag also surrendered after they witnessed Russia's determination.

"General Rachlav?" One of Rachlav's most trusted men came into the General's office and saluted.

"Yes Colonel Romanovros?" Rachlav saluted which allowed the other man to drop his arm to his side.

"Our plan for former Soviet domination has worked to our advantage. On top of Poland, we now have the Czech Republic, Slovakia, Hungary, Serbia, Romania, and Bulgaria."

"The United States of America will not know what hit them," General Rachlav smirked as he slammed his fist into the top of red oak desk.

Rachlav turned the war around without anyone to stop him. Six months later there were two battlefronts; one in Russia, and one in U.S.

"The Americans do not know what to do. Never before have they fought such a battle on their own ground. This will be a victory for all of Russia. The Americans are weak," General Rachlav boasted to anyone within hearing range of his statement.

"The United States is a Super Power that is not to be under estimated, General."

"The only super powers the Americans have are their egos, and their egos will be their downfall. Pride is conqueror of all men, and their pride and self worth will blind them. They will make mistakes, and when they do…America will fall."

"Yes General, you are right…Americans do have pride in their way of life. Pride like no other, but don't under estimate pride for weakness. The Americans are strong."

"Do you question my judgment, Colonel Romanovros?"

"No, of course not. I was just…"

"You were just saying that we cannot beat the egotistical Americans at the game of war."

"No sir, General Rachlav."

"We invented war…this war…we cannot be beat."

"General, why are we fighting this war? Yesterday, the Americans were our allies, and today they are our enemies."

"We were never allies with the American scum. Our country pretended to put up with the American ideals for the sole purpose of the trade industry, nothing more."

"General, there is more to our allegiance than trade. Think about when we were boys; did the Cold War not end?" Colonel Romanovros questioned an unquestionable fact about World History.

"The Cold War never ended…it is still today. We no longer are pointing our missiles at one another like the American television programs made it out to be. But there are still counter measures to put a check on our so called allies," Rachlav moved within inches of Romanovros, and corrected his trusted Colonel's way of thinking.

"Like what kind of counter measures?" Romanovros asked unsurely.

"The American 9/11 attacks."

"What? I thought…Russia did not have…"

"We supplied the terrorist groups with arms for a fee that they could not pay. So in exchange for these weapons, the terrorists would have to bruise the American pride by attacking their homeland. Once again diverting their eyes from us."

"The terrorist attacks of 9/11 devastated not only the Americans, but it hurt the entire world," Colonel Romanovros' voice sounded in sorrow for the thought of America and her people.

"A minor set back for the good of Mother Russia. In the end the Americans will fear us, and they will beg for our mercy. Just like they begged for our help in the *Great Patriotic War*. It was the Russians that beat *Hitler* and the *Nazis*…not the Americans or any of our other so called Western Allies. *Stalin* was right to be wary of western influences, but time changes everyone, except for the Russians. The Russians were and are the most superior superpower in the world."

"General we are not terrorists…you are not a terrorist. Why?"

"They ruined our way of life. They killed my father. They killed my Nika. Americans have no honor…just greed. They take what they want, just like they took my wife. I hate the Americans!" General Rachlav turned his back to the Colonel, and Romanovros took the General's action as a cue that the conversation was no longer up for debate, and to leave his office at once. Colonel Romanovros did just that; shutting the door behind him with a hollowed echo.

General Rachlav used the neighboring armies to keep the overseas Americans busy fighting; while his own forces made a move on the United States. The Russians devised a plan to invade Germany, thus increasing their strength, but spreading their armies thin. The plan was a deliberate ruse, knowing that the American forces would intercept the transmissions, and send forces to protect Germany. All the while as the deception took form, Russia swiftly moved thousands of soldiers through Siberia, around the world and hit the West Coast of the United States. Never before had the United States fought such a battle on their own soil, and it was the first time since 9/11 that Americans felt so unsafe.

"General Bachmeier der deutschen Luftwaffe spricht mit Ihnen jetzt," a Corporal in the German Air Force spoke into the phone receiver to an unknown US military leader.

"Hallo. Dieses ist General Bachmeier."

"General Bachmeier? General Adrian Bachmeier?"

"Yes, who is this?"

"It's Colonel Jack Braden from America."

"Brother Jack! How are things in the war with our Russian neighbors?"

"Not so good. We have Intel that states that the Russians have attacked your country. We would like to send some of our troops that are in Russia to aid you in your time of need. We don't need this to become an all out world war."

"Jack, my brother. I assure you that the Fatherland is not under siege. Your Intel is mistaken. I am sorry."

"I'm sorry too brother."

Jack Braden hung up the phone, ran his fingers through his hair, and looked at a photograph that he had hung on the wall of Russian General Rachlav standing next to President Ubiikobyla after the Russian Presidential election. "What are you guys thinking? Germany was never a target. So what the hell are you guys doing?"

CHAPTER 4

Jessica Farmer was a stereotypical tomboy growing up in Clayton County, Georgia. There were only a few girls that were around her age, so she mostly associated with the boys in her neighborhood. She had some female friends at school, but her entire nine years on Earth were mostly spent climbing trees, playing tackle football; and according to Jessica's mother, those were not appropriate girl type activities. Never the less, Jessica continued to do what she had always done, and that was to have fun. Except when it came to school. The third grade was especially hard for Jessica, and so she continued to struggle through the year.

"But why do I have to go to school? Couldn't I be home school with the Taylor's'?"

"No way young lady. All you would do is bug that Jesse Taylor, and his mamma already has her hands full with her young ones. Besides, public school is in our price range right now," Lisa Farmer countered Jessica's argument with a great big bear hug. "Now finish getting ready, and I'll walk over to Millie's house so that you can catch the school bus with her. Okay?"

"Yes momma."

Lisa loved her daughter, but it was hard on the both of them. She wanted to be there for Jessica, but she needed to support their little family of two. Lisa worked part time at the local city library, and she filled in at Jerry's Diner whenever they could spare her any extra hours. Times were hard, but they had always been hard, and so in Lisa's mind, that thought made their lives bearable.

"Jerry, what about Tuesday night? Jeannie Rae is off...or wants it off so that she can go to the drive-in with Billy. I already have a sitter, and everything. Besides...I really need the extra money, and you don't have anyone else."

"Now is that a fact Mrs. Lisa Farmer?" Jerry asked sternly then smiled slowly. "If I need you then I need you, and according to you...I need you. So be here at four thirty, and be ready to run. They're playing Bingo down at the church hall, and we're supplying the food."

"Who would of thought that Bingo and Chicken Fried Steak went together?" Lisa joked as she walked towards the backdoor of the restaurant.

"Don't go joking around about my Chicken Fried Steak. It won..."

"I know, I know…second prize in the State Fair," Lisa mimicked Jerry as he defended his cooking.

"Two years in a row," Jerry yelled out as Lisa opened the door to step out into the unusually cool weather.

"Two years Jerry…we've been living with that story for two years."

"Well if you feel so strongly about it, then I won't include you in the telling of my story when I win it again this year," Jerry playfully shouted.

"Win? I thought that second was your place. Thanks for Tuesday Jerry. Good night." Lisa closed the door behind her before the conversation with Jerry continued.

"I'm claiming first place this year," Jerry mumbled to himself. "Mrs. Fleming doesn't stand a chance, or at least this year. That old cheating bag and her store bought gravy. Damn woman wins first place every year, and every year she rubs it in my face, 'Maybe next year Jer.' Jer? She can't even say my name right. But not this year…this year is my year, and I'm taking home the Blue Ribbon and the fifty dollar gift card to the *Wal-Mart*…" Jerry quickly stopped talking to himself when he realized that his voice had gotten louder due to the heated nature of the subject, and that everyone in the diner may have overheard him.

Back at the Farmer household, both Lisa and Jessica were excited about Michael's upcoming release from the Federal Penitentiary in Atlanta. It had been a long time since Lisa had a chance to hold her husband in her arms without guards and bars looming all around them. Jessica on the other hand, never really knew her father. She saw him four or five times a month when they could afford the short trip, but visiting someone in jail was a lot different then growing up with them in your household. Things were going to be different when Michael returned…a lot different. A difference that would affect the entire Farmer family.

"Mom? What was Daddy like before he went away?" Jessica asked her Mother as Lisa brushed out her daughter's long thick hair.

"Like he is now. They say that prison changes men, but your Daddy has always been a good honest person. He worked hard, but sometimes that's not enough and people do things against their nature. That doesn't mean that they're bad people. It just means that they fell onto hard times, and they did what they thought was right for their family at that exact moment."

Jessica turned around on the bed that her and her mom were sitting and faced her mother, "Is that why Daddy went to prison? Because he was doing right by us?"

Lisa tried to hold back the tears, "Yes dear. Your Father did what he had to do for our survival. It wasn't right, and I don't condone it, but your Dad fell into a place that kept him from seeing the light. I think that he felt trapped and desperate, but all the time and his actions that have lead up until today…just remember one thing…that your Dad's thoughts have always been about you and me. Your Daddy loves you very much Jessica, and so do I. And when he gets home…we'll be a family again. A real family, and nothing or no one will take that away from us again. I promise honey." Lisa then crying, took her daughter securely into her arms and kissed her forehead lightly as they slowly rocked back and forth. "I promise honey that things will get better."

Lisa had a rough time with town folk right after Michael's mishap, but she never quit and she never gave up. Lisa had a newborn baby to feed, and they both needed a roof over their heads. Michael left them with a few essentials and some stolen money that had got them by for almost a month. Lisa knew that not turning the stolen merchandise in was a crime, but she needed to get the power turned back on, and so she did. That morning Lisa Farmer fed her baby, changed her diaper, and then drove down and paid what bills she could.

"Sorry that I'm late with power money Rose Ann, but if I put down one hundred and twenty-five dollars…would that be enough to get the lights back on?" Lisa asked her one time friend.

"Let me check with Ross in the back, but this should be fine." Rose Ann picked up the U.S. currency and counted it out, "This isn't the missing money from the robbery is it?" The power company teller asked in a rumor seeking whisper.

"What missing money?" Lisa lied.

People shunned her because of who she was; because of whom her husband was. One day after job rejection after job rejection, Lisa literally ran into Judge Fall in front of the local diner. She told him about life after Michael's arrest and conviction.

"I'm so sorry Judge. I'm a space case right now." Lisa blurted out after she almost knocked the Judge to the ground as he took his hat off before he entered the diner for lunch.

"It's okay Lisa. No blood no foul, right? So how have you and the baby been?" Judge Fall asked while he bent over to pick up the hat that he had dropped when he and Mrs. Farmer bumped into each other.

Lisa answered the Judge's question with complete and brutal honesty. She felt refreshed to get her thoughts into words about what she had been going through. Judge Fall stood there and listened to Lisa Farmer without interruption.

Judge Fall knew Michael, and what he had done; although wrong, was out of love for his family. He also knew that he was not going to allow this young woman be the downfall of her husband's actions based on gossip and rumors. The Judge waited until Lisa was done letting her emotions and thoughts out before he said a word. He told her to stay right there, and he went into Jerry's Diner alone.

"I see that the most of the town's influential characters are having their lunch, like they do everyday." Judge Fall pointed out in a very angry and mocking tone. "I am also sure that the town folk that aren't here this very minute will hear about what I have to say within moments. Isn't that right Mrs. Baxley? Mrs. Robertson? And not to leave out Mrs. Johnson, and anyone else that hurts innocent young women and children because of their constant bickering and banter. ENOUGH IS ENOUGH! DO I MAKE MYSELF CLEAR?"

"Judge...I must say..."

"Mrs. Baxley, you say enough already, and that's the problem. Lisa Farmer is a good woman, who is trying to raise a baby on her own.

Sure, what Michael Farmer did was wrong, but he was a desperate man trying to do his family right. You cannot fault a man for trying to put his family first. And you most defiantly cannot and will not fault his wife for trying to make things right with you people…with all of us. Think of little baby Jessica. What did she do to deserve this kind of treatment from our so-called high society? This town makes me sick when I think how quickly we turn on our own…good people that we call friend and neighbor. Well what kind of friend are you to Lisa and Jessica Farmer? I think that you should all take a good look at your own lives, and see what kind of people that you really are. Do any of you have things that you don't want the town to know…things that might embarrass you if they got out in the form of gossip and slander? We teach our children about the "Golden Rule," but as adults we spit on it when we find it convenient to do so. Look…I can't legally make you do anything against your own will. However, as your friend, neighbor, and as a member of this community…I beg you to please make it right with the Farmer family, and anyone else that may think differently then you. We have a good town, and I want it to stay a good town. Mrs. Baxley, don't you yourself have a brand new grandbaby…your eldest son's boy, right? How would you feel if the sins of the father were passed down to that precious little angle?"

"Judge Fall?"

"Yeah Jerry!" The Judge turned his attention away from the diners and towards the owner and head cook of the restaurant.

"I have a opening here at the diner. It's only temporary. Lisa Sue is going to be taking maternity leave, and I need someone to fill in for her. I can guarantee fulltime for now, but after she comes back…"

"I appreciate it…and Jerry why don't you give Lisa a call over at the house this evening…her and the baby are coming over for supper."

"Yes sir, Judge Fall."

After Judge Fall exited the diner there was a lot of commotion from the flabbergasted town folk who were still inside.

"Can you believe the nerve of that man, and to think that he may run for mayor? Not on my watch."

"Shove it Mrs. Baxley. The Judge was right, and we all know it." Jerry jumped the Judge's defense.

"Well Jerry…I have a clear mind to inform the entire town of your hostility towards me. Especially in front of my friends, and in a place of business of all places." The proud, self proclaimed town leader of doing what was right for the community got up in a hasted rage from her seat to leave.

"Mrs. Baxley? Mrs. Baxley…please look at me. Now Mrs. Baxley…you know that I have the right to refuse service to you or anyone else that I see fit to do so." Jerry pointed to the sign that hung on the back wall above the cash register.

"Well if you do, I'll get the entire town to boycott your establishment. Let's see how long you can survive in this dump with no customers." Mrs. Baxley fired back.

"Mrs. Baxley…let me finish. As I was saying, the Judge has a good point. I made a promise, and I'm going to give Lisa Farmer a job here at the dinner. If that does not suit you, then you can take your business down to the new *McDonald's* in Creek Water."

"Creek Water!" What nerve…Creek Water is over ten miles away. Nobody in their right mind would ago all the way to Creek Water for a town luncheon…especially when their not allowed in their own town diner. Do you know how fast a rumor like that would spread?"

"Yes Mrs. Baxley, I can say that I can. All that I am saying is give the poor woman a chance…that's all. You don't have to invite her over for sweet tea and biscuits…even though that would probably be nice. Just be courteous…that's all."

"Courteous? Courteous…do you realize what that woman's husband put this town through? Put you through? He tried to kill your brother. What would you have done if that woman's husband had succeeded in killing your only brother? You would be missing your brother terribly…and us without a sheriff. Or did you forget that your brother has been sheriff of this town for over thirty years now, and as a member of this town's Board of Trustees…he should be here now discussing the fate of Lisa Farmer? Don't you think…Jerry?"

"I see your point Mrs. Baxley, but like Judge Fall reminded all of us…it's not her fault. The son…err…and in this case the daughter, and wife…should not bare the sins of the father…and husband. We…I have been a total and obvious jerk towards the Farmer women for quit sometime, and it's not their fault for what Michael did. Hell, we grew up together…Michael, Lisa, and me. I know that it is not an excuse, and what Michael did was wrong, but the mill doing what it did to him…was also wrong. We all need to change as a community. We need to re-find our compassion, and the reasons that God put us here."

Jerry looked around after his little speech, and to his surprise the entire diner was silent. Jerry turned and walked towards the kitchen with a smile on his face. A smile that represented standing up to a lifetime of backing down to people like the Baxter family.

Outside of the diner, Judge Fall walked with Lisa Farmer for a short time saying absolutely nothing, until they came to little park in the center of town and sat together on one of the six black wrought iron benches.

"Lisa, will you join a foolish old man?" Judge Fall asked Lisa as he patted an open spot on the bench right next to him.

"Of course Judge." Lisa sat down and crossed her legs at the ankles, and brought her knees together.

"Lisa honey, I know that times have been tough on you and baby Jessica. And I know that they go way back before Michael's mishap. I also know that the town folk haven't made it any easier either. For that I am so very sorry." The Judge looked down and pulled a piece of lint from his jacket.

"Judge don't be. You have helped my family more than you know. You were probably the only one who hasn't turn your back on us, or spoke about me when I was standing right there."

"Lisa...I feel somewhat responsible for what has happened to Michael."

"You were just doing your job." Lisa smiled at the Judge.

"I know, but I could of helped prior to the robbery. You see...Michael came to me after the accident. His hand was so messed up, and he was in pain. The mill closed and didn't pay what they should have. I knew that he couldn't continue fixing cars like that, but at the time I didn't do anything about it."

"How could you have? You weren't even involved." Lisa looked confused.

"But I was. You see after it was all over, and Michael felt lower than low; that's when he came to me. He asked for my help in reviewing the case that he was planning to bring forth against the mill for damages that he received while on the job."

"But the mill closed, and filed bankruptcy, or something. There was no money to be got." Lisa was confused on where the judge was going with his story, but stayed with it never the less.

"But there was, and Michael knew it, and I knew it. Michael could have sued the plant owners. Sure they filed bankruptcy and closed the mill, but somebody made money off of the deal...someone always does. He could have gone after *OSHA*, and the good old U.S. of A. He may not have won, but they probably would of settled for a nice chunk of change. No matter what...Michael should have tried, and I should have helped him. I told him no, and damn near spit in his face. I told him something about the mill closing had hurt a lot of families, and he should just suck it up. A couple of days later, Michael was brought in on charges of robbery, attempted murder, and well you know the rest."

Lisa seemed to be taken back by Judge Fall's words. She had no idea that her husband had gone to others for help. She took a moment to take the new information about Michael's actions in before she said another word. "We'll be fine Judge. It wasn't your fault…you had no way of knowing that anything was going to happen. Michael had always been a good man. Nobody knew. Times are tougher because of Michael, but he is my husband. I cannot and will not fault him for making a huge sacrifice to give me and our daughter one last ray of hope; even if he knew that it would be his last."

"I admire your strength." Fall stated as he grabbed Lisa's left hand and gave it a light squeeze.

"I'm not strong Judge…I'm a wreck. I'm just determined to survive, and to raise my daughter up right, unlike the people of this town. Sure I know what Michael did was wrong, but my daughter didn't do anything." Lisa Farmer carefully pulled her hand away from the Judge in a way that would not seem in haste, and upset her family's only friend.

"I know, and that is why that you and baby Jessica are coming over to the house tonight for supper. I know that it's last minute notice, but I insist, and Janet has probably already set you a place," Judge Fall stood up from the park bench that he had been sitting on. "You know my wife...once my wife has made up her mind about something...there is no changing it. So it might just be easier if you came peacefully," the Judge snickered at his own comment about his wife's thought process.

"Judge, I can't..."

"You can and you will. I will not take no for an answer, or I might have to find you for contempt of the court. Besides I have a feeling that your luck my somehow turn around tonight." Judge Fall smiled.

"My luck? How's that?" Lisa had a questioned expression on her face.

"Supper my good lady. I will see you around six...ish?" The Judge bowed to his soon to be dinner guest.

"Thank you, but..."

"No buts...see you at six." Judge Fall waved goodbye to Lisa.

"Okay..." Lisa walked off even more intrigued by the day's happenings.

"And dress nice," the Judge shouted back at Lisa. "It's not everyday that you get to dine with the most prestigious judge in the entire county. Besides, you may never know who may come by. Plus I heard Janet say that women feel better about themselves when they look the part…or something about husband's spending money on frivolous things that make our wives look pretty. That last part was my own interpretation. Please don't tell Janet?" Judge Fall put his hands together in a motion of pleading, or praying if Lisa told his wife what he had said about her spending habits.

"No problem…it's our little secret," Lisa told the judge as she gave him a little wink.

A few minutes before six o' clock p.m.; Lisa, who was carried baby Jessica, rang the doorbell of her evenings hosts.

"Good evening Lisa, and there is little baby Jessica. It's amazing, she looks more and more like you everyday." Janet Fall answered the door to her home in the most welcoming manner.

"Thank you Mrs. Fall, and I must say that you have a lovely home. Thank you so much for inviting us tonight. I hope that it wasn't too much of a bother."

"Nonsense child. It was no bother at all. In fact, I should have insisted on this a long time ago. You know, your mother and I use to go swimming up at Potter's Landing years ago, before husbands and children. Even though sometimes they can be one and the same…husbands and children that is. You'll learn all about that when Michael…when…"

"It's okay Mrs. Fall. Michael did what he thought that he had to do. Michael is my husband, and I love him, but that doesn't make his actions right. Never the less; he is serving his time, and when he gets out we'll make the best of it. Just like we are doing now. Okay?" Lisa said her piece; and was happy that they got that part of the evening out of the way, and that she had finally stood up to one of her elders.

"Enough said. I didn't mean to pry. It was just that…"

"It's okay. If there is anything that you would like to know; I'd appreciate it if you asked me rather than the town. The town is small enough without the added weight of good southern gossip." Lisa put on a fake smile to show her gracious host that there were no hard feelings.

"Amen Lisa. Now Janet, you're not interrogating our guests before they even take off their jackets, are you?" Judge Fall butted in to break up what could have become a very heated debate.

"It's okay Judge. Your wonderful wife was just curious on how we've been getting along." Lisa commented as she held her smile, and her tongue.

"The whole town is just wondering how you all are getting along, and that's the problem. Nobody has time to get anything done, but they always have time to worry about what other people are up to. Right Janet? Judge Fall asked his wife.

"And how would I know. I barely have a moments rest being the wife of a judge." Janet Fall seemed to be offended by her husband's tone.

"I'm sure all that shopping wears you to a nub," Judge Fall said as he moved his right hand across his wife's lower back to calm her down.

"You want me to look presentable don't you?" Janet fired back in an eased and more playful tone.

"Of course dear," said Judge Fall as he winked at Lisa Farmer. "Lisa and I were just talking about that this very afternoon outside of Jerry's Diner."

"Talking about the way I dress?"

"Yes dear, but more like the way it makes you feel. Woman like."

"Woman like, what's that suppose to mean?"

"You see what I mean Lisa? I try and compliment the women, and she does a one eighty on me. Go figure." The Judge threw up in the arm to show that he had given up on understanding women.

"You better go figure how you're going to make your own dinner if you keep talking about me like that," Janet Fall said smiling.

Judge Fall could not contain his laughter any more, and so he let it all out; startling the baby who had been sleeping in her mother's arms.

"Judge and Mrs. Fall...you remind a lot of those old married couples on those old black and white TV shows. Still having that spark for one another."

"What do you mean old? I'm still as spry as the next geezer. Janet on the other hand is old."

"I am not...we're the same age."

"No we are not. You're thirteen month older than me. So no matter how old I get, you'll still be older than a geezer." Judge Fall playfully pointed out while he ran a few feet back to be out of his wife's arm reach, and to avoid any repercussions such a comment might have brought with it.

"Enough with this geezer talk. Lisa are you ready for supper?" Janet turned her attention back to her dinner guests.

"Yes I am, thank you. Where do you want me to put these?" Lisa asked as she took off Jessica's jacket and hat.

"Here I'll take them," Judge Fall said as he walked over to Lisa with his right arm out.

"Thank you Judge Fall."

"It's no problem. Please make yourself at home," The Judge whole-heartedly stated as he took the Farmer's outerwear.

"Yes dear…like the old geezer said, make yourself at home. I'm going to go get supper on the table," Janet slapped her husband lightly on his shoulder when he walked by, "and that's for telling my age."

Just then the phone rang, and Judge Fall went down the long hall to answer it.

"Who would be calling at a time like this?" Mrs. Fall wondered out loud.

"Telemarketers," Lisa joked as Mrs. Fall looked on.

"Like I was saying, you and the baby make yourselves comfortable while I get supper on the table," Janet Fall said, paying no obvious attention to Lisa's telemarketer joke.

"Mrs. Fall?"

"Yes dear?" Janet turned around in mid step to reface her guest.

"May I please use the restroom?"

71

"Why of course dear. It's down the hall, and the second door on the left." Janet pointed the way with thin pale fingers as she gave Lisa directions to the first floor bathroom.

Lisa took Jessica with her down the hall, where they passed Judge Fall hanging up the phone. "It's settled then…we'll see you in about an hour or so…okay…bye bye."

"Honey?" Janet asked her husband as he returned from using the hall phone.

"Yes dear?"

"Who was that on the phone?"

"That was Jerry Albright. I told him to come over this evening to offer Lisa a job at the diner. I think that it will work out beautifully between them. By the way where is Lisa?" The Judge asked as he looked around.

"She went to the bathroom."

"The Judge scratched his head, "I am getting old. I just saw our guests down the hall a second ago. Wow!"

Is that why you had the Farmers' over for supper, to get Lisa a job at the dinner?"

"Well sort of…you see…I had a few words with some of the town folks earlier, and Jerry said that he had a opening that he needed filled, and that Lisa Farmer would do just nicely. And so I may have mentioned that she and the baby were coming over to the house tonight for a little supper. That's it."

"That's it?" Janet Fall looked sternly at her husband. "What will I be hearing in town tomorrow that you're not telling me tonight? What did you do?"

"That's it…nothing else. So hurry up and get supper on the table so that Jerry doesn't come over during the meal and eat us out of house and home," Judge Fall motioned to his wife to hurry it up, "he'll be here in less than an hour.

By that time Lisa had exited the bathroom, and was headed down the hall towards the living room, carrying baby Jessica in her arms. When she was about half way down the hall, she heard her hosts in the kitchen talking about something. So she turned around, and made sure that they heard her, so there would be no confusion of her eves dropping on their conversation.

"Mrs. Fall, are you in here?"

"Why yes dear, come on in." Janet gave a quick glare at her husband.

"Do you need a hand with anything?"

"Well," Mrs. Fall said as she scanned the kitchen. "I could use a hand filling those glasses with that tea over there."

"It would be my pleasure Mrs. Fall."

Lisa stepped into the kitchen, but stopped like she forgot something."

"Please give me one quick minute. I left Jessica's carrier in the living room, and I need to go get it so that I can put her down."

Lisa left the kitchen and headed down the hall, to the living room. When she reached the spot on the floor where she had left the baby carrier, Lisa squatted down and placed Jessica in it. Then she buckled the safety straps and picked the entire thing up, baby and all.

As Lisa walked back down the hall towards the kitchen, she had an uneasy feeling about what the night might bring. Why did she have to dress up in her fanciest dress for dinner with people she knew her entire life. However, she did realize that it was dinner with a judge and his wife; both of who were the most influential people in the entire county. Lisa thought to herself, "Stop being so paranoid, it's not like your going to a job interview or something. Its just dinner. Dinner at a home that you were never invited to before. Weirder things have happed...I'm sure of it. Now pull yourself together, and be a gracious guest."

As Lisa reentered the kitchen, she saw the Judge carrying a dish filled with boiled potatoes into the dinning room. Lisa quickly, but carefully put Jessica in her baby carrier down on the floor, and jogged over to the Judge. "Here let me get those for you."

"Well at least someone appreciates me around here. Thank you Lisa, but I think that Janet told me not to let you lift a finger…a guest and all." The Judge gave an apologetic smile.

"Hog wash! Guest or no guest, I can still carry a bowl of potatoes to the table. Besides it is the least that I can do. Mamma always said that you got to earn your keep. Right?" Lisa flashed her own smile back at the Judge.

"I believe that my mother told me the same thing, and we all know that our mothers are always right…even when they're wrong."

"What are two gabbing about over there? The foods going to get cold if you don't get it on the table. Now move it…both of you. This food isn't going to eat itself," Janet demanded in a stern but pleasing tone; obviously after hearing the conversation between her husband and their guest.

"Yes dear." Judge Fall winked at Lisa.

"Yes Mrs. Fall." Lisa smiled and giggled softly so that Janet Fall would not hear.

The three adults and the baby all went into the dinning room to sit down to eat.

"Mrs. Fall, do you have an old kitchen chair or stool that I can use for Jessica?"

"What's wrong with one of those chairs," Janet said, pointing to a small group of chairs that were around the unused part of the dinning room table.

"Nothing! It's just that these chairs are so nice, and I want one that I can flip upside down right here next to me."

"Now why on Earth would you want to do something like that?" Janet looked at Lisa like she had just heard the dumbest thing on the planet.

"For the baby. You see…if you turn the stool upside down; it makes a nice little holder for the car seat carrier. That way Jessica can be up here with all of us, and not on the floor."

"Wow! I never thought of that. So, it's like a self made high chair for babies that are too young to use a high chair." Judge Fall chimed in as he took a fork full of food from his plate to his awaiting mouth.

"Exactly," Lisa exclaimed proudly as she sat up straight. "It's a lot easier than carrying a million different baby things around with me everywhere I go. This way I can just improvise and leave all the big stuff at home."

"I'll get something," the Judge said as he looked up from cutting his Pork Chop.

Judge Fall got up from the table, and went into the kitchen. He went to the backside of the island and got one of the bar stools that they had there. He picked it up and looked at it. He turned upside down while he was holding it, and examined it. He thought to himself, "I had never heard of such a thing, but times have changed, and the youth of this great nation know a lot more than the youth of my generation. They're more resourceful then my generation. Like this damn upside down stool. I never would of thought of that, yet it is so simple."

"Dear, are you coming back? Lisa would like to eat sometime tonight."

"Yes…. just one sec," Judge Fall answered his wife from the kitchen.

"You better not be in that pie I have on the counter." Janet shouted towards the kitchen.

"No dear," Judge Fall answered as he broke a little piece of the crust off of the Strawberry Rhubarb pie that his wife made earlier that day.

As the Judge walked back into the dinning room, the doorbell rang.

"Damn," the Judge whispered loudly. "Hide the Pork Chops dear before Jerry invites himself to stay awhile."

"Jerry? Jerry Albright from the diner?" Lisa looked at her guests, first at Janet and then her husband. "What's going on here?" Lisa asked confused.

Judge Fall looked at Lisa with his soft warm eyes; eyes of a person who really cared for her well-being. "I informed Jerry Albright that you would be here tonight, and that he should stop by AFTER DINNER to offer you the position that he needs filled at the diner."

"What?" Lisa stood up in disbelief. "Why?"

"Because," the Judge started to explain, "you needed help, and the people of this town weren't giving you a break."

"So you made them?" Lisa questioned the Judge's motives.

"No! I asked them to walk a mile in your shoes."

The doorbell rang again, and everyone looked towards the direction of the sound.

"Judge?" Lisa looked uneasy and confused.

"Lisa," Judge Fall walked around the table and took her hand, "this is a legitimate offer from Jerry to you. This isn't a handout, but a break. And the way things sound…you need a break. In a moment the offer will be on the table. Here Jerry out, and if you don't like it, then don't accept it. Do what is right for you, and there will be no hard feelings between any of us. Okay?"

"Okay Judge." Lisa gave Fall a hug, and then straightened her dress. "I'm ready."

CHAPTER 5

Joe Adams remembered the first time that he met Charles Jenkins. It was hard for him to believe that old childhood friends like them would die on the same day in different parts of the country. Life had been hard growing up in the poorest parts of the Los Angeles area of California.

"Hey you, what's your name?" This little scrappy looking kid came up to Charles as he watched his father and uncle unload their rented moving truck into their new apartment.

"My name is Charles. What is your name?" Young Charles answered back.

"Joey. Hey you want to be friends?" Joe asked as he ran off to play.

Charles' mother looked down at her son, "Go ahead and play with your new friend."

Charles ran off to catch Joe. "Hey Joey wait for me."

Joe Adams stopped and waited for the new kid to catch up. "I'm going to go into the First Grade after summer vacation," Joe pointed out.

"Me too," Charles replied.

"Maybe we'll have the same teacher? Hey, do you want to come to my birthday party? I'm going to be six in two weeks."

Charles had felt that this move was their best move so far. He had never met a friend on his first day at a new place before. "Yeah I'll go. What do you want for your birthday?"

Joe thought about his answer for a brief minute, "*G.I Joes*, *Transformers*, and boy stuff like that."

"Yeah, I hate little girl stuff. One time I found this doll, and I cut all of its hair off," Charles boasted to his new friend.

"We're going to good friends Charles," Joe exclaimed as he ran off again.

Life had been real hard for a lot of families in that part of California. Crime was up, but for a lot of people it was the only area that they could afford to live. Desperate people sometimes did desperate things to survive. The problem was when those desperate people turned to crime, and they ended up liking the feeling that it brought with it.

"This is Amelia Ortega with the Six o' clock Nightly News," the Jenkins family's television blared. "Our top story looks at the rising crime rate in our area compared to that of the rest of the nation. What are expectable levels, and what the police are doing to curve those numbers?"

Joe Adams grew up in the projects a few doors down from where Charles Jenkins grew up. When they were kids they always played together; everyone in the neighborhood did. There were no issues, just kids playing. To live in the Sunnyside Estates, your family had to be a low-income family, and have children under the age of eighteen or still in school. Which meant that all of the neighbors had kids, which made childhood fun for kids like Joe and Charles. The mothers would sit out gossiping and doing each other's hair and nails as they watched out for each other's children; while the fathers would be out working, looking for work, or whatever else that they did to bring home some money.

"Did you hear about Jo Jo's husband the other night?" One of the mothers asked as they sat out in the apartments community yard.

"Now Wanda...you know that your man is no better."

"Read the hand bitch. At least my man comes home at night," Wanda replied to the statement by putting her hand in front of the other ladies face. All the women paused for a moment to let the tension build up, then they all started to laugh hysterically.

"None of our men are good for nothing. Their mommas should have raised them better."

"Mommas? You should see my mother-in-law? She has more back hair than a gorilla," one of the other wives named Maria jested.

"That would explain his eating habits," another wife chimed in.

"That's funny bitch," Maria stated, "but true. I can't argue with that. That stupid son of a bitch has no manners at all, and our little Pedro is growing up just like him. Probably have back hair like his abuela too."

Life was fun for many years in the lives of Joe and Charles. They lived by one another, they went to the same school together, and they came home together to hang out and play together. As the boys and girls of the neighborhood matured into their young teenage years problems that were common in South Central Los Angles started to occur. Gangs and drugs were the biggest issues that faced the children in the area. The Sunnyside Estates that Charles and Joe grew up in fell in the middle of two rival gang's turf, and so there had been a constant battle for the land; resulting in bloodshed over the splitting of the land. Unfortunately, both Charles and Joe grew into their teenage years as active gang members; the once friends became rival gang members to one another.

"I don't care holmes. Keep that dead flag out of my face," Joe informed Charles as he tried to grab the red handkerchief out of Charles' hand.

"Fuck the scrapas homie, and their colored flue rags. This is the red side…catorce. The big Norte. You don't know anything about that Joey." Charles came back as he defended his new North side gang, while he proudly insulted Joe's South side click.

Joe Adams did not agree with the Notenos and how they did things. Charles Jenkins felt the same way about the Surenos. They could not convince each other to join the same gang, and so they went their separate ways; neither as enemies, nor as friends. Joe was courted into the PBS gang after school one Friday, which consisted of him standing in a circle of ten Play Boy Surenos, fighting them at the same time for thirty seconds. It was the longest thirty seconds of Joe Adam's life.

Charles also got jumped into a gang on a Friday after school, but his was with a Norteno gang. The way that they did things was that every Norteno gangster that was present could jump in and fight the person being courted in for an undetermined amount of time. There would always be one person who stayed out of the coronation to keep track of the time. In reality, the timekeeper was nothing more than a referee that ended the fight when he felt that the new person had enough.

"Simón holmes. You did it bro."

"What's my tag holmes?" Charles asked as he stood bloody from the fight of the gang coorination.

"Fuck that holmes. You have to earn that shit." That was the only answer Charles received about the topic of earning a new tag name; the street name that every other gang banger knew one another as. A street gang member could go through life without ever knowing another gangster's given birth name. A name that Charles Kenkins would soon receive.

"Check this out holmes," Dumbo threw an article of clothing at Charles Jenkins.

"Hell yeah," Charles stated as he unfolded a black sweatshirt that had red letters spelling out the name Bloody Loc in the *Old English* style of lettering.

"Check this vato out," Dumbo joked, "he's all crying and happy and shit because he's somebody now."

After years of living next to one another, but never speaking; Joe and Charles grew accustom to their separate but similar lives. It was not until Charles was allowed to retire as an OG from the Norteno

Red Ridaz that he actually approached Joe on an individual level as an acquaintance rather than as a rival. Joe Adams did not know how to take the new Bloody Loc. They were friends, then rival gang members, and then Charles wanted to talk again after more than half a decade as enemies.

Joe had always liked Charles, and Charles had always liked Joe. That was the main reason that the two never fought in all of the years as potential enemies. Their gangs rumbled with each other or with other rival gangs, and if one or two gang bangers were out alone there was always a chance that they would be jumped or shot at. However, if Joe and Charles were both involved then they would step out. Both parties had the respect of their peers to be allowed to accomplish that feat. That was why when Charles went to Joe's house; Joe let him inside.

"What?" Joe asked rudely as he answered the door after someone had knocked.

"What's up Joey?"

"Well…well…if it isn't Mr. OG Bloody Loc. I heard that you retired?" Joe Adams stated sarcastically.

"I did holmes." Charles shook his head, but never taking his eyes off of Joe.

"So what do you want ese?"

"I want to talk Joey."

"About what holmes? We have nothing to talk about. You're Norte and I'm the right way…entendes?" Joe took the blue handkerchief out of his back pocket and ran it slowly through his fingers.

"I get it, but we used to be cool. I'm no longer that vato who banged, but I'm no little kid either ese. Just let me in holmes." Charles refused to back down to Joe's obvious attempt of intimidation.

"Orale," Joe replied to Charles plea.

The two former childhood friends talked about their lives and what had changed for them. They both liked the idea of letting things between them fall in the past; no matter how difficult that may have been. One of the biggest hurdles that no longer existed was that Charles was no longer an active member of the Notenos; although he would still be associated with them for life.

"Do you remember when we were little chavalos getting into trouble, and our moms getting all mad at us?"

"Simón Chuck, but check it out. We're no longer those little chavalos playing hide and seek like we used to, or playing football in the streets. We've grown into different adults; we're men now."

"I get it, but did you ever have the urge to hit me even though we weren't cool?" Charles put up his fists like he was about to box, but them put them down again to show Joe that he was giving an example.

"Never holmes."

"Why is that you think?"

"I don't know. It just never felt right." Joe shook his head in what seemed to Charles as remorse.

"I know Joey…me too. I don't bang any more, and so we don't have this color thing between us. It's just you and me…entendes?"

"So why don't you bang holmes?" Joe asked even though he had heard the answer on the streets before he had even asked.

"After I got shot at Baby G's funeral, I woke up eight months later vato. The world had passed me on, but it was only a minute for me. And when I woke up, there was this girl who saved my life."

"Sorry about getting shot holmes, but I didn't have anything to with that." Joe gave his one time friend his condolences as he sat down on the living room couch.

"No worries…I know." Charles stated as he sat down on the opposite end of the green vinyl sofa bed couch.

"Seriously homie...that was messed up. They killed that vato's familia and everything. That shit's fucked up." Joe spoke about Baby G's family and their deaths.

"I know, but there's nothing we can do about it now," Charles frowned.

"Yeah there is...I'm through too holmes."

"What do you mean through Joey?" Charles questioned his old friend Joe Adams.

"I mean like you. No more banging. No more putting in work. No more dirt. It's over holmes."

"They're not just not going to let you walk away bro." Charles tried reasoning with Joe as he repositioned himself from the edge of his seat to a more comfortable position against the back of the couch.

"Simón, pero I have an idea. You know those pinche Chicanos Por Vida?"

"Yeah I know them. They shot up Chico's party." Charles answered in a pissed off tone.

"They're like those *Borg* vatos from that TV show *Star Trek*. They come in and take over gangs. They conquer them, and make them part of their own gang. It makes them big but weak."

"How's that?" Charles asked sort of confused.

89

"It's like the United States holmes...*Civil War*."

"Like the *Civil War*?" Charles understood the concept of Joe's description. Charles then laughed at himself because he himself never picked up the comparison between TV sitcoms, U.S. history, and the CPV's.

"Simón ...they take over gangs that use to be enemies and then they tell them that they're on the same side now. Then those gangsters who are thrown together as CPV's in the same gang then have to fight against other Sureno or Norteno gangs that used to be their allies. There are too many vatos who don't want to work together to put their differences aside to keep the CPV's from falling apart...like the *Civil War* in the North and South...just like us bro...the North and the South."

"So how are they going to help you?" Charles again looked confused.

"The PBS's are fighting them right now...for the last two or three months. Pretty soon the Play Boys will be no more, and I'll walk away from a member less gang."

"That works?"

"Hell yeah. How can I be part of a gang that isn't around no more?" Joe excitedly proclaimed.

"True." Charles nodded in agreement, and finally understood the point that Joe was trying to make.

"We should do something else holmes...like be cops or something."

"Cops? What are you a narc?" Charles sat up rather quickly.

"Fuck that...I'm just saying vato, that our lives are ours. If we can be cool again, then we can be anything we want. You know like that one kid's old man who used to take us on patrol with him when we were all little chavalos?" Joe thought back to his childhood.

Charles also thought back to his childhood for a moment. "You mean that little kid Paul? That vato was cool for a little kid, and having the police for his dad. Officer Myers? Now he's a bad ass cop; he cared and shit." Charles looked at Joe, "I'll bet that little kid will grow up and the hura too, just like his old man.

"Si...like him...Officer Meyers." Joe thought deeply about the man who made a difference in their neighborhood.

"But cops?" Charles threw up his hands.

"Yeah bro I know...I was just using the extreme. So tell me about this girl who saved your life? And I heard that you found God in the rich part of high society. Is that true?" Joe asked in attempt to learn more about his old friend that had returned.

"Simón Joey." Charles nodded.

CHAPTER 6

Three years after the first attack...

"Mr. President?" Secretary of Dense Andrews spoke to get the war weary President's attention.

"Yes John!" President Mason looked up from behind his desk.

"We have captured General Rachlav here in the U.S., and he is...uncooperative to say the least."

"Hmmm..." the President quickly pondered the course this news brought.

"Sir...we need him alive." Secretary of Dense Andrews quickly pointed out before the President could make any rash and uncalculated judgments.

"Move him to the Black Site at Camp Delta. As of now Rachlav is your number one priority. He has become our highest value detainee."

"But sir, he's a POW?" Andrews tried to make the President understand that they had captured a General in the Russian military, and not some random terrorist.

"As far as the United States is concerned, General Rachlav is missing in action. And John...no paper trail on this one." President

Mason stood up face to face with Secretary of Dense Andrews to make sure that his instructions were clearly understood.

"Yes sir!" John Andrews turned and left the Oval Office.

"And dammit! Give me something that I can use," POTUS proclaimed as Andrews was still within his normal hearing range.

Camp Delta, Guantanamo Bay, Cuba; a Black Site for prisoners who need to stay quiet and outside of the legal jurisdiction of the U.S. government. A place that has little public and political say. That's the way that POTUS likes it, and that's the way General Fox runs it: don't know, don't tell.

"Roger that; November, 4, 4, 7, 6, Sierra. You are free to land."

Dressed in a standard orange jumpsuit, General Rachlav entered his new maximum-security home, simply known as *Camp 3*. Here was where all detainees go when they first arrive at *Camp Delta*, and based on their cooperation and level of security risk, inmates could move up or down into other camps and possibility to more accommodating living arrangements. However, General Rachlav was not one of those accommodating type of individuals, and after a moth of interrogating the Russian leader, the U.S. knew no more of Russia's plans for the Americans then they did before they captured Rachlav.

"I want my lawyer." The Russian General demanded.

"You don't have a lawyer," Lieutenant Colonel Mitchell reminder Rachlav.

"I have studied the laws of the United States, and I know my rights." General Rachlav tried to stand, but with no luck of success.

"Perhaps, but then you would have read that under Article 17 of the I Don't Give A Shit handbook, that it clearly states that any stupid ass political bastard that attacks my home and kills my family, willing revokes his rights. And those who refuse to give up their rights will get the living shit kicked out of them. Am I clear...General?"

"America is weak. You have nothing to offer. Even if you kill me, Russia will conquer your pathetic nation." The General smugly remarked before he spit the Lieutenant Colonel's face.

"GUARDS! I think the General here as earned a little R & R." Lieutenant Colonel Mitchell looked back at the two-armed Marines behind General Rachlav.

"What is this R & R?" The General asked as he looked at the faces of the three United States Marines in the room with him.

"Oh it stands for lots of things...like Rock and Roll, but in this case it may stand for Rape and Re-rape. Just like your dead wife...right General? You couldn't stand the thought of her being with a real man...an American man. So you killed her, just like you killed millions of my people…you murdering piece of shit." Lieutenant Colonel Mitchell grabbed General Rachlav by the upper part of his orange jumpsuit and flung him to the floor, chair and all.

"You can't touch me! I am a General in the Russian Military. Am I not a Prisoner of War?" The General made his point as he looked up from his position on the floor as he tried to sit up.

"General, we don't have any POWs here at Gitmo…as far as I know you're an unknown terrorist," Mitchell stated as he helped the Russian leader back into his chair.

"The Geneva Convention clearly states that I am a Prisoner of War," Rachlav spoke as he slammed his cuffed fists into the wooden fold up table that he sat behind.

"You're an enemy combatant, and until I hear further, that's what you'll stay. Besides, nobody knows that you're here…General." Lieutenant Colonel Mitchell reminded the Russian General who was in charge as he spat in Rachlav's face.

Two more months ago by and General Rachlav was allowed access to *Camp Echo* to meet with his lawyers, after Presidents Mason and Ubiikobyla agreed to meet for peace talks in a secured location in Seattle, WA. Both sides demand that the other surrender, and release key individuals who were taken as hostages. The peace talks broke down, and as President Ubiikobyla left the Seattle location, he was flocked by hundreds of reporters and cameras from news stations around the world.

"The people of the United States of America," Ubiikobyla started, "it is my pleasure to inform you that I indeed have been in communication with my famous General Rachlav from your secret prison camp in Cuba. I will also say that I feel sorry for the prisoners of the United States of America, and that I will rectify an unjust undoing by your country by allowing you to turn against the ones that have caged you like animals by joining the ranks of Russia's forces, and help make America something that you can be proud of."

"President Ubiikobyla," a reporter yells as he raised his hand, "what are saying?"

"I am saying that Russia's forces will focus their attacks onto maximum security prisons, super max prisons, and your not so secretive Black Site prisons. We will do this to give the people of this country a choice on how they want to live their lives. Even if these caged animals do not join with Russia, they will still wreak havoc on the civilians of your precious America."

"Mr. President! Mr. President!" reporters scream as President Ubiikobyla's security team forced individuals out of the way of the President's car.

"I have nothing further to say to you people." The Russian President stated as he looked down upon the people who swarmed him.

Within minutes of the news, maximum-security prisons around the country came to life with the rumble of riots, and the anticipation of President Ubiikobla's promise of an early release.

"Yo Joker, here comes the CO," Puppet informed his cellmate as he looked down the tier with an illegal small piece of mirror.

"Hola Officer Jenkins. Why don't you open these bars and let us burn this puta down?" Joker confronted the Correction Officer as he ran his fingers back and forth along the cell bars.

"Back away from these bars Ramirez," Officer Charles Jenkins demanded.

"Chale, holmes! I got your back ese. Open these doors vato and you can go home to your wife and kids ese." Joker Ramirez tried to calm the Correctional Officer down with a threatening but pleading tone.

"STEP AWAY FROM THE BARS!" Jenkins screamed out loud to his prisoner.

"Check it out Puppet, this chignon has balls."

"Orale carnal!" Puppet agreed with his cellie.

"Check it out holmes! You can let us out and you got my word that you can go home. If you don't, I'll show your wife some respect of my own," Joker threatened Officer Jenkins.

"That's it! You're going to hole Ramirez." Jenkins was then beyond mad.

"Your punk ass comes into my house ese...I'll shank you holmes," Joker Ramirez threatened the Officer's life.

"Against the back wall," Officer Jenkins demanded, "both of you levas."

"Orale! But when the pinche Russians get here; I'm no longer going to be locked up holmes. Entendes?"

"The Russians aren't coming to get your sorry ass," Jenkins said not backing down from Joker's meaningless promises.

"Check it out holmes...they're coming. That vato on the TV said so. I don't give a fuck; if they come, they come. I ain't scared...I'll bang the color of Russia red. Cause red is red...no matter whose hood you're from," Joker boasted proudly.

"Orale holmes," Puppet agreed.

Hours later it started; maximum-security prisons up and down the West Coast were targeted with missiles, and taken by the Russians. With the attacks of the invading army on the outside, and the prisoners on the inside; prison officials had nothing else to do except surrender.

"Surrender your prison or die like your comrades; Officer Jenkins?" Russian Commander Demidov gave the grave choice to the kneed Corrections Officer after they captured him when the Russian military took *Folsom* prison.

"That's what I like about you Ruskies; you're not afraid to use cheesy ass ultimatums. Man…what the hell. Kill me bitch!" Officer Jenkins exclaimed. "There is some quote that says something like I'd rather die on my feet than live on my knees."

"Yes…I have heard of this quote that you speak of," Commander Demidov shook his head in agreement. "It is a good policy to follow."

Correctional Officer Jenkins chimed in and said, "Yeah, but I have a better one."

"And what is that Officer Jenkins?" The annoyed Russian Commander asked.

"Fuck Russia, and fuck your two bit whore of a mother," Jenkins proudly proclaimed as he flipped his right middle finger up for the entire prison to see. "The U.S. is going to kick your sorry asses, so like I said before…kill me bitch."

"Принесите мне архивы на пленниках. Хотеть быть свободно первым.

ТЕПЕРЬ!"

"Командир права отсутствующий."

"Hey Commander Dumb ass…here in America we expect you to speak our language…English…Bitch," Jenkins smugly said due to the fact that he was a red blooded American who was about to die.

"I'm so sorry Officer Jenkins…I meant no disrespect to your last moments of life. I simply told my man to bring me the files on the prisoners. The most wanting to be free first. Then I yelled the word "now" to have him hurry up." Commander Demidov explained to the captive prison guard.

"Why hurry…where are you going in such a hurry? America is nice this time of year." Jenkins joked as he tried to stand up.

"You are an American comedian…no?" The Russian Commander kicked Officer Jenkins back to the ground.

"Огорченно к interupt. Здесь командир архивов."

"На английском языке."

"In English, Commander?" Commander Demidov informed another Russian officer.

"You dare question me soldier?"

"No Sir…never…sorry Sir," the lesser-ranked officer apologized to his Commanding Officer.

"Good! Then repeat what you told me…in English. For we are guest in these people's country, and we have no secrets from our gracious hosts." Russian Commander Demidov said as he looked around the prison yard with his arms opened in an inviting manner.

"Yes commander! Like I said in our Mother tongue…Sorry to interrupt. Here are the files, Commander."

The Russian soldier handed over the files to his Commanding officer, "Thank you," said Demidov.

"Why do you want those files Comrade?" Charles Jenkins asked. "You can already see that this prison houses some of America's finest specimens of lowlifes on the face of the Earth…well until I met you putos."

"Nicely said Officer Jenkins," the Russian Officer said clapping. "However, I'm looking at these files to find me just the right person to kill you where you kneel."

"Don't want to get your hands dirty?" Jenkins spat at the Russian Commander, but missed.

"No Officer Jenkins...I do not mind getting my hands...dirty. I am giving my new American followers what they want. Something of their own...what you would call a gift, or possibly a sacrifice...depending how you look at it. Either way, I'm giving them a chance to kill their capture. One of them sacrifices you...I give them all their freedom. A fair offer in my mind...do you not agree?" Demidov squatted down so that he was face to face with Jenkins. "Check mate," said Commander Demidov as he then spit in Correctional Officer Jenkins face without missing.

"You can't do this." Jenkins pleaded.

"Yes Officer Jenkins, I can...and I have. Inmate 778129 Lance Flanders, please come up and join us." The Russian Commander looked carefully over the sea of *Folsom* inmates as he looked for movement among the masses.

After the initial shock of hearing his name being called by a Russian military officer; Lance Flanders made his way through the bodies of alive and dead prison personnel; both prisoners and prison employees alike. When Lance got closer to the Russian Commander, two Russian soldiers grabbed him by his arms and escorted Lance the rest of the way.

"Mr. Flanders. I am Commander Demidov of Russia." The Russian Commander opened his arm with his hands palm up in a social greeting, even though Lance Flanders was not allowed to touch him in any way.

"A pleasure, I'm sure Commander, but why me?" Lance looked confused.

"In your file, Mr. Flanders, it reads that you are on your way to serve prison time until you are dead from old age. Is that true?" Commander Demidov asked as he rescanned Flanders' file.

"Yes Sir, but so are a lot of these other guys." Lance turned around and pointed hastily at the other inmates.

"This is true, but I'm giving you a chance to prove that you are more than a wife beater in front of your American peers…as well as all of Russia before you."

"Prisoner Flanders, get back to your cell, and I'll testify that you cooperated with prison officials during the time of the attack," Officer Jenkins demanded.

"Officer Jenkins…your words fall on deaf ears. Mr. Flanders does not want to go back to prison if he does not have to. Is this not right Mr. Flanders?" Commander Demidov put his large right arm over Lance's shoulder.

"Yes Sir Commander Din…Demrof…Dem…" Lance Flanders stuttered over the Russian leaders name.

"Demidov…Commander Demidov." Commander Demidov corrected as he removed his arm from the American idiot.

"Sorry…Commander Demidov." Lance said with a shaky voice.

"It says in your personnel file that you Mr. Flanders originally were sentenced in a Texas maximum-security prison for killing in-laws, and family." Commander Demidov looked at Lance with an amused look on his face.

"Well between you and me Commander," Lance said with more confidence. "I killed my cheating wife's parents, her sisters, and their families. They tried to hide her from me. They thought that I was crazy, and might do something. The only reason that I didn't get the death penalty is because I told the cops where the bodies were."

"And now Mr. Flanders; how did you get here to this prison so far from your home?" The Commander looked around as if he could see Texas from inside the prison walls.

"As I was saying Commander…my wife was hiding from me, and a while back I found her lying ass from prison. I got to her, and she got scared and had the harassments stopped. One night as I was cursing my life…this CO came into my cell and ripped up my last letter to wife…right in front of me. I ripped out his throat for ripping my letter…he'll never laugh at anyone ever again. So for security issues they shipped me here…to this hell hole," Lance started to laugh. Then he turned to Officer Jenkins and kicked him in the face.

"This is why…Mr. Flanders…that I have chosen you to end the life of your capture, and to be free to make amends with your wife…face to face back in your state of Texas."

The Russian Commanders drew his weapon from its holster and handed the butt of the gun to Lance Flanders; who took it in his trembling hands.

"Choices Lance…you have a choice here Lance…we all do." Charles Jenkins tried to get his point across to the dazed and confused inmate.

"SHUT UP…you…your not…your not my CO anymore Officer Jenkins." Lance Flanders yelled at Officer Jenkins from mere inches away. Charles could feel the spit as it stuttered out from Lance's trembling lips.

Lance Flanders raised the gun to make contact with Officer Jenkins's forehead.

"Lance…I have a family…a wife…" the Correctional Officer pleaded for his life.

"And how would you feel if she testified against you?" Lance asked as he pulled the trigger.

A single gunshot, and all was quite as Commanding Officer Charles Jenkins fell to the ground…dead.

"Release these prisoners, and gather them for a speech in the main prison yard." Commander Demidov commanded his troops.

The Russians commanded the remaining prison guards to release the prisoners who were not already freed of their cells. In the yard, every individual in the prison, including the warden, stood crowed together. There was a massive rumble between the prisoners and the guards, the prisoners and other prisoners, the guards and the Russians, and the prisoners and the Russians. It was complete chaos, until the AK's started to fire, which loudly ripped through the prison. Multiple shots were fired; some overhead, and some into the crowd. Then there was only silence, and complete attention was then focused on the Russian Commander.

"I am sorry that I had to have my men shoot at you," Russian Commander Demidov apologized. "My actions were only to get your attention. It must be hard to be in a situation where you can finally fight back against your capturers, but aren't allowed to. I ask you for your patients. At this very moment Russian forces are taking other maximum-security prisons. Within a few months, every prison shall fall into our hands. The United States will fail to stop us. Every prison we take for ourselves increases our military numbers by the hundreds. Of course, you do not have to join the Russian military. This is the land of the free, and with that you are free to make choices. You can go on your own and fight against the ones who took you freedom, and maybe you will get killed because you are out numbered. The United States will hunt you like dogs. You can choose to die, or you can choose to join our forces and take back your country. Together our numbers will increase. Your military is fighting battles on two fronts. This is impossible to overcome. It is a matter of time before this land is ours...all of ours. So join us, and together we will make America great."

CHAPTER 7

Nathan Fox watched as the coffin was lowered into the grave. Once friends, his dead counterpart laid at rest along side his wife. Nathan did not attend the funeral to morn the passing of Mike Striker, or to visit the grave of Mike's wife Brenda. In fact he had hated the Striker couple since high school. Nathan Fox had attended the funeral that Saturday to observe their only son under pressure from loosing both parents.

"What do I do Dad?" Eric thought to himself as he looked down into the grave that his Father's silver coffin was lowered into. "That bastard is here, and he is starring at me. How dare he show his face after all these years? What do I do Dad?"

All Nathan knew about Major Eric Striker for sure was that he was an only child whose mother died during childbirth, and that his father Mike raised him in a military home. Nathan Fox looked into Eric's personnel files once in a while, to see what kind of a soldier he had become. As far as he could see, Eric only became a military man because of his father. But unlike Mike Striker, or even Nathan Fox himself; Eric did not join the Marines to lead people, but to be a fighter pilot with ambitions to fly into space one day. However, that dream would never be a reality in Nathan's eyes, because Eric was a sub class soldier who made rank of Major because of his connections rather than by merit. Eric had no real family left as far as Nathan knew, but even if he did; no one would ever miss Major Striker if some unseen mishap was to occur that lead to his death.

As Fox looked around at the people who attended Mike's funeral he smugly thought to himself, "I was right. There are a lot of Military personnel, but not a lot of civilians. Eric has no family, and so I'll welcome him with open arms into my extended Marine family. Where he will die, as all Strikers should."

Nathan Fox looked down at the hole in the ground, then back up to the solemn looking man across from him, and confirmed that he made the right choice in life. This so-called fighter pilot before him would lead the act that would betray a nation to save it. Eric Striker would either be a hero to the United States, or a devil in disguise; but no matter what, Eric Striker would be dead and all of Nathan's past mistakes buried along with the final remaining Striker family member.

Nathan Fox thought back to high school, and his choice to go into the military despite his own father's warnings. Nathan and Mike Striker decided that they would join the Marines together. Nathan had always considered Mike to one of his closest friends, if not the closest.

They did everything together, but even a friendship as tight as theirs could easily be broken up over the love of a girl. Brenda was no girl, and Nathan loved her from the start; Mike knew that. Mike betrayed Nathan by stealing Brenda away from him. Sure they had troubles, but they were young, and they had always worked out their problems before Mike butted into the relationship. As far as Nathan remembered, he and Brenda's relationship was on the right track. Nathan was finished up with school, and had started down a very promising career and future within the ranks of the United States Marine Corp. Their future was to be set in stone, before Mike convinced her to betray her true feelings of love.

Nathan remembered one of the conversations that he had with Brenda before Mike ripped them apart. It seemed like a lot of their conversations somehow involved Mike Striker. Nathan drifted off into a daydream state as he thought about his own truthful words to Brenda, "Mike came up to me today and asked my permission to ask you out. I guess the guy has been crushing on you for ever, and didn't do anything because we were buds or something."

"Brenda," Nathan's voice just barely audible, "my words were meant to show you what a creep and stocker Mike was. They weren't meant to drive you away…they were meant to protect you. I loved you, and you killed me when I was most vulnerable. Your dead, Mike's dead, and soon your only child will be dead."

At the time of their falling out, Nathan felt that he had been betrayed by the two people that he cared for most. So to balance that pain, he attempted to hurt them. Nathan left for basic training along with his former friend Mike. They had a huge falling out prior to their departure, but they still had to go on with their decision to be part of something bigger. They had to become Marines like they signed up to do while they were still friends. After boot camp, the two former friends were stationed at different bases to finish their training in their specified fields. This decision was a delight to Nathan, because he was tired of seeing that back stabber Mike everyday and night.

Nathan recalled that the only time he had heard from Brenda after their break up, was in the form of a letter that she had written him after he had finished his run at basic training. He almost did not reply to the letter, but he thought that he should reply in a way that was both fitting and reflective of his still broken heart, and so he did. That was the last time that he had contact with either Brenda or Mike prior to the Mike's funeral. Over the years, however, Nathan secretly checked in on the Striker family from time to time to see how things evolved within their lives. To Nathan, the Striker family was a project gone wrong. With the death of Brenda, and Mike; Eric would be the last to die before Nathan could be free of their hold over him.

It was at this time that Nathan's full idea to help end the war with the Russians came into complete mental view. He needed Major Eric Striker to be on board to pull it off, and so approached the young man after the funeral was concluded.

"Major Striker?" Nathan Fox walked up to the hurt young Marine.

"General Fox, what a surprise to see you at my father's funeral?" Eric Striker saluted the General that stood before him.

"Well, we are in the same branch of the military," Fox answered as he returned the salute. "At ease Major. We can be formal here."

"Yes sir, but excuse me I didn't realize that you and my father were acquainted," Eric lied. In fact, Eric Striker knew all about his father's past with Nathan Fox. He knew about the secret that devastated his mother, and the letter that said it all. Eric knew enough about Nathan Fox that he never had to meet the man, to hate the man.

"Did your father ever talk about me? As you may or may not know, we're from the same town. We even went to high school together; your mom, dad, and myself. We were quite close for a while, but life happens and people move on." The General spoke in a slow and calm voice as he tried to put Eric at ease while he tried to extract as much information as possible from the Major.

"I didn't know that," Eric lied again. After he read the letter that his dad gave him a few months before he died; Eric investigated what had really happened, and whom Nathan Fox and his parents really were.

"He never mentioned me?" General Fox looked pleasantly surprised.

"No...why? Should he have?" Eric thought about his answer after he saw the smirk on Fox's lips.

"No, but when people get sick...sometimes they dwell on the past, and your father and me had a falling out years ago. I thought that maybe he would have talked about it with you."

"To ease his conscience General? No offence sir, but my father was great man. If he had any guilty feelings; he never shared them with me. Knowing my father, if he had a falling out with someone; it wasn't his fault...sir." Eric's words and tone bordered the line of what some would call slander of a higher ranked officer, which could have resulted in a court martial.

"Maybe you didn't know Mike Striker as well as you thought that you did," Fox replied. He picked up Striker's tone and knew that he had pushed the pilot too far, and that any guarded information about the Striker family would stay guarded on that day.

"Maybe you're right, but he's dead and we'll never find out." Striker dropped the attitude, and looked back at his dad's gravesite.

"He is dead, and that is why I'm here. To offer you a position that could save America from total disaster with the Russians."

"You're here, at my father's funeral, on business?" Major Striker turned his attention back towards the General.

"Yes…yes I am. If I knew Mike Striker at all, he would do what was right no matter the outcome." Fox's own words made him think back to his troubled past. "Son, your country needs you."

Eric thought that it could be the moment that he needed to get close to General Nathan Fox. He knew that he hated him, but he needed to validate his own feelings about the man. The only way to do that would be to work along side him. In time Fox would trust him, and let his guard down. Then and only then would the true Nathan Fox come out. Eric needed General Fox to trust him, but he did not know that Nathan Fox planned to play him too, and that Nathan needed Eric's trust as much as he did.

"Okay General, what did you have in mind?" Eric asked as if they were old friends, or father and son.

"Let's go somewhere a little more concealed." General Fox looked around with his eyes.

The two military men walked along paths that lead to the General's limousine. Once inside, General Fox continued his discussion with Eric Striker.

"Major Striker...may I call you Eric?" Fox briefly put his right hand on Striker's left knee.

"Of course General."

"Good! As I was saying by your dad's grave, your country needs you. Quite a few years ago...many years ago...Russia lost a couple of planes. Intel never gave us a concise picture of what happened to them, or at least that's what we tell the people that we are trying to protect...or hide them from." Fox sat back and examined the look on Striker's face, and if he could comprehend what was going on.

"Are you saying that we have the missing planes?" Striker made an intelligent guess based on the General Fox's roundabout story.

"Yes we do, and nobody knows about them...not the Russians, or even our own President. It has the highest most level of security clearance in our nation. Knowledge of this mission could be considered treason if taken too lightly."

"Of course sir, but what does have to with me or my father?" Striker was panicked and felt that he was in over his head. He tried to show no emotion as he spoke to the General.

"Your dad owed me one, and frankly I feel as though you are the right pilot for this exact mission." General Fox slapped Striker's left leg again.

"Pilot?" Striker asked while his mind started to race with the possibilities of was to happen with the pieces of knowledge that Fox had gave him.

CHAPTER 8

Paige Flanders was scared, happy, relieved, and overwhelmed when the judge handed down a thirty year to a life sentence to her husband of sixteen years, Lance Flanders. To be honest, it was the greatest day of her life. Paige never knew what ailed her husband, but whatever it was; it haunted his dreams. Paige lived everyday of her married life in a state of unknowingness. She never could judge how the day was going to go; was her husband going to be happy, pissed off, depressed, loving, charismatic, or full of rage? No matter how Lance's mood happened to be, it always started and ended with a few beers.

"Paige! I'm out of beer. Make sure you get the right kind this time. I'm tired of drinking this light shit." Lance through his empty beer can at his wife before he got up from the breakfast table.

Paige touched her face as she remembered the one and only time that she questioned Lance about his drinking before work; his answer was still visible in the bathroom mirror reflection after twelve years of trying to cover it up.

"You stupid bitch. Look at what you made me do?" Lance held the back of Paige's long dark hair so that she could see the glowing red burner on the stove. "You made me burn your face. I work and work for this family, and all I get is hell for having a beer once in a while. Don't I deserve some peace and quite sometimes."? Lance let go of his wife as she fell to the floor bawling. "Clean this shit up, your burning flesh is making me sick."

Paige held he face as she pulled herself up. The pain was unbearable, but she had to endure it for her own survival.

"Were the fuck is my breakfast?" Lance asked while still in a rage.

Paige was sure to be home and have dinner hot and ready for Lance when he came in the door, no matter what time it was. Sometimes Lance would come home happy and almost seeming like he enjoyed life, and to end off the perfect day, Lance would have himself a half rack of *Coors* to celebrate. Most days however, Lance would come home hating the world and the trailer that they lived in because it was like his momma's trailer. Lance would finish off those days with enough beer to make him man enough to beat Paige for all of his problems, and then when he thought she had enough, he would continue his drinking binge until he passed out. Paige would wait until

119

he passed out, then she would put her husband to bed, because if she forgot to; she would get it worse in the morning; reason being, God fearing Christian wives took care of their husbands. So Lance would beat the Devil out of Paige, freeing her of her demons and immoral ways.

"Where are my pants Paige?" Lance asked in a demanding tone. "It's Tuesday, and you know that I have to go to work so that I can bring home the money that feeds your fat ass."

Paige looked at herself in her full-length mirror that hung on the closet door, as she got dressed. Her one hundred and fifteen pound frame did not seem big to her, in fact she thought women like herself looked a little bit better with slightly more weight on them.

"In fact," Lance continued as he looked over towards his dressing wife, "why don't you go on a diet and save us a few bucks. It's not like you couldn't skip a few meals."

Paige just stood there as tears streamed down her face. She cried quietly as she finished getting ready for the day.

Paige had no one to turn to, or to even talk to when it came to serious matters like Lance and his drinking. Paige was allowed to visit with her friends when her chores were done, and as long as she was home and waiting for Lance when he came home. Her friends consisted of a few neighbor women in similar situations. The entire trailer park knew what was happening, but no one ever spoke of it, because if it ever got back to one of the husbands; there would hell to pay. Paige knew in her heart that she loved Lance, she also knew that her body and mind could not take much more of his abuse. She considered leaving a few times, but knew what the Bible and The Almighty preached about divorce; besides Lance would track her down and murder her before she got out of the glorious state of Texas.

"Why Lord did you put me in such a place?" Paige Flanders' prayed while she fell to her knees. "What lessons am I to learn from this madness? How am I to save my husband?"

When Paige first met Lance, she fell in love with this mystery that surrounded him and his family. She was never allowed to come over to his house, or inquire about his family. This intrigued Paige so much that she made finding out about Lance Flanders her pet project. Paige herself came from a middle class family that owned their own little fifties style ranch home in the middle of town. The Pottersmith family owned and operated a general store named The Lone Star Corral; which sold everything from milk and pizza sauce; to clothing, toys, and toilet paper. Paige liked working for her parents, and being one of the only kids in school with a paycheck; made her a little bit more popular they she would otherwise had been. By no means were the Pottersmith family the richest family in town, but by no means were they the poorest. Paige received a car on her sixteenth birthday, just like her older sisters, Nancy and Beth, did when they turned sixteen. The car was not new, but it was the nicest gift Paige had ever received, and she was grateful for it.

"Here you go honey. Happy birthday sweetheart." Mr. Pottersmith handed his youngest daughter the keys to her very own *Ford Mustang* convertible.

Paige invited her friend Lance to her sweet sixteen party, but he never showed. It upset Paige, but she knew the reasons why. So instead, after the party she loaded up her new birthday car with a blanket and leftover birthday cake and drove over to Lance's house. As soon as she pulled into the parking area in front of Lance's trailer, he came bolting out screaming at her. Paige started to cry, and Lance consoled her, and then left in the car with her to help celebrate her very special day.

"I'm sorry Paige," Lance whispered as he held her. "I'm embarrassed of where I live, and my family isn't the most well rounded family in the county. I didn't mean anything by it. I swear I'll make it up to you."

"You swear?" Paige looked up at Lance, and saw him for the beautiful person that he was on that moonlit night.

"I swear," Lance confirmed smiling.

"Good then," Paige slapped her empty front passenger side seat. Lets go! It's my birthday, and I want to celebrate."

That night the two friends confessed their love for one another; crossing the threshold of friendship into that of lovers. Late that night after Paige was home in bed, Lance climbed up to her window and proposed marriage. Tree weeks after Paige's seventeenth birthday; Paige Pottersmith became Mrs. Paige Flanders.

"I do," Paige said as she answered the Pastor's question about taking Lance to be her husband.

Paige looked around her parent's backyard, and how it had been transformed into a beautiful setting for her wedding day. Her only regret was that she did not fight harder for a church ceremony. She had always dreamt of being wed in a church, but Lance had strong convictions against it. In the end, Paige felt that the place was not as important as the whom. She was to be married to her love, and it made no difference if it was in her backyard or in stone building; God would be with her either way, and that thought made her heart smile.

The Pottersmith's did not approve of their daughter's choice, but according to Dennis Pottersmith, "Whatever their daughter wants, their daughter gets. Even if it means slumming it with the trash of the town."

Paige had felt early on in their marriage that she had made a mistake when it came to marring Lance. He was abusive and demanding, but he always made up for it. Lance worked as an apprentice for a small automotive technician. The job consisted of long hours, sometimes seven days a week, and all for little pay. The only perk was that the owner of the shop allowed Lance and Paige to stay in one of singlewide mobile homes that he owned rent-free. Paige talked to her mother numerous times about her marriage to Lance, and every time the answer was the same. Catherine Pottersmith felt that her daughter and Lance were young, too young for marriage. She felt that Lance had a very stressful situation at work, and that Paige needed to be there and be supportive of her new husband.

"Paige honey, you need to focus on the positive. Lance has a job…kind of, and you don't. You realize that once you got married and moved out that we couldn't afford to pay you a proper wage. We had to let you go. It was a smart business decision. And it hurts me to think that if you left your husband…and I'm only looking at the financial side of things. How would you be able to pay your Daddy back for the money that he wasted on your farce of a wedding? Do you realize how much we spent? It far exceeded your other two sisters."

Paige was shocked by her Mother's candid reaction to life. It was as though she had no feelings towards her daughter. Paige just sat there in a daze as her Mother changed from the person she grew up with, to the person that she actually was and had always been.

Catherine also thought that Lance and Paige's living arrangement were below par, and that they should strive to do better. The worst part, at least in Paige's mind, was that her mother was okay with spousal abuse.

Her mother basically said that, "It happens from time to time, and that it is the wives fault for not being there for her husband, and not supporting him in his time of need."

Until that time, it never dawned on Paige that her mother had been living as mentally and physically abused wife for over thirty-five years.

The last thing that her mother said on the subject was, "Paige, your father is a good man. He has supported us for all of these years. He has supported me, and he has supported you and your two sisters your entire lives. I have never asked you girls for anything, because I felt that it was my place as your mother to protect you and watch over you. Your father and I have had some rough patches, but so does everyone else. I have learned when to speak and when not to speak. Your father works hard for us, and in doing so he is allowed a few bad days along the way. Don't you think? Lance is having a rough time trying to do right by you. It's true that we don't entirely approve of him or his family, and I'm sure that's part of it, but he is trying. It is your place to make him feel needed and loved when he walks through that door at night. And sure, he'll have some bad days. Deal with it...we all do! So he kicks your ass from time to time; at least he's not out whoring around like some other husbands we know. He's kind of like your father in that way, they both are very emotional men who don't know how to express themselves, and when they have taken all of what they can handle they explode. Sometimes with their words, sometimes with their fists...it's very primal. I saw this thing on *Oprah* the other day...but anyways, like I was saying...your husband is your husband, and you only get one. Otherwise you're living in sin, and sinners go to Hell. So in short, you go home every night and support your husband and learn to deal with his emotional barriers, or you go the alternative route and go to Hell. And who says that Hell will be any better, and besides your Daddy already said that if you leave your husband you can't come home. We will not support a Hell bound tramp in our family…we have a reputation to uphold, and you've already made it difficult on us with your choice in men. You made your bed…now sleep in it. Am I clear?"

"Ye…ye…yes….ss…ss…Mother," Paige replied crying uncontrollably.

"Now come over here and give your old mother a hug. There's no reason to cry. You're a grown woman with a husband at home. Enjoy it…these are your honeymoon years…cherish them…they won't last forever."

CHAPTER 9

President Mason looked around at the Joint Chiefs of Staff, and shook his head at the thought of what he was about to do. Congress overwhelmingly approved the Presidents request for a nation wide Martial Law to start immediately.

Constitution, Article 1, Section 9; clause 2: *The privilege of the Writ of Habeas Corpus shall not be suspended, unless when in cases of Rebellion or invasion the public safety may require it.*

Constitution, Article 1, Section 9; Clause 3: *No Bill of Attainder or ex post facto Law shall be passed.*

"Mr. President...Rich...do you know what you are saying? It's the Constitution; it's what we've based our lives on. It's what we've sworn to uphold. Martial Law or not you can't just change it...plus it's...it's wrong." Secretary of Defense Andrews put both of his hands on the desk in the Oval Office and leaned slightly over it as he tried to sway the President's decision.

"Damn it John, I know, but we are in a state of emergency and it's got to be done." President Mason stood up abruptly and ran his fingers through his grayed hair.

"Rich come on there has to be a way…" Andrews stood up and turned around with the fingers of his left hand messaging his weathered forehead.

"Sorry John, it's an executive decision. Gather the Joint Chiefs of Staff, and have them ready in fifteen minutes." The President ordered as he sat back behind his desk and weighed the fate of his country…the fate of the world, on his mind.

Fifteen minutes later the President of the United States stood in front of the Joint Chiefs of Staff, with Secretary of Defense John Andrews by his side.

"Gentlemen," President Mason started, "thank you for your quick response in this matter. I know you are all aware of what has been happening these last few hours…hell the last few years. I want you all to know that my thoughts are with you and your families. I've been talking with John Andrews, and decided that all of the maximum security inmates in the entire U.S. prison system need…to be…they need to be executed immediately…"

"Mr. President you can't do that…what…what about Congress…there are laws…" Chief of Naval Operations Moody exclaimed.

"As of 2:30 Eastern Standard Time, the United States of America is under Martial Law. *Habeas Corpus* has been suspended, and both a *Bill of Attainder* and *ex post facto* have been past. Along with myself, Secretary of Defense John Andrews, and the United States military, we will win this war that has plagued our nation. We also have attained the services of General Nathan Fox, who has just flown in from the Guantanamo Bay Naval Base in Cuba. General Fox will act as our Combatant Commander..."

"Sorry Mr. President," Chief of Naval Operations Moody blatantly interrupted, "but as a member of the Joint Chiefs of Staff, we won't let you do this. Come on, you're actually going to kill thousands of human beings that may or may not escape from prison? Hell, half these guys are probably up for parole in the next year or two."

"Sorry," the President said as he shook his head in what seemed to be remorse. "I understand your concerns...I have the same ones, but it's for the good of the nation and the majority of the people in it. I'm also sorry to say...that you've are all dismissed. May God protect you and your families." The President turned his back to his Military leaders and started to walk away.

"YOU CAN"T DO THAT!" Moody screamed as he ran towards the President, but was stopped short by two Secret Service officers.

"I CAN AND I WILL!" The President shot back. "The law clearly states that under the *Goldwater-Nichols Department of Defense Reorganization Act of 1986*, that I the President of the United States of America can and will speak directly to the Secretary of Defense. Who will in turn speak directly with the Unified Combatant Commanders who are led by General Fox; bypassing in all of their glory...you...the Joint Chiefs of Staff. Good day sirs...and John could you ask Nathan to join us?" President Mason again turned his back on the Joint Chiefs of Staff and continued towards the door that led out of the conference room.

"MR. PRESIDENT..." Chief of Naval Operations Moody again raised his voice to the Commander in Chief.

"YOU ARE DISMISSED!" The President angrily yelled without looking back at the men who were still sat around the brown wood boardroom style table.

"What about the 5th Amendment...the whole part about no person shall be deprived of life, liberty, or property, without due process of the law?" This time Chief of Staff of the Air Force Becker stood up to face the leader of the free world head on.

President Mason turned around with an eased but worried look on his brow. "I know the law, and that same Amendment also says something to the fact of except in cases arising in the land…in time of war or public danger. Gentlemen, you are dismissed!"

"How is this even legal? Congress couldn't have Okayed this…there's no way." Chief of Staff of the Air Force Becker pleaded for the lives of the American people.

"I wish there was another way…" Mason shook his head in sadness of his decision.

"Mr. President, are entire existence as a people are based on these documents, and you are handing them…" Becker tried to reason with POTUS, but was cut off.

"I am using the laws that are fore fathers set before us incase something like this ever happened, and unfortunately it has.

"But why death?" Chief Staff of the Army Freeman calmly asked as he too stood up from his seat.

"The parts of the Constitution that we're talking about give us the power to reevaluate a prisoner's sentence without certain laws getting in the way." The President explained as he tried to convince the

Joint Chiefs, and himself that what he had to do was the right thing overall.

"Getting in the way? Those laws are who we are." Moody spoke up again, but in a calmer tone.

"And that's what I'm trying to protect." Mason said as he sat back down in front of his audience.

"By changing their court appointed sentences into automatic death sentences?" Freeman asked as he to sat back down with the rest of the dismissed Joint Chiefs.

"I know it is hard to understand," the President put his arms on the table with his palms up as he tried to get the men to see his reasoning, "but to preserve our way of life we needed to implement a mandatory nation wide death sentence for all maximum security inmates from the little old city jails to the big bad federal penitentiaries. It is the only way to stop the Russians from turning our own prisoners against us."

"Don't you understand Mr. President, that you are turning our nation into something that we have always fought against?" Freeman begged in the form of a question.

"It's done! The decision has been made, and the men have their orders." President Mason stood up once again from the table to leave.

"What man would follow those orders?" Chief of Staff of the Air Force Becker asked sarcastically.

"We have built the Unified Combatant Command team with key individuals from different branches of the Service. They will follow their orders."

"And what about the war in Russia?" asked Commandant of the Marine Corps. Fischer.

"Those who are still in Russia will fall back and return to the U.S. to defend their own," the President answered.

"And the prisoners; do they know?" Freeman sincerely asked.

"The news would cause a massive panic…giving the Russians an even greater edge over us. So no, we have to keep this quite!" President Mason explained as he leaned on the table and faced the men in front of him. "We'll move in, take the prisons, and perform mass executions. I know that this sounds like a fictional story from some book, but it's real. These laws have always been here, and they've been used in the past. Maybe not here in our lifetimes, or those of our fathers, but they have been used. They are put there to protect us. I know this may sound like a cheap excuse, but these men…these women…these prisoners, knew what they were doing when they committed their crimes. They understood the law when they were arrested, and they knew the law when they were put behind bars. They should know that laws can…and in this case…change. I will admit that this is a drastic move on the part of the United States government, but I assure you if there was another way, we would have taken it. Maximum-security inmates are there because they want to be. Nobody made them commit these crimes. They originally did something that automatically placed them at the maximum level, or they did something while in prison to be raised to that level. Either way, they are there on their own accord, and no one else's. You can blame the entire world for your problems, but at the end of the day, it was your choices that led you to where you are. And we believe if they were given the chance to do it again, the majority of these inmates would. That is why that we have to stop them before the Russians let them out. We cannot afford to let dangerous individuals out into a world where they have no consequences."

"Isn't that nice!" Moody exclaimed in disgust for the President.

"Gentlemen, war is never nice."

"But it's covenant, just like the laws…right Mr. President?" Moody hammered back.

"Once again gentlemen, I'll ask you to leave. If you refuse you too will become enemies of the state…and you really don't want that.

GUARDS! Would you please escort these men out of the building?"

The President threw up his hands and walked out of the room.

CHAPTER 10

Charles Jenkins was a dedicated father with two beautiful kids who shared his passion for the outdoors. Maggie was the oldest; at seventeen. She had a way about her that made other people around her happy. Fabian, who was eleven, was rougher around the edges than his older sister. The one person, who Charles Jenkins loved more than life itself, was his beautiful wife of twenty-three years, Charlotte. To Charles, family was the center of his entire existence, and without it he felt that he had no self worth. Being a father, and a husband was what defined him. His family's needs always came first, and that was how Charles liked it. He felt good being the supporter and backbone of the family. Charles thanked God every night for his family, and prayed every morning for their safety.

"Lord I thank you for another beautiful day filled with the love of my wife and children. Please protect them, and let them live long, pain free lives. Help me to be a stronger person so that I can continue to do your work. Lord, thank you for saving my life by sending me Charlotte. In Jesus name I pray, Amen."

His life was not always like that, because before Charles had found Charlotte and the Lord, he was on a path down the wrong road.

At thirteen, Charles joined the Norteno Red Ridaz street gang, and began to go by the tag name Bloody Loc. By the age of seventeen, Charles "Bloody Loc" Jenkins was ruthless, but somehow always avoided being brought up on charges. Charles was involved in anything and everything; ranging from petty theft, to drug trafficking on the street corner, to attempted armed robbery, to attempted murder in a drive by shooting. Charges never stuck, as he once again slipped through the cracks of the system; plus it did not hurt that he also had a suave way about him that helped him get his way with other people.

Charles was given the tag Bloody Loc after he repeatedly stabbed three rival Surenos that jumped him in an alley behind the corner grocery store. When Charles walked out from the unlighted dark alleyway, he was covered in blood; some of it his, but most of it was from his three attackers. Charges were never brought up because no one testified to what happened, or even cooperated with the on going police investigation. All three of the Sureno stab wound victims survived, and swore to handle it on the streets. After the attack, Charles' fellow gang members gave him the tag name of Bloody Loc to signify what he had accomplished during his attack.

"Check this out holmes," Dumbo threw an article of clothing at Charles Jenkins.

"Hell yeah," Charles stated as he unfolded a black sweatshirt that had red letters spelling out the name Bloody Loc in the *Old English* style of lettering.

All of that changed when Bloody Loc attended a funeral for one of his fallen homies, Baby G. After the church service and viewing of the body, all the of the family and friends of the slain young man, got up to say their last wishes and prayers, and then went outside. The pallbearers carried the casket of the young dead gangster out the front doors of the church to the parked black hearse. Outside of the church, waited two carloads of rival Sureno gang members, all of which had aimed their weapons at the front doors of the church. The Surenos waited briefly until a large majority of the people were outside, and a lot of Norteno red was waved in the summer breeze.

The first shot rang out, followed by a massive amount of other bullets. Baby G's mother fell, his grandmother fell, and so did twenty-six of his fellow Norteno brothers who had just paid homage to his memory and life. Baby G's casket crashed to the ground when the pallbearers who carried it were shot.

Bloody Loc took three slugs to the chest, and one to the head. When the paramedics arrived at the scene of the dead red rags and carnage, they could not believe that anyone hit that many times in life threatening locations on the body could still be alive, when so many other had perished with less injuries.

"We have one still breathing over here," radioed a paramedic. "I don't know how he is still alive. Lets get him to the hospital before we loose him."

Charles "Bloody Loc" Jenkins was in a comatose state for eight months before he regained consciousness from that day at the funeral. After his awakening, Charles had to remain in the hospital for quite awhile until he was cleared to go home. During his wakeful stay in St. Elizabeth's Hospital, Charles began taking therapy on a daily basis to help him walk and regain his fine motor skills. Therapy was a daunting task that frustrated Charles. He knew how to walk, but he could not get his body to do what it had once done.

"Walking is something that this vato will never take for granted again. I didn't know it would be like this." Charles who was very frustrated said to himself.

"I know...I'm just a little farther along than you. By the way, my name is Charlotte."

Charles turned around to see who was speaking to him. To his surprise it was a beautiful girl about his age who happened to be in a wheel chair similar to his.

Charles did not know what to say. He had never been bashful around females before, but he had never been in a setting like that before either. So instead of speaking, Charles just stared at the girl with her hand out.

"Aren't you going to shake my hand?" Charlotte waved her hand back and forth to get Charles' attention.

"Um…yeah," the dumbfounded Charles stuck out his hand to meet Charlotte's in a quick handshake embrace.

"Again, my name is Charlotte. What is yours?"

"Um…Charles, but you can call me Chuck if you want to." Charles looked away from the lovely young lady to hide his embarrassed face.

"What do you prefer?"

"Prefer what?" Charles looked back with a confused look on his face.

"Charles or Chuck…you silly vato," Charlotte laughed. "Isn't that what you called yourself? What does that mean? Is a nickname or something?"

"What vato?" Charles put his arms slightly up to show that he had never met anyone who did not know proper street slang before.

"Yeah." Charlotte shrugged.

141

"Oh, it just means like dude or something in espanol. Charles…Chuck it doesn't matter. It's whatever is easier on you." Charles started to babble as he answered two questions in the same breath.

"What does everyone else call you?" Charlotte leaned back and did a standing wheelie in her wheelchair.

"You mean like my friends?"

"Yeah…like your friends." Charlotte answered coyly.

"They actually call me Bloody Loc." Charles answered as if someone else was speaking for him. The tag he used on a daily basis seemed somewhat foreign to him.

"Are you like in a gang or something." Charlotte dropped her wheelchair back onto all four wheels and rolled over so that her knees touched Charles' as they sat face to face.

"Yeah…something like that." Charles looked at his legs as they touched that beautiful stranger's legs.

"Wow…I never actually met a gang member. Is what you see on the news real? Do you actually go out and rob and beat up elderly people for no reason?" Charlotte asked loudly and excitedly.

"Naw…it's not like that," Charles explained. "I'm sure that when someone gets roughed up, they like to blame it on gang activity, but it's not like that. We mostly just hang out, and fight some scrapas when they come around. But mostly we just hang, doing nothing but listening to music or cruising around."

"So it's not like the TV?" Charlotte almost seemed disappointed. She had never met a stereotypical bad boy before.

"Man the TV is all messed up. They take something and blow it all up like it's the end of the world or something. Gangs have been around forever, and most of the time its just bangers messing with bangers. No one else even knows what's really going on, and one someone else accidentally gets hurt; then the news makes us out to be attacking old people." Charles started to get defensive over the only life that he had ever really known.

"Okay then, what does your family call you?" Charlotte asked when she noticed her new friend got upset over life in a gang.

"Chuck mostly…most people call me that. Except my mom…she calls me Charles." Charles shrugged uncaringly.

"Then Charles it is. I like to feel special, and call you by a name that no one else really does. If that's okay?"

"Um…yeah…if you want." Charles again looked a little bit embarrassed.

"So why are you here in the hospital…Charles?" Charlotte reached over and tapped his leg that was still in close proximity to hers.

"I got shot four times by these rival gang members called the PBS…"

"PBS, what does that stand for?" Charlotte sat straight back in anticipation of a good shoot them up story.

"Actually it stands for Play Boy Surenos, but we like to make fun of their name and call them other things. Like Peanut Butter Sandwiches, Period Blood Stains, *Public Broadcasting Station*, and those Poor Bastards Suck. Anyway, a homie…a friend of mine…was killed, and at his funeral these rival scrapas ambushed us. When we came out of the church, there were a couple of cars full of the PBS scraps that opened fire and killed a bunch of people who didn't deserve to die. I'm the first one to admit that there are always consequences for choosing this life, and what goes around comes around. I lost twenty-seven homies, including Baby G, whose funeral we were at. It's hard to loose a bunch of people you know, especially at the same time; but they knew the outcome, either dead or in jail. The sad part was that in this case, innocent people really did suffer. Baby G's mom and grandma both died, when all they wanted to do was wish their little boy a safe trip to Heaven."

"I saw that on the television like almost last year." Charlotte looked like she could almost remember the news story. "That was a huge tragedy. Wow…you were involved in that?"

"Yeah! I got lucky. I was shot in the chest three times right here," Charles unbuttoned his shirt to show Charlotte his scars on his chest and upper abdomen.

"I thought that you said that you were shot four times?" Charlotte asked to make sure she had her facts straight. "I only see three scars."

Charles pulled back his hair that had not been cut in eight months. "The fourth is right here," Charles pointed to a spot on the right side of his head and another one in the very back towards the base of the skull. "The bullet entered through the side of my head and exited out of the back of my skull."

"Have you been here that whole entire time?" Charlotte asked with a concerned look on her face.

"Yeah…in a comma. I just like woke up a little while ago…this month." Charles looked as though he tried to remember what had happened to him over the last few months.

"You kind of talk funny…I like it. It's so street like." Charlotte slapped Charles' leg like she had just made a joke.

"So this whole thing might be old news to you," Charles turned away from Charlotte and her uncaring humor, "but it just like happened yesterday for me. I can't get over it, and I can't do anything about it with these stupid legs that don't work." Charles slammed his right fist into his muscle less limp right leg.

"What is there to do? I think those guys were caught…weren't they?" Charlotte again thought back to the huge news story.

"Yeah some of them, but I heard that this one guy, Peanut, is still out on the loose somewhere." Charles thought about what his brother had told him when his family came to visit earlier that week.

"Peanut, why do you call him Peanut?" Charlotte asked inquisitively.

"Because, that's the size of his brain. I don't know…other homie give you your name, and his is stupid," Bloody Loc answered in a foul tone.

"What are you going to do when you can walk to this vato named Peanut? Did I say vato right?"

"Yeah…you did alright. I don't know, just find him I guess." Charles again shrugged.

"And do what?" Charlotte asked as she grabbed her new friend's shirt and moved in close so that their nose almost touched.

"I don't know…just stuff," Charles said as he pulled his head back. "Let's change the subject cause I can't walk anyways, so what's the point about talking about it? That little leva is free walking around, and I'm in here shot to hell in a messed up old ass wheelchair."

"Okay then, what do you want to talk about?" Charlotte rolled back a foot or two.

"Well you know all about me…"

"Not quite, but okay." Charlotte teased her new acquaintance.

"Let's talk about you or something." Chuck smiled.

"Okay, what do you want to know?" Charlotte crossed her arms and clenched her lips tight as to avoid being interrogated by the enemy, or to throw a childish fit.

Whatever the reason for Charlottes face, it made Charles laugh out loud. "Are you rich or something, because you talk all proper and shi…you just talk very nice? Not like someone from the ghetto."

"My parents are okay. We're not rich…middle class I think." Again Charlotte shrugged her shoulders in an uncared manner.

"Did they buy you a car when you turned sixteen?" That was a question that Charles had always wanted to ask someone if he had ever had the opportunity to do so.

"Yeah, but it wasn't nice or anything." Charlotte but two thumbs down to signify her thoughts on the automobile.

"It don't matter; they bought you a car. I have to walk everywhere. Well I did."

"Now you can be "rolling with the homies,'" Charlotte joked as she waved her arms in the air.

"Funny." Charles did not laugh, even though he found the joke quite humorous.

"It was funny, just like that homie song. If you can't laugh at yourself; at least let someone else in a wheelchair laugh at you." Charlotte smiled and rolled back and forth in her wheelchair without going anywhere.

"Whatever." Charles slightly threw up his hands.

"Sorry, I was just trying to play around with you. No hard feelings or anything. I was just trying to be friendly."

"No worries Charlotte. This just sucks, you know?" Charles looked down at his body and the mobile chair that he was in.

"Yeah." Charlotte looked down at her own chair.

"So what happened to you? Why are you here…get shot in a drive-by?" Charles smiled, and then started to laugh.

"There you go…that's funny. No, actually I was in a car accident."

"In the car that your parents bought you?" Charles laughed. "No wonder you gave it two thumbs down."

"Yeah, a classic Mustang from the beginning of the century or something…. 1492 or something. Anyways, my Dad got this real great deal on it, and had it all cleaned up. It still had an old time pre-CD player in it and everything."

"Still…it was a car…for free…a present on your birthday." Charles shook his head in disbelief.

"Yeah, yeah. So I had it a while, and I got hit head on by this boat of a car. This low rider I think it was called. I was messed up bad…broken neck and everything. I had to wear this thing called a halo that keeps your head on while your body heels. And so I can never ride horses or anything ever again, because my neck is still like totally broke, even though it is fused. But the funny part is that this all happened around eight or nine months ago. I was picking up a friend who worked at this taco restaurant in the bad part of town. So driving there, this car full of TV like thugs come out of nowhere and hit me head on. I believe that the driver died, and I was crushed inside my car. I found out later that they were all high on some kind of hallucinogen

149

drug, and were wanted by the law in relation to this mass assignation of these funeral party people. So I think…don't laugh…but I think that we were supposed to have met. I think that we were both hurt by the same group of people, and ended up here at the same hospital taking physical therapy together. Is that weird or what?"

"That's nuts, but kind of a cool story. Messed up, but cool. Do you know what I mean?" Charles put his hands up for approval, and to see if Charlotte understood what he meant.

"Yeah I do. So maybe we should be friends? Since we were supposed to meet and all." Charlotte rolled right back up next to Charles and stared at him.

"I like it…Charlotte?"

"Yes, Charles?"

"Would you like to be my friend? Since it's destiny and all."

"I would be honored." Charlotte happily accepted.

The two new friends continued taking physical therapy together. Charlotte was further along than Charles, and so she came in and gave him moral support when her appointments were all through. They grew into a strong couple, and soon Charles was allowed to go home. He was confused on where he should be; on one hand he had the street life that he had always known, and on the other hand he had

Charlotte and the completely opposite life that she had always known. Charles felt a sort of gratitude towards the fact that he was shot. If it were not for that incident and the things that were a direct outcome of the shooting, Charles never would have met Charlotte.

At home, Charles' family seemed glad that he was home and okay, but he seemed to be in the way. Life had gone on without him, and the family had grown accustom to having one less member in their small home. One morning, a few days after Charles got home, he got dressed in the style of clothing that he had always worn; black *Dickie* pants that he perfectly creased, a white t-shirt, and a black and white pair of *Nike Cortez*. As he headed down the short hall towards the kitchen, Charles heard a knock at the front door. He had not seen anyone since his triumphant return from the dead, and he had secretly hoped that Charlotte was there to rescue him from his life. Charles opened the door and sadly saw two of his friends, Smiley and Dumbo, standing there. It was not like Charles was sad to see his friends; it was that something had changed inside of him, and Charlotte filled that gap in his sole.

"Orale Dumbo. Orale Smiley," Charles exclaimed to his comrades as he held his hand out to shake theirs; which was a time-honored tradition that they always had done when you first greet a person, and then again when they part ways.

"What's up fool?" Smiley asked Charles. "When is your ass coming out?"

"No idea holmes…right now I guess." Bloody Loc shrugged his shoulders.

"Right now?" Dumbo asked with anticipation.

"Simón…right now after I eat some grub. Come in and eat some food dudes."

"Dudes…what this dudes? We're vatos…not dudes. Entendes?" Smiley defended his Spanish slang against the American version.

"Orale Dumbo. Sorry for insulting you…shit." Charles slipped back into his old self for a moment.

"Lets go fool. Hurry and eat. There's this low rider show today at the fair grounds and Kermit's girl Lisa is working at the ticket counter, and she's going to hook us up for free. So hurry your ass up." Dumbo grabbed Bloody Loc's black sweatshirt for him.

"Calm down Smiley. I just got up. Besides I don't know if I want to go."

"What do you mean that you might not want to go? What else does your shot up ass have to do today? Mr. OG to big for us vatos who still put in work? Shit Loc…you better remember who your homies are. Besides Dopey's older brother Lobo put his Impala in the show. You have to go…all the homies will be there." Smiley argued in a mild threatening way.

"Naw holmes, I'm just going to kick it right here in the casa today. Get my shit straight before I see everybody. Entendes bro?" Charles held out his hand for his friends to take with a friendly handshake.

"Fuck you Loc. Everybody said that you lost it, but I'm like hell no…Bloody Loc ain't lost shit. He ain't afraid of anything, but I guess I was wrong." Smiley threw his hand up and stepped back.

"Smiley it's not like that, and you know it. I'm just not ready to face everyone yet." Charles replied with his right hand still out.

"Damn holmes you don't have to worry about nothing. You're an OG now, and have nothing but respect," Dumbo said as he threw the black sweatshirt back on the living room couch.

"So then respect me." Charles spoke with authority.

"Alright holmes…We'll hit you up manana." Smiley said with a big smile on his face.

153

Smiley and Dumbo shook hands with Charles as they left, and Charles went back to making his morning breakfast.

"What should I do today?" Charles asked himself. "Charlotte," was the answer he gave himself.

After Charles finished his morning meal and cleaned up, he walked down to the city bus depot to look at the daily schedules. He never rode the bus before because one of his friends or family always had a car available for use; either in the form of a ride, or by letting him borrow it for a few hours. That day was different, he could not ask his family after all they had done for him over the last year, and he could not ask any of his homies after what he told Dumbo and Smiley. The bus would be his only form of transportation to get him around the city.

"According to this list...I'll need to take three stupid buses to get to Charlotte's pad." Charles whispered to himself as he shook his head in confusion.

"Did you say something son?" an older man in passing asked Charles.

"No sir...I was just talking to myself. This route...bus thing is all messed up."

"It can be a little confusing if you don't know what you're doing. Do you ride the bus much?"

"No sir I don't." Charles looked back at the bus route map.

"Well let me help you out, or at least point you in the right direction. Us bus folks need to stay together. Now where are you trying to get too?" The older man nudged his way next to Charles so that he could see the map as well.

"Right here," Charles pointed to a spot on a city map that was hung on the bus depot wall.

"All the way across town. That's a long way from our side of the tracks…if you know what I mean? What's going on over there?" The older man nosily inquired.

"A girl," Charles replied.

"Well in that case you'll need to take the Number 3 until Canal Street and 5th. Get off there and wait until you see the Number 6 bus going towards Fremont. Don't take the Number 2…that's where most people make the mistake and end up where they don't want to be. The Number 6 is the second bus to that stop. They arrive about ten minutes apart from each other, so don't sweat it. It depends on exactly where you are going, but I would get off the Number 6 at that new *Wal-Mart* on Division and then transfer to the Number 7. Take that until you see your stop, or until that you are so lost that you end up back here at the end of the day," the helpful gentleman smiled and then winked at Charles.

"Thank you sir. Number 3, then 6, and finally 7 until I get to where I'm going. Got it!" Charles smiled back.

"Good boy. Now you better hurry, the buses leave in five minutes exactly," the man looked down at his wristwatch.

Charles walked off towards the bus that he needed to start his day trip on across the city. He followed the older man's directions, and when Charles got on his third and final bus; he was surprised to find the helpful gray haired man that helped him on the bus.

"Well I'm glad that you made it this far son," the man winked.

"Thank you sir, but I didn't know that you were the bus driver."

"You didn't ask. Besides, I didn't want to brag," the older man smiled a huge smiled that made Charles giggle softly.

"Why did you make me take all of those buses if you were coming over here anyhow?" Charles bent over and asked the bus driver quietly.

"For the experience son…for the experience. It means more when you do the work rather than getting a handout. Sure, I could have taken you with me, but you wouldn't have learned anything. If this girl is special, then I assume that you would want to see her again. And if you didn't learn the route today, then you would have been in the same boat next time...dazed like a deer in the headlights. I did you a favor son, and now it's your turn to watch out for her stop so we don't pass it." The bus driver patted Charles on the arm and gave him that big old smile again. "Take a seat son. Safety first on this boat."

Charles was not exactly sure where Charlotte lived, but he had a partial address from an envelope that she tore a piece off of when she used it to write on the back of it when they were both in the hospital. He thought to himself that maybe trying to find her was a bad idea. She had never actually invited him to do anything with her, but she had come to the hospital to see him after she had been released. However, Charles had not heard from Charlotte since he had been home. A lot of back and forth thoughts about Charlotte and their possible feelings for each other went through his mind while he was on the bus. Charles looked up and saw the street name on a street sign that matched the one on the envelope.

"Marion Drive," he whispered to himself.

Charles pulled the brake cord that hung above the window that told the driver to stop at the next bus stop. As the bus came to a complete stop, Charles quickly rose to his feet, and walked towards the front of the bus to get off.

"Good luck son," the bus driver said with an encouraging smile.

"Thanks." Charles shook the older man's hand for all the help that he had given him, and to show his respect for his elders.

Charles got off of the bus and walked back four blocks towards the street that he believed Charlotte lived on. As he walked down the debris free sidewalks, Charles noticed how clean everything looked. From the well manicured dark green grass of all of the yards, to the graffiti free houses and fences. Charles "Bloody Loc" Jenkins felt a moment of embarrassment for the life that led and the area that he lived. He felt that no one from this side of the city would ever leave all of that for someone like him and the hood. Still, Charles kept walking down the tree-lined street towards the addresses on top of the steep upcoming hill.

Once Charles made it up the hill, he stopped and turned around. He thought about his childhood and how a hill like that would have been great to race his bike down. Then he though about how much it sucked when a person who had been shot and was out of shape tried to climb it on foot. When he turned back around, he saw Charlotte as she came out of her house. It was a two-story Colonial style home, with a red brick facade.

"Charlotte," Charles yelled loudly for her to her.

Charlotte looked up and waved to him. "What are doing here?"

"I came to see you. I figured that the barrio was too far away for a girl with a crashed up car, so I would come and see her instead." Charles joked.

As the two friends spoke, Charlotte's parents came out of the house dressed up and ready to leave.

"Oh, I'm sorry Charlotte. I didn't think that I was interrupting something today. I just wanted to see you. You guys going somewhere?" Charles asked as he looked around at Charlotte and how she was dressed.

"We're going church," Charlotte replied with a lovely smile.

Just then her dad walked up to where the two friends stood. "And who is this?" Charlotte's dad lightly grabbed Charles' shoulder and smiled with a warm inviting glow.

"Dad, this is my friend Charles Jenkins from the hospital. Charles this is my dad, James Worthington III."

The two guys stuck out their right arms and shook hands.

"So Charles, our little Charlotte here tells us that you were her only friend in the hospital, and that you saved her life."

"Well sir, it was more liked she saved my life." Charles looked shyly at his friend.

Charlotte's mom walked up behind her husband, and put her tanned left hand on his back. "Well dear, who do we have here?" As she looked over at Charles and his urban style clothing.

"Honey this is Charles; Charlotte's friend that she has been talking about from the hospital. Charles, this is my wife Bunny."

Charles stuck out his hand, "it's a pleasure to meet you."

Bunny took his hand in hers and pulled him towards here. "Well Charles, what is this that you are wearing? Urban chic perhaps?"

"Mom, stop it." Charlotte looked embarrassed by her Mom's obvious dislike of her friend.

"Sorry dear. I just was admiring young Charles' clothes, nothing else."

Charles stepped back to his original spot on the Worthington's massive driveway.

"Dad, can Charles go to church with us?" Charlotte clasped her hands together in a pleading sort of form.

"I don't know sweetheart, does he want to?" James looked at his daughter then to Charles.

Charlotte looked at Charles and asked him to go with them. "Will you please go with us? There's lots to do, and I'll show you around."

"I guess…if you want me too, and your folks don't mind." Charles stammered unsurely.

"Nonsense son," James Worthington replied. "We would love to have you as our special guest this morning."

Charles loved the idea of the Worthington family. He loved the way that they did things together as a family. When they had a party, everyone came; young and old and celebrated life together. Even more, Charles fell in love with Charlotte, and she with him. Charles had also found the Lord alongside Charlotte. At first, the Stone Church was big and it overwhelmed Charles, but as he continued to go, it became smaller and more inviting. Charles liked his new life better than his old.

"You're a fucking leva," Dumbo exclaimed to Charles. "You never want to kick it anymore. All you ever worry about is some bitch, and God. What's really up G?"

"I don't know holmes. I'm just different, you know?" Charles stepped back in a defensive manner.

"I know that you're different holmes. So, are you going to kick it or what, or should I tell all the homeboys that you pussied out again? What's it going to be holmes, you down or what?" Dumbo was pissed at his long time friend and fellow gangster.

"I was going to hang with Charlotte tonight."

"Man you hang out with that girl all the time. What about us? You've barely kicked it since you got shot." Dumbo reminded Bloody Loc Jenkins.

"Alright Dumbo …alright…you win vato. Let me call Charlotte and tell her that I can't go with her tonight, and that I'm going to a party at Chico's house. One time holmes…that's it...I'm done."

"Tonight's the night homie. You go this one time, and I'll leave you alone; entendes?" Dumbo got instantly happy.

"Simón vato. Now let me call my chic." Charles went into the other room to use the phone to call Charlotte and to explain what he had decided.

She was more than happy for Charles to hang out with his old friends, and so Charlotte decided to do the same. She called up a couple of her girl friends that she had been neglecting for a while. The female friends decided to go out and have a girl's night out for old time sake.

"Hey Ashley…this is Charlotte. What are you guys doing tonight?" Charlotte asked her friend over the phone after she hung up with Charles.

The full intention of the Norteno gang that Bloody Loc belonged to was get him to Chico's party and make him forget that rich girl that he had been dating, and make him remember where he came from. Charles walked around the party in a daze. The world that he had once knew, felt so foreign to him. Charles observed some friends as they sat on a couch smoking Marijuana, as they got high. He also saw people that he grew up with so drunk that they could not walk, or being able to hold anything in their bodies. Charles also saw a drunken girl go down the hall towards the bedroom with three or four of his so called homies. Charles Jenkins was shocked at the life before him. He was shocked that he once lived for that life. He was done; whatever the consequences were, he would deal with them, but Bloody Loc was no more.

As Charles started to make his towards the front door, bullets started to rip the house apart. Charles dove to the floor, and crawled quickly towards the window, making sure that he stayed low to the floor. He slowly peeked out the large picture window that had been shattered from the gunfire. Charles looked through a small opening in the corner of the curtain, and was able to make out two of the cars that had slowed way down to make sure that the right house was hit during their attempted drive-by shooting. In a matter of moments, the rival gang had sped away, and the sounds of police sirens filled the night air.

"Who was it? Bloody Loc? You see who did it?" Negro asked.

"Simón! It was those fucking CPV's Toker, Trippy, and Chapo."

"Let's go holmes…lets get them." Chico chanted.

The Norteno Red Ridaz fled Chico's house and the scene of the crime to track down and retaliate against the rival gang who had attempted to end the life of every single member of the N double R, Noteno Red Ridaz gang.

Charles rode in the backseat of one of the four cars that were out looking for the CPV gang that shot up their party. All he could think about was Charlotte, and how his life could have ended on that very night.

"Let me out." Charles demanded to the driver.

"What?" Smiley looked back not wanting to believe what he heard from the O.G. who sat in the backseat.

"Let me out," Charles repeated himself.

"What the fuck for? You see what those vatos did to us? They tried to kill us, and now we're going to go out and find those sons of bitches and murder every single one of them."

"Let me out." Charles demanded once again.

"Are you serious?" Smiley looked over his shoulder into the eyes of his friend.

"Smiley…let me out. Nobody got hurt tonight. Nobody got shot…nothing. You do what you got to do, but let me out first." Charles tried to reason with his friend. He talked in a tone that somehow convinced Smiley to see his side of things.

Smiley reluctantly pulled over his maroon *Buick Regal*, and let Charles out in front of a *Taco Bell* restaurant.

Smiley looked at Charles and nodded. "No worries Loc…I got this."

The gang that Charles once bragged about being a member of drove off to commit a heinous crime without him. Charles was completely done with that part of his life. He walked up the restaurant and stood in front of the payphone that hung on the outside of the building. He dialed Charlotte's cell phone number and waited three rings before she answered.

"Hello."

165

"Charlotte, can you come and get me?"

CHAPTER 11

Rachlav and Nika were happy together, even though his military life sometimes kept him away for long periods of time. Nikolaevna had little to do around the house when her husband was gone because of the grand life he had given her. Nika was bored when Rachlav was far from home, she was a newlywed and her husband should have been home with her. She found that she was intrigued with the American culture, and how they perceived themselves.

"One day I too will go to America with my husband, and I will be carefree as American surfer babe from California." Nika said to herself in a full-length mirror as she struck a surfing pose.

Nikolaevna became obsessed with the American way of life. She went to the University to learn English as her second tongue. Rachlav did not approve, but he loved Nika so. It was harmless stupidity, but he allowed it.

"Why must you pursue these foolish American ideals?" Rachlav asked one night, as he got ready for bed.

"Why do you fight it so?" Nika countered as she brushed her hair out from the long day of having it up.

"Nika listen to me," Rachlav stopped what he was doing and stood there as he looked towards his wife with his shirt off, "the Americans are destroying our way of life. They have been destroying it for years, and every year it gets worse. My father Nika! You yourself saw what it was like, I just want to protect you."

"And I love you for that," Nika put down her brush and walked over to her husband. "But you love me because I am a strong woman. So please let me continue my education."

"But why America?" The General questioned as he put his hands on his wife's shoulders.

"America is not your enemy, and they are not mine. Russia and the United States are allies." Nika looked deep into her husband's eyes.

"Одобренное Nika, я доверяю вам."

"And I trust you too, my love. Thank you my by big strong General. Will you please learn English with me…together, or at least let me teach you to speak it better?" Nika put her arms around her husband's waist and pulled herself into his strong arms.

"Nika please, I don't want to talk about the Americans no more…allies or not, they are still destroying us," Rachlav begged as he held his wife.

Rachlav also started to master the American dialect himself, even though he hated the Americans with a deep passion. It took convincing on Nikolaevna's part, but she talked Rachlav into studying English at home. Nikolaevna felt great pride in herself for making the great and powerful General do something that he did not want to do. In reality, however, Rachlav knew that learning English and the American ways would only help him in his quest to avenge his father.

Months later a great world-sporting event happened in Moscow that pitted the Russians against the Americans in swimming. It was to be a three day event to showcase each countries young talent, most of which were going onto the next Olympics. Athletes from both countries showed equal strengths and heartaches. On the American team there was three or four stand out swimmers. They did not stand out because of their amazing abilities, but because of their out of the water body language. They were good looking guys, with bad attitudes and suave ways.

On the second night in Moscow, the Americans celebrated a narrow victory of day two's events. Those same stand out American guys had celebrated a little more than the rest, having shots after shots. The rest of the team refused even drinking because it was against the rules, and more importantly they were in the middle of an equally matched swimming competition with the Russians.

"Hey bro lets go find some Russian love," Chad said as he leaned back in his chair and looked around the bar.

"Hell yeah…Russia has some good-looking chicas," Ryan happily chimed in.

Nikolaevna was on her way home with a fellow English student when they saw the Americans from across the street.

"Hey aren't those the American swimmers?" Nika asked her friend.

"Nika, you are a married woman. Too bad you're not одиночно like me." Ekaterina laughed.

"My husband would make me quit school if he knew I had friends like you…single or not." Nika playfully pushed her friend.

"It don't hurt to look a little. Besides they are leaving in a few days, and you'll never see them again." Ekaterina pushed her Nika back.

"Hey chicas bonitas, why don't you come over here and talk to us?" Ryan yelled in a drunken state of mind.

"No thank you. Ekaterina, let us go, I have a bad feeling about this." Nika pleaded with her friend as she started to walk again.

"Girls wait don't leave, we're sorry. But for real though…have either of you been banged by four Americans?" Chad said as he stepped of the curb and onto the street that separated the two parties.

Nika felt strange in the pit of her stomach, and a little bit afraid because the four Americans were loud and obscene as they directed their words towards her and her friend. This was not how people from the land of the free were supposed to act. Never the less the American swimmers ran across the street and came after them.

"RUN EKATERINA! БЕГ! Please run…run fast." Nika shouted as the two female friends realized the severity of their predicament.

Both girls ran as fast as they could, but the guys were quicker. Nikolaevna fell when she was pushed from behind during mid run. As her head hit the payment, the last thing she remembered were two of the Americans standing over her as she quietly said to herself, "Ekaterina run, please don't stop running."

Nikolaevna awoke to find her husband as he sat in a chair next to her bed in her private hospital room.

"My love…I am sorry…" Nika started to cry even though she was not really sure why.

"Shh Nika…it was the Americans not you." Rachlav walked over and sat on the edge of his wife's hospital bed.

"Ekaterina?" Nika asked quietly.

"I don't know." The Great Russian General lied to his battered and bruised wife.

"You lie…if I was one of your soldiers…General…what would you tell me?" Nika was furious within a moment. "Tell me the truth."

"The truth Nika…the truth," The General stood up and ran his hands over his tired and unshaven face. "You were brutally raped and beaten, and left in the street to die. You've been in a coma for seven days. For seven days I have wondered if you would live."

"Ekaterina?" Nika asked again.

"She was like you," Rachlav said as he turned away from his wife. "Beaten and rapped by the same American swimmers. She was found four blocks from your body. She didn't survive the attack. Her funeral was three days ago."

"And the Americans?" Nika dared to ask.

"They are being held for their crimes. The people of the United States must know that they cannot walk over us like ants." Rachlav angrily punched and broke a mirror that hung on the drab wallpapered wall.

A week later Nikolaevna was allowed to leave the hospital, but she was scarred. She was frightened about being alone, and she was frightened of people being around her. She was scarred of the life she had; she was scarred of America. She could not get past it; it was everywhere. Her father did not speak to her, her husband seemed to be away more, and people in general seemed to treat her differently. They all blamed her for something she did not deserve. They blamed her for Ekaterina. Nika heard a women tell her companion, as they passed her in the street that, "It was her own fault for wanting to be an American, and disgracing her family and Russia."

Nikolaevna fell into a deeper depression. A month later, Nikolaevna found that she was impregnated during her attack by one of the rapists.

"This will never end," Nika told herself as she looked into the bathroom mirror.

She could not go on living in a world that she feared, and with a child created by that fear. Nika went to her husband's office and opened a box that he kept in the third drawer of his desk. She felt the coldness of the object and understood her own. She needed to overcome by the coldness to feel whole again, and so she let it overcome her.

Rachlav returned home after he spoke with Nikolaevna's doctors to find his wife dead on the bathroom floor. She had used one of his pistols; two shots. One into her abdomen, and one to her head.

"Nika…I'm sorry…I'm sorry…Nika please…I'm sorry." The mighty general cried uncontrollably.

Rachlav held his wife's lifeless body close to his. His medals on his chest meant nothing to him; they were useless; he was useless. What could he have done?

"Lord take my wife, and her unborn child to a place that will protect her from pain. Lord give me the wisdom and the strength to defeat the Americans," Rachlav prayed out loud.

"ВОЙНА! Я ОБЪЯВЛЯЮ ВОЙНУ НА ВАС! For you American scum who are in your little homes in your safe little country, I shall repeat myself in your tongue so that there is no confusion of my words. WAR! I DECLARE WAR ON YOU!" General Rachlav yelled as he laid his wife's limp body down and ran out his front door.

Rachlav went to Ubiikobyla's house with his clothes still wet as they dripped with Nika's blood. He ran up to the front door and kicked it in.

"Mr. President I need you. I need your support" Rachlav went right up to the startled President.

"General…the blood…are you…"

"Nika!" The General looked down at his blood soaked hands and uniform.

"Nika?" The President asked in shock.

"She is мертво…dead! The Americans have killed her." General Rachlav started to cry again as he thought about his wife.

"Dead, but how? They are locked up awaiting trial. General they couldn't have done it." President Ubiikobyla tried to make sense of what his friend was trying to say.

"They killed her that night, just as they killed Ekaterina. It just took longer for my wife to die." Rachlav charged the President but stopped a few feet short of reaching him.

"My friend…how did she die?" Ubiikobyla took the needed steps that gapped the friends, and embraced Rachlav with open arms.

"By the hand of God. He helped her ease the pain from the hell she was living. She had no one, not even me. The news of the pregnancy must have put her in a place so unimaginable to you and me."

"A pregnancy…General, what pregnancy?" President Ubiikobyla stepped back in surprise of the breaking news.

"Those American rapists, those American murders, they implanted their seed into her. She found out today; I found out today. I always leave a loaded weapon by my bed, and one in my desk…Nika…Nika used one of the weapons on the unborn child, and then on herself. She is in a better place…a place of understanding." Rachlav dropped to his knees as the tears came faster.

What can I do?" President Ubiikobyla asked with a mixture of sincerity and rage.

"Объявите войну!" Rachlav growled.

"Declare what? Declaring war is not an option," Ubiikobyla stepped backwards and sat down in one of his black leather armchairs. "General, countries do not create war over the actions of a few people. It is sad what has happened to your wife and to your father, but you can't blame the Americans for everything bad in your life." Ubiikobyla tried to reason with the insane General.

"Declare war on the United States, and I will promise you a victory." The General swore as he rose to his feet and then kneeled before his President.

Rachlav then left the President's house and went straight to the place where the American swimmers were held. He released the guards of their duties, and unloaded two clips of ammunition into the four caged prisoners.

"Почему вы изнасиловали и убили моего супруги? Sorry let me translate that for you dumb Americans," Rachlav sarcastically said as he looked over their dead bloody bodies. "Why did you rape and murder my wife?"

Nothing, only silence answered Rachlav request. He just stood there and watched the motionless bodies turn cold before returning to his home.

CHAPTER 12

"Guantanamo Bay Naval Base is where you'll be." Secretary of Defense Andrews informed Colonel Jack Braden as they sailed off of the Florida shore in the Gulf of Mexico.

"Why, isn't there only terrorist in Gitmo?" They're no concern of mine...hell I nailed Bin Ladin years ago." Braden countered smugly as they walked downstairs to the galley.

"Sorry Jack, but you have no say in this one." Andrews sat down and jokingly frowned.

"Alright John, what's up? Why all the secrecy?" Jack took a seat next to his boss.

"You already know that we have Rachlav in Cuba. We kept it a secret as long as we could, but somehow word got out that he was there. After that all hell broke loose, and we had to change his status from enemy combatant to that of a P.O.W. We played it off as well as we could, but POTUS is getting it from every angle. Hell...we broke every law out there. Not just ours, but the Geneva Convention, you name it." John Andrews flipped through the files that he had been looking at.

"Tell me what you need John?" Braden asked outright.

"I need you to go in as a prisoner." Andrews found what he had been looking for and pulled out a picture of Russian General Rachlav in an orange prison jumpsuit.

"A what?" Braden shook his head in disbelief.

"I need you to get to Rachlav," Andrews calmly said. "We need an inside man, and this is what your trained for…you're the best of the best."

"Some of those soldiers down there might know me." Braden stood up and grabbed a water bottle out of the tiny refrigerator. He then held one up as if to ask John if he wanted one.

"We're counting on that," John Andrews answered as he shook his head yes, and caught the flying object as Jack tossed him a cold bottle of water.

"They'll blow my cover John." The uneasy Colonel pointed out.

"No they won't, because no one really knows who you are. They know you are a take charge kind of guy with untouchable security clearance."

"Until now!" Jack exclaimed sarcastically.

"We'll get you in, and throw your name around, so it looks like the real deal," John Andrews quickly said before taking a big gulp of water.

"What's the charge?" Braden looked over at Andrews' files.

"Treason!" Andrews tossed his files over to Jack Braden.

"John…come on…that's not just something you walk away from afterwards." Colonel Braden pleaded his case.

"I know, but Rachlav has to trust you," Andrews informed the Colonel. "If we don't do this, the Russians will eventually break Rachlav out, along with every other maximum security inmate in the country."

"How do I get in?" Braden tossed the file onto the empty chair next to him.

"It's got to be on the up and up…those damn Russians have spies everywhere. Lucky for us you'll be found guilty under Martial Law. No judge, no jury!" Secretary of Defense Andrews said smiling to help ease the tension that his assignment brought.

"That's death sentence!" Braden jumped up in awe.

"We still have enough pull to keep that from happening. We have bigger issues to deal with first; like the Russians, and thousands of newly released prisoners. So no one is going to be killing you anytime soon," Andrews reassuringly said to mental prepare Braden for the role of a traitor.

"Once I'm in, how long do I have?" Jack asked as he committed himself to his new assignment.

"I don't know it's out of my hands once you're in. But I do know that they are going to move some of the prisoners from Guantanamo Bay to an ultra secret Black Site within a few days of your arrival." Andrews picked up the file that Braden had set down.

"Where's that?" Braden sat back down after he had paced back and forth along the galleys wood floor.

"Under Area 51!" Andrews pulled out another picture. It was a satellite photo of the area around the controversial base.

"What…I thought…I heard…believed that Black Sites were never on U.S. soil." Braden was shocked at what his job entitled him to know about top-secret security issues.

"They're not…and this one doesn't exist either." Andrews made sure that his point was well taken.

"An alien cover up?" Colonel Braden joked.

"Come on Jack, would you look for war criminals in UFO central?" Andrews playfully played along. "Why do you think we let those rumors slip out, and allow all those people to monitor our actions?" Andrews produced another photo of people as the camped out as close as they could get to the base without being in direct violation of the law.

"I thought the military kept those people away?" Braden examined the picture.

"Just enough to keep their interest peaked. It's a perfect alibi! People watching that place day and night, and they've never reported a prison inmate." Andrews smiled as if Area 51 were his idea.

"John! Someone will eventually catch on," Braden said as he handed the photo back to the Secretary of Defense.

"They never saw *Saddam*."

"*Saddam*?" Braden repeated.

"We needed to keep him locked up and alive until his trials began." Andrews informed Braden about an unknown fact of American history.

"What about Bigfoot?" Braden laughed out loud.

"Jack its time to get serious," Andrews insisted, as he turned solemn. "We need you to go in and gain Rachlav's trust. Keep him alive because he is our only bargaining chip. And Jack, just like always; nobody knows of this mission except us. It is strictly off the books, but I'll do what I can for you."

"Of course!" Braden walked back up the stairs to the upper level of the sailing yacht and waited for it to fully dock before he stepped off the floating palace.

"God speed my friend." John Andrews said towards Braden as he watched him walk away.

CHAPTER 13

Marie Onzuga was a in her fifth and final year at *UC Berkeley*. Her sister Blanca was the Assistant Records Keeper at *Folsom State Prison*. Even though the two single sisters lived a couple of hours apart, it seemed as though they were always together. They were as close as two sisters could be, in fact one would say that Marie and Blanca were the best of friends.

When the news of the attacks on New York City had spread to the prison system on the West Coast, the *University of California, Berkeley* closed their doors until further news was available. Marie took that opportunity to drive to her sister's apartment and stay with her for a while. Both sisters had watched the news when they saw a replay of Russian President Ubiikobyla's speech on television. They could not believe what they had heard and seen on the TV screen. Marie knew that the Russians were the reason that they closed the school down, but she had not gotten the entire picture of what that meant until she sat there with Blanca.

"Blanca you need to quit your job…right now." Maria grabbed her sister's leg in concern, which caused Blanca to jump from being startled. "The Russians are taking over the prisons, and letting the inmates do whatever they want. You don't want to be anywhere near that. That stupid job ain't worth your life. Whatever you do, don't go back...promise me."

Blanca agreed, and called her supervisor, but all she got was the office voice mail.

"Stupid machine." Blanca said as she held the telephone receiver to her ear.

"What is it?" Maria asked.

"I got Joan's voice mail. Should I quit over a recording, or call her back tomorrow?" Blanca wanted her younger sister's advise.

"There might not be a tomorrow. Just quit already. She'll understand. That's why she's not there right now, because she quit too." Maria looked scarred, but was still able to reason with her sister.

"Shh..." Blanca told her sister as she spoke into the phone. "Hey Joan, this is Blanca Onzuga...sorry to this over the phone, but I just saw the news and what that Russian President said really scared me. I know this is bad timing with Melissa on maternity leave and everything, but I need to quit...for my own piece of mind and safety. Nobody knows what's going to happen, but still...I need to be with family right now. Please call me back when you get this message, and I can tell you more. Take care, and if it's cool...I'll go pick up my stuff later on this week. Thanks...bye."

Blanca hung up the phone, and turned to her sister, "I never know what to say on those things. Am I talking too much, too little? I swear that I just ramble on and on."

"Who cares...you did it." Maria jumped onto the couch. "Can you believe if you didn't quit, and the prisoners came after you? Your fine and all, but some of those dudes probably haven't seen a woman in twenty years. They'd be all over you quick like. Maybe you shouldn't have quit, and then you could get yourself a man." Maria laughed and held a throw pillow in front of her to keep Blanca from hitting her.

"Your lucky that you're my sister or..." Blanca held up her fist in a playful mood.

"Or what?" Maria threw down the pillow and acted tough.

"Really though...thanks for coming out here to stay with me, and for making me quit my job. I need the money, but my life isn't worth being around that." Blanca crawled across the floor and gave her sister a hug.

Maria and Blanca sat on the couch for days on end and watched the country that they loved be destroyed by the Russians, but what the two sisters found even more devastating was the fact that a lot of the destruction had been done by uncaring US citizens.

"Prisoners or not, they should be on our side. They are Americans...aren't they?" Maria threw a piece of buttered popcorn at the television screen.

"Yeah Maria, but to a point...America sentenced them to prison. Then we changed the game, and they're all going to die. Wouldn't you want revenge on the country that did that to you?" Blanca tried to get into the mind of ravenous freed inmates.

As they were watching the news, the Charles Jenkins' story came on.

"Hey Maria...I know him," Blanca informed her sister as she turned up the volume. "He's a guard down at the prison. Dude he's a keeper. He's a bad boy turned good guy. He's got the attitude, but not too much...you know. His wife is lucky."

Then they saw the rest of the news piece...Charles Jenkins was dead.

"Chuck's dead? No way...I just saw him yesterday." Blanca started to cry.

"Were you guys close Blanca...or just a dude from work?" Maria grabbed her sister and held her tight.

"Kind of both…we were cool like that…you know." Blanca laid her head down onto Maria's gray sweatpants covered lap.

Blanca Onzuga thought about the day that she first met Correctional Officer Charles Jenkins. It was her first day on the job, and her supervisor, Joan Green, had her go and make copies in the guard's office, because the copy machine in the Records Room was broke.

"Blanca, would you be a dear and go make me about a hundred or so copies of the flier for our company picnic at Fulbright Park next Saturday?" Joan asked her newest employee. It had been the first time Joan had help in roughly two years.

"Sure Joan," Blanca replied as she grabbed the piece of paper from Joan's hand and started to walk towards the copy machine.

"You'll have to use the one in the guard's station," Joan said without even looking up from her computer monitor.

"Why?" Blanca blatantly asked her new boss.

"Because this one is out of order, and the repair man can't get here until next Tuesday," Joan answered as if tired of all Blanca's banter.

"Okay…sure. Where is the guard's station?" Blanca stepped one foot out of the office and looked down the hall.

"Unfortunately you'll have to go through part of the prison to get to the nearest one, but don't worry, you shouldn't run into any of the inmates. At least the deadliest ones that is." Joan looked up to make sure that she had not scared the new girl too badly with her remark. "Just go down this hall, and turn to the right after you see the second camera on the wall. There'll be two sets of bared doors that you'll have to be buzzed through. They should see you coming, and let you through without any trouble. If they say something, ask to talk to CO Jenkins…he'll know what to do."

"Great," Blanca shrugged as she started towards the door.

"Blanca?" Joan spoke coldly.

"Yes Joan." Blanca turned on her heels quickly to face her boss.

"Can you make those on yellow paper…it's more spring like, don't you think?" Joan smiled.

Blanca Onzuga strolled down the hall looking up for the cameras.

"The last thing that I want to do is get lost," Blanca thought to herself, "and have to be stuck in an all male prison overnight. What if something happened? My pops would never talk to me again…he would blame me because I chose to work at a prison."

Blanca saw the first camera as it came into view up a few feet ahead of her. Then she wondered if the guards could see her. Blanca remembered something about staying close to the wall when you walked the halls so that the cameras could pick up your image.

"Was it the right side? Or the center of the hall that I'm suppose to stay on?" Blanca's question echoed silently down the hall.

"What's up hyna? You looking good…you must be new around here. What's your name chica?" A prison inmate approached Blanca.

"I shouldn't be talking to you. You're a prisoner in this prison…aren't you?" Blanca looked scared.

"Si, but that doesn't mean that we can't see a lot of each other…does it?" The inmate moved in a little bit closer as he licked his lips erotically.

"The cameras…the cameras…they'll see you…us. I need to go now." Blanca tried to reason with the young man.

"You can stay right here. The pinche   guards can't see shit. The cameras don't get right here." The inmate put his arms straight out and spun around without a care in the world.

"How do you know that?" Blanca nervously asked.

"Because I run the pinta, that's why. Now what's your name?" The young tattooed inmate demanded.

Blanca knew that she had to keep the inmate talking until someone came down the hall to help, and so she replied, "Blanca Onzuga."

"A mexicana…no?" The inmate rubbed his hands together with delight.

"Si, and what's your name?" Blanca asked to keep him busy until help arrived.

"Cali Ramirez, but everyone calls me Joker."

"Is that what got you in here…banging?" Blanca resorted back to her old neighborhood slang so that she would seem to fit in with Joker without seeming above his economic class. Middle and upper class seemed to piss off a lot of ghetto gangsters.

"Simón, pero that's not all. I'm down for my shit; Norteno red ragger kind of shit, but what got me in trouble with the One Time. You see this puta I was with; she was my ruca and shit, but she fucked all that up. I caught her giving some head to a cracked out scrapa leva for some mota or coke or something. So I fucked them both up, and when the cops came; I fucked them up too." Joker boasted proudly.

191

By this time Blanca was too scared to move. She did not want to hear anymore about Joker Ramirez, but she had to hold on until someone came to look for her.

"How long have you been in here?" Blanca forced herself to ask.

"Tres anos. Three long fucking years, with twenty to go." Joker spat on the cold concrete floor.

"I'm sorry, but I need to go make some copies before the guards start worrying about me." Blanca held up the paper that Joan had given her.

"Go! What are talking about? You're going with me. Fuck! What are they going to do, give me another twenty years? Three years I have had no panocha, and today I'm getting some of yours." Joker started to unbutton his prison issued blue jeans.

Blanca screamed, and tried to run, but Joker grabbed her around the waist and pulled her towards him.

"Get on your knees bitch and suck it." Joker Ramirez threw Blanca to the floor.

Joker pulled out a prison made knife and stuck it to her left eye. Blanca responded by slowly unzipping his unbuttoned prison blue jeans.

"First you're going to suck it, then you're going to fuck it." Joker thrust his pelvis area into her face.

Blanca started to reach into Joker's unzipped pants, when she was knocked to the floor by a prison guard who had tackled Joker. They both fell to the tiled floor, before the guard came up with Joker's handmade weapon.

"Stay on the floor Ramirez," the Correction Officer ordered.

"Orale holmes, but it's not my fault. This bitch came on to me…talking about wanting to slum it with a real gangster and shit." Joker nodded at Blanca as he licked his lips again.

"Enough Ramirez." The CO slapped Joker in the face with the back of his hand.

By that time there was a team of correction officers armed with non-lethal rubberized beanbag guns that took Joker Ramirez into custody. The CO that saved Blanca's life then turned his attention towards her with a concerned look about him.

"Are you okay…Mrs.?" The CO held out his hand to offer her a hand up.

"Blanca…and yeah I'm alright I guess. What happened? I thought that all inmates were locked up behind bars in prison?" Blanca reached down to straighten her outfit.

"Usually," the guard started to explain, "but some like Ramirez are allowed to hold down jobs while inside, which gives them access to some non essential areas of the prison in some cases."

"Non essential? It's my life that we're talking about. He said that the cameras couldn't see us here. So how did you know?" Blanca looked around still shaken from her near rape experience.

"He's right about the cameras…unfortunately, there are some spots that we just can't cover. Somehow the inmates find things like this out, and use them to their advantage when they need too." The CO looked at one of the cameras and shook his head with disgust.

"How did you know that I was here?" Blanca asked her hero.

"Joan in Records. She called my desk to see what was taking you so long, and when I didn't see you…"

"You put two and two together and saved my life." Blanca smiled widely.

"Yeah, but I'll probably get fired for it though." The CO looked at the back of his hand that he smacked Cali Ramirez with.

"Why…. you did a good thing here?" Blanca also looked at her hero's hand.

"Yeah, but I used physical force on an inmate…an inmate that was armed with a blade. I used unsafe judgment, and a thing like can get you killed. By the way my name is Charles Jenkins…Correction Officer Charles Jenkins."

"Yeah…I got that part," Blanca joked, "the correctional officer part that is."

Jenkins looked down at his uniform. "It's that obvious huh?"

Blanca stuck out her hand, "Blanca Onzuga. Nice to meet you."

Charles accepted her hand in a handshake and replied, "Nice to meet you Blanca Onzuga."

CHAPTER 14

Adrian Bachmeier was sixteen years old when Jack Braden left the United States to live with him and his family for a season. The Bachmeier family decided that they would like to volunteer as a host family for foreign students who wanted to come to Germany to learn about the culture and its people. American students were by far their first choice, because America was so interesting; and by sharing information about Germany, the American student would in return tell the Bachmeier family of America.

Braden was excited to go to Germany, and literally jumped at the chance to sign up as an exchange student. As the sign up sheet was being posted, Jack Braden jumped in front of Maggie Thatcher, a girl from his third period Chemistry class, who in turn stepped back and knocked over two other students who were also interested in signing up as foreign exchange students. As the teenagers fell, others turned to look, except Jack. Jack in turn signed his name to the top of the list, and being the first name on the list gave him first pick on where he would like to go from the list of available places to stay.

"Mr. Braden...I see that you picked Frankfurt as a possible choice of where you would like to spend your summer." The History teacher looked over the list of places available to travel.

"No, Mrs. Graded, Frankfurt, Germany is the only place that I would want to go." Jack Braden pointed out.

"And why is that?" Mrs. Graded looked up from behind her black-framed glasses.

"Mrs. Graded...have you ever wanted to study history?" Jack sat down in one of the hard office chairs across from the teacher's desk.

"I do make up half of the History Department along with Mr. Brown." The teacher gave a faked half smile.

"No! I mean have you ever wanted to study history from an unbiased source?" Jack scooted the chair up so that he could lean his elbow on the desk.

"Well of course, but that is a rare find Mr. Braden." Mrs. Graded did not look impressed with a student moving her furniture around.

"How about if you could piece together the truth by studying both sides of proverbial coin per say?" Jack brought his fingers together and pulled them apart like he had preformed a magician's illusion.

"Okay…keep going." The History teacher waved him on to silently tell him that her time was valuable, and that he had been wasting it.

"World War II is a terrible time in the world of man, but a great piece of our history. What if I could take what you and Mr. Brown have taught me, and combine it with the history that has been taught to the citizens of Germany." Jack brought his hands together to represent unity. "Learn their truths, and combine them with our truths. Then, maybe then, we can find the real and holistic truth about that little piece of our worlds history." Jack sat back and smiled for he had impressed himself with what seemed like it could have been the truth.

"Very good Mr. Braden…very good. I'll put you in contact with the host family in Frankfurt, and the people that will help us and your family on your journey of truth." Mrs. Graded smiled. She felt as though all of her years of teaching had been worth it. One student was all that she needed to reach, and she had done it. Mrs. Graded took a sigh of relief and relaxed.

"Thank you Mrs. Graded." Jack bowed as he stood up and pushed the maroon office chair back to its original resting place.

"Thank you Mr. Braden for opening my eyes. Now would you please send Billy Maxwell in?" The teacher waved Jack out of the office.

The truth was that Beth Anderson was to travel with her family to Speyer, Germany to visit her father's roots. Frankfurt just happened to be the largest and closest city that Jack could move to and still see his beloved. In fact, Speyer to Frankfurt was no more than an hour away. Jack thought that he was a true genius and grinned at the way that everything had worked out. All he had to then was to tell Beth of his summer plans.

"It's a great idea." Jack threw his arms out and smiled a huge fake smile.

"No it's not Jack. What if we get caught?" Beth pointed out. "And stop smiling like that. You look like a creepy used car dealer."

"Get caught doing what?" Jack shook his index finger at Beth like she had thought of something naughty.

"Hello? You are planning a romantic summer vacation for the two of us in Europe. Does my father ring a bell? Or Mrs. Graded? Mr. Brown? Does any of this sound feasible to you?" Beth threw up her arms in frustration.

"Beth, come on. Just think about it, you and me picnicking on the River Rhine. Spending our days studying the history of…"

"My father, and where we came from. There is no way that my parents would ever let me go out alone with a person who came up with well thought out and deliberate plan to stalk their daughter around the world." Beth felt as though she could not get that parent point through Jack's thick skull.

"I'm not a stalker, just a love sick boyfriend. Who happens to be a World War II history buff." Jack tapped on his History book that he had brought to the school library with him.

"Since when?" Beth glared as she thought about the lie that her boyfriend fed her.

"Since you were going to Germany, and there was an available host family a few miles down the road from where your grandparents grew up."

"No Jack." Beth leaned back in her hard plastic chair.

"Just think about it. Germany is a country of romance and mystery." Jack looked up as though he could see the country right before him.

"No, Germany is a place of your murder if my Dad catches onto your plan," Beth whispered loudly as the school Librarian walked by.

"It happens to be a coincidence that we both ended up in the same part of a foreign country at the same time. In fact, I'll be there first. So if you look at it that way, you are stalking me." Jack put his hands behind his head and smiled smugly.

"No way Jack. You're the stalker. I'm just the beautiful girl that you can't live without." Beth threw a piece of wadded up writing paper across the table and hit Jack in the chest.

"Maybe, but never the less you have to convince your parents to let you see me this summer." Jack picked the paper off of the floor before the Librarian came over to see what they were up to.

"I'll try." Beth glared playfully.

As the school year came to a close, everything had already been set into motion for the summer events. Jack had become good pen pals with his exchange brother to be, Adrian. Beth and her family would leave the United States for Germany for their four-week excursion after the July 4th holiday; which happened to be a month after Jack was scheduled to leave.

When Jack arrived in Frankfurt, Germany, the Bachmeier family greeted him. They held a sign for him that read:

Willkommenes Haus Jack Braden

Welcome Home Jack Braden

Jack had always secretly wanted one of those movie moments where he got off the plane, and there were people, familiar strangers that held a homemade sign so that he could find them. The Bachmeier family had done that for him, and he was glad. Jack came to a country where he had little mastery of the dialect, and to be lost in an airport would have been the worst. Luckily, Jack had a caring family that made a sign in both English and German for him to read.

As he walked up to them for the first time, Jack became overwhelmed by the emotion of the trip and the summer. He was greeted by a great big Bachmeier family hug that devoured Jack in love and kindness. Never would have Jack seen that sort of greeting in the United States. An entire family that embraced and welcomed a virtually complete stranger into their home with hugs and kisses like they had known him for years.

"Brother Jack?" Adrian asked with his arms opened to embrace his guest at any moment.

"Brother…Adrian?" Jack responded unsurely.

"Welcome to Germany." Adrian hugged his exchange brother warmly.

"Thank you. Thank you for having me at your house for the summer." Jack felt uneasy about the greeting, but overjoyed and welcomed at the same time.

"This is my Mother and Father. I mean our Mother and Father. Here you are family. An honorary Bachmeier...yes?" Adrian introduced his parents who took Jack into a deep and powerful embrace.

"Yes...I'm honored and happy," Jack muffled out from inside of the Bachmeier family hug.

"From your letters brother Jack, you do not speak my language too well." Adrian smiled.

"No, but you speak English very well," Jack pointed out. In fact he was surprised on how fluent Adrian was.

"All children are taught English and other languages of the countries that border us. There was a U.S. military base close to our home when I was much younger. My friend Eric moved here from the United States to live with his father on the base when we were boys, but later moved around whenever his father was transferred. The education is there, but the problem is that our parents do not speak

English too good; and so to help you, we'll teach you German." Adrian was a helpful and gracious host from the moment Jack got off of the plane.

"That would be great. I want to learn all I can about the culture while I am here," Jack said in upbeat tone.

After he retrieved his luggage, Jack Braden followed the Bachmeier family out the doors of the airport to their family car.

"Wir sind in keiner Zeit an allen Haupt," Mrs. Bachmeier exclaimed as her husband opened her car door.

"Mother said that we will be home in no time at all. It's an American slang term that she heard on the American cable MTV." Adrian put his arms out as if to say that parents want to be hip, and never grow up.

"You guys get American TV here?" Jack asked surprised and excited.

"Of course Jack. On the satellite television. This is the twenty first century is it not?" Adrian thought that Jack's question was quite odd.

"Yeah it was just…it was just that this is Europe, and not the States. I mean…I knew that there would be TV; just not what I was used too…that's all I meant Adrian." Jack tried to cover up and explain his obviously dumb question.

The two boys sat in the back of the Bachmeier's family Volvo station wagon as the parents sat up front and left the two of them to talk. Adrian told Jack about life in Germany, and in return Jack told Adrian what it was like for him to grow up in the United States.

"So Adrian, what do you want to be when you grow up?" Jack asked a very common American style question.

"That is a funny question coming from a person which is the same age as me. Who says that I will grow up? I may be like your Peter Pan." Adrian flapped his arms as if were able to fly.

"Perhaps, but really. What do little German boys and girls grow up to be?" Jack actually wanted to know.

"Right now I am a skater that is going to school into communications." Adrian answered Jack's question with pride.

"You skate?" Jack looked surprised. He and Adrian had written back and forth for a while, and Adrian had never mentioned skateboarding once.

"Of course. If I do not a become famous skater, then maybe I will join the German Luftwaffe as a Communications Officer." Adrian grabbed his sweatshirt as if he were wearing a uniform jacket.

"What is Luftwaffe?" Jack asked as if he should have known that one.

"I think it is similar if not the same as your United States Air Force," Adrian said after a moment of thought.

"Yeah…I'm going to do that whole military thing too," Jack said while he too grabbed his shirt a he wore a military uniform jacket.

Jack looked out of the car window for a moment before he turned back towards his exchange brother.

"So what do you know about Speyer?"

"The village?" Adrian asked as if the question intrigued him.

"Yeah, the town…village…whatever Adrian. What do you know about it?" Jack anxiously wanted to know about the town where Beth would be.

Jack and Adrian spent a lot of time together doing things that two brothers would. They became real close; a closeness that would last a lifetime. When Jack was not hanging out with Adrian and his host family, he would e-mail messages back and forth to Beth. Jack was excited to see Beth. That first part of the summer had been the longest that the loving couple had been apart from one another.

"Absence makes the heart grow fonder. Is that not what *Shakespeare* had written?" Adrian asked Jack as he looked over one of Beth's e-mails.

"*Thomas Haynes Bayly*." Jack corrected his brother.

"What brother Jack?" Adrian looked confused.

"*Shakespeare* didn't say that. It was a famous poem or quote or something from this guy *Thomas Haynes Bayly* who wrote this whatever it was, titled *Isle of Beauty* back in the mid 1800s."

"Americans are very smart." Adrian smiled and slapped Jack on the back.

"Not really, but some of us are. Luckily for me, I happen to be dating an intelligently beautiful girl who loves poetry." Jack smiled at the thought of seeing Beth.

"Amazing," Adrian added.

"Yeah, who would have know that a poem could bring peace to the world. It stopped us from getting into an international argument. We could have started World War III." Jack tossed his bed pillow at Adrian.

"What other poetry do you know?" Adrian asked as he picked up Jack's pillow and placed it under his head as he laid on the bedroom floor.

"Not much, but when Beth gets here, she could probably quote you some. Hey speaking of world wars, what does your old history books say about Hitler and World War II?" Jack looked up to see Adrian's reaction to the question.

A couple of weeks later, the Anderson family landed in Frankfurt. Before the family started their trek to Speyer and the German countryside, Beth was allowed to spend part of the afternoon with Jack and Adrian, both of whom had waited impatiently at the airport for the plane to arrive.

"Jack, I've missed you so much," Beth happily cried as she ran up to Jack.

"Me too. Hey this is my German brother Adrian. Adrian this is my American girlfriend Beth." Jack stepped back and pointed each of them out. The two strangers hugged as they met for the first time.

"Hey…you make it sound like you have another girlfriend. Mr. This is my American girlfriend." Beth slugged Jack a little to hard.

"Beth, you know that isn't true. It's just when you're here, it's hard to separate things unless you specify where they come from…like my American girlfriend…my one and only girlfriend." Jack tried to back peddle his statement.

"That's better." Beth grinned and hugged jack again.

Beth then turned her attention back to Adrian. "So you are Adrian, huh? Jack as told me a lot about you and him having fun over here in Germany without me." Beth smiled to show Adrian that she had been light hearted with her statement.

"He has told me a lot about you also," Adrian said as he returned Beth's smile. "If you want to have fun, you have come to the right place."

"What, the airport?" Beth joked.

"No...Germany. It is the greatest country in the world. United States is second, but a close second...yeah?" Adrian looked at his two American friends and then laughed loudly.

"Well I can see that Jack was right about you." Beth positioned herself between both boys and entangled her arm within theirs.

"What does that mean? Jack? Beth?" Adrian asked worriedly.

"Don't worry," Jack exclaimed. "It's another one of those American sarcastic slang terms. Beth likes you...no worries brother. Now lets get the hell out of here."

CHAPTER 15

The Jenkins family was devastated when they heard of the news of what Russian President Ubiikobyla was doing to destroy America. The prison system was in place to protect the innocent and punish the unjust. The only thing that Charlotte Jenkins could focus on was the thought of Charles' last kiss before he left for work, as he knew the risk of what the Russians had been doing to other prisons up and down the West Coast.

"Charles, I beg you to stay home. I have a bad feeling that something is going to happen to you today," Charlotte cried in the hope that her husband would stay home.

"I can't stay home every time that you have a feeling. Believe me, I would love too, but these groceries and house don't come cheap. No worries…I'll see you tonight."

Charles Jenkins was a dedicated husband and father, who showed that dedication at work, and everything that he did. He always gave one hundred and ten percent every minute of the day. He felt that he could do more good at work, then he could at home. He was needed and so Charlotte let him go. Then the Jenkins's family waited in front of the television together, and waited for any news on whether or not that the Russians had attacked the prison that Charles worked at.

When the news came; it was too late. Prisoner Lance Flanders had assassinated Correctional Officer Charles Jenkins as Russian Commander Demidov stood by to supervise the execution of prison law enforcement.

"No! This can't be happening," Charlotte cried. "It can't be true. Not my Charles." Charlotte took the children into her arms and cried in an uncontrollable manner.

The Jenkins' family television roared loudly as the program continued. "This is Nina Cordova with Channel 6 NEWS at six. We are going live to a feed of Russian Commander Demidov inside of the Federal Correctional Institution here in our area; where we have late breaking news to the apparent assassination of a senior prison guard. The feed is coming in live, like I said. The speech is in Commander Demidov's native language of Russian. We have a Russian to English translator for this NEWS station on the way, and we will re-run the report as soon as that translation is made available to us. In the mean time, let us go live to Mark Johnson at the prison."

The television NEWS channel changed its view from the newsroom to the field reporter Mark Johnson.

"Mark are you there?" Nina Cordova asked as she looked at the television camera that was focused on her smiling face.

"Yes Nina, and thank you," the field news reporter answered. "As you can see behind me there is a lot of commotion about the happenings that have taken places just moments ago. I must warn you that the pictures and images that you may see could be disturbing to certain viewers. Like always…Parental digression is advised." Mark turned to the side so that the cameraperson could zoom in on what had happened.

"Mark, what is that thing lying by who I assume is the Russian Commander?" Nina asked from the news studio. That was the first time that had the chance to see the actual footage as it came in from the field report.

"Nina…that is the body of Correctional Officer Charles Jenkins…who moments ago was brutally shot one time in the head by convicted inmate Lance Flanders." The cameraperson zoomed out, and once again focused their imaging on Mark. " Inmate Flanders, as I believe, was under the direct order of Russian Commander Demidov. The most disturbing piece of this story is that the execution took place in front of the entire prison, and to my record…this may be the first time that Correctional Officer Charles Jenkins' family has had any news of the situation. Our hearts go out to his family and friends. Here is Russian Commander Demidov now."

"Люди Соединенных Штатов by far слабе что одно о мысли. Хорошо для людей России. Офицер Jenkins делал его работу как хорошая собака, тем ме менее все собаки должны умереть. Он вымолил на его жизнь, но на жизни его семьи. Умолять не будет почетный trait в России. Одни умоляют получают съемку. По мере того как вы все знаете, планом России будет освободить ваших пленников от их клеток тюрьмы, и команды с ими для того чтобы сделать остальнои ваших жизней как ад. Россия превалирует, и америка не будет стоять. Офицер Jenkins был ничего больше чем потеха для меня. Испытание для моих новых следующих, но важно пример мы охотно готовы сделать для того чтобы задавить американскийа образ жизни."

"Wow Nina, I have no idea what Russian Commander Demidov just said, but it did not seem very good for the people of this city, or our fair country." Mark gave his opinion from outside the gates of *Folsom* Prison.

"I'll have to concur on that point Mark, but like I said we have a newsroom translator who just shown up. While we wait, I would like to again send out our deepest condolences to the Jenkins family for the

213

unneeded tragedy that has happened earlier today. As far as we know, this newscast may have been the first time that the family had heard about Charles Jenkins." Nina put her head down and was silent for a few moments to honor the brave Mr. Jenkins before returning to her job. "Our Russian translator is ready and as far as I understand he will translate Russian Commander Demidov's words as close to possible to our own English language. Isn't that right Mr. Deedle?" Nina Cordova turned her body and chair slightly to the right so that she could both face her guest and the camera.

"Yes it is Nina, and thank you. My condolences also go out to the entire Jenkins family. My name is Bobby Deedle, and I am a translator for the news station. I travel around the world on assignment, and I am fluent in five different languages, Russian being one of them. I'm happy to be here, but I don't think Russian Commander Demidov is. So the following images you see will be of Russian Commander Demidov's speech that he gave a few minutes ago. We will replay the entire speech for you, but my voice will be dubbed in to replace the Russian Commander's voice." Bobby Deedle picked up some papers from the desk in front of him.

The speech is replayed on televisions across the area, as the words of Russian Commander Demidov come to life in English.

"The people of the United States are by far weaker that what one would of thought. Which is good for the people of Russia. Officer Jenkins was doing his job like a good dog, however all dogs must die. Not only did he beg for his life, but for the lives of his family. Begging is not an honorable trait in Russia. Ones who beg get shot. As you all know, Russia's plan is to free your prisoners from their jail cells, and team with them to make the rest of your pathetic lives like Hell. Russia will prevail, and America will stand no more. Officer Jenkins was nothing more than fun for me. A test for my new followers, but more importantly an example of what we are willing to do to crush the American way of life." Bobby Deedle put down his notes after he was done with his translation, and turned his attention back to Nina. The cameras followed suit and zoomed in on Nina Cordova.

"Thank you Bobby," Nina said. "This is a cold day in America today. We will keep you posted as this story continues to break. Until then, this is Nina Cordova with Channel 6 NEWS at six. Good night." The newsroom went dark, and the cameras stopped sending images.

After the translated speech and interviews were over, the off aired Nina Cordova turned to her British friend Emma Watson, who Nina had gotten onto the list of journalists to go to *Folsom* Prison that day. "Can you believe that? He was shot on national television. One of us media happy, story grabbing parasites is going to win a Pulitzer for this one."

"Amen," Emma replied.

"Hey Emma, why don't you consider working here in America. You did great on TV tonight, and we have an opening for a field reporter," Nina informed her friend.

"I like working for the paper," Emma sighed.

"Then do both," Nina said with a big smile. "Let's get some dinner. What do you say…fish and chips?"

"Funny," Emma laughed.

CHAPTER 16

Colonel Jack Braden was convicted of treason for conspiring against his country for the good of an invading nation.

"Colonel Braden, you are hear by found guilty on all charges. You are hereby stripped of your rank in the United States military, and for your actions against the country you swore to protect; you are sentenced to death. Do you have any final words before these proceedings are concluded?" General Nathan Fox handed down the sentence to the enemy of the state. General Fox was the judge and the jury appointed by the President. Nathan Fox could have been as ruthless as he wanted with no one to stop him.

"General Fox...is it?" Braden approached the court. "I did what I did for the greater good of this country, and if those actions make me guilty, then kill me. But kill me as an American...not as a Commie sympathizer." Colonel Braden threw his handcuffed arms into the air and turned around for the witnesses to see that he wanted his last request to be granted. "I am an American. Let me die with dignity."

The evidence against Braden was unimaginable. He could not believe how well John Andrews and the U.S. government had set him up. He was in so much trouble, he almost believed it. The only thing that kept Braden alive was the word of his good friend and boss, Secretary of Defense Andrews. The word came down through the Secretary of Defense to the Combatant Commander General Nathan Fox that Jack Braden was not to be touched until further notice, and that he was to be immediately sent to the Black Site in Guantanamo Bay, Cuba.

"Remove the prisoner from the courtroom," Fox ordered two armed Marines.

The thought of leaving the traitor alive angered the General. Fox had felt that the law should have solely fell under his jurisdiction; instead Mason and Andrews scrutinized him. "We'll never get our country back when they keep tying my hands," General Fox said out loud while alone in the empty courtroom.

"Roger that; November, 4, 4, 7, 6, Sierra. You are free to land."

"Man oh man! So that was the old Guantanamo Bay Express, aye?" Braden asked as he stepped onto the island of Cuba for the first time.

"Shut your mouth traitor," a Marine bluntly said.

"Hey I heard ya'll got three planes that fly in and out of here...well at least three planes the world knows about; isn't that right?" Braden looked around, and then smiled at the guard that had escorted him away from the plane.

"I said shut your mouth," the guard screamed as he hit Braden in the face with the butt of his rifle.

"That's just like you guys…all stressed out from being in the heat of action." Braden looked up at the guard that had knocked him down. Braden then licked the blood from his teeth, and then spit on the ground after a brief moment of consideration to spit on the guard. "Hey no offense, but I'm just trying to make small talk here. So back to these three prison transport planes. We flew in on the N4476S, right? So that means that the N44982 and the N221SG are around here somewhere. Unless ya'll house them somewhere else." Braden looked around as he tried to remember the layout of the base.

"Don't you know how to follow orders soldier? I said shut your mouth." The Marine had increased his level of madness towards the former Colonel.

"Okay, okay, okay! Come on though, you have to have other transport planes, right?" Jack smiled and shook his head in an attempt to get the Marine to talk.

That was the last thing Braden remembered before the guard struck him in the back of the head with his weapon.

"Rise and shine, you sleeping bag of shit," said the never cheerful Colonel Jackson.

"Uhh, my head! How long have I been out?" Braden open his eyes to screaming Marine and a massive headache.

"You can't ask any questions…Colonel! This is my house, and in my house I set the rules. Someone up there must like you, because I can't kill you. I hate the fact that your traitor ass is still alive. I can't lay a hand on you, and that is a direct order from my CO. I also received a direct order from my CO that I am allowed to lay anything else I saw fit on you…like this here bat I found just laying around the other day. Yeah, do you see this blood right here above the handle? That blood belonged to no other than the famous Russian General Rachlav himself," Colonel Jackson boasted as he flung his wood bat around.

"No kidding…Rachlav himself, aye?" Braden smiled a huge grin.

"You got a smart mouth, and I'm itching to beat someone. Ever since it slipped that we had we had the General down here, all hell has broken loose. Now I can't touch that murderous bastard, and we can't house him here either. That damn KGB wannabe has more rights than me. Lucky for him though, but very unlucky for you." Jackson was nose to nose with Braden. Jack could feel the spray of Jackson's spit as he loudly spoke.

"You know what; I am glad that we are getting to know each other. That whole thing with you and Rachlav is amazing, and the entire baseball bat fetish is a little weird, but to each their own, right? But to tell you the truth…I'm hungry. So, when do we eat?" Braden knew how to get at a guy like Jackson, and his tactics seemed to have been effective in doing so.

Beatings became a daily activity for Braden, but on the plus side he was also allowed to secretly communicate with other prisoners, especially with General Rachlav. Colonel Braden remained in isolation twenty-three hours of the day. He was allowed one hour of exercise per day in a secluded outdoor location. It was there that Braden used his background knowledge of certain guards to blackmail them into passing messages back and forth between him and other inmates. If the guards kept their end of the deal; then their past dealings would not become public to their families and to their country.

"Give this letter to Rachlav, and wait for his answer if possible." Braden held a piece of folded up paper for the guard to take.

"You are a low down son of a…" The guard started to say.

"Hey watch it Malone! Do your children know what kind of language you use?" Braden looked directly into the guard's face.

"You keep my children out of this." Malone pushed Jack into a concrete wall.

"They are out of this...aren't they? But speaking of kids; isn't your daughter in a school play next week? What's her name again...Mary?" Jack shrugged his shoulders to get his jumpsuit to fall back into place.

"I swear if you touch..." The guard stepped towards Braden again.

"Shut up and send the message," Braden commanded as he turned his back on the guard. Braden then started his daily exercise program as he walked laps around the roof free concrete enclosure.

Braden knew that he had to get in touch with Rachlav more often, and he also knew that the General would never trust an American. Luckily the charges against Braden were so believable that he did not have a hard time convincing Rachlav that he was indeed against the American way. However, he could not look too eager either, Braden had to show that he did not trust the Russians any more than he trusted the Americans. That part was easy, he told the truth. He hated the Russians for what they did to his homeland, and to all the people that he had ever known. Nobody was immune from the carnage and the damage that Russia brought with it. That made his story even more believable, and Rachlav bought it.

Survival was the key, and escape was the only way to keep either one of them alive. Braden knew that if the Russians reached them first, then he might stand a chance given his obvious situation as a traitor to his country, which had been locked in a secret military prison cell similar to the Russian General Rachlav. It was also clear that his former American allies would kill him if they got there first. Rachlav stood in the same situation; he needed his troops to get there before the Americans. Rachlav needed Braden to help him get out and back to his people, but then it would be over and the American traitor would be killed. Braden needed Rachlav as a back up plan incase he needed to use the Russians as a survival tactic. However, his main objective was to keep Rachlav out of both countries' hands until further notice by his *Pentagon* contact. He could not allow the American military to kill their only bargaining chip, but he also could not allow the world's biggest war criminal go back to his country and pick up where he left off.

Braden bowed his head and prayed, "Lord protect us, and save our people. All of our people, the people of this world. Do not let borders divide us, for we are all one. Do not let race separate us, for we are all one race. Let us solve our differences quickly, and again make brothers out of our enemies. In Jesus name, I pray. Amen."

CHAPTER 17

Michael Farmer had thirty-nine days left on an eight and a half year prison sentence when he received word from the Government that his sentence had been re-categorized from a standard prison sentence handed down by a County Judge to a death sentence handed down by the President of the United States.

"This can't be happening…what about my daughter?" Michael wadded up the official letter and tossed it onto the cold cell floor.

Michael Farmer had always been a good man. Even when the judge and jury convicted him for his crimes, the judge recognized him as loving father.

"All rise!" Demanded the court bailiff, as the people rose to their feet.

"Has the jury reached a verdict?" Judge Fall looked towards the jury box as he asked his question.

"We have your honor," answered Brenda Lee, who was one of the jury members.

The court bailiff walked over to the jury box and accepted a piece of folded paper from the head juror, and then walked it back over to Judge Fall.

The Judge unfolded the paper, read what it said, and then refolded the jury's verdict as he sat up in his chair.

"Mr. Farmer; would you please rise?" Michael looked at his lawyer, and then back towards his wife before he stood in front of Judge Fall. "The jury has found you guilty on all counts presented to them, but to tell you the truth, I believe that you are a good man and a loving father who took a desperate risk for his family that did not pay off. I admire your heart and compassion for your family, but not what you did. So instead of charging you with the three separate offenses of 1st degree armed robbery, 1st degree assault, and 1st degree attempted murder of a police officer; I'll do something a little different. Since I really do believe that you are a good man who has made a bad choice for the good of his loved ones, I'll combine the charges against you. That way instead of there being three Class A felonies, which are also known as Strikes, there will only be one. Otherwise the *Three Strike Law* would have you behind bars for life, and none of us want to see that, especially your wife and young baby Mr. Farmer. However, there was a weapon involved, and so that makes it fall under the Federal Law. So, in short; I sentence you, Mr. Farmer, to a term of no less than eight and half years to be carried out at the Federal Penitentiary in Atlanta."

Michael Farmer bowed his head in a quick prayer, before he looked back at his wife, and then to the Judge.

"God almighty…please keep my girls safe until I return. Please keep me safe until I return to them. Amen!"

The judge continued, "I would like you to use your time as an opportunity do learn a trade, and to go to school; so that you'll have knowledge to fall back on, rather than robbery. Atlanta is right down the road, and so you'll have a chance to see your daughter grow into a young lady that is loved by both parents."

"Yes sir!" Michael nodded at the Judge.

"And Mrs. Farmer…I ask you to please give your husband that chance to be in both of your lives. He is a good man at heart, who fell on bad times do to desperation." Judge Fall looked past the Defense's table so that he could address Lisa Farmer directly.

"I will your honor." Lisa looked at her husband with tears as they rolled down her face.

"Mr. Farmer, is there anything you would like to say before this ruling is complete?" Judge Fall asked as he turned his attention back to the armed robbery case in front of him.

"Yes your honor," Michael said as he again turned to his wife and looked directly at her as he spoke to the Judge. "I would like to kiss my wife, and tell her what she means to me one last time so that she might remember me without any cuffs, bars, or prison attire." Michael turned his head towards the front of the courtroom. "Please, Judge Fall?"

Judge Fall smiled and waved his hand towards the bailiff. "Of course son. Bailiff, would you make Mr. Farmer's dream a reality before you escort him out of the courtroom."

"Thank you, your honor." Michael smiled at the Judge, and then held his hands out so that he could be un-cuffed.

Before he was sentenced to prison, Michael Farmer was a man who could never seem to get a brake. His mother had said that he was cursed, and his father had thought that he was a looser; but no matter what anyone said about him, Michael knew that he was truly lucky because Lisa loved him with all of her heart.

Times were always hard for Michael and Lisa, but after Jessica was born things just seemed to get worse. There never seemed to be enough money for food, bills, and other essentials that women and babies need. There was always love, but Michael knew that would not keep them full and warm during the long days and nights ahead.

With Lisa out of work because of newborn Jessica; Michael had to pick up the slack as he worked two jobs. He worked full time at the mill, and fixed cars on the side. Michael would get up at four o'clock in the morning to go to work at the mill, and then he would work on as many cars as he could in the evening to bring in any extra money. Sometimes Michael would not climb into to bed until well after midnight. He was tired and hungry, but he always kept it to himself, and smiled and laughed when he was around his wife and baby.

"Good night babe," Michael would say as he climbed into bed at night. Lisa had been asleep for hours, but he liked the thought as he wished her well and kissed her unwrinkled forehead.

One day when Michael and his partner Bill had attempted to change the blades on the milling machine, a crewmember for the swing shift that had just came onto duty, turned on the machine with Michael and Bill still in it. Bill was killed instantly in a mangled mess, while Michael somehow got wedged in between the gigantic old blade that he had changed out and the spinning new blade that had been quickly shut off. When the swing crew found him, Michael was pinned between the inside wall of the unit and the new set of blades. The only thing that saved Michael's life was that the new blade grinded itself to a halt when it hit the old blade that Michael had been caring. It took three men to pry Michael loose, but they did it. Michael was a mess both mentally and physically. He had seen his best friend and co-worker get chopped up like applesauce, and Michael himself sustained an injury that would later hurt his family. Michael's right hand was crushed during the ordeal; resulting in every bone in his hand being shattered.

"Michael," the doctor said as he came into his patient's room smiling. "The good news is that we were able to save your hand."

"Great attitude Dr. Joe," Michael groggily said with a huge dose of sarcasm. "Now what's the bad news?"

"Well Michael it looks like you'll have little or no use of your right hand. We did what we could. I installed pins and small rods where I could, but the truth is…your hand was too far-gone. It was crushed beyond belief. That is why I smile Mr. Farmer…your hand was able to be saved." The Doctor checked Michael's bandages and said, "that they looked good."

The mill had been in financial trouble for a little over a year preceding the accident, and it had been rumored that there had been a possible closing planned in the near future. Nobody wanted that, because it would kill the town. After the accident, *OSHA* closed the plant down pending an investigation. Safety was an issue that was never followed, and safety was an issue that would be costly to fix. So instead of fixing the problems, the owners decided to close the plant for good.

"We've decided to close this location to better help restructure financial obligations within our own network," read one of the company's attorneys during a press conference days prior to the mills closing.

Michael and his family had no insurance; the mill would not pay him for the accident, and he was told that he could not sue the company because they closed their doors for good when they went out of business; and with a crushed hand he could not stay a mechanic. A man that worked so hard for his family finally broke down and cried. For two weeks Michael looked for work; willing to do anything, but with seven hundred other skilled workers who were also out of work, and that all had two good hands; it was tough.

"Sorry Mr. Farmer," said the young hiring manager at a famous nation wide fast-food restaurant," but without the use of both hands I feel as though learning our complicated computerized cash register may be too much for you. We like our employees to succeed, but I believe that if you were given the chance to work here…that we would be setting you up for failure. Neither one of us wants that, and so I must thank you for coming in."

Both gentlemen stood up from the red Formica table and Michael shook the manager's hand with dignity.

"Thank you sir for your time and consideration," Michael lied. In fact, he was pissed that his disability kept him from landing the simplest of positions.

As he walked away, Michael heard the hiring manager tell him, "Don't forget to tell your friends and family that kids eat free every Tuesday and Saturday with a paid adult combo meal."

The final eviction notice came in the form of a nice young man as he served Michael papers as he stood in the welfare line. The power and phone were cut off, and his baby was starving and out of diapers. Michael broke down once again, but this time he decided to take matters into his own hands. He had a gun that his daddy gave him when he became a man. The gun was dirty, and Michael could not afford bullets for it, but nobody else knew that.

"I'm done with this shit. I can't find work, and my family is counting on me. I'm no fucking looser," Michael cried to himself as he sat on the edge of full size bed and looked at the pistol.

Michael walked into the local general store that he shopped at his entire life, and started to shop. He grabbed a shopping cart, and filled it with groceries, baby formula, baby food, diapers, and a new rattle. He then walked up to the cash register, pulled out the gun and demanded money. The cashier stepped back and started to dial 911.

Michael got scared and hit the cashier with the side of the gun, grabbed the money and ran out of the store as he pushed the shopping cart. As he started to drive off, the local sheriff tried to stop him. Michael, who was determined to get home to his family, drove straight at the cop; not trying to hit him, but to get him to move so that he could get home.

"Move Roger…move," Michael yelled at the ageing sheriff.

All Michael cared about was getting home to his family. Thoughts went through his mind so quickly that everything seemed like a blur, but he knew that he had to stay focused for his family's sake. Michael retained enough sanity to realize that if he got caught before he got home, then his actions would have been for nothing. These were good people that Michael hurt and stole from; people that he had grown up with, and he knew that under any other circumstance that he would never have committed such a negligence act against anyone; especially friends and neighbors. But none of that mattered then; all that mattered was the outcome.

"I got to get home. I doesn't matter what I've done. Lisa and Jessica need some kind of hope. They need food in their bellies and a warm home," Michael kept repeating to himself.

Michael turned left onto Faust Street, and that is when he saw the local sheriff's car in his drive way. The lights and the sound from the blaring siren attracted all of Michael and Lisa's neighbors. The entire neighborhood was out on their front porches, or had come down the street to witness all the commotion first hand. Michael used this still functioning mental madness to do a u-turn in the middle of the street without being noticed, and go around the block. With everyone focused on the gossip and the speculation of what the truth may be, Michael decided to go in the backdoor. He parked his vehicle two blocks away on Mercer Street, and nonchalantly walked home like he had done it everyday. Except that time he cut through Fred Thompson's yard, and tossed the groceries and the other items over the back fence that he and Fred shared.

For a moment Michael starred through a hole in one of the slats of the fence that separated himself from his family. Michael started to pull himself up and over the fence when he saw his wife come into the kitchen with the sheriff. He quickly got down before they saw him through the window, but he knew that he had to turn himself in before it got any worse.

"I can't do this to my family. Lisa is a good woman that deserved the best. I'm sorry honey," said Michael out loud.

Michael ran back to his car, and drove home. The crowd had really grown by that time, and Michael had to honk his car horn to get

234

people to move so that he could get into his own driveway. Sheriff Roger Albright came out to great him at the door, along with Lisa and their baby. The arrest went down without incident. Michael Farmer gave himself up, and was allowed to tell his wife and baby good bye.

"Michael...I'm sorry for this. Please love me." Lisa felt guilty for Michael's actions.

"Baby don't cry, it's not your fault," Michael whispered softly. "I'll always love you, like I've always had. And Lisa, make sure that you finish mowing the backyard." Michael winked at his wife as he the Sheriff walked towards the patrol car.

Lisa went inside crying, while the sheriff drove off with her husband in the back. Lisa looked out the window as she held baby Jessica. She watched the crowd break up and head to their own homes, their own lives, and their own problems. Lisa thought about her husband's last statement and thought how strange it was.

"Why would he even care about the stupid backyard at a time like this?" Lisa kicked a throw pillow that had fallen off of the family's handed down couch.

As Lisa rocked the baby to sleep, she could not get Michael's words out of her head... "Lisa, make sure that you finish mowing the backyard."

"What was he thinking…we worked on the yard all weekend? Why would that be the last thing that he said to me?" Lisa shook her head with frustration.

So Lisa decided to go out back to ease her mind and answer any possible questions that she had about her husband's state of mind. Then she saw what he meant. There were a dozen or so grocery bags from Grayson's General Store filled with food, diapers, other necessities, and a huge wad of money.

"Thank you Michael! Thank you for risking your life for your family. I'm sorry that it had to come down to this, but even now you thought of us first. I love you always." Lisa looked towards the sky and kissed baby Jessica as she slept soundly in her mother's arms.

CHAPTER 18

Rachlav wanted to escape as soon as it was possible, but Braden needed more time; he needed to stall until the prison transfer from Gitmo to alien central happened. Braden did not have to wait long. After lights out, guards rushed in and attacked both Braden and Rachlav. They were beaten, blindfolded, gagged, and thrown into the back of what must have been a truck. The two prisoners never saw one another, or knew what had happened. Braden thought it may have been the transfer, but then it may have been his day of execution. The prisoners were knocked unconscious by some kind of gas, and moved from the truck into a plane bound for Area 51.

"Lets just kill the un-American bastard," said one of the Marines who was sent to take Rachlav and Braden from their cells to the transfer area.

"Which one are you talking about?" asked another Marine.

"Does it matter?" answered the first soldier with a smile. He drew his side arm and pulled back the slide. "Lets do them both, and say they tried to rush us once we got them together. Hell, as far as we know…they could have been in cahoots the entire time."

It was predawn when the plane landed at its destination. The prisoners were unloaded, and carried into their new cells deep below the surface of the base. After they woke up, Braden knew what had happened and that it was indeed the transfer that he had been waiting for. The unknown was Rachlav; what did he know, was he still alive, and who else was transferred with them? Braden had to get his bearings; he knew approximately where he was on a map of the United States, but he did not know much else. He needed to influence a guard to help him fill in the gaps, and get a message to General Rachlav.

"Man John this is a rough one," Braden mumbled to himself as he thought about some of the assignments John Andrews had given him. "I need a n aspirin and a beer, and you are defiantly going to buy me the coldest one available."

General Rachlav woke up with a splitting headache from the actions of the night before. As far as he knew it had to be from the previous night, but he could not be certain. The small cell he was in did not have any widows or natural light coming in from any place that he could see. The room was dimly lit, and sparsely decorated; it only housed a bed, a sink and a toilet; all of which were metal and all bolted to the wall. Rachlav looked up when he heard the squeaking of the peephole in the door as it opened and shut rather suddenly. Then a folded piece of yellow paper was slipped under his door. It was from Colonel Braden asking if he knew his whereabouts, and if he had any injuries.

The Russian General yelled, "No" to the guard that had waited outside of Rachlav's cell for an answer.

The war was ruthless, and took a toll on the people of the United States. The Russians did what they had promised to do, and they did it well and efficiently. The Russians simultaneously fought the war with the Americans, and attacked maximum-security prisons. The Americans could not do much to stop them, except to do what they were ordered to do. The Americans held back the Russians, and they too attacked the prison system in what history would later say was the deadliest war ever fought on U.S. soil. It was a race of sorts; the Russians would attack prisons to release the prisoners, and the Americans would attack the prisons to execute the prisoners before the Russian could succeed with their plan.

"America is weak," stated Russian Commander Demidov after another prison had fallen into his hands. "They let us walk over them like cockroaches. Do they not care? Why do they waste time in killing their own prisoners when they could use their forces to attack us head on with their pathetic armies?"

Rachlav was not sure where he had been moved, or long he had been out. As far as he could see the future was uncertain. If he was still somewhere on the island of Cuba, then maybe he still had a chance for communication with his President and his homeland. His future was defiantly unknown. Rachlav despised the thought of trusting his life to an American, even if that American was a traitor to his own people. But as far as Rachlav could see, he had no other choice. Rachlav's government would never find him before the Americans came to kill him and every other prisoner in that complex. Rachlav smiled at the thought of Americans killing Americans, and that he would proudly die if his death aided in the destruction of the United States.

"Nika, why did the Americans have to take you from me?" General Rachlav asked out loud as he laid on his hard cold bunk.

Secretary of Defense John Andrews had just entered General Fox's mobile command base when he bumped into the President as he was leaving.

"Mr. President…I'm sorry, please excuse me." John said as he grabbed the President's shoulder to keep from falling.

"No need old friend," President Mason said, as he held out his right hand in a traditional greeting. "I was just checking on how this mess is going." The President looked around as he talked.

"And how is it going?" Andrews asked as he accepted the President's handshake.

"Bad! And I mean that I can't even take a crap without wondering if there is a bomb on the toilet. I have the Russians, the prisoners, and every red blooded American hating me…wishing that I was dead. Hell, the only ones that like me are the Democrats, and that's only because after this stunt they'll probably end up in office for the next two hundred years." Mason showed a smile as he spoke, even though his tired face looked worried.

"Rich…come on," Andrews addressed the President. "You made a call, and in my opinion…it was probably the right one, and I think that everybody knows that. They might not admit it, but deep down somewhere we all have a respect for your call; even if it is just a little, the respect is still there. Nobody would have made that call but you. The Russians defiantly didn't see that one coming; it takes bold moves by bold leaders to win wars, and Mr. President you may have won us the war." John Andrews built the distraught leader up as much as he could without too much unneeded flattery.

"That's B.S. and you know it. Now, why did you really come down here?" Rich Mason laughed at his old friend as they got back to business.

"I need to speak to you and General Fox about one of our prisoners." Andrews held up a thick manila file folder.

"Rachlav?" The President asked cautiously.

"No, Jack Braden!" Andrews slapped the file with his free hand. The sudden snap echoed in President Mason's ears.

As Secretary of Defense Andrews followed President Mason into General Fox's fortified dwelling to inform them of Braden's true purpose in the prison system, that he was still undercover, and that they needed to get him out before he was killed by uninformed personnel. Unfortunately before he could take a step into the command center, a short-range missile struck a supply truck that had been parked only feet from John Andrews's position. The blast flung the Secretary of Defense into the President, who had crossed the threshold of the door. John Andrews was killed before he could utter the words that would have saved Jack Braden's life.

"Mr. President? Mr. President?" Within moments of the attack, military and emergency response vehicles were on the scene. The lone terrorist bomber was located and shot on site.

"Roger that. I have the suspect in my sites. Awaiting orders." The U.S. Black Ops sniper held his steady finger on the trigger as he awaited his command.

"Take the shot. I repeat. Take the shot." The sniper pulled the trigger as he had been trained to do. The scene around the President and the Secretary of Defense was so overwhelming, that nobody saw the terrorist fall to his death as he tried to flee the scene.

Back in Russia, President Ubiikobyla was furious that his Intel could not locate his friend.

"People do not just vanish off the face of the Earth. I want General Rachlav found immediately." Ubiikobyla slammed his fist into his family's wood dinning room table.

Ubiikobyla knew that the American government could not afford to harm Rachlav, but then again Ubiikobyla felt as though the American government had made bad choices when it came to killing their own people to spite Russia; and in his mind unpredictable actions by the U.S. made their downfall harder to plan.

"General Rachlav promised me a victory. I see no victory," President Ubiikobyla said in a loud sarcastic voice.

After the rouge guard returned to Braden's cell with the one word answer from General Rachlav; Braden tried to get additional information from the prison guard.

"Colonel…the Russian prisoner just said no." Private Loren whispered to the prisoner so that he would not have been overheard.

"That'll do…hey wait…"added Braden as he thought about what he needed to say. "I need to make a call, or send a message to the Pentagon in Washington D.C."

"No can do…and I know that I owe you one…or two, but I can't. I would be sent before a court martial." The young Private bowed his head as if ashamed of his lack of actions.

"The Iranians would have killed you…twice." Braden reminded the young soldier.

"Fine! Who else do you need to blackmail to try to save your ass?" The Private seemed to come to life as he raised his quite voice into a raged sarcasm.

"Secretary of Defense John Andrews." Braden started to write down a quick message to give the guard.

"No can do amigo…John Andrews is dead." Private Loren threw up his hands and shrugged his shoulders.

"DEAD?" Braden had been taken back by the news.

"Yeah he's some sort of hero. A lonely Russian on a suicide mission tried to take out the President with a bazooka or something. He missed POTUS, but killed your contact."

"Are you sure?" Braden ran towards the locked cell door and got as close as he could to his inside contact.

"Man you prisoners really are secluded. It's all over the news. Braden...I'm sorry, but I can't help you." Private Loren closed the window opening on the door and walked off.

Braden just sat on the cold concrete floor in the corner of his cell, and tried to absorb this new information about John; about his mission.

"I'm screwed. He was the only one that had knowledge about this mission, and my cover. What do I do?" Braden bashed the back of his head into the concrete wall.

Braden knew that he had to survive, and without a paper trail or something to show that he was whole heartily not a traitor to his country, left him with limited choices. He had to get out of the country and take on a new identity; something low key and off the map. However, the mission was constantly on his mind. He had never walked away from an assignment, and the thought of doing so left an uneasy feeling in the pit of Braden's stomach. If something went wrong; every scenario would lead to his death. If Braden did nothing, then he would be executed for his crimes against his country. If Braden escaped by himself, then he would be shot on site; unless he got out without anyone's knowledge, but then he would be hunted wherever he went. He could wait for the Russians, and trust General Rachlav with his life. The only problem with that was that the Russians needed to know about and find a top secret Black Site on U.S. soil under UFO central, that only a select few knew about. The fourth scenario would allow Braden to finish the job that he was assigned, and that was to gain the trust of General Rachlav and gain information that would be useful in ending the war. Helping a guy to escape a death sentence was a great way to earn the trust of an enemy in a hurry. Just like the other scenarios, that one also led to his Braden's and the confirmation that he was indeed a traitor to his nation. In Braden's mind, the fourth option was the only option. He had to escape, and he had to do it with General Rachlav. The Russian General was too valuable a prisoner to ignore. The U.S. needed Rachlav; all Braden had to do was convince Rachlav to help take down Russia, or at least trick him into it.

Area 51 was indeed a challenge in itself. Braden did his homework on the area itself, including some need to know information that John Andrews had shared with him during their last mission briefing. *JANET* flew back and forth daily between Las Vegas and the surrounding base area. The commuter plane would be easy enough to highjack, but they would be easily tracked, and probably be shot down before they left Area 51s air space. Groom Lake had at least two functioning runways; the 14R/32L, and the 14L/32R, which happened to be the main one in use. That area also housed numerous other aircrafts that would make their escape a whole lot easier once they had attained a plane. The two main problems that Braden could see with that idea were that a plane of military design would be a lot harder to get to. Plus a few Russian fighters were permanently housed there, which would be the second part of the problem. Explaining to General Rachlav, and possibly the Russian government, on how and why the United States attained those fighter jets. Not to mention the fact of how long those fighter planes were in their possession, and if they were top secret at the time that the Russians had lost them to the Americans.

CHAPTER 19

Nathan Fox was a brilliant child, who grew into a brilliant adult. His entire life was about strategic planning. In fact if one were to describe Nathan Fox in one word it would be strategy. As a young man, Nathan had two loves; the military, and Brenda Logan.

The military was a way for Nathan Fox to be in a world devised of discipline; which he lacked at home. Nathan's father was a former Marine who could not cut it over seas. Drugs took over his life, and soon afterwards Bill Fox was sent home as an unfit soldier.

Bill Fox would sit up for hours on end looking over the paperwork that the military had given him before he was sent home. "Dishonorable Discharge is a load of crap. They don't know what it was like. All they know is how to get chauffeured from their million dollar mansions to their offices. 'Look at me…look at me…I work in Washington. I wear a suit.' Stupid ass bastards don't even care about the common man who puts his life on the line day after day trying to protect theirs."

"Now Bill," Nathan's mom Jackie would say, "I'm sure that they felt that they had a good reason to let you go." She would always have a cold beer ready for her husband when he slipped into one of his depressed moods. "Here you go honey. Now why don't you go and drink your beer in your comfy recliner and rest awhile."

"Don't start with me Jackie. You know what those bureaucrats did to this family. I had a good thing going, and look at me now…welfare from the same morons who left me to die on the streets." Bill Fox would go through the same routine after every one of his pathetic episodes. First he would contemplate ripping the paper into shreds. Then he would decide that wadding it up would be best. He would then throw the balled Government letter onto the floor. Then finally after a few minutes he would pick it up, smooth it out, and then put it back into his bedroom nightstand.

"Well thank God that you have me and Nathan." Nathan's mother said to her husband.

"Two more mouths to feed," Bill replied as he emptied the last swig of beer into his mouth. "Nathan? Damn…where is that boy"

"Yes dad," Nathan answered as he ran down the hall.

"Where were you son?" Bill looked around his towering son to see where he had come from.

"From my room. Why?" Nathan knew why. He knew better than anyone, but he always came when his Father called to him.

"Promise me son that you'll never go defending the country that did this to your old man. Promise me." Bill tried to stand up to look his son in the eye, but collapsed back into his soft dirty brown recliner.

"I promise Dad." Nathan rolled his eyes as he lied to his dad.

"Good, because it was those damn government officials back in D.C. who were running the military operation that I was on in the Philippines. Those were the people that got me hooked on drugs. Those are the same people that we rely on now. That same people that say that if I'm not enrolled in a drug treatment program, that I'm going to loose my government checks. They're trying to take away the money that I earned in our country's name. I fattened Uncle Sam's pocket, and now he wants more. No more...I fought for this country. I deserve to be treated like a hero...not a zero." Bill Fox slammed his left fist into his right palm as if to drive his point home.

Nathan stood there and listened to his father, and when the speech had ended Nathan dipped his head and walked down the hall into the waiting arms of his mother.

"Mom why does he put us through this?" Nathan asked as his mother gently held him in a hug.

"Oh dear…Nathan…you know he gets like this when he needs his medication." Jackie pulled back and looked at her almost grown son.

"Mom! It's not medication…it's freaking crack rock. We lost what little we had. If it weren't for welfare aide…we would be on the streets. Literally…in a cardboard box." Nathan pulled away and looked at the stark white kitchen wall as though he could see his Father, who happened to be on the other side of it.

"It's not that bad dear. I swear…you kids exaggerate about everything these days." Jackie grabbed a green dishtowel and wiped the already clean counter.

Unfortunately for Nathan it was no exaggeration. His home life was less than par…with a drugged out father, and a mother who was oblivious to the world. Nathan's only retreat was school, and in his mind he felt that he should study hard and do well. School was a safe haven, and by doing his part by doing what was asked of him on a daily basis; school in turn gave him the balance of discipline and reward that he had missed elsewhere in his young life.

"Damn bro…you got a hundred percent of Mr. Jones' Geometry test," Mike Striker said as he looked at Nathan's score as they walked down the senior hall towards second period History.

"I guess that I got lucky," Nathan said as he slapped Mike on the back of exposed neck.

Besides, school up that point had been the only place that he could see Brenda Logan. Brenda was a grade below Nathan in school, but even as a higher classmate; Nathan never had the nerve to ask out Brenda until the beginning of his senior year of high school. The school had a job fair day in the gymnasium, and Nathan had just spoken to a Marine Recruiter about his future, when Brenda walked by. Nathan turned and watched her closely, he looked at her through the eyes of a man in love; totally forgetting the Marine before him.

"Excuse me son. I was speaking to you," the Marine Recruiter said confidently.

"Uh what…what…I mean yes sir…sorry sir. It was just that…" Nathan stuttered.

"I know son. You talk to her yet?" The Marine looked towards the young lady that had caught his recruit's eye.

"No sir I can't…you see my…" Nathan faded off as he looked down and his feet slide back and forth nervously.

"To be a Marine you need to confident. Confident in God. Confident in the Corp. Confident in yourself. Missing any one of those, and well…sorry son…a Marine you will not be. Now if I were a strapping young man of seventeen, I would go over there in front of the entire school and ask her out. A man with confidence could do that. A Marine could do that. The question is…are you a Marine?" The Marine Recruiter stood there proud of who he was. His level of confidence filled the room, and it gave Nathan what he needed.

"Yes sir," Nathan said with enthusiasm.

Nathan Fox turned away from the recruiter and proceeded to ask Brenda to go out with him. To his surprise the whole confident thing worked. Brenda accepted his invitation to the schools Welcome Back Ball, which is held every September on the second Friday after school started for the year.

"Excuse me ladies, but could I steal Brenda away from you for a moment?" Nathan asked as he approached a small group of female students.

"Hi Nathan," Brenda waved. "Do you want to talk to me?"

"Um…yeah. Do you want to go to the dance with me?" Nathan looked back at the Marine Recruiter who stood strong against the back wall, and then back to Brenda.

"I was hoping that you would ask." Brenda blushed, "I mean that I would love to go to the dance with you." Brenda turned and hurried off back towards the safety of her friends.

The dance was a successful first date in Nathan's eyes. Throughout his senior year of high school, Nathan and Brenda dated off and on. The problem lied with Nathan; he was so focused on his upcoming career within the military that he sometimes forgot about his so-called boyfriend duties. Brenda on the other hand, never forgot about her first love Nathan Fox. She tried and tried to fully win his heart, but she could only capture it for a minute at a time. The routine was almost a game to their friends; Nathan would blow off Brenda so that he could spend more time working out and reading up on the history of war. Then Brenda would try and get his attention away from such trivial things, and in the end she would eventually fail and she would break up with him. The act of breaking up with him would always bring Nathan back, and he would always come back more loving than before. Nathan liked the idea of romance, but he did not practice it on a regular basis.

"I said that I was sorry. It's just that going into the Marines is a big thing for me. My Pops failed at it, and I really think that the structure is something that I need right now." Nathan apologized to Brenda as he entangled his long thin fingers into her braided hair.

"And what about me?" Brenda asked as she pulled away from her hurtful boyfriend.

"You know that I love you, and I'm doing this for us. Picture it," Nathan said as he swooped his arms apart in the air, "Hawaii, Paris, Bob's Chicken Shack…"

"What?" Brenda cut in.

"Just playing. For real though…what if the Marines stationed me in a beautiful romantic place? You could fly out and we could be married somewhere spectacular." Nathan smiled as he hoped that his words spoke louder that his actions.

"At Bob's Chicken Shack?" Brenda playfully glared at him.

"It's a thought," Nathan said as he two on again daters kissed briefly.

It was that on again off again choppy relationship that finally got Brenda noticed by one of Nathan's friends, Mike Striker. Mike had always had a thing for Brenda, but he never acted on his feelings due to the fact that he and Nathan Fox were pretty good friends. In fact, Nathan and Mike signed up for the military together. Mike Striker waited patiently for Brenda and Nathan to break up for what seemed like the millionth time, before he made his move. Mike had heard through some mutual friends that the couple had a huge fight that seemed to be the end of them forever. Mike put his plan into action to win the heart of Brenda Logan, even though he may have lost a good friend; in Mike's mind it was a chance that he had to make.

It was near the end of school, and the senior class had prepared for graduation night. Mike felt bad that he had to willingly stab Nathan in the back, and so he went to him an honest man.

"Nathan?" Mike said as his friend opened the front door to the Fox's house.

"What's up bro?" Nathan fired back as the two friends shook hands.

"Hey…you know you and Brenda aren't alright…right?" Mike tried to plant a seed of doubt in Nathan's mind.

"Yeah bro, it's over for good this time. She's tired of the bullshit, and I can't blame her man." Nathan showed his partner into the house. The two guys went into the kitchen, and Nathan grabbed two cans of cold soda out of the refrigerator.

"Is she free of you then or what?" Mike tried to seem nonchalant about the topic.

"What kind of question is that…is she free of me…yeah she's free of me…why?" Nathan tossed one of the cans at Mike.

"You know?" Mike shrugged.

"What?" Nathan asked as he looked in the cupboard for some chips.

"I like her, and want your blessing to ask her out." Mike paused and looked down, as Nathan turned around at looked at him.

"What the…dude whatever…ask her out. It not like she puts out any ways." Nathan threw his half emptied can of soda in the sink.

"You know Nathan, you're a real jerk sometimes." Mika followed Nathan out of the kitchen.

"Forget you Mike. I hope that you and Brenda are happy together." Nathan opened the front door and gestured for Mike to leave.

Nathan did not like the fact that one his friends, or any guy in fact wanted his girlfriend. Broke up or not, Nathan decided to get Brenda back before Mike did anything about it. Nathan drove over to Brenda's house, and ran up the front steps just in time to catch Brenda as she opened up the door.

"Nathan…what are you doing her?" Brenda jumped back in surprise. "You scared me."

"I'm here for you." Nathan got down on both knees.

"We're done Nathan. No more of your crap," Brenda said as she pushed past him.

"I know, and I'm sorry. I'm not here to win you back like every other time." Nathan turned around while still on his knees so that he could look at Brenda as they spoke.

"Then why are you here?" Brenda sat down on one of the front porch steps that led up to the house.

"I'm here to try and save our friendship." Nathan crawled over and sat next to Brenda.

"Our what?" Brenda asked sarcastically.

"Friendship. We have all the same friends, and I don't want it to be awkward when we're all hanging out. I still love you Brenda, but I know I screwed up. And since I can't win your heart…I'll settle for your friendship instead. If that is even possible at this stage?" Nathan held his palms together as he pleaded with his love.

"Yeah…I think that we could work something out." Brenda smiled as she laid her head on Nathan's shoulder.

"Good…let's go, I have something to show you." Nathan jumped up and grabbed Brenda's hand.

"I can't right now. I'm meeting Mike and the gang over at Tony's house." Brenda got up, but pulled her hand away from Nathan's.

"So you'll…we'll…be late. No one cares, except us. Come on, friends don't let friends beg." Nathan stated to get back down on his knees.

"Alright, but make it quick. We need to get over to Tony's house. I promised Mike that I would be there." She pulled Nathan back up by his underarm.

"No worries." Nathan smiled enormously.

Nathan drove Brenda out to the lakeshore. He had already set up a little romantic picnic area before he picked up Brenda. As they pulled up, Brenda saw what Nathan had done, and she started to question his motives.

"I thought that you wanted to be friends?" She strongly stated.

"I do." Nathan tried to put his arm around Brenda.

"Then what is all of this?" Brenda pointed towards the blanket illuminated by the cars headlights. "Keep your arm off of me…we're friends…right?"

"It's a little friendship meal by the lake. We've had lots of meals by the lake with our friends over the years. What's one more?" Nathan undid his seat belt.

"Just friends?" Brenda smiled.

"Just friends," Nathan confirmed as he turned off the cars ignition and opened his door.

The two friends walked over to the moon lit blanket, and Nathan squatted down and lit an old railroad lantern that he had found in his grandparents barn.

"Wow Nathan, you were never this romantic when we were a couple; two of my favorites; cherry pie and *Vanilla Coke*." Brenda mimicked an old television commercial by licking her lips as she rubbed her belly.

"Nothing but the best. Why don't you come down here and nibble on a little bit of this pie I bought from the store, all by myself." Nathan patted the ground to show Brenda where he wanted her to sit.

Brenda sat down on the blanket as she laughed at Nathan's pie joke. "I miss you Nathan. Why can't you be like this all of the time?"

"I just…I have no excuses. I'm a jerk, and now it is too late. I'm sorry." Nathan broke off a piece of the pies crust and shoved it into his mouth.

"Don't be sorry, just be honest. I needed a boyfriend who was there for me…not part of the time, but all of the time. The only times that you paid attention to me is when I broke up with you, or some other boy looked at me. Just like tonight." Brenda sat up on her knees so that she would get too comfortable around her old boyfriend by letting her guard down.

"Is there some other guy in your life?" Nathan looked at her.

"No you idiot. I'm talking about breaking up with you. We had the worst break up ever, and now your kissing my ass harder than ever before." Brenda shook her head in disbelief.

"I don't mind kissing your ass if you want me to," Nathan replied as he reached out massaged Brenda's exposed left leg.

"Nathan stop it." She slapped his hand away from her bent knee.

"I'm sorry...I just thought that we could start over somehow." Nathan made a move again.

"How? Your freaking military career is starting in a couple of weeks. I'll never see you." Brenda did not stop him as Nathan rubbed her leg again.

"Just for a few weeks, until after boot camp. Then maybe we can get back together...permanently...like husband and wife?" Nathan smiled at her and reached up and kissed her forehead lightly.

"Nathan...how do you always do it?" Brenda blushed.

"Do what?" Nathan smirked.

"Win my heart back?" She kissed his lips with hers.

"I'm just that kind of guy I guess," Nathan said as he slipped his hand under her dress without any resistance.

The couple made love for the first time under the moon lit night on the spot that Nathan had picked out earlier that day. After they got dressed, Nathan looked at his watch and realized that they were late in meeting their friends.

"We have to go." Nathan grabbed his car keys out of his pants pocket.

"What Nathan?" Brenda looked at what Nathan was doing.

"We have to get to Tony's before it too late." Nathan stood up quickly.

"Why? Can't we just stay here?" Brenda laid back down on the blanket.

"No…you said yourself that we couldn't be long, and that Mike and the gang were waiting for us…you. So lets go." Nathan pulled at the warm thick blanket.

The couple got situated, and was ready to go. On the drive out of the woods that led away from the lake, Brenda could not stop staring at Nathan as she thought about what he had said about her being Mrs. Brenda Fox.

"Mrs. Brenda Fox. Mrs. Fox. Brenda Fox. Mrs. Nathan Fox." Brenda kept repeating different versions of her married name out loud.

At Tony Brown's house, the couple arrived two hours late. As the couple stood at the front door and waited for someone to answer their knock, Nathan turned to Brenda.

"Mike came up to me today and asked my permission to ask you out. I guess the guy has been crushing on you like for ever, and didn't do anything because we were buds or something." Mike smiled proudly.

"What?" Brenda asked in disbelief of the conversation.

"Mike likes you. He's maybe even in love with you...hell I don't know." Nathan shrugged his shoulders.

"And why are you telling me this?" Brenda asked in complete confusion.

"Just being honest like you wanted." Nathan laughed out loud.

"Is that why you came over tonight? Is that the reason you set up shop at the lake? To get into my pants...because of Mike Striker?" Brenda stepped away from Nathan, and started to cry.

"Well...yeah...honestly." Nathan shook his head in agreement.

At that moment, the door opened and the party of friends saw Brenda slap Nathan across his face. Mike Striker ran to the door and asked Nathan what had happened.

"What's up Nathan? What did you do?" Mike looked out the door and saw Brenda as she ran down the driveway.

"I fucked her. Now you can have the slut." Nathan looked Mike in the eye like he had won a prize.

Mike knocked Nathan on his ass from a right blow to the side of his head. Mike than ran after Brenda, who had ran down the sidewalk towards her home.

"Brenda wait up." Mike shouted as he caught up with his heart broken friend.

"Not now Mike. He did this just to get at you. He used me…my feelings…to get to you. Why?" Brenda pushed at Mike's chest.

"Because I love you Brenda. I always have. I told Nathan that I have waited long enough, and that friends or not I needed to be with you. He did this so that no one else would want you, but that's not true. What I can give you is much more that Nathan Fox could ever give you, because I truly do love you Brenda." Mike understood that she

needed time and a lot of space. Never the less she allowed him to drive
her safely home.

"Good night Brenda," Mike said as she got out of his Dad's
Jeep.

Brenda did not reply. She went straight into the house, and
never looked back to see if Mike had been watching her.

CHAPTER 20

As Jack Braden laid in his small isolated cell, his mind wandered to better times; times before the war; times with Beth. During college of their freshman year, the two decided to go to Cancun, Mexico with all of their friends for what everyone had said was to be the wildest Spring Break ever. All of their friends also warned the two not to attend the festivities that year because of their resent engagement.

"Dude, you can't take your wife to Mexico on Spring Break." Jack's roommate informed him.

"She's not me wife…yet." Jack stood up for his and Beth's relationship. "We have a strong bond that will span time and space. We are unbreakable. So kick back dude, because we're going to Mexico."

"It ain't the point. What if some hot blonde wants to hook up, and you have the old ball and chain wrapped around your ankle, dude? You know I love Beth, and I'll step into your place as her husband if something should happen…" Paul was happy to mention that last part.

"Thanks a lot Paul, but nothing is going to happen to me." Jack gently pushed his friend in the chest.

"That's the problem...nothing will happen with the wife in tow. We all know that Beth's a babe, and all the guys want to hook up with her, but for some reason she has chosen your ugly ass to marry. And when she breaks your heart when she meets some other dude south of the boarder...don't come crying to me when you're all of the sudden single, lonely, and sad because nobody wants to hook up with a marked man." Paul pointed his finger at Jack, "Believe me dude."

"Marked man?" Jack tried to slap his roommate's hand away, but missed.

"Some dimwit that brings the spouse to a smorgasbord. Just leave her here incase you get screwed up...and down...if you know what I mean." Paul thrust his hips back and forth in a rocking motion.

"Exactly, and I don't want to screw that up by listening to your dumb ass." Jack sat down on the edge of his bed and looked at the clothing items that he had picked out for the trip.

"Ok, but look at it from this point of view. All the guys that want to get with her here...will be ten fold down there. They'll all be trying to get some..." Paul started to thrust his hips again.

"And I'll defend her." Jack threw a soiled shirt at his friend's face.

"You'll be thrown in a Mexican jail. Can you say 'No burrito en mi culo?'" Paul put his hands on his own butt to act out what the term "cover your own ass" meant in literal terms.

"Nothing is going to happen. We love each other, we are going to be married, and Mexico seems like the right thing to do." Jack got up and grabbed a small black and red suitcase out of his cramped closet.

"I'm just saying dude, that there will be a lot of temptation, and I don't know if you have the pants to fill Beth's needs." Paul grabbed the crotch area of his pants with his right hand and thrust once again.

At the same time across campus, Beth's friend Janie Miles tried to talk her out of going to Mexico.

"Beth you can't go." Janie jumped onto Beth's bed, and bounced into a seated position.

"And why not?" Beth stopped what she been doing and looked at her friend.

"Because you and Jack are a cute couple, and I want to see you guys make it." Janie picked up one of Beth's tops and examined it.

"And who says that we won't?" Beth grabbed the shirt from Janie and folded it so it would fit into her compacted travel suitcase.

"Paul Wickersham is over at Jack's dorm right now trying to talk Jack out of going with us; just like I'm trying to do to you." Janie picked up another one of her friend's tops. "Can I barrow this one tomorrow night?"

"I know Paul Wickersham, and Paul Wickersham is trying to talk Jack into breaking up with me before we go so that he has a free pass to a guilt free conscious." Beth looked at the pile of clothes that she had pulled out of her tiny closet.

"Possibly…but that wasn't the plan. The plan was for us to get you guys to change your minds about going to Cancun for Spring Break, and do something else that involved less of an orgy type of atmosphere." Janie continued to go through her friend's wardrobe as they spoke.

"Don't worry Jack and I are fine…and very much in love." Beth picked up a picture of Jack and herself that she kept next to her bed.

Cancun, Mexico would have been the ultimate test for a couple that were not as secure in their relationship and love as Beth and Jack were in theirs. Beth was beautiful, and held her own against the rest of the half naked women on the beach. Jack was also an attractive person with a finely fit body. Both of them had gotten a lot of looks, and a lot of offers; but neither swayed.

"Beth?" Jack asked as the two lovebirds sat together on a log that had washed ashore.

"Yes my love." Beth turned to Jack.

"Cancun may have not been the best idea for the two of us." Jack turned to face Beth.

"What…why?" Beth looked worried.

"It's too freaking crowded. I can't even hear myself breathe. Lets leave tonight, and find us some secluded beach somewhere down the coast where it'll be a little more Spring Break like…Jack and Beth style. What do you think?" Jack stood up and put his hand out for Beth to take in agreement of his idea.

"I was wondering what was taking you so long to ask me." Beth accepted her boyfriend's hand as he pulled her to her feet.

Jack and Beth borrowed Janie Miles' car and drove south along the coast, and away from the Spring Breakers. A little over an hour later, the couple came across a little villa that was not on any map. There however, was a widowed lady that rented out a room in her beachfront hacienda. By the looks of the place, it had once been a grand estate, but time takes a toll on everything. The owner was more than excited to have young guests that were so in love like her and her husband once had been. The old widow lady just stood and watched the couple for what seemed like an eternity. All of the sudden she herself was back in her late teen years being called on by her soon to be husband.

"Sr. Guzman, me honrarían para tener su Esmerelda como mi esposa para ahora y por siempre. Vengo aquí hoy pidiendo su permiso en pedir su mano en la unión."

Esmerelda and her three younger sisters had hid around the corner to eves drop on the conversation that her true love Manuel had had with her father.

"What did Manuel say? What did he say?" Esmerelda asked as she tugged on her sister's dress.

"Calm down Esmerelda…I can't here." Her sister Maria pushed her back.

"Shhh!" Exclaimed one of Esmerelda's other sisters Manuela.

"Oh mi dios!" Maria had gotten very excited.

"What? What?" Esmerelda asked her younger sister.

"Manuel just asked Dad if he could marry you." Maria turned around and hugged her sister.

"Word for word…please?" Esmerelda stopped the embrace. She put her hands on her sister's shoulders and pulled back so that she could see Maria's entire face as she repeated the conversation between the two men.

Maria strutted like she was Manuel as he came to the front door of their small house. Her reenactment even included sister Manuela as she portrayed the girl's father. "Mr. Guzman, I would be honored to have your Esmerelda as my wife for now and forever. I come here today asking for your permission in asking for her hand in marriage."

"Wow! Are you sure?" Esmerelda quietly hopped up and down on her toes.

"Yeah...something like that," Maria giggled as she replied.

"What did Dad say?" Esmerelda asked nervously.

"Shhh! I can't hear Dad over you." Maria waved her hand at her sister to quite her down.

Back in the other room, Miguel Guzman had been pacing back and forth as he mumbled to himself just loud enough to make Manuel nervous. He knew that Manuel came from a good hardworking family. He knew his father Juan very well. In fact he and Juan have had that very same discussion a number of times. The answer would of course be yes, but he needed to make sure that Manuel knew who was in charge, and that he was not just going to sit back and let his eldest daughter up and marry any two bit bum that rode into town; besides Miguel liked to see Manuel sweat a little, it was good for him.

Finally after Miguel Guzman felt that young Mr. Ramos was close to his breaking point, he gave his answer. "Sí. Mi respuesta es sí. Le doy mi permiso de casar mi Esmerelda. Ahora va a ella con mi bendición mi nuevo hijo."

Esmerelda's sister screamed loudly when she overheard her father's decision.

"What is it Rosa? What did Dad say?" Esmerelda asked as Maria and Manuela covered Rosa's opened mouth.

"He said yes. My answer is yes. I give my permission to you to marry my Esmerelda. Now go to her with my blessing my new son." Maria repeated as she helped hold her sister down before their father heard them.

"Really?" Esmerelda held her hands over her heart and spun around; her dress spun lightly in the air.

At that moment Manuel came around the corner to find four very excited young women screaming and jumping up and down with more enthusiasm than Manuel had ever seen.

"Manuel, did my father really call you his son?" Esmerelda ran to her boyfriend.

273

"Yes my love...he agreed to our marriage." He embraced his fiancé with an enormous hug. Manuel then took Esmerelda's hand in his and kissed the top of it gently.

"Esmerelda Ramos...Señora Ramos...Mrs. Esmerelda Ramos. I will never get over this feeling of happiness and weightlessness Mr. Ramos...husband to be." Esmerelda had been overjoyed with the emotion of love and happiness.

"Señora Ramos? Señora Ramos? Are you okay?" Jack Braden had asked his hostess.

"Sí." Esmerelda Ramos came out of her brief daydream.

"¿Cuánto para el cuarto?" Jack asked as he pulled his black leather wallet out of the front pocket of his khaki shorts.

"In English please...I need the practice." The homeowner waved her hand as to say that she would not accept any monetary payment. " Have some time with me after supper tomorrow evening, and the room is no charge."

"We can't except. Please let us pay something for your hospitality." Beth entered the conversation.

"Young love like yours...like me and my Manuel...is always payment enough in my house. Now go and enjoy yourselves. Walk on the beach, and I will get some food for you to eat for when you come back." Esmerelda waved the beautiful young couple away.

"Thank you…from the both of us." Beth took Señora Ramos' hand as she thanked their new friend.

Jack and Beth took the advise of their hostess and decided that a romantic beach stroll would be the perfect thing to do in Mexico. At first there were a few houses and small structures that helped make up the scenery, but after a mile or two along the coast; they were finally alone.

"Wait here," Jack said as he stopped Beth in her tracks.

"Where are you going Jack? There is nothing out here," Beth called out.

Jack ran into the dark green jungle, but not far enough to loose sight of Beth. There he collected an arm full of wood and carried it back to the beach.

"One more sec." Jack dropped the wood and kissed Beth on the cheek.

Jack ran back into the woods, and came out a minute later as he dragged a six-foot log behind him.

"This should make a great fire. It's nice and dry." Jack patted the log after he dropped it next to Beth and the other wood that he had collected.

"A fire on the beach Jack? That's romantic…even for you," Beth said smiling.

"I know…it just came to me. Honest!" Jack winked at his fiancé.

"I'm sure." Beth smile grew even bigger.

Jack found a perfect spot to build their little bon fire. He dug a shallow hole, and filled it with small pieces of wood and dried grasses. Within a few moments Jack had a roaring fire that any *Boy Scout* would envy.

"My lady?" Jacked asked as he held out his hand to help Beth down to the ground. Then he himself laid on the ground next to her. Beth followed suit, and with both of them laid out on the ground as they held each other close; the beautiful moment overtook them. The warm night air, the feeling of the sand below them, the coolness of the ocean mist, the heat of the fire, and the love for one another made a perfect moment.

Jack looked deeply into Beth's eyes and knew that he could not live without her. "I love you so much," he whispered.

"And I you," she said as she snuggled closer into his arms.

Jack pulled back so that he could look Beth in the face, and as she looked up towards his, they kissed. Jack knew that this was not just any normal everyday kiss, but the first kiss. Jack thought to himself that they had kissed hundreds of times, but not this kiss; it just made sense in his sole to consider this kiss the first kiss.

Beth knew it too. There was a strange sensation that came over her as she lay in the sand with the man that she loved. Kissing Jack had always been okay, but that night he had been a new man, with a new passion for love. Beth thought that it must be some thing in the water; which made here giggle out loud.

"Are you okay?" Jack looked into Beth's eyes once more.

"Perfect! Why?" Beth kissed Jack's cheek.

"You just laughed, and sometimes you laugh when you're nervous." Jack scanned Beth's face as he tried to read her thoughts and emotions.

"I'm perfect." Beth smiled softly.

"Yes Beth, you are." Jack kissed the lips of the woman he planned to marry.

That night the two lovebirds became lovers. Neither one of them had ever been touched like that before, nor would they ever want to with anyone else. It was perfectly awkward, rejuvenating, and when the feeling came over them; it was the most unexplainable feeling that neither Jack nor Beth wanted to forget.

"It was like my love…my sole…left my body. I was close to God…I was close to you." Beth tried to explain the feelings that she felt when she climaxed.

"Beth, I do love you with all of my heart, my sole, and you know what," Jack smiled from ear to ear as he pointed towards his nether region.

"I love your beautiful…er…thing too." Beth's eyes followed Jack's sculpted body down to the area of topic. "But more importantly, I love you with all of my heart, my sole, and my body." Beth laughed freely when she realized that Jack had noticed her checking out his manhood. In fact it was probably the freest that Beth had ever felt. However, she knew that the only reason that she felt that way was because she had just made love to the man that she loved; the man that she wanted to…needed to…spend the rest of her life with. That was no random fling in Mexico. That was the real deal, and she was certain of that.

Jack felt Beth's presence even stronger than before. He loved her so much, but the more important realization was that he knew for a fact that Beth loved him as he loved her. She was the one that he would spend the rest of his days and nights with; he was sure of that.

"I love you Beth. I will always love you. We will be together for eternity. Through life, and through death." Beth snuggled up to Jack as he said those words.

CHAPTER 21

Almost every maximum-security inmate on the Eastern Coast of the United States had been put to death by the hands of the United States military. On the opposite coast, practically every prison had been taken over and over thrown by the Russian military. The majority of the war seemed to be focused on the inmates in the prison system rather than the two opposing nations in the heat of battle. President Ubiikobyla addressed the nation he fought against in a satellite press conference from an unknown location somewhere outside of Moscow.

"People of the Unites States of America. I have come to update you on the status of the war being fought in your streets and neighborhoods. We, the Russian people are allowing your country's worst prisoner inmates to run free raping your women like your country raped ours. Your government's answers to these threats are to kill these violent criminals before we get there. True, this tactic may work for some, but what of the others? Your government's armies are in the eastern part of your pathetic country, and rarely seen in the western part. So I speak to you, the Western Americans, what has your country done for you? They have forgotten you, or more likely written you off as casualties of war. There is a solution to this terrible situation. You, the people of the western side of the United States could declare a Civil War, separating you from the ones who don't care about you. I give you my word as the President of glorious Russia that the common man would be protected under our rule. Together we will un-unite the United States, and show the world that Russia cares for its people."

"Nathan, we need to stop the Russians." President mason turned to Nathan Fox after Ubiikobyla's speech had aired.

"Mr. President...I have an idea..." General Fox started to say.

"I'm not going to like it, am I?" President Mason sat up in his office chair.

"No sir, but we can make it work." Fox pulled some plans out of his briefcase that he had drawn up on legal paper.

"Between us?" Mason asked as he looked over at what the General brought with him.

"Yes sir! Lets nuke the bastards." Fox pointed to schematics of a nuclear missile and of a plane capable of firing it.

"General, did that blast we took give you a bigger concussion than we first thought, because that's the dumbest idea that I..." Mason pushed the paper aside, and sat back in his chair.

"We use Russian planes." General Fox slid some photos of Russian military planes across the Oval Office desk.

"What?" President Rich Mason grabbed the pictures from his desk.

"We have a few Russian planes in a base out in the middle of nowhere." Fox showed aerial views of Area 51.

"How come I didn't know about these planes before?" The President was taken back by all of the news.

"Need to know…you know how it works," General Fox replied. "So anyways, we use a few of these planes. Arm them with the nukes, and target large Russian populations within the West Coast. We already control the East Coast, and you heard what that fat ass president of Russia said. He's trying to make Civil War, and if that happens we are going to kill our fellow Americans in war anyways. So why not target Seattle, Los Angeles, San Francisco, Salt Lake City, Las Vegas, and wherever else we need to, like those fucking prisons. We kill the Russians, we kill the prisoners, and in the end the Russians get blamed for it. That is more than enough reason to get support from our allied nations to nuke Moscow, and split up Russia." General Fox pushed all of his files towards the President and stood up.

"We would weaken ourselves against other attacks from other nations. What if the Chinese made a play? With United States and

Russia both out of the game…there wouldn't be anyone to stop them."
Mason also stood up to match Fox's intimidation play.

"We pull our guys out first. We only target key areas. Hell, most of the innocent bystanders have already pulled out and are heading east. We'll take a loss, but we'll pull out ahead." Fox slammed his right index finger onto the top of Mason's desk.

"Who would we get to fly the Russian planes…none of our guys would volunteer to nuke their own homes?" The President looked right at Fox as he asked the question.

"So we lie to them! We pick a handful of pilots who would anything for their country. We tell them what they need to know, and that's it. None of my men would disobey a direct order." Fox had all of points covered before he arrived to meet with POTUS.

"And what about after? How is the famous General Nathan Fox going to explain to these lucky pilots that they carried out a nuclear lie that destroyed the lives of people who didn't have to die?" mason slammed his fist into his desk as the discussion heated up.

"We don't cross that bridge. Those brave pilots…those United States soldiers…those men of honor will have died serving their country in the line of duty. They were never in those planes. The United States have never had in their possession, at any time, Russian fighters. Those men will be remembered as heroes defending the American way," General Fox proclaimed proudly.

"And what about their families?" Mason countered.

"Mr. President, all you do is give those grieving people a bigger check. That way, when this is all over, you can sleep better." Fox started to pick up his scattered paperwork from the desk.

"There is no way to do this." Mason turned his back and paced a few steps while he thought for a few moments.

Mr. President…you have Congress approved Martial Law. We can do anything we want. And now with Secretary of Defense Andrews out of the picture you just relay everything to me, and I'll get it done." Fox sat back down with a calm look on his face.

"You're a monster!" Mason turned to Fox and pointed at him.

"We're monsters! You started this whole thing by reevaluating prisoner's sentences and giving them an instant ride to Hell." General Fox flew to his feet in a rage, and pointed his finger right back towards the President.

"How dare you! I'm the President of the United States of America." Mason quickly ran up to General Fox and got right up to his face.

"And I'm the man who does the work you can't stomach to do on your own. No matter how you pronounce it in you upper class society…you are still a murder. Now if you'll excuse me…Mr. President…I have some more of your killing to do in the name of freedom." Fox did not back to his leader. He stared at the President eye to eye for a brief second, and then turned and walked out of the Oval Office with his briefcase in hand.

CHAPTER 22

Emma Watson was a young and upcoming journalist for the London Times, when she decided to go to the United States of America to get a first hand look and a level headed story of what the war in America was really like. All flights to and from the United States were cancelled, but Emma used some of her connections and got a flight into Vancouver, Canada. From there she bordered a charter bus and rode it to the US-Canadian boarder. The boarder was closed as she had suspected and heard prior to her arrival, but Emma was no rookie at those sorts of odds. She got off of the bus with a bunch of tourists who wanted to see the devastation in America for themselves, but were denied. Emma went into a small café in Surrey, British Columbia and had some cherry pie and a *Coke*. Being a journalist by nature, Emma had no problem as she engaged local town folk to sit and talk with her. She told them that her name was Gretchen, a divorced housewife of three young children who were with their father and how she came all the way from the UK to stand in the two North American countries at once. Within a matter of moments, Emma had two ride offers to take her to Peace Arch Park.

"I would be more than happy to give you a lift young lady. I'm going that direction anyways." Joe jumped up and grabbed his cup of coffee to go.

"Thank you," replied Emma. "I would like that." She then took his hand in hers and shook. "It's a pleasure to meet your acquaintance Joe. My name is Gretchen."

At the park, Emma saw the famed Peach Arch that peacefully separated Canada from the United States. She casually walked over to the two country's dividing line, put one foot in America, and left her left foot in Canada. Then she totally stepped into America, as she left Canada behind. There was a lot of commotion at the park with people, who tried to cross the boarder, and so Emma easily slipped into the United States without much struggle; or so she thought.

"Ms.? Ms.?" A boarder control guard asked as he jogged over to her.

Emma turned around, "Yes?"

"I'm sorry, but that gentleman over there on the Canadian side said that you left your wallet in his possession. If this is true, then I will need you to accompany me back across the boarder." The guard reached out his hand to take Emma by the elbow.

"I'm sorry, but I think that you have the wrong person. I've been in America for the longest time now," Emma lied.

"Then if there is a misunderstanding, I apologize. But until then, please come with me so we can get this straightened out." The guard pulled Emma towards him as he stepped away from their standing location.

"Of course." Emma smiled and walked alongside the border guard.

Emma Watson knew that there would always be that connection that men had to her. She flirted for a living, but it never went any further than a ride or a good story. A few years prior, Emma developed a trick to discredit possible witnesses that aided her, like Joe who had given her a ride from the Surrey restaurant to Peace Arch Park. Emma knew that if she crossed the boarder, then her ride Joe would have said something.

Emma carried five pocketbooks in her purse, one was red and the other four were black. She had an unknown friend that had a knack for purse nabbing tourists, mostly American women if at all possible. Emma did not agree with his tactics, but never the less she would collect those women's ID's and stage them when needed. The red pocketbook was Emma's actual pocketbook, the other four were decoy pocketbooks made up of stolen ID's that threw off the credibility of the person who tried to identify her when she "accidentally" left one of her black pocketbooks behind.

"Okay Mrs., this gentleman here…" The guard stopped in front of Emma's accuser.

"Joe…Joe Rumage," The Canadian man quickly said.

"Yes Joe, thank you. As I was saying, Joe here believes that you were his companion that he picked up at Rosie's Café up in Surrey, BC. However, you disagree Miss, is that correct?" The guard looked back and forth between the two individuals as he spoke.

"Yes," answered Joe.

"Yes," answered Emma.

"I'm going to need to see some identification from the both of you if you don't mind," the border patrol officer said as he held out his right hand.

"Not at all officer," Emma replied as she reached into her purse.

Joe Rumage pulled his wallet out of his back right pocket of his blue jeans. In his left hand, he held a small black pocketbook that he held out towards Emma. "Are you looking for this?"

"No sir," Emma replied as she pulled her red pocketbook from her purse that she had draped over her shoulder. She opened up the wallet and pulled out her ID. "Here you go officer."

The boarder patrol officer took the ID card from Emma, and thanked her. "Thank you, and sir may I have yours?"

Joe stood there dumb founded. "I don't know what that is that she gave you, but I assure you officer that that ladies name is Gretchen, and I gave her a ride in front seat of my truck over there. I met her in at Rosie's and we came down here. I have her wallet that she left in my truck right here in my hand." Joe slapped his opened palm with the small black purse before he offered it to the officer.

The officer took the black pocketbook from the confused Joe Rumage, and opened it. "Well if there were any money or credit cards in here, they're gone now…" The officer did not look up as he accused Joe.

"What about a driver's license?" Emma tried to look over the guard's arm.

"Well let's see. The ID shows a picture for a Gretchen Hardy out of Shreveport, Louisiana, and it doesn't match the lady before us." The guard reported as he held up the photo ID for everyone to see.

"What? Let me see that," Joe angrily grabbed the driver's license out of the officer's hand."

"Calm down sir. I can see that you may have been confused. Just to be sure, I'm going to escort you over to one of the Canadian officers over there, and let them sort this whole mess out." The guard lightly grabbed Joe's elbow to lead him in the way that he wanted him to go.

"What about me sir?" Emma asked as she stood there and waited for direction from the border official.

"Yes, Ms. Watson," the officer replied as he handed her ID back to her. "You are free to go. Sorry for any confusion or embarrassment this may have caused you."

"Not at all…things happen. Thank God that you were here to sort this entire thing through." Emma smiled and lightly rubbed her hand along the sleeve of the guard's uniform shirt.

After she was completely and safely into the United States, Emma walked confidently into the city limits of Blaine, Washington. The first hotel she came too, Emma called her only American friend and fellow journalist, Nina Cordova who worked at Channel 6 in Sacramento, California.

The phone rang twice and Nina answered before the third ring started. "Hello."

"Nina? This is Emma from England."

"Emma? I'm so happy to here your voice. Where are you?" Nina excitedly asked.

"I'm at some inn here in a town called Blaine, Washington. I made it into the States without too much trouble," Emma explained to her American friend.

"Good! You can tell me all about it when you get here. Take a bus, a taxi, or whatever to the SeaTac Airport in Seattle. It should take you a couple of hours to get there. I'll have a ticket waiting there for you at the *Alaskan Airlines* booth this evening. You'll travel from Seattle, Washington to Sacramento, California. I'll pick you up at the airport here in Sacramento. If you have any trouble call me back at this number. It automatically roles over to my cell phone if I don't pick up at home. Any questions?" Nina made sure that her directions were short and to the point so she would confuse her foreign friend.

"Nope...got it. Seattle to Sacramento. See you tonight," Emma repeated back.

"Okay, good bye...and Emma...?" Nina paused.

"Yeah?" Emma hated awkward pauses in conversation.

"It'll be good to see you again," Nina finished saying.

"Same here." Emma was relieved, and was happy to be on her way to see her gal pal.

The two friends hung up, and Emma worked on a way to get to Seattle, Washington. She decided that a taxi would be the way to go. It would probably be the most expensive, but the quickest and most direct route. Besides the newspaper back home was to pick up the tab.

"Here you go lady. SeaTac International Airport. Which airline are you going with again?" The cab driver asked.

"Alaskan," Emma replied as she looked out the backseat window.

"Okay. Alaskan is just around this bend up here on the right. We'll have you there in no time." The cabbie looked in his rearview mirror and smiled.

"Thank you sir," Emma replied without towards the driver.

The taxi pulled over, and Emma got out. She did not bring any luggage because that may have hindered her arrival into the United States. Instead she pre-shipped her items to her friend Nina in the US. She paid the driver, and went into the airport.

"This is quaint," Emma thought to herself as she looked around comparing that airport to others that she had been to.

Emma made it to the airport in Seattle, and made her flight to northern California. On the flight, Emma reclined her first class seat and remembered how Nina and she first met.

Nina Cordova used to be a news reporter in New York City when she had first done an on location report on an oil spill off of the coast of Iceland that may have been terrorist related. Television stations and newspapers from around the world sent their reporters to cover that late breaking story. The London Times sent a good Essex girl named Emma Watson to cover the story for them.

Emma grew up in Essex, but she loved London ever since she could remember. As soon as she was of age, she moved to London with one of her classmates from school. Together the flat mates got jobs at the London Times doing odd jobs and freelance assignments. Emma's work was extraordinary, and the newspaper knew it. Soon after she moved to London, the London Times offered Emma a fulltime job writing for them. At first the columns and the interviews were small and meaningless to most people, but Emma was overjoyed to see her work in print in one of the finest newspapers in the world. Emma Watson continued to improve herself in her chosen profession, and she eventually landed her first big front-page role that made her a household name throughout the United Kingdom.

"You are a beautiful reporter that is on her way to Iceland. You're in the big times baby," Emma sang to herself as she danced in front of her bathroom mirror.

The oil spill off of the coast of Reykjavik, Iceland was the first of its kind, and the way that it happened made headlines. A Russian oil tanker traveling across the North Atlantic from the Russian Federation to the Republic of Iceland exploded and quickly sank on the outskirts of Reykjavik harbor. The explosion was not massive, but big enough to rip a gapping hole in the side of the oil tanker; which resulted in the pouring of crude oil into the sea, and all fifty crewmen to parish under the frigid waters when the ship went down. The circumstances to the explosion were questionable, and the news media loved questionable stories; it sold papers, and Emma wanted to sell lots of papers.

The London Times put Emma up in a quaint little Bed and Breakfast not too far from the harbor. Moments after Emma arrived in Iceland, she checked into her room and went straight to where all of the other reporters had gathered. Emma glanced around and saw a few newspaper reporters, but most of the media at the harbor were television personalities. Emma laughed silently at the thought of the television reports looking bad on television during the frigid weather that they have had in the area during that time of year. All Emma had to worry about was Emma. There was no television crew, no makeup artist to make her look good in front of million of television viewers, and no one to tell her to cut when she was on a role.

"Hi, my name is Emma Watson and I should have a reservation under the London Times." Emma pulled out her red wallet as he talked to the owner of the small B&B.

"Yes Ms. Watson," the owner replied, "I have your reservation right here."

After the check in process was complete the owner asked, "Would you like me to have your bags sent up to your room?"

"Yes please, and could you tell me where the big oil tanker had sunk?" Emma asked as she looked out over the panoramic view that the huge picture windows allowed.

The news reporters all took the same shots of where the ship was, the search party, and they all talked to the same witnesses. Emma Watson wanted more, and so she paid a young homely looking fisherman to take her out to the site where the Russian tanker had sunk.

"Please…I'll give you kr100," Emma said as she held out the paper money.

"No," replied the young fisherman, "kr1,000."

"What?" Emma gasped. "My final offer is kr500." Emma pulled some more money out of her purse.

"Okay," smiled the boat driver. " One kiss and kr500."

"Fine...kr1,000 it is," Emma laughed as she pulled out her money and handed it to the fisherman.

At the site, Emma was allowed to board a British Royal Navy Carrier that had been in the area, and was sent to aid the Russian tankers distress call. Being a fellow Brit, and the only reporter cleaver enough to get out to the area in question; Captain Grant allowed Emma to ask a few questions to some of his men, and to look around. He also assigned Lieutenant-Colonel Oliver to escort Emma Watson during her stay on the ship.

"Well Ms. Watson," Lieutenant-Colonel Oliver started, "how did you come about getting aboard?"

"It's a long story that involves the London Times, sinking ships, and horny Icelandic fishermen." Emma watched Lieutenant-Colonel Oliver's face as she spoke.

"What?" Oliver broke in. "I feel as though you should fill in those gaps. Perhaps over dinner? Especially the part of the horny fishermen."

Emma laughed loudly. "The last part was a small exaggeration. The guy wanted a ridiculous amount of money to bring me here to your ship, or a smaller amount and a kiss."

"And you settled for…" Lieutenant-Colonel Oliver stared to question.

"The larger amount of money of course." Emma set the Lieutenant-Colonel's mind at ease. "What kind of girl do you think I am?"

"I don't know," Oliver replied, "but I'd like to find out. What about Six o clock?"

"I think that I can…possibly do that," Emma joked. "Will we be dinning on the ship Lieutenant-Colonel Oliver, or on land?"

"On land, and please call me Gordon." Lieutenant-Colonel Oliver bowed slightly at his dinner guest.

"Gordon it is. Now please show me around the accident site if you would. I actually came here for a reason you know." Emma liked the young Lieutenant-Colonel a lot.

The London Times had the story that no one else in the world had. Emma Watson became famous overnight. Emma also had found a male friend named Gordon Oliver that she wanted to spend more time with.

"Well Ms. Watson, I see that your hard hitting inside scoop is paying off. I saw your name in Icelandic today," Gordon playfully teased.

"Did you know Lieutenant-Colonel Oliver…that I like having dinner with you?" Emma rubbed Gordon's hand as they held onto one another from across the restaurant table.

"And I you," Gordon replied sweetly.

"Excuse me?" The dinner couple was interrupted by a third person. "You're Emma Watson, are you not?"

Emma looked up. "And you are?"

"Nina Cordova. I saw your piece, and wanted to…" Nina started to say.

"Interrupt my dinner," Emma smiled harshly.

"No…interview your boyfriend." Nina pointed at Gordon.

CHAPTER 23

Rachlav grew more anxious everyday. He would pace back and forth wondering why he had not been released from his American prison cell. His government should have secured his release before then, or at least have found the prison that he had been detained, and forcefully taken it over.

"I am a highly decorated General in the Russian Army. I demand to be treated as such, and be allowed communication access to my country," Rachlav's voice screeched through the metal cell door.

There was a bang at the door that informed Rachlav to tone it down.

"And what about that American traitor Colonel Jack Braden, why had he not upheld his promise to escape the prison walls?" Rachlav thought quietly to himself.

Rachlav felt as though Braden was stupid for waiting so long to implement the original escape, because they had been moved to a new unknown location somewhere in the world. Rachlav tried once again to get his bearings on where he was, but again he had no luck.

"Guards, I demand to speak with my lawyer." Rachlav slammed his fists against the locked door.

"Shut the fuck up...what do I look like a Russian telephone operator? Now get a way from that door before I beat your ass for the third time today," the military officer yelled back.

Rachlav backed away from the door like he was told, but before he could fully turn his back to the entrance to his cell; a note was slipped under it by one of the guards. General Rachlav went over to where the piece of paper laid and starred at it for a moment before he picked it up and read the very precise directions:

TAKE OUT GUARD 05:30

Rachlav knew what he had to do, but how would he do it? Two guards always came into his cell; one with his weapon drawn, and the other with shackles. They would shackle Rachlav to the wall every morning so that his U.S. captors could talk to him before breakfast. Some of those morning talks were harder on the Russian General than other days, but never the less he gave out no useful information.

"How does the Colonel expect me to take out two armed guards who are just waiting to shoot me anyhow?" Rachlav mumbled to himself.

Even without knowing the time, Rachlav knew that his morning rendezvous would start at any moment. All night the General laid in his hard bunk and thought of ways to pull off that impossible feat, when it came to him that it did not matter. Then he saw Nikolaevna in the corner, and he sat up as his wife came to him. She sat on the edge of the bed and told him what he needed to do.

"Trust the American Colonel...not all Americans are bad...he will help you." Nika rubbed her hand over her husband's dirty cheek.

"What if we fail...what if I fail?" The general pleaded as his eyes welled up.

"Do not worry husband...if you do not succeed as you have planned...I will be waiting for you on the other side." Nika kissed the General on the lips with a kiss so soft that Rachlav could not tell if it was real.

"Nika...I have missed you." Rachlav took Nika's hands in his.

"And I you, but I have been watching and I see a grand life ahead of you." Nika stood up from where she sat.

"It's hard to go on without you...I was wrong, and I am sorry...I am sorry...I am sorry. Nika, forgive me?" Rachlav sat up and hugged his wife's waist.

"There is nothing to forgive...there is only love between us." Nika ran her fingers through Rachlav's oily hair.

"Nika?" Rachlav looked up as his wife started to fade before him.

"Now close your eyes." Nika slid her hands over the General's face.

As Rachlav closed his eyes he could feel Nika's lips upon his own as they kissed their last kiss; the kiss he had never truly given her.

The little window slid open on the door as one of the guards looked into General Rachlav's cell before he proceeded to unlock the cell. As the guard came in, Rachlav rushed him at the door, knocking both of them to the hard cement floor.

"Hold it," the second guard shouted as he placed the end of his rifle on the side of Rachlav's head.

General Rahlav looked up in time to see his gun wielding guard get taken out by a blow to the back of the head by an unknown third guard.

"Get up! Both of you...now," the third guard said with his side arm drawn.

"Frank...what are you doing? Think about this...you'll be tried for treason. Damn it Frank...he's the enemy." Private Johnson pleaded.

"Sorry...Suzy and the kids...I have no choice...I just need..." Private Frank Mitchell rambled.

"That's enough soldier." Private Johnson shook his head in disappointment, but with an understanding.

Everyone turned to look at the opened door as Colonel Jack Braden walked in.

"Now as I was saying…that's enough excuses from you. They don't care about why you did it, but rather that you did it in the first place." Braden explained to Private Mitchell.

With that, Braden reached over and took the pistol from Frank's hand and shot Rachlav's two guards without warning. Then Braden turned the gun onto Frank himself and gave him a choice.

"Is this something that you can live with…or do we end it now?" Braden alternated the guns position from Mitchell's head to his mid section.

"Colonel…my family…I betrayed my country for them…" Frank cried.

"No one needs to know." Braden put down his arm that held the gun, and then brought it right back up just as quickly.

And with that Colonel Braden shot the third guard with an un-fatal wound in the abdomen. As Colonel Braden and General Rachlav left the cell, Braden kneeled down and whispered something in the wounded soldier's ear.

"You are not a traitor to your country. It is hard to believe now, but Frank, you have just helped end this war. Your wife and kids would be proud of you soldier."

The two newly armed military leaders quickly walked out of the cell and down a dark corridor. With the Intel that Braden had from his mission briefing with Secretary of Defense John Andrews, Frank Mitchell's keys and codes, and basic general U.S. military protocol; getting into the locked Control Room went as planned. After the prisoners temporarily relieved a pair of soldiers from their camera duty, did the two finally speak.

"So you are the infamous traitor to the United States, Colonel Braden? Rachlav smirked.

"And you my Russian partner, are General Rachlav. We both know that each of us did their homework on the other. So lets put the bullshit aside and get the hell out of here." Braden turned his back on the Russian General and walked away.

"Agreed…Colonel…for now." Rachlav followed suit.

Dodging in and out of rooms and corridors made the process of getting to the elevators and to the ground level tedious, but effective. Once the two escapees were where they could see freedom for the first time was when the plan of escape became the most difficult of all.

Braden had not fully executed the escape plan in his mind from that point forward. He knew what had to be done, but before he actually saw the layout of the confines in first person, and the people in and around the base; Braden did not know how he was to pull it all together until he actually got there with General Rachlav. The idea was simple enough; General Rachlav and Colonel Braden would walk out into the open wearing the uniforms that they barrowed from a couple of unwilling guards that they met earlier that morning. The sun was not completely up at that time, so the predawn light gave them the perfect cover. It was light enough for other who where at a distance to see that the two men that walked through he base had worn United States military uniforms, but not bright enough to actually make out any details like the names on their uniforms, or more importantly their faces.

"So what is the plan Colonel?" Rachlav asked after they knocked out two guards.

"Take their clothes, assume their identities, and walk out the front door," Braden answered the Russian General as he stripped his prison garments off.

"Just like *John Wayne* and American Western movie…no?" Rachlav did not look happy with Braden's lack of discipline or escape plan.

The two inmates stepped out of the building, and into the crisp morning air.

"Wow, that's refreshing," Braden stated as the coldness overtook him.

"This is nothing," the General disagreed, "in Russia we swim in this weather. For us…this is like summer."

The two allied enemies briskly walked across the grounds, but slow and carefree enough so that they would not draw any undo attention to themselves.

"There is the front gate." General Rachlav pointed with a nod of his head. "Where do we go now without being overly suspicious, because the front gate looks a little too well guarded?"

"There," Braden answered.

CHAPTER 24

Lance Flanders grew up poor in a small trailer park in Texas. He was the youngest of three brothers, and two sisters. Lance never had any privacy, and at times he hated his own existence. Lance's mother was a known Meth user, and his part time daddies were known for their tempers and drug making abilities. It was no surprise to the local law enforcement when Ben Beemer shot his wife, Norma Flanders-Beemer, twice in the face, and then put a 45-caliber bullet into his own head on Lance's twelfth birthday.

"I'm sorry son," the sheriff told Lance. "You go on now with your Aunt and Uncle. They'll take you and your siblings in."

Norma had been married six times after her late husband John Flanders was killed in a botched arm robbery attempt outside of Waco. She felt that her children needed a man around for support, but she always hyphenated her name so that her children would always have some connection to her, their father, and their roots. All of the guys that Norma hooked up with were similar to one another, at least in the eyes of the children. They were all low life, two bit drug dealers that made Meth in the backroom of the family's two bedroom singlewide trailer. The Flanders children hated their mom for the life that she gave them, especially Lance. He had seen things that no child should ever see. Like the late nights when his Mom's body gave out from the day's alcohol and drug consumption. Lance's step dad, whoever it was at the time, would enter into the bedroom that all of the children shared and would have his way with the two young girls in front of the rest of the children, who cried silently and pretended to be asleep.

Lance stood up for his sisters once, and only once, and after that he stopped caring; until the day that he met Paige Pottersmith.

"Leave my sisters alone you son of a bitch," Lance grumbled as he jumped out of bed.

"Lay your ass back down, and mind your own business before I come after you with the belt," Bobby snarled and pointed his finger at Lance.

"Make me...bitch." Lance ran towards is step dad and hit him in the side of the head with a baseball-sized rock that the kids found at the lake.

Bobby slid off of the bed that the two girls shared. He shook the throbbing pain away, and pulled himself off of the floor.

"Your dead now you little shit." Bobby stood up and pointed to Lance.

"Come and get me Six." Lance stood ready with the large round stone in his hand.

Lance was no match for the strength of a full-grown man in a rage. Bobby knocked Lance to the floor with a right cross. Bobby stood over the scared boy, and slowly unbuckled his brown leather belt.

"Please don't Bobby. I was just doing right by my sisters," Lance pleaded.

Bobby whipped Lance with the buckle end of his belt for fifteen full minutes. When Lance stopped crying; Bobby stopped the beating, and then undid his pants.

"Your no good bitch of a mother never puts out. You break up my shit when I try and show your sisters how to treat a man. So tonight…you're my bitch." Bobby grabbed Lance off of the floor and carried the kicking and screaming boy into the bathroom.

"No Bobby don't…please don't," cried Lance as he tried to kick at his stepfather.

"I need to get my rocks off, and you did this shit to yourself. Maybe you'll learn to stay out of other people's business," Bobby informed Lance.

"Mom…Mom…please Mom…Mom please help me." Lance shouted, but help never came. That night Bobby Roland rapped young Lance Flanders in the family's only bathroom.

Lance was about eleven years old when his mom's marriage to Bobby Roland was at its end. Bobby was the worst husband and dad to Norma and the kids in a long list of bad husbands and dads; number six is what the Flanders children called him, which Bobby did not like very much.

At that time in Lance's life, nothing seemed positive. Lance's oldest brother John Jr. was serving his second year of a life sentence for a double homicide of an elderly couple that he was burglarizing when they came home early from dinner. One of Lance's other brothers, Mark, ran away from home because living on the streets was better than living at home. Lance's third brother, Billy, lived at home because the family could not afford to send him somewhere else. The doctors had explained that the TBI had caused cerebral hemorrhaging due to the bullet and bone fragments in Billy's brain. Not only did Billy survive his attempted suicide, but he was also paralyzed due to the fact that the bullet that entered his temple, bounced around in his head, and became lodged in his spinal cord.

"What the fuck is TBI?" Bobby asked the doctor.

"Please calm down Mr. Roland. TBI stands for Traumatic Brain Injury. It is caused when something real bad happens to a person's brain." Billy's doctor pointed to his own head to illustrate what had happened to Billy.

"Don't talk down to me Doc. I know something real bad has happened to Billy's brain, you fucking moron. He took a fucking bullet to the side of his fat fucking head. Shit-head couldn't even do that right, fucking dumb ass...SHIT!" Bobby threw his hands in the air, and then kicked over one of the chairs in the waiting room.

"Mr. Roland please? Billy's injuries are severe, and we don't know to what extent until after he wakes up," the doctor tried to point out.

"How much is this fucking thing going to cost?" Bobby quickly turned to the surgeon in a threatening manner.

"Mr. Roland, this is your son that we are talking about." The doctor shook his head in disbelief.

"He's not my fucking son. His whore of a mother popped him out with all of her other fucking brats. I just pay for his shit. Stupid motherfucker couldn't even die right. SHIT! Now I gotta pay for this fucking mess. It's always something with these fucking bastards." Bobby kicked at another chair and missed, which made him even madder. Bobby picked up the chair and threw it through the large picture window. The chair sailed down eight stories before it landed in six broken pieces on the top of another patient's red pickup truck.

It did not take long for husband six to leave when he felt that all of the Flanders family's problems had become his.

"But baby, why are you leaving?" Norma begged her husband to stay.

"Shit Norma! You have fuck-ups for children. They're always in the way, they're always in my shit, and I never have any fucking privacy. I'm not ready for a fucking family." Bobby pushed Norma away from him.

"Bobby...baby...maybe we can go away...just the two of us. We can go down to Mexico or something." Norma tried to hug Bobby.

"And how are we going to do that...sell your trailer?" Bobby snapped back.

"Maybe I can get the kid's grandparents to take them in for a while so we can have some alone time as a couple. What about that?" Norma followed her soon to divorced husband out of the house as she tried to pull him back in.

"Norma…I'm just not ready for a trailer trash family…especially yours." Bobby pushed Norma onto her butt and laughed.

After Bobby left, Norma drank herself into a two-week blur of emotional suicide. Then one Tuesday afternoon, the children were surprised to see their mom come out from the back of the house all dressed up and her makeup on.

"Where are you going momma?" Norma's youngest daughter asked.

"To get us some money," Norma replied.

"How?" Lance asked as he came into the room.

"This morning as I was laying there, I heard bells like in that one old movie about bells and angels. So I looked up and that gold cross on my dresser…the one that Daddy got me before he died…was shinning from a single ray of light that was coming through the rip in my drapes. I knew it was a sign from God, and I knew at that moment how I was going to use my gift." Norma looked up as if she could see the face of God in the ceiling of their trailer park home.

"How Momma…how?" Lance's sister jumped up and down in a very excited manner.

"Bingo! I have it all worked out. It's all true…God does work in mysterious ways." Norma pulled out the last of the money that she had stashed after she took it out of Bobby's wallet before he left.

That night Norma came home with seven hundred and forty-nine dollars that she won from hitting it big on the Mega Blackout Bingo Tournament. She not only came home with the cash in hand, but she also brought home some groceries, *McDonald's* take out, and Ben Beemer.

"Oh kids…it was love at first sight. I was sitting there next to Ms. Billy playing my standard four cards; when I noticed Ben sitting by the entrance looking all cute and smoking a cigarette like he was the *Marlboro Man* or something. Then it hit me…play the odds, and so I did. I grabbed a fifth card because five is an odd number. And what do you know…the very next hand I won the whole enchilada. After I yelled BINGO, I got to go up on stage in front of everyone, and they paraded me around like I was *Miss America* or something. They were going to give me this check, but I told them that I would rather just have the cash…and well they understood. And as I was coming down the stairs, Ben was there with his hand out to help me off the stage like he was my *Prince Charming* or some other kind of prince. It was the

315

most perfectly romantic moment in my entire life." Norma smiled as she shared the events of her magical evening with her children.

"Yeah kids…your mom here is one fine piece of ass," Ben chimed in.

"Oh Ben stop…you're embarrassing me." Norma playfully slapped Ben's arm.

"Momma, why did he say that about you?" Lance asked quietly.

"Well Lance…" Norma started.

"Son after your momma here won that money I took her to the store and to that burger joint to get y'all some grub. Your momma was so grateful and so in to me that I fucked her in the back seat of my car." Ben butted in to Norma's explanation, and explained his earlier comment in his own way.

"Ben's got a black 81' Trans Am with a t-top! I've always loved those cars…so manly and fast." Norma bounced on the edge of the family's torn couch with enthusiasm and excitement.

"Calm down babe…there's more of Benny the Super Stud to go around…in fact why don't we go around right now." Ben rubbed Norma's left knee.

"Okay Super Stud! Kids eat your burgers and fries and then go play outside for a while." Norma waved her kids on.

"But momma it's dark outside…" Lance pointed out.

"Here's five bucks…go to the store and buy yourselves some dessert. Now hurry up because me and Ben want to have some adult time without you around. That's why Bobby left…remember." Norma reached into her leopard printed purse, and pulled out some cash for the kids to have.

"Bobby…who the fuck is Bobby? Don't be talking about some other guy dicking you in front of me." Ben stood up in a rage.

"I'm sorry Stud…Bobby was my ex and it still kind of hurts. You know?" Norma pulled at Ben's rough hand so that he would sit back down.

"You're either with me or your not, but yeah I understand. I had a bitch who did that to me too." Ben sat back with a solemn look on his face.

"Don't talk about other women that you've been with!" Norma lightly slapped Ben's arm.

"Then don't be talking about Bobby!" Ben slightly pushed Norma's crossed legs.

317

It was not very long before Norma and Ben were wed in a small ceremony at the county courthouse. Ben was not big on the entire wedding idea, but Norma told him that what they had been doing was not right in the eyes of the Lord unless that they were husband and wife. So husband and wife they became.

"Lucky number seven…huh Lance?" Billy slurred his words.

"I don't think so. He's like everyone else…wants our mamma, but not us." Lance threw a ball of tape into the air.

"At least Ben's got a job…a new one for this family." Billy defended their Mother's decision.

"It don't matter though, as soon as he's tired of us he'll leave…just like those other five wannabes, and our real daddy." Lance caught the masking tape ball and threw it up again.

"Stop it Lance…Daddy didn't leave us. He died trying for us." Lance's sister butted into the conversation.

"Daddy didn't try…he took what he wanted. He got greedy, and that's why he died." Lance threw the ball across the room and tried to hit a picture of him and his father.

"Did not!" Suzy Flanders cried.

"Did too! If Daddy tried, then he would of got a real job, and he would be here with us now." Lance stood up and laid the picture face down.

"Mamma! Lance is…" Lance's sister Suzy started to tell on her brother.

"Go tell Mamma…she don't care, and Ben don't care either. I bet if you tell Ben that I was talking bad about our real daddy, he'll take me out to get an ice cream, because he don't like Mamma thinking about no other guys, no matter who it is." Lance ran out of the house and down the dirt road that led up to the trailer park.

The months that led up to Lance's twelfth birthday were pretty good through the eyes of the Flanders' children. Ben got drunk a lot, and he hit their mom, but he always did it in the backroom with the door closed; and as long as the kids gave him his space, he would give them theirs. Ben had a decent job as a mechanic, and he took young Lance under his wing and showed him a few things under the hood of a car. Ben was by far their best dad since their real dad. He bought the children school clothes, and taught them how to shoot his 45. School was important to Ben too, since he dropped out in the ninth grade; he figured that school was a proper means to an end.

"School time kids. Get your butts up." Ben would yell the same thing every weekday to get Norma's children out of bed.

Their mother on the other hand, was worse then ever before. Since Ben had a steady job, buying the ingredients for Meth was no problem. All of the children's part time daddies made Meth, and so through their eyes the ability to make the drug was not even a factor on if they liked Ben or not...he was just an Average Joe to them. Norma had always been depressed since John's death, but her increased Meth consumption had made her violent and suicidal. The teeth she had, rotted away; and the sores on her face increased in a most expediential way. She was scary to look at, and for the first time in their lives; the Flanders' children felt sorry for one of their mother's husbands.

"Lance get up here," Ben commanded.

Lance rolled the creeper he was on out from under Ben's Trans Am, "Yeah Stud?"

"It's your birthday next week, and me and your mom were kind of thinking that you might like a gift or something." Ben winked at the young mechanic.

"Yeah you know...I never got nothing before. So I don't get excited about things like that." Lance shrugged his shoulders slightly.

"Hey little bro, your with me now…with the Stud. So what's up?" Ben loudly slapped his chest with both hands.

"Well…there's this kid down the way that's got one of those phat chopper bikes like we saw on TV. Well that dudes always flaunting it like he's all that, and it would be so bad ass to roll up on him and his little posse, and you know…show him what's up." Lance stood up from the excitement of the possibilities that the conversation brought on.

"Okay, okay! Let me talk to your mom, and in the mean time lets finish my ride, so I know that you're still earning your keep." Ben pointed to the empty creeper.

Later that week, Lance heard Ben and his mom fighting in the living room. He snuck out of bed and overheard Ben telling his mom that he needed to get Lance a gift for his birthday, no matter that he lost his job.

"Stud…I know that you mean well, but we have priorities that come before some stupid bike." Norma sat hunched over on the flower printed couch.

"You know that Lance is like the son I never had…or ever will have. I need to do this." Ben almost seemed to beg for permission from Norma.

"You don't have a job! How are you going to do that...sell your precious car?" Norma came to life.

"If I have to." Ben sat down next to his wife and put his tired head into his calloused hands.

"What about my needs? I need my meds." Norma turned to her husband with a sick look on her face.

"There not meds...it's drugs, and you use up everything I make, so I can't even sell it." Ben stood back up and started to pace the carpeted floor.

"I need it Stud. I need it bad. What are we going to do?" Norma felt herself start to tremble.

"I'll get another job, but no matter what I'm getting Lance that bike." Ben walked over and stood in front of blank television.

"So you can sell it later, and tell him how someone stole it?" Norma tried to stand.

"I'm not like that." Ben turned his back to the TV.

"We're all like that...that's who we are...how society defines us." Norma succeeded to stand on her third attempt.

"I'm not letting him down." Ben sat back down on the couch for a quick moment, and then stood up and walked out of the house.

"All you need to do is worry about me…your fucking wife…not my snotty nosed punk kid. Now get your no job, lazy ass off my couch for good, which happens to be in my house, and make me up my oh so needed fix. Understand…Stud?" Norma tried to get all of the words out before the door slammed shut, but ended up talking to a quite room.

CHAPTER 25

The two military escapees walked nonchalant through the openness of Area 51s confines, to a hanger that allowed them access to a top-secret hanger that housed the Russian fighter jets. Colonel Braden and General Rachlav ducked behind some shipping crates so that they would not be seen, but yet able to see the door that led to the hanger that would potentially give them their freedom. Two armed guards stood on either side of the door, plus there were soldiers in and out of the hanger that they had currently been in. If Braden and Rachlav tried to take out the two guards, then it would also raise a concern with the other soldiers; even though airplane mechanics are still mechanics, they are soldiers first and foremost.

"Colonel…why not just attack these two men who are blocking our way?" General Rachlav asked in the most authoritative way.

"May I remind you General that we are in an unknown and secured location with a room full of men and women that will their duty to stop us," Braden replied in a hushed voice.

"They are nothing more that simple airplane mechanics." Rachlav shrugged off the United States military.

"Look." Braden pointed to a small group of mechanics who had been working on a newly redesigned F/A-22 Raptor. "Do they look like your everyday mechanics? Look at their side arms."

"So what," Rachlav exclaimed, "we are armed as well."

Braden shook his head, "It ain't going to happen."

The two semi-escaped convicts sat back and tried to evaluate the situation. Time was not on their side; within minutes their escape would be known, and the base would be shut down. If they acted with aggression, then their escape would be known, and they would be shot for attempted escape. They had no choice but to take their chances with the two guards, and they hoped that they would do it without any extra attention that might get them killed.

As Braden and Rachlav started to make their move, Braden stopped his crime partner in mid step and pointed.

"Look," Braden whispered.

One of the guards took out an electronic key and swiped it through the security lock. The soldier then opened the door, and as the two guards stepped back a few feet from their post, Braden realized that they had more company then they could deal with. A small group of pilots followed General Nathan Fox and a few other men walked quickly through the opened door. Once all the visitors were inside the secret hanger did the two guards relock the door and return to their posts.

"Colonel Braden? That is the door that we need to go through?" Rachlav pointed as he spoke.

"That's the door, and we don't have much time to do it in either." Braden looked back at a half opened bay door to see if it had gotten lighter outside.

Prior to his arrival at Area 51, General Nathan Fox went through numerous files on sub par soldiers that happened to be decent pilots in their own right. Soldiers that would never make his level of rank, and who barely received their wings by the skin of their teeth. Soldiers that General Fox hated, but soldiers that would not be missed by more than a few people, like his own illegitimate son. Fox's plan was to take those misfits under his guidance, and train an elite fighter squad; or so at least that was what they were told. They called themselves the Red Squad, and their first mission was to fly top-secret Russian planes into Russian controlled areas the United States, and fire non-nuclear missiles at maximum-security prisons and Russian strongholds.

"The military rejects will unwittingly destroy the Russians with a nuclear blast." Fox laughed at how easily he manipulated and lied to those young men. "They have no idea on the actual makeup of their weapons."

The fight would take the Red Squad into the hearts of most of the largest cities on the West Coast, and it would be there that the nukes would be used to stop the Russians from advancing in the war. General Fox warned that direct hits were necessary to protect the lives of the American citizens who had not yet fled their homes for a safer eastern location.

"Remember that the Russian aircrafts before you are necessary to keep the illusion." Fox waved his arms towards the planes. "The Russians will not realize the danger until it is too late. When we attack; we do it without mercy, or remorse. You un-average soldiers will be remembered in the hearts of all your fellow Americans." Fox internally giggled at how true his last statement was.

After the Red Squad learned what they needed to know about Russian technology, weapons, and fighter planes; they were ready to depart on their mission.

"Good luck, and God speed," Fox saluted his Red Squad pilots.

Braden and Rachlav waited at their hidden site until they heard a knock from the other side of the hangar door. Again the two-armed guards left their post to unlock and open the door for whoever was on

327

the other side. General Fox and the few unidentified men returned through the door that they had entered minutes before. However, the pilots did not come back through with them. Braden knew that in order to get into that hanger, he and his Russian counterpart had to act quickly. Timing was crucial for that whim of a plan to work. Colonel Braden and General Rachlav needed to get to the thick metal door before the guards relocked it, but after General Fox and his men were far enough away so that they would not be an immediate threat for at least a few seconds. They also did not know what was on the other side of the hangar wall, except for some American pilots who were interested in Russian technology.

"Okay General, are you ready to do this?" Braden looked back at Rachlav as he prepared to run.

"I'll take the one on the left." Rachlav nodded at Jack.

Braden and Rachlav got as close as they could to the hangar entrance without being detected. As General Fox and his followers walked away from the opened door, Rachlav and Braden sacked the two guards who had still been saluting a higher-ranking officer. The two escapees took out the guards, entered the top-secret hangar, and shut the door before anyone else in the room could even react.

"Holly shit…I can't believe that worked." Braden glanced at the Russian General for a reaction. Braden had been trained to deal with similar situations, but never with an enemy of the state, or against his fellow countrymen.

The American pilots had taken to the air as Braden and Rachlav entered the hangar. Braden had not counted on the U.S. using enemy fighters, and especially the planes that he had been trying to steal himself. However luck was on Braden's side because there was still one jet left, and it looked to be an old, but modified, prototype of the Su-27UB. Braden thanked God that the only way out contained a two-seated fighter, and an opened hangar bay door. Colonel Braden informed General Rachlav that they did not have time to discuss the plane, and that they needed to go if they were ever to get out alive. Rachlav swallowed his anger and pride and let Colonel Braden take control of the situation and the plane.

"What does your country need with Russian military technology?" Rachlav stopped Braden as he grabbed his arm. "These are some of our missing planes…no?"

"Yes they are," Braden truthfully answered, "but we have to talk about this latter.

The reinforced door had been pounded by something from the other side, while the two inmates could clearly hear vehicles as they came towards the open bay door.

"You and me will do this later." Braden waived his right index finger between them as he spoke. "Right now…we have to get out of here. Okay?"

"Agreed Colonel."

The two officially escaped inmates blasted off into the morning light that the ever-rising sun gave off.

"And that ladies and gentlemen, is how you escape from a military prison," Braden joked as he looked back towards the top-secret base.

General Nathan Fox was furious that his top two detainees were gone; and not only were they gone, but they flew out of Area 51 in a Russian fighter plane that had never existed according to the United States. General Rachlav and Colonel Braden had inadvertently blown a hole in General Fox's plan to nuke the West Coast. There had been no way for anyone to relay a message to the American fighter pilots in the Russian fighters because all communication devises were removed from the planes prior to the plan being initiated; all the planes, and that included the Su-27UB that Colonel Braden and General Rachlav escaped in, except for the two seated jets internal com link.

Braden knew that they could not go east, because the United States military had a heavy presence there. Their only hope was to get into one of the remote areas above Seattle, Washington. From there they could dump the plane and travel by car to Seattle; where they could get a message to the Russian government. Braden needed to stop the war, and he needed General Rachlav's help to do it. Going to the Russian government was the only way; especially since the United States government was out of control.

"Where are we going in my stolen plane?" General Rachlav sarcastically demanded.

"A remote air field a couple of hours above Seattle. From there we should be able to obtain transportation and get in touch with your government," Braden spoke into the working helmet com link that he and Rachlav shared internally.

CHAPTER 26

Eric Striker was born to be a fighter pilot; his name said so. A military man like his father before him; Eric worked hard to live up to his father's expectations of what a good soldier should be. Eric grew up all over the world, moving from military base to military base with his father Mike. The two of them were the only people that the each of them had. Eric's mom died when he was an infant due from complications with the birth; at least that was all that Eric was ever told about it. After Brenda Striker's death, Eric was sent to live with his paternal Grandparents until he was old enough to attend school full time, and when that time came Eric made the move to Germany to live with his father full-time. That was the only way that Mike could raise his son on his own; while he was at work, Eric would be at school.

"Why Papa? Why do I have to move to Germany to live with my Dad? Why can't he come her to live with us like he does at Christmas time?" Young Eric Striker asked his Grandfather as they sat at the dinning room table.

Eric grew to be a brilliant child; he loved to study, and often took it upon himself to learn more about a subject then what had been taught. After a while brilliant was not enough and it was replaced by boredom and rebellion, which looked like ignorance in the eyes of his teachers. Eric had actually flunked quite a few classes in high school because he did not care about doing what was asked of him. His dad ultimately made the decision for him.

"You are going to get your grades up, and join up with the Marines like your old man." Mike roughly rubbed his son's neck to help get his point across.

"The Marines Dad?" Eric disapproval of the idea was obvious as he broke away from his Dad's iron grip. "The first to go the last to know kind of thing, kind of bothers me to be honest. How about the Air Force…I could be a fighter pilot?" Eric turned towards Mike as he spoke.

"You're killing me son. Whatever you chose to do; do it well, and do it with all of your heart." Mike walked over and took down a plaque off of the wall that meant the world to him.

The plaque was actually a glassed box that hung on the wall. Mike's wife Brenda made it for him years ago. It contained the folded American Flag that Mike's Grandmother received when his Grandfather Bill Striker had died. A few of his Grandfather's medals from his years of service, and a black and white photo of Bill shaking hands with *President Reagan*. However, one of he most important pieces to the artistic tribute was a quote carved into the front of the wood frame.

"Some people spend an entire lifetime wondering if they made a difference in the world. But, the Marines don't have that problem." - Ronald Reagan, U.S. President; 1985

"I know Dad," Eric said when he saw his Dad run his fingers across *President Reagan's* words.

"Yeah...I know. Let's see those grades of yours, and then tell me 'I know." Mike hung the plaque back up on the wall slowly so that he could get it lined up straight.

"Why do you always have to be like that? We're all cool playing around, and then you got to be all like I'm one of your flunkies. Drop and give me twenty kind of thing. I know that Great Grandpa's memorial plaque means a lot to you, but I don't think that I'm cut out to me a Marine, and I know that it hurts you to hear me say that, but it's the truth. I don't even think that the military in general is the right thing at this time. School is boring, and so I drop a few tests...so what? I mean...it's my life...right?" Eric tried to use teenage logic on the man who raised him in a strict military setting.

"Sorry Eric, but grades are important, and so is your future. So you can't fault me for caring about you. We're the only family that we have, just the two of us." Mike looked at a picture of Brenda that also hung on the wall.

"I know dad, but can you chill out sometimes?" Eric smiled a big cheesy smile.

"I'll tell you what. You get your grades up, and check out the Marines...or...the Air Farce...I mean Force...I said Force, and we'll go on a trip together. The two of us; anywhere that you want to go. Father and son, just like the old days. Deal?" Mike stuck his hands in the air. "Hey what ever happened to that German kid you use to hang around with? What was his name...Adrian Bachmeier...or something like that?"

"Wow Dad, having a memory laps, that was a lifetime ago. Kids grow apart when they're Army brats. Too bad to, because he had this cousin from somewhere in England...Emma something that Adrian gave me a picture of once. She was fine, but you never transferred to England," Eric joked.

"Sorry to hold you back son," Mike Striker threw a playful punch at his son's shoulder. "Seriously though...grades up, and then a trip. Deal?" Mike stuck out his hand.

"Okay deal, but you better come through when it's time. No more of this war just happened to break out right after we planned our trip. Okay?" Eric had a real smile on his face that time, and he reached out and took his Dad's hand as they shook on their agreement. His Dad pulled him in, as their handshake became a hug.

"Okay! Now go study, or the only trip you'll be going on is the trip to the clean the portable latrines down at Mile Marker 36." Mike released his son, and pointed down the hall.

The two Striker men never got the chance to make that trip. Less than a year later, Mike Striker was diagnosed with Testicular Cancer. The surgeons removed Mike's right testicle, and the doctors started him on treatments. However, the Chemotherapy made him sick; too sick to go anywhere with his son.

"Mr. Striker, I must tell you that there is a ninety to ninety-five percent survival rate with this form of Testicular Cancer. I think that we found it early, and we got it out before it spread to other parts of your body. I'm almost confident that within a year, you'll have this entire experience behind you. Then you and Eric can go on that trip to Greece like you both wanted," Dr. Yarrow informed his patient with confidence.

Mike Striker did not know what his life expectancy was, and he refused to take any chances either.

"I'm Eric's only family. His Mom is dead, and so are both of his Grandparents on both sides. He needs to know that he is not alone in this world," Mike said to himself as he waited in his hospital room for his son a few days after his surgery.

Eric took his dad home, and helped him into bed. The pain medication that the Doctor subscribed made Mike Striker groggy and light headed.

"Son?" Mike's voice was low and semi shaky.

"Yeah Dad?" Eric looked concerned.

"Can you hand me my wallet over there on the dresser?" Mike raised his right arm slowly and pointed towards where the dresser sat.

"Sure Dad. You want to show me that picture of you and Mom again?" Eric made light of the situation so that his Dad would not see his deepened sadness.

"Not today, but there is something that I want to show you. You see, I loved your Mom so very much, and I did everything that I could do to make her happy. Honestly, the happiest time in her life was when she got to hold you in her arms right after you were born." Mike shut his eyes as the pain shot through him as he tried to sit up.

"I thought that Mom died in child birth?" Eric asked in a surprised tone as he repositioned his father's pillows.

"Technically she died from complications from child birth. She got to hold you for a few precious moments before we lost her. I know without a doubt that she died happy. Happy because of you." Mike struggled to keep his focus as it faded away.

Mike opened up his wallet slowly, and pulled out a folded up piece of paper. Mike unfolded the letter, and read over the painful words once again.

"This broke your Mom's heart, but the outcome was well worth it. I've carried this letter in my wallet ever since we found out that your Mom was pregnant with you. You're a good son…a good man. No father has ever been more proud of his boy, then I am with you. I want you to have this letter incase something happens…" Mike handed the worn letter to his son.

"Dad, nothing is going to happen to you. The doctor said that the survivability rate is…" Eric's face showed his emotion. His rock was slipping away despite what the doctors had said.

"I know what the doctors say, but their not always right. They're human, they make mistakes; we all do…all of us. That is why you have to take this letter." Mike grabbed his son's arm and pulled him close.

"Okay Dad," Eric said as he opened his hand.

Mike handed the letter to Eric and said, "remember son...you're not alone in this world."

CHAPTER 27

There was chaos in the streets, but as the prison inmates who were freed under Russia's plan, made it worse as they avenged their prison terms on the hearts of the American people.

"I'm going to get that bitch Onzuga who wanted to blow me." Joker announced to anyone in hearing range.

Joker Ramirez broke into the Records Room after the Russian informed them that they were all free to do, as they wanted. He had been looking for Blanca Onzuga, who he believed got him sent to the hole after a brief communication error. Instead he found Blanca's supervisor Joan hidden under her desk.

"Where's that bitch Blanca? We need to finish what we started." Cali "Joker" Ramirez pulled Joan into the open by her hair.

"I do...don't...don't know. Please don't kill me?" Joan pleaded as she looked at her attacker's feet.

"What's your life worth? Maybe Blanca's address, and where she's at?" Joker pulled Joan's head back so that he could look her in the face.

"I don't know where she's at...I haven't seen her today," Joan cried as she told Cali the truth.

Joker approached Joan's face with his face as he flipped a knife in his right hand. "Where's her personnel file puta?"

"Over there," Joan pointed to a black five-drawer file cabinet, "in the corner. Top drawer, under O for Onzuga."

Joker Ramirez opened the file drawer and flipped through the files until he came to the one that he was looking for.

"Nice puta," looking at Joan, "you told me the truth. Now what's your last name, so I can look at your file too?" Joker ran his knife along Blanca's file folder.

"Why? Please just let me go…I'll do anything. Just don't hurt me." Joan pulled her knees up to her chest.

"Hurt you? Why would I hurt you? Since Blanca isn't here, I'll need to release some of this sexual tension into you. Love never hurts when you want it." Joker undid his pants as he walked over towards the prison's Records Clerk.

Joan started to cry even harder, as the inmate slid the knife blade softly against her throat.

"You do want it don't you?" Joker whispered into her ear.

All Joan could do was shake her head slowly in an up and down motion. She would say anything to get out of this situation alive.

"Good. Let's see what you got then." Joker helped Joan to her feet and made her undress in front of him.

While naked, Joan removed items from her desk and laid on it. "Please don't do this? I just want to go home."

"You will," Joker replied as he entered her forcefully.

Puppet and other free roaming inmates, who had walked in on what had happened, raped Joan repeatedly. After the men were through with her, they slit her throat and threw her bruised and battered body on the floor like garbage. One of the men who walked in towards the end of Joan's last minutes on Earth was Lance Flanders.

"Hey you're that vato who took out the CO?" Joker pointed to Lance.

"Yeah, and you're Joker from my neighboring cell block. What the fuck is going on here?" Lance looked around in disgust.

"This puta was just helping some of the homies get a little pussy before they hit the streets. Want some?" Cali nodded his head sideways towards Joan sprawled out naked on her back.

"No...I'm saving it for my homecoming." Lance smiled coldly.

"You have an old lady vato?" Joker nodded in interest.

"Yeah, and she doesn't know that I'm coming home," Lance informed his fellow prisoner.

"WHAT THE FUCK DID YOU JUST DO?" Joker yelled the burning question at one of the other inmates, Pedro, who had just killed their rape victim Joan with a homemade knife.

"She could identify us, and I'm not coming back here," Pedro answered Joker's question in a muffled tone.

"Stupid leva! Remember the fucking Russians holmes? The jura ain't going to do shit to us ese. We run the streets from now on." Joker threw his hands in the air, and made his fingers form a one and a four to represent the number fourteen.

"Sorry Joker...you're right. I wasn't thinking. What do we do now?" Pedro looked down to avoid eye contact with the more powerful inmate.

Joker walked over to Pedro, took the bloody knife out of his trembling hand, and stabbed Pedro with it. Pedro Vasquez fell to his knees in agony.

"Why carnal?" Pedro asked Joker Ramirez as he painfully kneeled on the floor.

"You ain't shit to me. You ain't my carnal. If you kill a bitch, then you kill a bitch. Don't be a little bitch about it...fucking chavala. Admit the shit. Stand up for yourself, and don't cry around about it when asked why you did it. I stabbed you because your stupid, and I hate stupid people." Joker looked at the blood soaked knife and then flung it at Pedro's abdomen.

As Pedro fell over dead, Joker kicked the corpse in the face to make one last gesture of power over the dead man. Then he turned back towards Lance Flanders to finish their conversation.

"Where are you going homie?" Joker asked as his attitude went from that of anger to that of interest.

"Texas…why?" Lance asked cautiously.

"I need a ride out of this joint, and you have transportation. As I see it you killed the CO, and now you owe me." Joker ran his own knife over his own throat so that it made a slight red mark.

"Owe you? I don't owe you anything." Lance made his point known.

"Si pero no. As you see, I was going to kill Officer Jenkins myself, and he knew it. But the Russians had you do it. So as I see it, you took my kill, and now you owe me." Joker pointed the knife at Lance Flanders.

"You're messed up Joker, but I can't help you." Lance threw his hands up, as he shook his head no.

"Can't or won't holmes?" Joker asked as he stepped one step closer to Lance.

"Can't...no car. Entiendas?" Lance answered back.

"Don't lie to me holmes. I'll give you one lie since we're both cons, but that's it. I saw you take that vato Jenkins keys from his pocket after you blew him away. Entiendas?" Joker knew that he had Lance where he wanted him.

"Yeah. Fuck it...where are you going?" Lance shrugged his shoulders.

"Just down the way. As I see it Blanca's house is right there on your way to the big state of Texas." Joker nodded towards the wall that led to freedom.

Okay...let's go." Lance patted his front pocket that contained Officer Jenkins' car keys.

"Alright then. Just give me one minute," Cali said.

Joker went over to Joan's body and looked down on her. He stood there motionless for a moment, almost like he was studying her. Then he stepped over her battered body, and opened the drawers to her desk. He found her purse in the bottom left hand drawer, and took all of the cash that she had plus a *Chevron* gas card.

"Here holmes," Joker tossed the gas card at Lance, "so you have gas to get to Texas and kill your old lady."

The two newly freed inmates walked out of *Folsom Prison* through the opened front gates. They walked over towards the employee parking area where Charles Jenkins had parked his car. Lance pushed the alarm button on the key chain time and time again, until finally a green *Toyota Camry* beeped its horn and flashed its lights.

"Look at this piece of…the government needs to pay its prison guards a lot more money. You never know when they might get killed on the job," Lance joked as he looked at the automobile.

"Hey vato…a car is a car right now. And you shouldn't disrespect the dead, homie. How would you feel?" Joker's voice level raised as he defended the memory of Charles Jenkins.

"Like I was dead. What kind of stupid question is that?" Lance laughed at Joker's stupidity.

"Just watch it alright," Joker Ramirez made the cross motion over his upper body like they taught him at St. Joseph's when he was a young boy. Then he kissed his hand towards the sky…towards God. "Don't fuck with the memory of the dead, alright? That shit might come back and get you."

"Whatever dude, just don't let your superstition get in the way of me getting home." Lance pulled the driver's side door open and climbed in.

As the two inmates drove off, Lance tried to make small talk about a subject that he had been curios about.

"So Joker," Lance started, " what was with all of that hand jiving shit back there in the Record's Room?"

"What this?" Joker asked as he threw up the number fourteen with his hands again.

"Yeah...what is that?" Lance asked.

"It's a one four stupid." Joker looked at Lance with awe. "How long have you been locked up white boy?"

"Long enough, but I was never in a gang situation to learn the history on banging." Lance laughed at his own statement. "So what's the deal man?"

"All right then." Joker shifted in the passenger seat and started to explain gangs to his traveling companion. "The one on the first hand goes next to the four fingers on the other hand to make the number fourteen. Fourteen represents the letter N, which is the fourteenth letter of the alphabet. Entiendas?"

"Yeah...I think so." Lance tried to follow along.

"So N represents the *Nuestra Familia*, which was the original gang that fought against the Surenos. N also represents Norteno...or the North because that's where a lot of the *Nuestra Familia* gang came from...Northern California." Joker explained what he could in laymen terms to a person who knew nothing of the topic.

"So when you throw up fourteen, you are saying that you are a member of the Norteno gang?" Lance asked.

"Kind of...there are a lot of gangs under the title of Norteno, but yeah...basically I'm saying that I'm a member of a Norteno gang. Entiendas?" Joker tried to clear up the confusion.

"So it's like Geography? The United States is the whole thing, but it is made up of individual States. So Norteno would be the United States, and the individual Norteno street gangs would be the States that make up the whole enchilada." Lance almost confused himself on his analogy.

"Simón ese...kind of, but yeah...I think." Joker looked confussed.

"So what are these Surenos?" Lance asked.

"Surenos are the enemy," Cali Ramirez explained. "They represent the number thirteen for *La Eme*...the letter M for the *Mexican Mafia*."

"What's the difference?" Lance asked a simple yet direct question.

"Beliefs holmes. What we stand for. Entiendas?" Joker looked sincere as he spoke.

"Okay, enough on the subject. One last question though; what's the difference between you guys, to a guy like me, or is there one?" Lance felt that he was in too deep to get out of the history of gangs in America.

"Colors holmes. Norte is represented by the color red, and Sur trece is connected to blue." Joker shrugged at the ease of his answer.

"So you guys are *Bloods* and *Crips*?" Lance got excited that he knew something about the subject.

"Fuck that," Cali exclaimed. "We're nothing like those fuckers."

"Except you wear the same colors?" Lance pointed out.

"Just drive the fucking car holmes, and look your own shit up when you get home. I'm through ese." The enraged gangster turned towards the passenger side window and looked out at the passing cars on the freeway.

"What?" Lance asked his passenger. "What did I say?"

CHAPTER 28

"Mrs. Grayson! Mrs. Grayson! Jessie the Stealer stole my pencil." James Baxley told on his fellow classmate without raising his hand.

"I did not!" Jessica shot back as she looked directly at James.

"Did too! See Mrs. Grayson…that yellow one in her back pocket. She took it right out of my hands." James pointed towards Jessica as he excitedly hopped up and down on the gray tiled floor.

"Is that true Jessica…did you take that pencil out of James' hand?" Mrs. Grayson asked her student.

"Yes…but…but…it…" Jessica was so mad that she stuttered as she tried to talk.

"No buts about it; taking things that are not your is wrong," the teacher calmly stated.

"BUT IT WAS MY PENCIL FIRST!" Jessica yelled to get her point across to the opposing side.

"Was not!" James stuck his tongue out.

"Was too!" Jessica stuck her tongue out, but was caught in the act.

"That is enough young lady. Now you come with me this very minute. Mr. Combs the Principal will know how to deal with this." Mrs. Grayson walked between the rows of desks and grabbed Jessica by the wrist on her left hand.

As Jessica Farmer and Mrs. Carol Grayson walked out of the classroom, Carol Grayson turned towards her aide and said, "They're all yours...enjoy."

As the two entered the school office area, they were greeted by the school's secretary, Mrs. Beacon.

"Well good morning to the two of you on this fine day. Now Mrs. Grayson...young Miss Farmer wouldn't be in any trouble would she?" The secretary winked at Jessica as she turned her attention towards the irate schoolteacher.

"Good morning to you too," replied Carol Grayson. "Is Pete in his office this morning?"

"Why don't you go on in, and I'll watch over Miss Farmer here for a minute," Mrs. Beacon said to Carol Grayson as she pointed at the door to the principal's office.

"Thank you Mrs. Beacon," Grayson said coldly.

Then Carol Grayson turned towards Jessica and said, "I'll call for you in a moment or two...be ready little lady."

"Yes Mrs. Grayson." Jessica looked down at her worn shoes. She did not like being in trouble, but it seemed that trouble liked her.

As the door to the principal's office closed behind the schools only third grade teacher, Mrs. Beacon had to find out what had happened; even if meant that her news came from a child no taller than the counter.

"Okay little Miss Farmer…let Mrs. Beacon hear all about it." The secretary scooted her office chair away from her cluttered desk.

"Well…James Baxley stole my pencil from my crayon box after first recess. I knew that it was my pencil because mine was missing…" Jessica paused to make sure that she included every last detail into her story.

"Now you know that the world is filled with lots of different types of pencils, and some of them look very similar to each other." Mrs. Beacon opened her top desk drawer and pulled out a small handful of multicolored pens and pencils.

"I know…so I looked closer. His pencil had staples in it, just like mine did." Jessica looked at Mrs. Beacon's handful of writing instruments as she remembered the point that she made.

"Now why did your pencil have staples in it?" The secretary put the items back into the metal drawer and closed it softly.

"To hold it together of course." Jessica shrugged.

"Oh!" Mrs. Beacon nodded her head in agreement.

" You're silly Mrs. Beacon," Jessica giggled quietly.

"I'm not trying to be…see." Mrs. Beacon crossed her eyes and made monkey sounds. "I'm very serious."

"You see…we were all pencil fighting on the school bus on the way home from school yesterday." Jessica tried to finish her story, but Mrs. Beacon had made her laugh.

"I see." Beacon got serious again, and listened to the young student.

"And my pencil was the best…it broke everyone else's," Jessica boasted proudly.

"So how does this end with staples in your pencil?" Mrs. Beacon playfully scratched her right temple to show that she had pondered the point.

"Relax Mrs. Beacon…I'm getting to it. Now…as I was saying…my pencil and me made a pretty good team. I even broke James Baxley's favorite Batman pencil." Jessica jumped with excitement.

"Well that was kind of mean." Mrs. Beacon frowned.

"Not really! He shouldn't have been using it. My pencil was the best, and he got mad that my pencil broke his. So he took my pencil out of my hand and broke it. Then he threw the two pieces towards the back of the bus. I was so mad, but I didn't cry." Jessica looked at her feet once again.

"Okay…I think I see what's going on. So, did you staple your winning pencil back together?" Mrs. Beacon smiled when she caught on to the dealing of the Third Grade.

"Yeah, with my stapler that my Mom keeps on her desk upstairs. It happens to be my favorite pencil of all time." Jessica shyly looked back up at the school secretary through her hair that had fallen out of its ponytail.

"How did James know that you fixed your pencil…did you tell him?" Beacon sat back in her office chair, and took a sip of her bottled water.

"No…I showed him. I waived it right in front of his face, and told him that no matter what he does to my most favorite pencil…it will always beat his stupid Batman pencil." Jessica forced her arm straight out as if she still had her pencil in hand.

"And when was this?"

"This morning. Right before morning recess." Jessica looked at the big analog clock on the wall.

"Jessica…are you sure that pencil is yours?" Mrs. Beacon slouched forward so that she was eye to eye with the student.

"Yes Mrs. Beacon…I would know it anywhere," Jessica proclaimed.

"Okay honey, but I think that they might be ready for you in there now." Mrs. Beacon stood up and led Jessica Farmer towards the still closed office door.

"I'm scared." Jessica looked up at the friendly adult.

"There is no reason to be Miss Farmer, just tell them what you told me. Okay?" Mrs. Beacon lightly rubbed Jessica on the back, and gave her another wink for good luck.

"Okay." Jessica smiled.

The blue glassed door to the principal's office suddenly opened, and Mrs. Grayson stood impatiently for Jessica Farmer to finish talking to the office secretary. "Any day now Jessica."

"Yes Mrs. Grayson." Jessica jogged the last few feet that separated herself from her teacher.

The teacher closed the door behind Jessica, and motioned for her to sit down in a chair directly in front of the principal's cherry wood desk.

"And how are we doing today Jessica?" Mr. Combs asked as he looked over his desk.

"Not very well...I guess." Jessica put her head down and watched her feet as they swung nervously.

"And why do you say that?" Principal Combs asked warmly.

"Because I got in trouble from Mrs. Grayson for taking my own pencil." Jessica looked at her teacher from the corner of her eye.

Jessica was actually terrified to fully look over at her teacher, but she felt the cold chills that her Teacher's stare gave off.

"Your pencil? I heard that the pencil belonged to James." Mr. Combs looked at Mrs. Grayson.

"You heard wrong, because James stole my prized pencil from my desk during morning recess, and so I took it back." Jessica looked at the school principal.

"I see...and did you tell Mrs. Grayson all of the facts before she decided to bring you down here to see me?" Principal Combs asked Jessica as he continued to look at Mrs. Grayson, and then back to Jessica Farmer.

"I tried, but she just won't listen, " Jessica whispered as she cupped her hands around her mouth, so that only her and Mr. Combs could hear.

But Mrs. Grayson could still hear, and so interrupted Jessica's plea to the school principal, "You're just like your father. Once a thief…always a thief; and it looks like that old saying about the apple not falling far from the tree is proving to be quite accurate." Carol Grayson bent forward to look her student in the face as she spoke.

"Mrs. Grayson, that is quite enough," Pete Combs said with authority.

"But…" Carol tried to defend herself.

"No buts! Now Jessica would you please wait out with Mrs. Beacon while I finish up with Mrs. Grayson?" Principal Combs pointed towards the door.

Jessica Farmer got up from her seat, and opened the office door without looking back, but heard Mr. Combs say that everything would be all right.

Back in the principal's office, Pete Combs turned his full attention to his school's third grade teacher. "Did you give the girl a chance to defend herself, or was this a witch hunt?"

"That girl's father stole from my husband's store. A store that has been in this town, and my husband's family for over a century." Carol Grayson pointed her finger at the door as she spoke.

"Why blame the daughter…she was a baby when it happened?" Pete leaned forward and rested his elbows on his oversized desk.

"Because she benefited from it…just like her whore of a mother." Carol scooted back in her chair.

"Now how do you know that?" Pete asked with a mocked tone in his voice.

"Because the merchandise and the money were never recovered, but the poor Farmer clan suddenly had a little cash to spread around." Carol again pointed at the door to represent Jessica on the other side of it.

"You don't know that for sure," Pete shrugged.

"It's not hard to figure out…I just put two and two together…" Carol started to condemn the Farmer's even more when Pete cut her off.

"And hung an innocent child out to dry." Pete sat back.

"Pete! You have no idea what it was like being stolen from. You feel so violated. We welcomed those people into our town; our homes; our place of business, and this is how they repay us. This is not something that can be overlooked by any means." Carol Grayson tried to convince the principal that her point was valid.

"I understand your frustration if this was seven or eight years ago when this was all still fresh in the community's mind, but time has passed, and this little girl isn't to blame." Pete leaned forward and clasped his fingers together.

"She was part of it, and I know that she'll grow up just like that two bit thief of a father she has." Mrs. Grayson pointed towards the door once more.

"Judge Fall sentenced Jessica's father to serve prison time for his crime against you and this town. Now if the sentence was good enough for the law; then it's good enough for me, and it should be good enough for you." Pete tried to reason with the tenured educator.

"Good enough for me! Good enough for me! Well Pete…it is not 'good enough for me', and it never will be as long as there is retribution to be made. You weren't born in this town; you don't know what it's like to put sweat equity into building a town the same way that your parents did, and theirs before them, and so on. You obviously have no pride in your community. A community that accepted you into our homes; not as an outsider, but as one of us. A community that elected you to be in charge of our town's entire future; our youth. A town…a community…a family that I will personally see takes that responsibility away from you. We voted you in, and we'll vote you out. There were a few of us that didn't think that you were up for the job, but the 'majority' thought that you were. Well, I'll make it my personal mission to make sure that the 'majority' swings the other way this time, and sees it my way." Carol Grayson stood up as she spoke and put her finger in Pete Combs' face.

"Don't you come into my office and threaten my job, or my family's livelihood. As a matter of fact, I believe that the school board gave me the power of discretion when it came to running my school…the complete power of discretion. And with that power…as long as I still have it…I'm 'electing' to terminate your position at this school." Pete stood up the threat that was laid in front of him which made Carol sit back down.

"You can't!" Carol shook her finger at him from her seated position.

"I just did…you're fired." Principal Combs pointed his arm and extended his right index finger towards the shut door.

As Carol Grayson got up from her chair, she purposely knocked it over, and glared at Pete Combs. "THIS IS NOT OVER YET," she yelled as she yanked open the office door.

"I'm sure it's not," Pete mumbled to himself.

"Well it looks like your thieving family got away with it again. This time they stole my job. Fitting though; last time it was cash from the register...this time a paycheck from my pocket. I hope that you're satisfied you little tramp." Mrs. Grayson stood in front the scared child and looked down upon her with a deep rage.

"Mrs. Grayson, how dare you talk to little Jessica like that? Why don't you calm down, and think about what you said for a minute before you say anything else that you may regret." Mrs. Beacon came to the child's defense.

"Regret Mrs. Beacon...regret? Why don't you shut your fat mouth, and let me go about with my own business. Like the business that is between the Farmer family and me. Business that should have been taken care of eight years ago," Carol snapped at the flabbergasted secretary.

Carol grabbed Jessica by the hair and slapped her face once...twice before the school secretary could get between the young female student and the freshly dismissed teacher.

"Carol Grayson, what has gotten into you? You can't hit your students." Mrs. Beacon held the bawling child behind her.

"She is no longer one of my students Mrs. Beacon; or hasn't your eavesdropping methods worked for you today? I was let go because of this lying little bitch." Carol tried to reach Jessica.

"Carol?" Pete Combs' voice came from behind her, "I just phoned the Sheriff and Mrs. Farmer; they are both on their way. The school will be pressing charges, and I will strongly urge Mrs. Farmer to do the same." Pete shook his head with remorse. "Carol...you will be arrested."

Carol Grayson finally turned around to face Pete Combs. "Arrested...I think not. I am a prominent member of this community. I on the other hand will have your job, and the Farmer family will be dealt with in a manner fit for their type of scum." Carol turned back quickly and tried to grab Jessica's hair.

"Carol...listen to me. You will be arrested. We have laws against hitting children in the United States. Child abuse is not something to be overlooked...especially as an educator. The town will have no choice; they will hang you out to dry...regardless of who your family is or was. It will be a media circus around here...I'm warning you now, and since I don't know how the town will react to the entire situation...I also called a couple of television stations to make sure that this is aired in the right side of justice. Like I said, the town will have no choice." Pete slowly walked forward a few steps as he spoke.

"Fuck you Pete, and everyone else in this hokey town." Carol flipped off Pete, and then Mrs. Beacon and Jessica.

Carol Grayson collected herself, fixed her ponytail, and straightened her plaid suit jacket before she proceeded out of the office area of the school.

Pete Combs walked out after her. "Carol you can't leave just yet. The Sheriff is on his way, and believe me you do not want to be a fugitive from the law."

As Carol continued to walk down the hall towards the daylight of the outside, she was suddenly cut off by Sheriff Albright, and all thoughts of escape and prison entered her always thinking mind. Carol Grayson turned and ran away from the law, turned left down a side hall that ended in the cafeteria. She looked back and saw Sheriff Albright and Pete Combs as they ran after her in an attempt to stop her. However, her biggest concern at that moment stood right in front of her; Lisa Farmer. Mrs. Grayson turned her head back around to face forward as Lisa threw a mind-blowing punch that knocked Carol off of her feet.

"My daughter is a good person, a good student, and doesn't deserve any of your crap. Now get up you white trash piece of garbage." Lisa Farmer was ready for a fight. Years of hushed whispers and dirty looks about her family built up in Lisa's mind, and she was ready to let it out.

"I'm better than you." Carol Grayson wiped her bloody lip.

"Why…because you have money? We came from the same side of the trailer park. You married for money…not love. In definition, that makes you a whore. Isn't that right…teach?" Lisa slapped the dismissed educator with opened palm of her right hand.

"Go to Hell." Carol licked her bloody teeth, and smiled.

Sheriff Albright and Principal Combs caught up to the two women before any more could be said. "Carol Grayson…you are under arrest for the alleged…"

"Sheriff, I do not care what I am under arrest for. All I know is that if you follow through with this masquerade, I'll have your badge…just like I'll have Pete's job. Now release me before I get really mad, and maybe if I feel generous…you can still get a job in this town, unlike Mrs. Farmer and Mr. Combs here." Carol spit blood towards the principal.

"Keep talking Mrs. Grayson. Judge Fall is going to have a hay day with you." Principal Combs smiled.

"Judge Fall is going to thank me for cleaning up this hole from scum like you. Then maybe, the town can get back to more peaceful times without the heart ache of people who don't belong." Carol looked directly at Pete as she spoke.

The sheriff handcuffed the former teacher, and then turned towards Lisa Farmer.

"Mrs. Farmer, why don't you go with Pete and find your daughter and see if she is okay. I'll be back in a moment to get Jessica's statement, as well as everyone else's in a moment or two. Don't worry…things always seem bigger than they are when the heat of tension is turned up. Things will calm down, and fall back into place." The sheriff smiled as if he understood what Lisa had felt.

Lisa thanked the sheriff for all his help, and then walked with Pete Combs toward the office where her daughter sat crying in the arms of Mrs. Beacon.

"Jessie dear…honey are you alright?" Lisa tried not to cry when she saw that her daughter was okay.

"Mom!" Jessica Farmer got up and quickly ran over to mother who had squatted down with her arms opened wide to accept her daughter's shaking body.

"It's okay honey. No one will ever hurt you again...I promise. Look at me. I love you very much, and what you went through is not your fault. Some people blame us for your Dad's mistake, and they shouldn't, but they do. That may never change, but time will lessen the burden that you should never of had to carry. Sheriff Albright is going to back here in a few minutes to talk to you, Mr. Combs, Mrs. Beacon, and me. Just tell him the truth from the beginning, and then we'll go home and have some of that wonderful cake that Mrs. Billy brought us the other night. Okay?"

"Okay Mom." Jessica looked at her Mom and then pulled herself back in for another heart filled hug.

As the town's sheriff walked out of the school holding the handcuffed arms of the schools third grade teacher; they ran into mob of people who had waited outside to see what had transpired. There were news vans, TV crews, local newspaper reporters, and more than half of the town anxiously gossiping about what may or may not have happened.

"GET MY FAMILY'S ATTORNEY OVER TO THE JAIL HOUSE IMMEDIATELY. GET JUDGE FALL OVER THERE TOO...HE NEEDS TO HEAR WHAT I HAVE TO SAY," Carol Grayson shouted at the crowed as she was escorted to the backseat of the Sheriff's patrol car.

The media went crazy over the possibility of a small town scandal. The Sheriff and the former teacher were rushed by the mob of onlookers as they tried to get situated. The Sheriff pushed bodies out of the way as he made it to his car. After he secured Mrs. Grayson in the back, he turned towards the crowd and addressed them briefly.

"As all of you can see, we have Mrs. Carol Grayson in our custody. Mrs. Grayson, as you know, has been this school's third grade teacher for many of years. Mrs. Grayson has been arrested for conduct unbecoming of a leader of this community. Presently there is an investigation, and we don't know very much more at this time. As the story unfolds, and we ourselves know more; then, and only then, will I be able to answer any of your questions Thank you." Sheriff Albright turned around and started to walk around the front of his car.

"Sheriff wait...Sheriff..." A news reporter tried to block the sheriff.

"No more questions at this time. Now if you will excuse me, I have to escort Mrs.. Grayson to the holding facilities in our fine jail." Sheriff Albright pushed past the reporter.

The sheriff got into the front seat of his car, and started it up. The sirens came on, and the crowd started to slowly move as the Sheriff's car inched forward. The sheriff picked up the microphone to his patrol car's radio and spoke into it. "Robbie are you out there?"

"Go for Robbie, Sheriff. What can I do for you sir?" The deputy answered the call from his parked patrol car.

"Can you come over to the school and pick up the Farmers, and escort them home. Stay with them until I get there to make sure nothing accidentally happens to them." Sheriff Albright looked into his rear view mirror at Carol Grayson as he spoke.

"Yes Sheriff…right away." Robbie started his car.

"Thanks Robbie. Oh yeah, and tell Mr. Combs and Mrs. Beacon that I'll get their statements from them before the end of the day." Sheriff Albright cleared from the pedestrians, slammed on the gas and sped away.

CHAPTER 29

As Braden and Rachlav approached Seattle, Washington; they spotted two of the Russian fighters as they attacked the city.

"Fox is setting up the Russians," Braden mumbled to himself.

Braden turned his fighter to apprehend his fellow American pilots in stolen Russian aircrafts before they did something that America would never forget. One of the Russian planes turned to intercept Braden and Rachlav, as the other one fired a nuclear missile into the heart of downtown Seattle. All three planes took off to continue the fight elsewhere before the missile hit.

"Colonel Braden," Rachlav asked, "what is your military trying to do?"

"Set your ass up," Braden replied.

In the air, the dogfight continued. Braden and Rachlav in their barrowed Su-27UB ended the life of one the American pilots that they fought in a stunning blaze of fire and shrapnel. The two remaining planes were both violently forced down by one another in a bullet-flying version of *Chicken*. Neither plane wavered as they flew towards one another. A constant array of bullets ripped through the outer shells of the planes, until there was nothing left to do except hit head on. All three soldiers ejected moments before the planes hit in mid air. The blast pushed the survivors head over heals through the Pacific Coast air.

"Eject! Eject!" Colonel Braden commanded to his passenger.

Seattle took the blast of one nuclear missile, but that was nothing compared to the damage that Los Angeles, Las Vegas, Salt Lake City, Portland, San Francisco, and San Diego took. Those cities were bombed multiple times from multiple locations. Anybody left in those cities, or anywhere near the cities, had a zero survivability rate. Millions died, hundreds of thousands died within a day or two, and thousands would continue to die as the nuclear blasts spread through the West Coast of the United States. Whatever General Nathan Fox had planned for worked.

"Roger that Blue Leader. You have a green to go." The ground shook as the F-35 Lightning II 's roared to life.

"Lets kick some Russian tail," Lieutenant Jameson said enthusiastically.

"*Time to kick the tires and light the fires big daddy*," Iceman quoted.

"*Independence Day*…man…I love that movie." Lieutenant Jameson readied his men as they took to the air.

The U.S. military sent out all available fighter planes to apprehend the Russian assassins that took out the West Coast. The Russian fighters piloted by the American soldiers regrouped in mid air as they were ordered to do after their individual missions were completed. Their last step was to come in together; back to GITMO Bay, since Area 51 would have been compromised by the nuclear blast, for debriefing and a little R & R. The pilots noticed that two of their planes had not yet returned from their Seattle mission.

"Where is Striker and Campo?" One of the pilots mouthed to another pilot off of his starboard side.

One of missing pilots was their commanding officer, Major Eric Striker. The pilots decided that they could not wait around because of the fuel consumption that would be needed to get to Cuba. The unfavorable decision was made, and the other two planes would have to catch up. Nobody liked the thought of soldiers being left behind, one being their commanding office. That was a difficult decision to make, sense none of their radios worked, and all communication was done by relayed hand signals.

"What happened to Striker?" Jones relayed the question.

"*Mother Goose* lost the flock. Follow the *Yellow Brick Road* home." Was Jones' answer to his question. Pilots liked to use colorful terms to describe what they did.

The American pilots who flew the Russian fighters knew that what they did was wrong. Orders or not, they all dealt with what they did in their own way. A few of the pilots thought about their families, while others thought about the nation that they lived in and swore to uphold the American way. However, they did not have to think about things long, because on their flight towards Cuba; they entered an air space, which contained a massive amount of American fighters. The pilots in the Russian planes knew at that moment that they had been the escape-goats for a dirty and cruel plan. They were going to be killed by their military brothers, who did not even realize who they were; and that, for their family's sake, was probably for the better. All of the hunted men came to the same conclusion; they were going to die, they deserved to die, and they did not want to hurt any of their fellow American brothers. A couple of the Russian fighters fired a few non-lethal rounds of ammunition at the American planes, and hoped for a quick and painless death. They did not have to wait long; death came with a massive air attack that lasted mere moments.

"Roger that Blue Leader...enemy has been neutralized."

Letters went out to the families of the fallen pilots. Letters that stated that these men died for their country…these men were heroes. Only a select few knew exactly how these men died, and more importantly why they died. One of the select few was the President of the United States, Rich Mason.

The President sat in the Oval Office and wept to himself. He then got up and walked over to a mirror that he and his wife bought during a trip to Russia early in his Presidency. He looked at his own reflection and said to himself, "The pilots that shot these men down had no knowledge of who they were fighting; only that they were Russian. If the American fighter pilots who brought justice to the Russian bombers knew that their own men…their American brethren in the armed forces…were the ones who were commanded to nuke the West Coast by their Commanding officer…would it have made a difference in the outcome of the battle? Would have they tried to bring them in peacefully? Should I have…could I have fixed…change what has happened?"

President Mason turned away from the mirror to see General Fox as he stood in the doorway.

"Nathan…what are doing here?" The President asked.

"Well Mr. President last time I heard you were still my boss, and so I thought that I would check in." General Fox walked into the room and sat down.

"Nathan, the bombings were wrong. I have been receiving the numbers on the death tolls, and…" The President was almost too shaken to speak.

"The Russians are being blamed for it. Stop worrying!" Nathan Fox set his black briefcase on the table and opened it.

"I'm personally going to see each and every family of those pilots who died doing our dirty work. Damn it Nathan, those men never should have been in those Russian planes. Hell, we should never even had those planes." President Mason looked into the mirror once again.

"Those planes were a necessity…times were different. You know that; we did what we had to do, just like now. Mr. President, you cannot and will not visit those families. Everything on our end must appear on the up and up. If you start going to a few soldiers homes, and not the homes of every single soldier who has died in this war…or any war for that matter…things would look a little fishy to your voters. Don't you think?" Fox shuffled some papers in his briefcase, and then shut the lid.

"I don't give a damn about votes!" Mason turned towards Fox.

"I'm sure you give a damn about your family." General Fox stood up and glared at the President.

"That is two threats today. One more and you are finished." Mason took a few quick steps at the General and pointed his index finger angrily at Nathan Fox.

"We'll see!" Fox did not back down.

"I AM THE PRESIDENT OF THE UNITED STATES OF AMERICA! At this time in our current history I have complete Congress approved Martial Law. I am the leader of this country, and you my friend are a dime a dozen. You will not threaten my family or me ever again, and if you do…you'll be hanged for treason. Is that clear…General?" President Mason walked up to the four-stared General and ripped the ribbons from his chest.

"Yes, Mr. President…I was just…" Fox starred at the President's hand.

"You were just leaving, or did you have some other stupid ass comment to make?" Mason handed the ribbons back to the General, and pointed his finger in Fox's face as a warning.

"No sir…good day." Fox picked up his stuff and walked out without a further word.

CHAPTER 30

Colonel Braden, General Rachlav, and Major Striker all came back down to Earth in the same general area. It was an all out frenzy to see who could get out of their safety gear first. Major Striker wanted to get away from the two men who shot down his partner's plane and then had a head on collision with in mid air. Colon Braden tried to get free so that he could subdue the murder who nuked Seattle. In the end however, it was General Rachlav who got free the quickest. As Rachlav stood he pulled out his weapon that he got from the Area 51 prison guard earlier that day. He pointed it at Major Striker, and then at Colon Braden. As he slowly waved the gun back and forth between the American soldiers he spoke.

"You stupid Americans...did you think that you could hide our military's fighter jets from us forever?" Rachlav's face showed his disgust for the people of the United States.

"Um...yeah! Wasn't it your stupid military that lost those stupid jets in the first place?" Braden did not looked pleased at the Russian General's decision to point a loaded weapon at him.

"Shut up Colonel!" Rachlav demanded. "You have no right to speak about my country. I was right about you...all you Americans are

376

the same. You have no honor, and to tell you the truth…if I did not need a guide to get out of this wasteland of a country…I would kill you both. But I only need one guide, so I will only kill one of you. Which one of you is the bigger traitor to your pathetic United States?" General Rachlav slid back the slide of his semi-automatic *M9 Beretta*, and waited for the traitors to turn on one another. "Who is going to die so I can live free?"

As General Rachlav spoke, Braden and Striker freed themselves from their chute restraints and devised a plan with their hands and eyes to take down Rachlav. Colonel Braden started to stand, and that was all it took for Rachlav to move towards him to retake control over the situation. As Rachlav stepped, Major Striker tackled Rachlav. Both men flew to the ground, with Striker landing on top. The two opponents briefly wrestled for the weapon, before Colonel Braden walked over and stepped on Rachlav's clenched fist. Braden grinded Rachlav's hand into the ground until the General gave up his grip on the gun and offered it up without a sound. As Striker stood, both he and Braden pulled General Rachlav up as they grabbed his arms.

"Get your Commie ass up, and don't try that shit again," Striker informed the Russian General as he dusted himself off.

"Would you have me not try? For even free...am I still not a prisoner in this country?" Rachlav looked at Major Striker, and then turned his attention to Colonel Braden.

"I got you out alive, right?" Braden asked Rachlav.

"For this...I thank you." General Rachlav nodded with gratitude.

"So then trust me enough to keep my word." Braden stuck out his hand as a sign of peace, and Rachlav accepted the gesture.

Back in Russia, President Ubiikobyla waited for the latest news on the war in America. When the President of Russia received the news that the United States had been nuked, he was shocked.

"What has happened?" Ubiikobyla turned off his television set and tossed the silver remote control on a side table.

"Mr. President, our sources indicate that Russian fighters carrying nuclear missiles destroyed the entire West Coast of the United States," Press Secretary Andropov informed his country's leader.

"How is this possible? I did not order such a counter measure...who ordered this?" Ubiikobyla was clearly concerned about the unknown attack in North America.

"I do not know Mr. President," Andropov quickly shared his lack of information. "Our intelligent report stated that it was indeed a

Russian attack. However, we don't know where they came from, or who was flying the planes. Our spies in the White House in Washington D.C. inform us that the Americans are grieving from the attacks because of old wounds. But however or whatever caused these nuclear attacks helped the Americans more than it hurt them." Andropov handed President Ubiikobyla a file on his findings.

"What are you saying?" President Ubiikobyla quickly flipped through the data filled report.

"Mr. President…I am saying that despite a major loss of American civilians…our own troops, and we lost thousands upon thousands of good soldiers. The United States could take the upper hand." The Russian Press Secretary stepped back from the fear that his assumption might cause.

"What about the maximum security prisons? Are they not still a target for our plans?" Ubiikobyla looked up at Andropov as if had not heard a word that had been spoke.

The relieved Press Secretary was overjoyed that his lack of respect for the President did not lead to a prison sentence…or worse. "Yes sir, but with all honestly…the loss of so many men at one time has cut our military's forces dramatically. We cannot sustain our level of influence over the American prison system."

"I refuse to fail, and I refuse to surrender!" The President handed the report back to Press Secretary Andropov, and turned his back to him.

"Mr. President...I know that I am not you trusted advisor and friend General Rachlav, but please listen to me. The Americans will attack, and they have no reason to doubt it was our nation that attacked their western coast after what we did to their New York City. Their forces are strong!" Andropov took a bold move as he spoke to the President of Russia as an equal.

"Our forces are strong!" Ubiikobyla spun around and faced the Press Secretary.

"Yes, but their will is stronger," Andropov mumbled in a near audible tone.

As Press Secretary Andropov left President Ubiikobyla's office, Ubiikobyla grabbed his left shoulder from behind.

"Don't let me ever hear you talk to me in such a tone ever again," Ubiikobyla whispered in Andropov's ear. "A word of advise...do not portray yourself as General Rachlav's equal...he would not like it." Ubiikobyla let go of the Press Secretary's shoulder as he spoke the last of his words.

CHAPTER 31

Lance Flanders found his wife in the backyard weeding the garden when he finally made his way home to Texas. Even the best plans to hide rarely worked for most people. For one thing, Paige did not have a lot of money of her own. Her parents had done okay with their business, but once Paige got married; she and Lance were on their own. No matter what their situation was, Paige's parents let her live with her own choices, and whatever rewards or consequences came with those choices. Like her choice to marry Lance against her parents better judgment.

"You're a big girl now," Paige's dad said as the two of them sat on the white front porch swing. "If you want to marry, then marry. However, you should do it for love and not rebellion."

Paige looked at her father and said, "I do love him Daddy."

The Pottersmith's turned their emotional connection to their daughter off when she announced her womanhood during her wedding ceremony.

"Do you take Lance to be your lawfully wedded husband…" The Pastor started to ask.

"I do," Paige smiled as she answered the question.

Even without that parent daughter connection, Paige somehow talked her parents into letting her rent one of their small one bedroom rental houses; a business that they got into because it seemed fun, and they could make a little money for their later years.

"Please Mom. I'll pay the full amount that you would ask anyone else. Lance is locked up until the 15th, and I don't want to live in that trailer anymore," Paige pleaded with her parents.

"The full amount, and when your two bit hubby gets out of the County Jail for the nineteenth time…I don't want him around. You hear me little lady?" Paige's mother looked sternly at her daughter.

"I'm leaving him Mom, and I know that you don't agree in divorce, but he's not the man that I married." Paige's eyes welled up.

"I know honey, but I agree that you need to get away from him. When he gets out…we won't tell him where you went. Okay?" Catherine gave her daughter a hug.

So it was not hard for Lance to track down his wife in a small Texas town, where she lived in a house willed to her by her murdered parents; in fact it was quite easy. When he arrived at the house and saw his wife in the backyard, he decided that it would be a bigger surprise if he waited inside. That way they could have a little more privacy in case their reunion got loud or out of control. It actually surprised Lance that Paige did not seemed worried about his homecoming.

"She should have heard about the Russians," he mumbled to himself. "I know that me killing that prison guard made the national news. Why isn't she worried or scared? She's going on like she doesn't have a care in the world." Lance had a pissed off look on his face as he stared at his estranged wife through the small kitchen window above the stainless steel sink.

The increased mental images of Paige not caring made Lance even madder. "That stupid bitch will care." Lance tore through the kitchen drawers as he looked for a large knife.

The truth of the matter was that Paige Flanders feared for her life every moment of the day. She bought a hand gun that she kept on her person at all times, even when she was in the shower, that gun never left her side. Paige was amazed how her senses were heightened by her husband's ordeal. Like the fact that she noticed a strange car pull up and park across the street from her house. Her neighbors across the way where visiting their grandkids in Toronto, Canada. It was hard to miss a stranger in town, when the population is so small. Paige kept gardening like nothing was out of the ordinary. She did not want to seem tense, or alarmed in case it was Lance coming to get her.

"Calm down, and breathe," Paige told herself.

Paige nonchalantly reached for her gun that was in the front of her pants waistband and slid back the slide to cock it. She did it in a smooth motion from bending over to pull a weed, to sitting up almost upright as she tried to pull the weed from the ground. When the weed came free, she cocked her gun, and went back to the next pesky weed.

"Perfection!" Paige had been happy that she had mastered her weapon. She practiced with it everyday, and took a shooting class every Thursday and Saturday night.

Lance Flanders did not seem to notice his wife's gun, or that she was aware of his presence. He went out the front door to scan the neighborhood, and came back around the side yard that led to the back. Lance went back into the house through the back door, and went straight into the kitchen. He flipped through a stack of bills on the counter, and checked the answering machine for any old messages that Paige may have gotten since his departure. Finally, Lance opened the refrigerator and grabbed a *Coke* from the bottom shelf, and proceeded to sit down at the small dining room table that they had bought together from a yard sale right after they got married. Lance thought how empty the fridge seemed, and how bad off his wife may have been.

"Maybe she's been tortured enough?" Lance mumbled out loud.

"Maybe I have," Paige replied from the doorway. "I knew you would come back and find me. That's why I didn't try to hide…it would have been worthless."

"So you saw the news…saw what I did?" Lance was happy to have his fifteen minutes of fame as a reality star.

Paige started to cry; she tried to be brave in front of the man who haunted her, but all she could do was shake her head in an up and down fashion that demonstrated her agreement. Paige was terrified of Lance, and what he was capable of doing.

"Paige…why didn't you file for divorce if life was so bad?" Lance looked around at the smallness of the house. "Hell I could live here…it's bigger than my cell."

Paige wanted to file for divorce so many times; in fact she still had copies of the papers that she originally signed but chickened out at the last minute. Divorce papers would have definitely set Lance off.

"Because I love you Lance, "Paige lied in a shaky voice.

"Don't you dare lie to me bitch. Wives do not turn on their husbands, and get them sent to prison. I'm sure that you wanted me to get sent up. In fact you probably wanted me dead. Well I'm not dead…but you are." Lance picked up the butcher knife and twirled the handle so that its tip dug a small hole in the wooden table.

"I'm tired of being scared Lance," Paige informed her husband with a new found authority.

Lance cockily took a huge swig of his drink, and then slowly put the can down onto the table when he saw Paige with a gun pointed at him.

"What are you doing Paige? You don't have the balls to shoot me. Now put the gun away. Let me finish my drink, and then we'll talk about whatever you want, but you will die tonight." Lance raised his arm high and brought the knife down. A solid thud rang out when the blade sunk into the wood.

Paige just stood there with her finger on the trigger.

Lance picked his *Coke* back up, and examined the can. "Did you know that this is the first soda that I've had since I've been locked up?"

He put the open *Coke* can to his lips, and slowly put his head back to drink. Paige took two quick steps and shot her husband in the face without hesitation. She had been ready for that moment for a long time. Paige did not know how she was going to shoot Lance, but she knew that she had to do it before he killed her.

Paige walked over to the counter and picked up the phone. She listened to the dial tone for a moment before she dialed 9-1-1.

"9-1-1 operator, how may I assist you?"

"Yes, this is Paige Flanders. I have just shot and killed my husband who had recently escaped from prison." Paige looked over at Lance's drooped over body.

"Mrs. Flanders is your husband dead? Can you check to see if he is breathing?" The 9-1-1 operator asked from the other end of the landline telephone.

"He's dead," was the only response she gave the emergency operator before she hung up the phone.

She looked at Lance one last time before she headed outside and sat on her front porch swing and waited for the cops to show up. Paige could not believe that the worst part was over. Her fear of her husband had vanished. She really did not care what happened next, because whatever happed; she would be safe from now on.

"Thank you Lord for the strength that you have given me today, and everyday over these last few years." Paige looked up towards Heaven as she prayed out loud.

The sheriff arrived about ten minutes later, and Paige took him into the house so that he could examine her dead husband's body.

"You know Paige, this could have went the other way. I never liked the thought of you owning a gun." Sheriff Brown put his arm around Paige's trembling shoulder.

"I know Bill, but I had to protect myself. Did you see what he did to that poor prison guard? He killed him in front of the entire world. What if that guy had family...a wife and kids? Could you imagine what Edith would go through if that would have been you?" Paige looked at her old family friend with remorse for the thought of her husband's actions.

"I think about that everyday. Paige you know that I'm going to have to take you in. It's all preliminary. We know what he did, and how he did it. We also know that he came her to kill you. You defended yourself; you had the right, and the whole town will stand behind you. By the way...that car that Lance was driving; it belongs to a missing female employee of the prison he broke out of. Just thought that you should know. Luckily that sort of helps out your situation a little bit more." The sheriff pulled his car keys out of his pocket and said, "Is there anything that you need to grab before we go?"

"Thanks Bill, for everything." Paige briefly looked around the house and said, "No. I think that I have everything for now, but do you know what the funny part is?"

"What's that?" Bill opened the front door and held it so that Paige could walk out first.

"I don't feel remorse for killing him. I feel glad…relieved. Does that make me a monster?" Paige looked at the sheriff.

"No, it makes you human." Bill cared deeply for the last remaining member of the Pottersmith clan.

Sheriff Brown took Paige Flanders down to the police station, and booked her on first-degree murder of her husband, Lance Flanders. The evidence was clear cut, and over whelming in Paige's favor. The judge released Paige later on that evening on a verdict that she acted in self-defense, and that she helped bring down our Nation's most wanted American criminal.

"Paige, please stand. We have obviously found you not guilty. The town knows you and your family, God bless their souls. We knew what Lance did to you, and what he was planning to do to you. You did what you had to do to preserve your own existence. None of us can blame you for that. Not only was Lance a criminal in our minds, but in the minds of every free person in this here United States of America. After what Lance did to that correctional officer in front of the entire world; he jumped to the top of the FBI's most wanted list. You did a brave thing today, and America owes you a debt of thanks. You can go home now." Judge Macomb stood up and clapped for Paige Flanders'

deed, and the rest of the courtroom stood up and followed the judge's

lead.

CHAPTER 32

Brenda Logan and Mike Striker got real close, real fast after the incident at Tony's house on the night of the big blowout between them and Nathan Fox. However, Mike and Nathan got further apart. Their friendship was no more, and Mike took the higher road, and chose to spend his life with Brenda.

"Brenda, the past is whatever we make of it. Together we can make a bright future, it is ours to manipulate. The future is whatever we want, and I want you. Brenda, I would be honored if you were to take my hand in marriage." Mike Striker took one knee as he asked his future wife to be for her hand in marriage.

"Mike I love you..." Brenda started to cry a joyful, happy cry.

"I love you Brenda. I don't have a ring to give you; my heart is all I have. I also know that I'm going away to Basic Training, but I'll be back, and if you'll wait for me; I'll promise that I'll love you forever. Mike stood up and hugged Brenda as he hoped for a positive response.

"Yes Mike...I'll wait for you...I'll marry you." Brenda looked up and the two kissed as Brenda's mind and heart raced at the thought of a brighter future.

Brenda spent the next six weeks preparing for her upcoming wedding to Mike Striker.

"Mrs. Brenda Striker…I can live with that," Brenda thought to herself smiling.

A few days before Mike's return home, Brenda went to her doctor because she had not felt like her normal self; she felt like something was wrong. The doctor's office staff ran a number of tests during her visit, and told her that they would have the results in a day or two. Brenda went home and thought that it may have just been that she was excited that her fiancé would be home soon, and that they could continue their lives together.

"Calm down," Brenda said to her image in the bathroom mirror. "I know that you're in love, but don't kill yourself over it. He'll be home in a few days." Brenda took a few deep breaths. "Just relax."

The next afternoon, Brenda received two very important phone calls. The first was from Doctor Mitchell's office asking her to come in to go over her test results, and the other was from Mike stating that he was on his way home and that he would be there in time for breakfast.

Brenda got herself ready and went out for her follow up appointment with her family doctor to go over what she hoped would be nothing more than pre-wedding nerves.

"Brenda, thank you coming in again." Dr. Mitchell smiled as he entered Exam Room 1.

"So what's the news Dr. Mitchell, am I as sound as a...as a...as a something?" Brenda was nervous. She hated going to the doctor, and her blood pressure showed it.

"Well the good news is that you are as healthy as a horse. However the tests did show something. Whether it is good or bad is up to you. Brenda you're about eight or so weeks along in your pregnancy." The doctor sat down on his black medical stool and wheeled over to Brenda.

"My what?" Brenda was flabbergasted by the news. There could be no way in her mind that it was true. She had Mike had decided to wait until their wedding night before they became one in that way.

"You are going to have a baby." Dr. Mitchell took the pregnant girl's hand in his and gave it a little squeeze.

Brenda left the doctor's office in disbelief. She had only been with one person, one time. The night that Nathan used her to get back at Mike for falling in love with her. It was Nathan's baby.

"What do I tell Mike...Nathan?" Brenda had to take a seat before she fell over. So she sat down on the curb of the sidewalk and cried. She had so much emotion built up so quickly, that she had to release it, and so she bawled uncontrollably.

"Honey, are you alright?" An elderly woman stopped and asked out of concern.

Brenda could only nod, and so the woman continued on her way with the knowledge that she did what she could for the upset young female.

Brenda had not seen or spoken to Nathan Fox since that night at the lake. The night that she made love for the first and only time; the thing that Mike did not care about. That night never happened to him, and that their wedding night would be the first time for either of them. Mike would not let Nathan Fox ruin their life together, and so they went on like it never happened, but it did happen; the truth was about to be evident.

"Mike is coming home in the morning, what do I tell him?" Brenda laid her head down on the family's dining room table.

"Tell him the truth dear. Mike is a good man...he'll understand." Brenda's mother was as understanding as she could be.

"And what if he doesn't? Mom I can't loose him. We're too young to have a child...someone else's child." Brenda looked up at her mother for guidance.

"You could always not tell him." She reached over and rubbed her daughter's back lightly.

"And what...live a lie? As soon as he walks in the door tonight, I jump his bones and pretend that he knocked me up?" Brenda became sarcastic towards her mother and her marriage-ending dilemma.

"It's your call dear, but in my opinion, Mike deserves the right to know. Whatever you decide, I'll follow your lead if that's what you want." Brenda's mother stood up and kissed her daughter's forehead, which signaled the end of the conversation.

"Thanks Mom, but I did this to myself; young and blind to the reality of things. Mike is great and this is going to devastate him." Brenda rose to her feet, and walked into the kitchen to get a refreshing glass of cold lemonade.

The next morning Mike Striker arrived at the Logan residence in time for breakfast, just as he had promised. The greeting that he received was not the one that he had imagined in his mind. As the door opened, Brenda ran into his arms and pulled him in tight as she started to bawl uncontrollably. Mike did not know if that was a good thing or a bad thing.

"Are you really that glad to see me, or did something happen?" Mike pulled back so that he could look his fiancé in the face.

"Yes," Brenda replied quickly.

"Yes to what? The seeing me part, or the bad thing part?" Mike asked nervously.

"Yes to both." Brenda pulled Mike back towards her.

Mike and Brenda decided to go for a walk to talk about what had been happening in both of their lives since he had been a way. They stopped at a little park a few blocks away from the Logan's house, and sat on two of the swings that were next to each other. Brenda told Mike everything. She relived the night with Nathan for the first time since it happened; which was something that she had never went into detail before with anyone, especially with Mike. She told him about the baby, and how it was Nathan's; the conversation with her mom, and everything else that had built up inside her. All of the emotion came bursting out in the form of an uncontrollable crying fit that made it hard for Brenda to talk, but she got it all out.

"I'm so sorry honey. Mike...I never meant for any of this to happen."

Mike sat there on his swing as he watched her, and listened without saying a word. He felt hurt, and mad; but at the same time he felt a sense of happiness that Brenda could finally be open with him about anything. This made him love her even more, and that the baby would never be an issue.

"Like I told you on the night that I asked you to marry me. The past is what we make of it; the future is ours to manipulate. This baby is a blessing, a blessing that we can raise together if that's what you want. I want us to be together, as a family. Honestly it's a little sooner than I thought, but a family nonetheless. What do you say; you want to do this?" Mike got off of the park swing, and bent down on one knee. "Unlike six weeks ago…I have a ring to give you." Mike pulled the black jewelry box from his jacket pocket and opened it in front of Brenda. "Brenda Logan…will you do me the honor of being my wife? Will you please marry me?"

"Mike, how did I get so lucky?" Brenda started to cry again. That time the cry was a cry of relief and a cry of love.

"Well I believe that timing is the key, and I'm a great catch if I do say so myself." Mike stood up and slid the ring onto his fiancé's naked finger.

"Yes you are." Brenda looked down at her hand a smiled.

Mike and Brenda decided that they should continue on with their plans to get married. They would move back East to where Mike was to be stationed, and there they would have their baby. No one would any wiser, and that the young would move on with their lives.

Before any of that could happen though, both Brenda and Mike decided that Nathan should know the truth. He could do what he wanted once he knew, although they both hoped that he would just stay out of all of their lives. Brenda did not want to face Nathan, so they decided that a letter would be the best policy.

Dear Nathan,

I am writing this letter to inform you that I am pregnant with child. A child that you helped conceive on the night that you used my feelings, and tricked my heart into believing that you were more than you are. I do not care if this letter finds you in good health. In fact I wish that it did not. However, I have decided that I am going to go through with the pregnancy, and that Mike and myself will raise the child as our own.

This child was created out of love. Not the so-called love that you threw around to get what you wanted, but the love between Mike and I. The love between a man and his wife, and the love that God himself blessed us with when he found us fit to be parents to this innocent unborn child.

I do not wish to hear from you ever again, and I do not want anything from you. In fact this letter is nothing more than a courtesy between myself and a man who should know the truth and consequences of his actions. A man I consider to be no more than a common rapist. That however, is between you and God, because I have found piece with Mike and the baby that he and I share.

Brenda Striker

Brenda mailed the letter to the base that Mike confirmed that Nathan had been stationed at. Two weeks later, the letter came back with the words "*FUCKING LIER*" written diagonally across the page in black marker. When Brenda read what Nathan Fox had written, it made her cry. She did not know why she cried, but whatever it was had to due with the fact that she still had feelings for him somewhere deep inside of her.

Brenda thought to herself, "How could I not care? He was my first love, and if he was a creep or not; I need his approval. I want to be liked."

Brenda hated herself for crying over something so trivial, but Mike understood that she needed him at that moment regardless of his own personal feelings on the matter.

"It's okay, you can cry on my shoulder if you like, and get snot all over my clean shirt." Mike made a joke to try and lighten the mood.

Brenda hugged Mike with one big squeeze, and then held it there for as long as she could. Mike hugged her back, and for a moment they could feel the other's heart beating through their own chest because of how close they were to one another.

"Think of it this way Brenda, now we don't have to worry about any issues with Nathan and the baby." Mike looked down at his beautiful wife as he spoke softly to her.

Brenda thought to herself, "Mike was right. That is what I wanted when I originally wrote the letter. And now I have it. Stop crying you big baby, you got what you wished for."

Mike took the letter off of the desk where Brenda had laid it, and he stared at it for a few moments. Mike then folded it up and put the letter into his wallet.

"This will go in here so that I'll never forget how far we came." Mike kissed his wallet and tossed it on the dresser next to his car keys and cell phone.

The marriage and the pregnancy were both wonderful. The Strikers' did not want to know the sex of the baby until it arrived, but that did not stop everyone else from telling them what the baby was going to be. At Brenda's baby shower, the main topic of choice was Brenda's pregnancy, as it should have been. But when it came down to it, she really was not ready for the questions and suggestions. Especially from the older women who still believed in wives tales.

"You know Brenda, you shouldn't raise your hands above your head because it might strangle the baby with the umbilical cord," warned Brenda's grandmother on her mother's side.

"You know Brenda, I would of knitted a little blanket, booties, and a matching cap if you would have told me if the baby was going to be a boy or a girl. Sometimes you are so hard to read, "complained her other grandma; the one from her dad's side.

Her mom started to explain that being pregnant was the best form of birth control, "because you can do it without Mike putting on a rubber or anything, because you can't get pregnant while you have a bun already in the oven." Mrs. Logan slapped her knee after she embarrassed her daughter.

"Homemade bread?" asked Brenda's grandma.

"What Mom?" Brenda's mom looked over at her mother in disbelief.

"You said that you had some rolls in the oven, and I wanted to know if they were homemade. If I had known that there was going to be food, then I would have brought something. Hell, I would have made the rolls, I know how. Been doing it sixty-two years." Brenda's grandmother was upset that she had been left in the dark about the party.

"Mom...I was talking about the baby in Brenda's womb...not really a bun in the oven." Mrs. Logan sighed with disbelief about her mother's lack of hearing.

"Grandma," Brenda butted in, "are you hungry?"

"Yes I am, and I don't smell that bread yet. What temperature did you say that you set the oven too?" She got up and went into the kitchen to check on the progress of the bread.

"Grandma," Brenda called out, "there is no bread…it was a figure of speech."

Brenda ordered a couple of pizzas to feed the group, and that made everyone happy; except for Brenda's maternal grandmother who had still been upset about the rolls that never came out of the oven. The rest of the party went about the same, people gave lots of advise; some it good, but a lot of it was also bad. Like Brenda's Aunt Kathy who asked her if she had a hairy belly.

"Why Aunt Kathy?" Brenda leered.

"Because when I was pregnant with Nick, my belly got so hairy that I had to shave it twice a week. They say it was because that a woman isn't use to all of that testosterone that a man puts off, and so when you have a baby boy; his body is making testosterone, and so your body produces body hair like a man." Kathy talked like she had been an expert on the subject, and with nine kids; she should have been.

"Really?" Brenda's mother asked her sister with disbelief.

"Really, because you all share the same blood during pregnancy." Kathy jumped onto her older sister's lap. "Just like we're sharing this love seat."

"Well maybe I'm having a boy then, because I'm freaking hairy ladies." Brenda pulled up her shirt just enough to show off her enlarged belly.

CHAPTER 33

Michael Farmer knew that he had to try and escape from the prison that he had been held at for his entire sentence. He had a wife and a little girl that needed him. It was one thing to be in prison, but it would have been a total difference to his family if he were dead. He refused to die in prison for robbery; a robbery that he still felt was a needed risk for the time.

"I'm sorry that if I made your life harder that it already was," Michael spoke to a picture of his wife.

Breaking out of prison would be hard on its own, but doing it as the United States military came down on Michael was an extremely difficult task. There was a zero degree margin for error on Michael's side, and a win win situation for the government. If Michael stayed in prison, then he died. If Michael were caught as he escaped, then he would also be dead. Either of those ways ended well for the country that he loved. Michael felt that he only had one shot to get the escape right, but he did not have a solid plan in the works.

"Think damn it think." Michael Farmer looked around his cell for items of inspiration.

When Michael's wife and daughter heard the news about the killing of every maximum-security inmate in the country, which started on the Eastern Coast, they were devastated. Lisa told her daughter to get ready to go and visit her Dad in Atlanta. She also called into work and informed them that she would not be in that day. The two Farmer women got into their beat up old *Ford* pickup truck, and drove the longest drive of their lives.

"Jessica hurry up and get ready. We need to go and see your Dad, and find out what is going on." Lisa tied her left shoe as she called out to Jessica.

"Mom, are they really going to kill Dad just because he is in prison?" The young daughter asked her Mom.

"I don't know sweet heart…I don't know." Lisa frantically looked around for her light blue jacket that she kept on the back of the closet door.

"Can't we call someone? The governor, or someone? He only has like a month left before he comes home." Jessica found her *Atlanta Braves* hat that her Dad used to wear everyday.

"I know honey. We'll sort this whole thing out. Now please go make us some sandwiches for the ride over while I call Jerry. Lisa shooed her daughter out of the room.

Young Jessica went into the kitchen and pulled out the fixings for a couple of turkey sandwiches for her and her mother. Lisa stayed in the living room and dialed the number for the diner that she worked at.

"Jerry's Diner, this is Pam. How my I help you?"

"Pam, this is Lisa. I need to talk to Jerry." Lisa's voice seemed shaken and rushed.

"Sorry Lisa, Jerry is in the middle of a rush. We have been slammed all day, and my feet and back are killing me. I can't wait for you to relieve some of this pressure in the diner. What time are you coming in?" Pam carried on the conversation way to long for the restaurant to have been that busy.

"I'm not," Lisa replied.

"What…why not?" Pam's back tightened with the thought of working a double shift.

"That's what I need to talk to Jerry about," Lisa insisted.

"Like I said, we are busy, busy, busy. Can this wait?" Pam did not seem to understand Lisa's plea.

"No! Tell Jerry that I will not be in today, and that if he needs to know why, tell him to turn on the television." Lisa made sure that she upped her tone so that her fellow employee would pass the message along with a little urgency.

"Okay Lisa, I'll tell him." Pam almost sounded hurt.

Lisa Farmer hurriedly hung up the telephone and practically dragged Jessica out of the house.

"Did you grab everything that we needed?" Lisa looked at Jessica.

"Yes Mom, but why are we going today? Dad doesn't have visiting today, remember?" Lisa tried to pull away from her mother. "I can walk you know."

"I know that Dad doesn't have visiting today, but we have to try. For heavens sake they plan on killing the man for no good reason. He's only in there for us. He's not a bad man. He didn't kill anyone. He did what he did for us. Judge Fall saw that, and maybe the warden and others will also. We have to try, okay?" Lisa stopped in front of their truck and squatted down to explain her reasoning to her confused daughter.

"Okay Mom." Jessica knew that her Mom loved her Dad a whole lot.

When they arrived at the prison, miles of other cars whose occupants also had their same idea greeted the Farmers'. Unfortunately for all potential visitors, the prison was closed indefinitely. No one was allowed on the grounds for any reason. A guard came out from one of the towers and walked down to the front gates. People shut off their vehicles and got out to see what the officer had to say. Hundreds upon hundreds of people followed suit. They all quickly walked or ran up to see and hear the correctional officer with a huge megaphone to his mouth.

"Mom, what's going on? Why are all of the people getting out of their cars?" Jessica looked scared.

"I don't know, but something is going on up at the prison." Lisa rolled down her driver's side window and looked out.

"We can't even see the prison yet, it's still way up there." Jessica looked all around her at the massive amount of cars and people.

"I know, but we can't go forward or backwards because of all of this traffic. And since it doesn't look like we will be going anywhere, any time soon; we might as well follow the crowd. Maybe we can find something useful out." Lisa opened her door and stepped out.

The guard spoke slowly and clearly into the megaphone that he held in his right hand. "People, I know that you are all concerned about what you have seen on the news. No action has been taken against any inmate at this time. Nor will any be taken without probable cause. At this time, we have not heard anything more than you have. Please get back into your vehicles and go home and watch the news for any further updates. The prison is closed to all unessential employees and visitors until further noted. Please just go home. You can't do anything here today. May God be with you and your loved ones? I'm sorry."

The guard put down his megaphone and turned his back on the confused crowd of hopeful visitors, which made the question bound crowd turn into an angry mob of people that tried to break into the prison to save their loved ones. People grabbed the bars on the fist set of gates and tried to shake them back and forth. One person, who had their car parked at the beginning of the line; got into their vehicle, honked the horn, and drove into the gate. Other people who also had their cars up front followed suit. The prison tower guards were ordered to fire into the crowd, which they did, but the act only riled the mob even more. The guards stopped firing their weapons against direct orders, and retreated into the prison. Within a half an hour time period, the gates were opened and the mob ran towards the prison itself.

"Mom, what is going on?" Jessica asked as she heard the shots and angry screams from somewhere far ahead of them.

"I don't know, but we're going to find out soon enough." Lisa grabbed a hold of her daughter's hand and ran a little faster.

The two Farmer females continued their trek that took them across the black pavement of the road, and through a motionless congestion of empty parked cars. As they rounded the bend they saw what the commotion was all about. There was a riot, and people tried to get into the prison to get their loved ones out. Lisa Farmer wanted to rush up there and help open the prison up, but she rationalized in her mind that it would not be the right thing to do with her daughter at such an influential age.

"Mom lets go up to the front of the line and help get Dad out." Jessica tugged at her Mother's jacket sleeve.

"No honey; breaking out of prison is a crime, and we are law biding Americans." Lisa looked down a Jessica.

"What are they going to do, arrest Dad and give him more time for escaping? He already has a death sentence, like everyone else here." Jessica made a valid point that Lisa had a hard time arguing against.

"Yes, but what happens if we're the ones who get arrested for being accomplices to a prison escape? You would be taking away from us, and your Dad and I couldn't live like that with that over our heads."

Lisa thought about the reality of the situation. Jessica was right about Michael, but Lisa could get time for her part. "I can't do it honey."

Inside of the prison riots broke out with the news that there were people who believed in them, people who knew that the U.S. government was wrong. The riots both inside and outside of the Georgia prison caused riots around the country, especially in the East Coast, where inmates were scheduled to be executed by the new law of the land. As the news showcased the activities at the prison, other prisoners around the nation watched. As they watched, the prisoners grew extremely violent. Riots broke out in every prison from coast to coast. Guards took televisions and all commissaries away from the inmates, but that only added to their rage. Without the televisions to inform the inmates of riot like acts, the guards felt that things would die down on their own, but they did not. Prison guards were attacked, other inmates were attacked, and breaking points of the prison system were attacked. Inmates did not want to die, especially inmates who had thirty-nine days left on their sentence; inmates like Michael Farmer.

"I hope that Lisa and Jessica stayed home today," Michael thought to himself.

The riot outside was a perfect distraction for Michael to escape without being noticed. First he had to get out of his cell, and after that he believed that he would be caught up in all of the commotion from the people who tried to get in. Not all of the cells were closed when the lack of peace broke out, and so vast majorities of the inmate population were out of their tiered homes. Those who were not free to roam about their cellblock were set free by the other inmates, inmates like Michael Farmer.

"Step one, get free of my cell. Done!" Michael smiled to himself.

The prison guards did their best to barricade the individual cellblocks to keep the prisoners in and the angry mob out. The idea, which was well perceived, failed in a matter of hours. The outsides gates came down. The inside metal mesh screens came down, and the bared doors came unlocked. The state prison in Atlanta, Georgia came under the control of the prisoners and their families. The confusion and turmoil were immense, but the rage that fueled the act lessened as loved ones came together.

"This is Nina Cordova with Channel 6 NEWS at six. On location in Atlanta, Georgia is our very own Emma Watson." The cameras cut over from Nina to Emma. "Are you there Emma?"

"Yes Nina, and thank you. As you can see that prison right behind me has been overrun by friends and family of the maximum

413

security inmates who currently reside there." Emma Watson smiled as the camera recorded her every word.

The guards who were on duty still needed to maintain order, and not let any of the inmates get out of the prison alive. The time to end the lives of the inmates came sooner than first anticipated. The United States military was on track to enter the prison and take control before they exercised the plan for terminating life. The state penitentiary was not due for termination for a while, but the news that the prison had drawn made it a top priority. Riots were out of control, and that prison would be the example that America saw. Guards, who could, escaped out other exits and ran for their freedom. Other guards stood up for what they believed in and the job that they were paid to do. Guards like Joe Adams took what means that they had at their disposal and tried to take control of the prison situation before the military arrived; which could have led to a bigger mess.

"If I could survive banging, then I can survive this," Correctional Officer Adams thought to himself.

Joe Adams, who transferred from California to Georgia, was no stranger to confrontation in the prison environment. While working as a correctional officer for the State of California in *Folsom Prison*, Joe was attacked by seven inmates while he guarded them in the showers.

Joe's partner broke protocol and went off to talk to one of the medical staff while they were on shower duty. Inmate on inmate attacks and rapes while in the shower were down seventy-five percent over the course of five years. Joe had a beanbag gun for riot control, which would have been an immensely painful if hit while naked and wet. Joe thought nothing of his partner's actions, and assumed everything was in order. Joe Adams did not like the idea of watching other men as they showered, and so he looked on as he sometimes did. The naked inmates took advantage of that situation and attacked Correctional Officer Adams. They drug him into the shower, under the warm running water, and held him down. One of the inmates, Cali Ramirez, pulled out a knife that he had keistered and slowly cut off the correction officer's tongue. Joe Adams cried out on pain, but his missing tongue muffled the noise. The inmates stripped their CO and attempted to rape him. They would have succeeded in their attempt, but Joe's partner Ray Turner returned from his get together that jeopardized his partner's life. Correctional Officer Turner fired his beanbag gun right into Cali Ramirez's erection. Joker dropped to the floor in pain, and Cali's accomplices let Joe Adams go. After that Joe took some mandatory time off, and when the state felt that he could return to the work; Joe decided to move far away from home and the situation that haunted him daily.

"I would like to put in for a transfer," Joe informed his boss.

"Where?" The Prison Warden asked with compassion.

"I don't know…maybe Georgia. My Mom has this cousin down there…Lisa. I never met her or nothing, but I need to get out of here." Joe and the Warden talked about the issue at hand, and Joe was ultimately granted his transfer.

As one of the only guards left in the Georgia prison, Correctional Officer Adams stood up for the security of America. He knew that those inmates could not be freed to run the streets of his home.

"These convicted criminals are here for a reason, and they're not getting past me," Joe thought to himself.

Joe Adams reached the locked armory room that housed the weapons that were used by the prison guard up in the towers. The door had an electronic keypad that was inoperable without the proper number combination, which Joe did not know. However, he knew enough about the prison and electronic devises that if the power was ever totally lost that the door locks would be inoperable. That also meant that the doors that protected the inmates from the outside world, the doors that kept the outside people from reaching the inmates, and the doors that separated the remaining guards from danger would also be unlocked.

"Fuck it! No guts no glory," Adams thought. "Man, I wish that Chuck was here. That vato could fix anything."

It was a risk that he had to make. Correction Officer Adams needed to throw the switch to the main breaker off, and then shut off the power to the backup generator that restored power to key areas like the armory and other essential areas of the prison.

The generator was run on diesel fuel, and was housed in its own area outside of the main prison area to avoid any kind of tampering. The problem for Joe was getting from where he was at, to the other side of the facility where the backup generator was housed without being caught. As Joe Adams left his area, he past another guards room that had a small television on. Joe glanced at the TV screen and saw a prison guard photo of Correctional Officer Jenkins posted on it. Joe went into the room and turned the volume up so that he could hear the news flash clearly.

"Charles Jenkins is dead?" Joe whispered mentally to himself.

Correctional Officer Adams pulled out a wheeled office chair from a table, and sat down. He thought about the first time that he met

Chuck Jenkins. He thought about their falling out, and their reunited friendship. If they could do that to a guy like Charles Jenkins; there was no telling what they would do to him. He had to stop these inmates from being freed onto the world.

"I'm sorry Chuck." Joe's eyes welled up a little bit. "If you had been my partner back in *Folsom*, then I would have a tongue to sing out your praise. I never would have left, and you'd be alive today." Joe thought back to their childhood. "A homie always has his homie's back.

Joe had to make it to the backup generator if he was to stop what had happened to his friend from happening to others. Joe remembered that the maintenance service shafts and corridors that led throughout the prison. He located a maintenance entrance to one of those corridors, and cautiously went in. With any luck, the generator room would also have needed maintenance to maintain it properly, and so one of the metal grate floors might lead right to it.

As Joe Adams walked between the prison walls, and between the prison floors; he could faintly make out the sounds of riots as they progressed.

"At least they won't hear me banging on down here. They're too busy with themselves to care about my next move," Joe thought to himself.

Approximately ten minutes later, Joe found what he had been looking for. There was an access panel in the ceiling that was clearly marked "Generator Room." Joe Adams climbed the eight or so feet of the metal ladder rungs that led him up to the locked hatch that separated him from his potential disastrous plan. Unfortunately Joe did not have a key for the silver pad lock, but he did have a small screwdriver that he always kept on his person. Although it was against prison rules; Joe did not care. He was never going to be trapped ever again, and if a screwdriver gave him peace, then so be it. He could use it for prying, for stabbing, or taking out screws. There was a lock, but the old door hinges were screwed to the door from the bottom side, the side that Joe was on.

"I love old buildings," Joe thought to himself and smiled.

Joe removed the screws, and used the lock on the opposite side as the new door hinge. He pushed the access panel open, and climbed into the generator room. The generator was massive, just as Joe thought that it would be. Corrections Officer Adams went to the south wall of the room, and grabbed a toolbox from a small workbench. He rummaged through the toolbox until he found some wire cutters and an adjustable wrench. He took the wrench and turned off the flow of diesel that the generator needed to fire up. Then he took the wire cutters and cut anything electrical that he could find on the generator and in the room. Joe removed the digital control panel plate, and cut everything he could. Then he found a circuit breaker box on the wall, and he cut everything that he could find there after he threw the switch to the off position. When he thought that he was done sabotaging the generator, Joe went back down the hole in the floor, and ran through the maintenance corridor until he had reached the place that he had first entered through.

"Now it is time to kill the power, and see if I can get into the armory area," Joe grimaced to himself as he threw the main power breaker.

The entire place went dark almost instantaneously. The only glimpse of light was the fading of the light bulbs as they lost the power needed to stay lit. Joe waited for a few seconds to see if the emergency backup generator was going to come on. The power was not restored, and Joe's mission to damage the generator was a success. He turned on his flashlight, and followed the hall to the prison armory. Just like Joe had planned, the door opened with nothing more than a turn of the brass doorknob. Correction Officer Joe Adams stepped into a room, and was instantly overwhelmed with the massive amounts of firepower at his command. He grabbed a machine gun off of its rack, and loaded it methodically.

Michael Farmer, and everyone else realized their position when the power turned off. Locked doors opened, and inmates fled towards the exits. On the outside of the prison, it did not take long for the mob to realize that the electronic locks were shut off. People trampled each other as they tore into the stone penitentiary.

"Come and get it." Joe restored the power to the prison, and went to meet his fate.

As the power went up throughout the institution; doors relocked, and people were trapped. The only un-breached room was the cafeteria. The cafeteria had two unbreakable windowed doors that led into it, which were both electronically locked. On one side were the prisoners, and on the opposite side of the cafeteria were their family and friends.

In the center of the cafeteria stood Correctional Officer Adams, who had been armed and ready to retake control of the situation. Both sets of rioting mobs grew even more anxious, and frustrated; they could see each other through the windows, but they could not reach each

other through the last set of doors.

Joe Adams looked back and forth between the two groups and

smiled because he knew that everybody had been trapped deep inside

the prison, and that they could not anything about it.

CHAPTER 34

Blanca came home and found her baby sister sitting on the couch with the inmate who tried to rape and kill her when she first got her job at *Folsom Prison*. Blanca was in shock, and did not know what to do. All she knew was that she had to get Maria and herself a safe distance away from that killer.

"Hola Blanca baby. What's up?" Cali Ramirez nodded his head in the form of a greeting.

"How did you get here? Maria get away from him," Blanca demanded.

"Calm down baby, your sister likes it here by my side. Isn't that right my little college student?" Joker rubbed Maria's knee seductively.

"That's right Cali," Maria answered Joker's question and then turned her attention towards her sister. "What's your trip? You didn't tell me that you had a man in your possession this whole time. You're not trying to keep him all for yourself are you?" Maria winked at Joker.

"No Maria. You need to come with me this very minute." Blanca pleaded with her sister.

"Why Blanca? Cali is a your guest, and you're being a dick," Maria pouted.

"This man right here," Blanca replied to her sister's ranting while she pointed at their houseguest. "This man right here is no friend of mine. His name is Cali the Joker Ramirez. He is the inmate that the dead correctional officer from the TV saved me from."

Maria jumped up, but Joker grabbed her arm and pulled her back down, this time onto his lap.

"Where are you going bonita? We're not finished yet." Joker tried to feel up the young sister.

Blanca looked at Joker, "What do you want from us?"

"To tell you the truth I wanted to finish that blow job that you owed me. But now I find out that you have a sister finer than you, and she's smart too. I might just have to kill you, and take what you owe me out of her." Joker licked his lips and smiled joyfully.

"Please Joker, let my sister go? I'll go with you if that's what you want, but she doesn't have to be here. She is innocent." Blanca tried to reason with disturbed escaped inmate.

"That's nice seeing family caring for family, pero you know that doing sisters is a man's wet dream." Joker ran his hands over Maria's clothed chest area.

"Let her go Joker," Blanca tried to reason with their uninvited guest once again.

Joker Ramirez pushed Maria off of his lap, and onto the floor. "Okay baby sister, you undo my pants while your sister here blows me."

Blanca saw that Maria cried uncontrollably while she scooted toward their capture. Blanca did not know what to do; she could have run, but her sister would have taken the punishment for that. Joker grabbed Maria by the hair and pulled her towards him and then he slapped her across the face with the back of his tattooed right hand.

"Bitch when I say move it, I mean move it. You got that bitch slap for moving like a fucking dead person or something." Joker held Maria by the hair and spit in her face.

Maria stated to unfasten Joker's prison issued blue jeans, when she heard her sister speak.

"What do you want first? A BJ or some pussy?" Blanca slid her right hand over the crotch of her pants.

"Orale...now you're talking. I knew that you sisters were into doing the whole vato thing. Why don't you guys get naked while I watch?" Cali let go of Maria and leaned back in his seat.

"Do you mind if we pick out some music and dim the lights to get the mood right? It's been a while, right?" Blanca kissed the air with her pouted lips.

"Hell yeah Blanca, you can do whatever you need. Just make it fast, and stay right here where I can see you ladies." Cali adjusted his jeans.

Blanca helped Maria off of her knees, and then the two of them went across the living room and stood in front of the CD rack. Both sisters pretended to scan the music selection while they whispered quietly.

"Maria I need you to run when we get a chance," Blanca informed her little sister.

"What about you?" Maria asked worriedly.

"Look, when I'm sucking him off; I'll bite his raping dick off. Then we'll both run and get the cops over here. That vato is going back to prison if he doesn't bleed to death first? Okay?" Blanca rubbed her sister's back in a soothing manner.

"Okay, but do you really have to that?" Maria seemed grossed out at the thought of her sister performing oral sex for their survival.

"I can't see any other way. Survival of the fittest, right?" Blanca winked. "It'll be okay."

The sisters agreed on a classic *Marvin Gaye* album to get everyone relaxed and in the proper sexual mood.

"Hell yeah, this is the jam right here," Joker exclaimed. "Let's get this shit started."

The two sisters went over to the couch where Cali sat and impatiently waited for something to happen. Both women got down onto their knees; Maria reached out and undid Joker's pants, while Blanca started to tug on the pants to pull them down. It was obvious that Cali Ramirez was excited about what was happening to him. Maria started to caress their capture's bare leg in a light and sensual way. Blanca unbuttoned her shirt and reveled that she was not wearing a bra. Then she bent over and tenderly licked the tip of Joker's penis. Then Blanca looked to Joker's eye closed tight face, and then to her sister. Maria knew what Blanca meant, and so she carefully climbed onto her feet and sat in a squatted position; therefore when it was time to run, her feet would already have been under her. Blanca made sure that her sister was secure, and then she did what she promised to do.

Blanca did not completely sever the male membrane, but she might as well have because it was held on by nothing more than some fatty tissue. Blanca spit the blood from her mouth into Joker's face as she and her sister ran for the apartment door. As they ran for freedom,

427

all they could hear were the crying screams of a man in severe pain. They made it to another apartment three doors down within a matter of seconds.

Blanca banged on the white wooden door.

"Rachel let us in…Rachel please." Blanca begged her neighbor through the locked door.

Blanca's neighbor Rachel Guzman opened the door with a sleep-ridden face.

"What's up girl? Why you and your sister all crazy like? Ah shit…what's up with all that blood all over your face?" Rachel looked scared.

"No time to explain Rachel…can I use your phone?" Blanca set the tone of what she needed to accomplish.

"Sure Blanca, but someone needs to tell me what's going on. I mean you all come up in here like you just killed some dude with blood all over your grill and shit." Rachel stepped back to let the two impatient women in.

"Rachel, the phone?" Blanca demanded.

Rachel grabbed the cordless phone from the love seat and handed it to her neighbor.

"Here you go. Who you calling?" Rachel wanted answers.

"The police," Blanca answered as she listened to ringing on the other end of the line.

Maria filled Rachel on what had happened over at her sister's place while they listened to what Blanca told the local police.

"They'll be here in about ten minutes. What should we do until then?" Blanca was hyped up from adrenalin.

"You all need to quit bringing this mess down onto my house. You need to go check on your man and see if his sorry ass is still alive." Rachel pointed towards the door.

"He's not my man bitch. Hey Maria, what if he's dead...what if he's not dead?" Blanca looked at her sister.

The two sisters finally convinced Rachel to go with them. The three terrified, yet curious women each grabbed a knife from Rachel's kitchen counter and headed out the front door. They walked along the sidewalk cautiously making mental notes on any outside changes that may have occurred from Joker's injuries.

"Hey is that blood?" Maria whispered while pointing to a spot ten feet in front of them.

"No, I think that might be a penny or something." Rachel squinted at the object in question.

The girls walked a slow steady pace to Blanca's front door and looked down.

"Oh shit…it is blood." Rachel screeched.

"I told you Rachel that it was blood." Maria looked pleased that she was right, even though she was scared beyond belief.

"Shut up," Rachel demanded.

"Both of you shut up," Blanca scornfully whispered to her friend and to her sister.

The living room curtain was partially opened, and so the thee of them quickly walked past the apartment door, and tried to peak through he window. The problem that they had was that the couch sat against the far wall; which they could not entirely see. Armed with knifes, the three scared women decided to go into the dwelling to check things out.

"You know that the police to me not to enter the residence until they cleared it first. I like cops…they have a good philosophy. They go in first, and make it safe for the rest of us." Blanca looked at the other two for a reaction.

As they entered the house, they could see that Joker was not dead, or at least not dead on Blanca's couch. There was blood all over the couch, the living room floor, the kitchen floor, and some dishtowels that Blanca had left on the counter that morning. However, there was no Joker Ramirez present up to that point. The girls walked in a group of three while the checked the remaining rooms in the apartment. There was no blood present in the master or guest bedrooms, but there was a lot in the bathroom sink and bathtub.

"Where did this guy go? They say that you can't trust a woman because, how could you trust something that bleeds for a week at a time and doesn't die. Hell…this guy has lost more blood than all of my periods combined, and he's still out there walking around." Rachel scoured the hallway for clues.

"Too much info Rachel." Maria wrinkled her nose with disgust.

"Yeah neighbor, my sister is right. Too much information, and gross. Don't forget gross." Blanca copied her sister's facial remarks.

Cali "Joker" Ramirez was not to be found in Blanca's apartment. The three ladies went outside to wait for the police to arrive. After the police got to their destination; Blanca, Maria, and Rachel told them what they had been through, and what they had done. Included in their story was the fact that they actually went back into the apartment after the police strictly told them not to.

"Ladies…you know that a stupid stunt like that could of gotten you killed," the police officer scolded them with compassion.

431

The two male police officers informed the residences to stay outside while they investigated the home. Two more police officers joined the group five minutes later, and looked for any evidence that the escaped convict may have left if he indeed left the premises.

The original policemen who were first on the scene walked out of Blanca's front door, and confirmed that although there was a lot of blood; Joker was not in there. They radioed for the other officers to hear if they had stumbled onto anything that may lead them to the whereabouts of there bleeding fugitive. The officers could not find any clues to follow, and so they returned to the apartment to talk about what had happened.

"There was some blood on the sidewalk, and a little on the grass over there," the officer pointed to a playground area in the center of the complex, "but nothing else. We have to assume that he some how jumped that chain link fence over there, but again there is no blood present. What about the inside…pretty bloody?" One police officer talked to Officer Meyers about his findings.

"Yeah, this young lady did a number on that guy. She's a hero. She saved her life, and the life of her sister." Meyers pointed at Blanca.

"Yeah," Maria interrupted, "my sister bit his dick off."

"With all of the blood that Cali Ramirez has lost; he'll turn up at a medical facility soon enough, if he's not dead already. We'll keep the hospitals on the look out for a man fitting Cali's description and medical wounds. They'll notify us if he shows up needing medical treatment. In the mean time here is my card, and let me get you a case number. If anything happens…if you need to talk, or if he somehow turns back up here…please call me day or night. Here let me write my cell number on the back." The officer took his card back from Blanca, and scribbled his personal cell phone number on the back. He then handed it back to the bravest woman that he had ever met.

"Thanks Officer Myers." Blanca looked down at the card shyly.

"Paul…call me Paul," Officer Meyers insisted.

"Okay Paul. Thanks for all of your help. Unless you would like to come in and help us clean up?" Blanca pointed towards her apartment. "I swear that I'm never going to get my deposit back now." Blanca smiled at the young officer.

"I would love to…I really would, but I have to go and save the world and all. I'm a cop you know," Officer Paul Myers joked as he pointed to his badge.

CHAPTER 35

Colonel Braden, General Rachlav, and Major Striker had walked for a day and a half without a sign of another human.

"I hate this country," General Rachlav grumbled out loud.

Then late in the night, they came to a steep faced bluff above a small grassy valley where the trees cleared, and down in the valley there were a few older homes. The trio decided that if they were going to survive, they would need to steal a car from one of the locals. They climbed down the steep hill to the valley floor. They quickly, yet quietly came upon the first homestead. They could see that there was a light on inside the house, but the light looked as though the residents of the house turned it on every evening before bed. So for all they could see, the homeowners were fast asleep.

"Poor bastards," Striker said as he looked towards the house. "When they wake up in the morning, their *Buick* will be gone."

"American's talk to much. They would rather converse than do any work. That is why Americans are lazy." The Russian General looked into the darkness as he took watch of the area around them.

"It doesn't sound like the Russians talk any less," Striker joked as he neared the locked automobile.

"America is nothing like Russia, nor it's people." Rachlav started to get angry with his companion.

"Enough," Braden said as he looked at both of the men. "We need to get out of here. General," Braden looked at Rachlav as he spoke, "I need you to shut up for a while, and Striker," Jack turned his attention back towards the other man, "I need you to...well...work."

"Even another American can see that you are lazy, and will not work." General Rachlav laughed after Braden came down on Major Striker.

"General?" Braden grabbed the Russian General's shoulder as he walked by. "Please...we need to go now."

Major Striker broke the driver's side front window with his elbow. He opened the car door, and slid onto his back to get access to the wires under the dash. As he started the car, an old *Chevy* pickup truck came around the driveway along the side of the house. The driver, who happened to be the homeowner coming back from his swing shift job at a local paper processing plant, jumped out of his truck with a shotgun in hand.

"What in the hell is going on here," John Munster asked impatiently. "Now I want you petty thieves to put you hands up and freeze. Comprende?" Mr. Munster waved the twelve-gauge back and forth with his right index finger firmly on the cold metal trigger.

Striker tried to get out of the car to flee, but the homeowner blasted him in the chest as he tried to turn and run. Colonel Braden made it to the opposite side of the pickup truck, but General Rachlav was in the homeowner's sights.

"I said freeze," Munster reminded the trespassers. "One down…two to go."

Braden needed to act quickly because Rachlav was between the *Chevy* truck and the *Buick* that they had tried to steel. The homeowner took aim, and Colon Braden ran and tackled Rachlav as the shot went off. Rachlav was fine thanks to Braden, but Braden took some pellets in the right leg and in his side.

"Damn that hurt." Braden looked down at his bleeding leg.

"Why did you save me?" The General asked as he pulled himself into a squatted position behind the automobile.

"Some other time General." Braden waited patiently. "Right now, we have to get out of here, but I promise that we'll talk later."

"You sound like my wife." The General paused as he thought how odd that her memory would come back at such an inopportune time.

"Lets do it," Braden said as he briefly looked at his Russian counterpart.

As the homeowner tried to quickly reload his gun, Braden got up with his weapon drawn and told the homeowner to drop his weapon and go inside the house. Rachlav cut the phone and power wires that led into the log home, and then he and Colonel Braden lifted Major Striker into the back of the running pickup truck. Within a minute the three fugitives were off on their way to freedom.

"Sir...I do not want to shoot you, but I will. Do you understand?" Colonel Braden spoke slowly and calmly to the homeowner.

Mr. Munster shook his head to signify that he understood the Colonel.

"What is your name?" Braden pleasingly demanded an answer from the balding man before him.

"Munster...John Munster," was the shaken reply.

"Good...John! Now put your weapon down, and walk towards the house. When you have taken seven steps, I want you to drop your pickup keys in the dirt." Braden held his pistol out as he commanded the frightened civilian to obey his orders.

John Munster did as he was told.

"Sir, we need to barrow your truck. I know that you don't like the idea, but it will be returned to you. We need to get our partner to a hospital because of his injuries that were sustained by you." Colonel Braden tried to get inside the homeowner's head psychologically.

"Colonel we need to go," Rachlav informed the American hero.

"Help me grab his arms and legs so that we can load him into the bed of the truck," Braden instructed Rachlav as they reached towards the severely wounded Striker.

John Munster froze after he dropped his keys on the ground, and waited for further orders from his potential captures. "Wh...what wou...would you like...ike me to do now?" Munster stuttered.

"I'm glad that you're still with us John." Braden looked up from the wounded soldier. "My Russian friend here is going to cut the power so that we can get a head start. So, I need you to go into the house with him and grab what you need until your power is restored. It's easier to find things now rather than later. Flashlight, candles, extra batteries, just grab what you need." Braden nodded an okay to Rachlav, who followed John Munster into the home.

Colonel Braden went to slash the tires on the car that they had originally tried to steal, but changed his mind. "Tires are freaking expensive," Braden whispered to himself, "but I can't let this guy follow us or get to a neighbors house that quickly." Braden looked around and saw a lug wrench in the back of the opened truck bed.

"That'll do," Braden exclaimed to himself. He popped the truck release latch on the *Buick's* driver's side floor panel and walked around and lifted the truck lid. The Colonel lifted the carpeted flooring and fished out the car's lug wrench.

"As long as he doesn't try to go anywhere, this should work out just fine." Braden removed all of the lug nuts from the car's four tires, and tossed them in the back of the pickup next to the bleeding Major Striker.

Braden limped up to the house and walked in the front door. "Time to go General, and…oh yeah John…you won't be able to drive the *Buick* because the lug nuts are in back of the *Chevy*. So when you get your truck back, you should be able to drive both vehicles." Braden gave a single wave to the powerless homeowner. "Good bye John."

Colonel Braden drove the best that he could with his wounds, but it was Striker that he was worried about. They could not just show up at an area hospital, but they desperately needed a doctor. Braden and Rachlav had extensive medical combat training, but that nights situation was more than either of them could handle without proper supplies. Braden and Rachlav decided to ditch the stolen truck in front of a payphone booth. That way they could report the stolen truck, and the injuries to their traveling partner to the 911 operator. Rachlav and Braden found a used car lot a few blocks up the road, and commandeered the best looking one.

"American muscle." Braden examined the shiny red automobile. "A *1966 Ford Mustang*. What a car?"

Rachlav walked around the car and intrigued Braden when he exclaimed, "Not just a *Mustang*, but a *1966 Shelby GT-350 Fastback*."

"You know your cars?" Braden smiled at the Russian.

"Americans have good cars." Rachlav gave a semi half smirk.

The original plan was to get to Seattle, where there were a large number of Russian forces, so that Braden could somehow stop the war. He just did not know how, and then there was the dire situation of Seattle being in ruins. So, Braden had to find other means to accomplish his mission. Little did Colonel Braden know, was that he had already started peace negotiations with Russia by saving General Rachlav's life on more than one occasion.

Rachlav himself started to feel as though his precious Nika was right about the American Colonel Jack Braden; maybe he could be trusted, and maybe not all Americans are rapists as he once thought.

Time would tell, and for the first time since Nika's attack, Rachlav felt a little relief from his pain.

"Nika, why did you send me this American?" Rachlav looked up towards Heaven as he talked to his deceased wife.

Braden drove as far as he could before the pain of his injuries overtook him. They found a secluded spot off a dirt road so that they could pull over to let Braden rest. Rachlav insisted that the Colonel let him examine the wounds, because if it were not for him then there would not be any wounds to care for.

"Please Colonel." The Russian soldier looked at the American soldier. "Trust is the first step towards peace."

For a minute while Rachlav tended to Braden; Braden saw a less harsh side of Rachlav...an almost caring side. Rachlav got Braden patched up enough so that they could continue with their journey to freedom.

"There you go." Rachlav held out his right hand and helped Braden to his feet. "Not bad for a dirty Russian...no?"

Braden laughed, "No...not at all my friend."

The two running fugitives decided to get to the largest city they could get to in a day or two. A larger city made sense because they would stick out less there then they would in a smaller town. When they got to the city, a phone was the first thing they needed to find.

Rachlav and Braden knew that Ubiikobyla's phones would be tapped, and so Rachlav dialed a coded number and only spoke one word into the receiver…"Denver."

Within a matter of hours, Russian helicopters landed within the confines of City Park in Denver, Colorado. Colonel Braden and General Rachlav flew off to an undisclosed location somewhere north of Denver. There, Russian President Ubiikobyla awaited his friend's arrival. As Braden got out of the plane, he was immediately arrested by the Russian military, and taken to a small cabin on the south side of the complex. Rachlav could do nothing but watch his men take the American traitor off to extract information from him. General Rachlav then turned to see his friend waiting with opened arms to great him back from the dead.

"My General…how has you vacation to the United States been?" The Russian President joked whole heartily as he hugged his missing companion.

"What is the status of our war efforts?" Rachlav went straight to work. "I need the American Colonel released immediately for further investigation into the mind of America."

"This, I cannot do." Ubiikobyla looked shyly away from the General.

"You have no choice." Rachlav walked up to the President and stared him down. "I am taking back control of my forces, and with that control comes the power to decide on the fait of political and military criminals. The American is needed to help end this blood bath." Rachlav turned his back on his country's leader.

Rachlav convinced Ubiikobyla to release Colonel Braden into his custody. To make matters a bit more stressful, Rachlav invited Braden to dine with them; even though Ubiikobyla and every other Russian at the table strongly disagreed with the decision. However, Rachlav was known for making sound decisions for his people, and so they allowed it for the time being. As the group dined they spoke about living in America compared to living in Russia. Most of the conversation pertained to topics other than the war.

"America does have a lot to offer, but I do not see *Vodka* on the dinner table...no?" One of the Russian leaders spoke to Braden from across the table as the entire crowd laughed.

"*Vodka* no, but cheeseburgers...yes," Braden countered smugly.

After the meal was finished, Rachlav asked for a special meeting between himself, President Ubiikobyla, and Colonel Braden. Again Ubiikobyla was not happy with the decision, but he allowed it.

"President Ubiikobyla, it is vital to our survival that we speak strategy with Colonel Braden tonight." Rachlav paced back and forth of the seated Russian leader.

"I trust you, and you are my confidant, but how can I trust your decision after being brainwashed by the Americans for all of these months." Ubiikobyla made a valid point.

"I have seen the worst of the worst, and Colonel Braden is one of the good guys. If he believes that America is worth saving, then so do I." Rachlav stopped pacing and looked at the face of his friend.

"But why?" Ubiikobyla simply asked.

"Because I saw my Nika." General Rachlav waved his hand, "perhaps in a dream, but she told me to trust this man. He has saved my life, and for this I owe him a chance to right for all of us." Rachlav kneeled before his leader and asked for his support. "Please Mr. President...I was wrong."

"Okay General...okay." President Ubiikobyla took his friend's hand and patted it softly.

Rachlav told Ubiikobyla about the Russian planes that the American's had and what they had done with them. Braden continued to address the situation by saying that a few higher government officials tricked the American people, and so they should not be held responsible for not questioning orders, no matter how wrong they were. Rachlav told Ubiikobyla that the war was the wrong thing to do in the first place because he had one nation attack another nation over the death of a single individual. Rachlav understood that now, and he tried to convince Ubiikobyla of his mistake.

"Those were the Russian planes that fired nuclear missiles on the western coast of the country." Ubiikobyla was in awe of what the United States could fathom as the right course of action.

Colonel Braden was free to do what he wanted after that first night with Rachlav and Ubiikobyla. He was of course, heavily watched and for the most part his every move was with a few armed escorts. Braden needed to regain his innocents so that he could continue on with a semi-normal life. He told Rachlav that he needed to leave to search for some answers. He also asked Rachlav for some money, clothes, and a car to get him to New York. General Rachlav agreed, but only if they went together.

"I need to go tonight," Braden explained to Rachlav. "I am not, nor ever have been, a traitor to my country. I had a deep cover assignment to infiltrate the Guantanamo Bay Cuba Black Site to get next to you. We needed this war ended, and you seemed like the most likely point of contact. However, my inside man is dead, and I'm a traitor hanging out with the enemy." Braden had a worried look to his face. He knew what he had to do, and the consequences of his actions, but the reality had set in as his mission wound up.

"I will go too. I have never seen New York City, I have only bombed it." Rachlav looked embarrassed by his bad humored joke. "I'm sorry Colonel...I meant no disrespect."

CHAPTER 36

In New York City, the devastation of the war was still evident, even though the rebuilding process started a couple years prior. When Colonel Braden and Russian General Rachlav arrived in the city, they went straight to the *Chase Manhattan Bank* where Braden had some personal belongings in a safety deposit box. Colonel Braden walked into the bank as General Rachlav waited outside to absorb some fresh air. Braden went up to one the waiting tellers and informed her that he was here to close out his account and clean out his safety deposit box.

"Hello," Braden said as he glanced at the bank teller's nametag.

"What can I do for you today?" The teller smiled back from behind the high counter.

"Claire, I would like to close out my account if at all possible." Braden returned the cashier's smile to help make her feel at ease.

"Well, let's see what we can do for you." Claire typed on her computers keyboard. "*Chase Manhattan* would hate to loose you as one of our clients Mr. Braden, and we have a lot of different banking options to better help fit your needs."

Jack Braden surveyed the open banking area. "I appreciate all of your help, but I'm relocating to an area were you couldn't help me. I'm sorry." Braden made Claire feel warm and relaxed.

"I'm sorry too Mr. Braden, but I'll need to get the Branch Manager Mr. Perkins to aid you further." Claire looked around to see if she could spot her gray haired employer. "It's policy to get the manager involved when large accounts are closed out and or safety deposit boxes."

"No problem." Jack scanned the area for the Branch Manager. "Is that him over there?" Jack asked the young teller as he pointed towards the center of the room.

Claire followed Jack's direction with her eyes. "Yes it is. I'll be right back." Claire left her post and quickly walked behind a long row of counter space and bankers.

The teller went and got the branch manager, who came and spoke to Colonel Braden and welcomed him back. He seemed surprised that a low-key customer like Jack Braden would come in twice within a month's time. Which only made Braden play it off like he had indeed been there, but in reality he had not been to this bank in over a year.

"Mr. Braden," Perkins stuck out his hand to greet his account holder. "What a pleasant surprise having you back so soon. Usually we only see you once a year, not twice a month."

Braden accepted Mr. Perkins' hand in a quick embrace. "Business called and so I rose to the occasion."

"I understand that. Now, what can we do for you here at *Chase Manhattan*? Young Claire here tells me that you are thinking about closing your accounts with us?" Mr. Perkins briefly put his left hand gently on Claire's clothed shoulder as he mentioned her name.

Jack glanced over to Claire. "Yes, Claire is correct. You know business?" The Colonel shrugged nonchalantly.

"Indeed I do," the bank manager nodded. "However, if I could urge you to keep at least one of your accounts active, then we could easily continue our relationship if business ever swings back the other way."

"I like you Mr. Perkins, and so I'll consider it." Braden gave a suave sort of smile to the two bankers. "In the mean time, how about my safety deposit box?"

"Of course." Perkins and Braden once again shook hands as they left each other's company.

The bank manager then called over one of the senior bankers to escort Mr. Braden down to the vaulted area. In the safe Braden found a few of his different identities in the forms of passports, identifications, social security cards, and credit cards. There were also stacks of cash from different countries around the world, but most of it was in U.S. currency. As he put all of the items into a black duffle bag that he had also stored in the box, Braden noticed a large manila envelope under his two black 9 mm pistols, and platinum rings. He hid the weapons, put the rings in his pocket, and pulled out the envelope. Inside he found pictures of himself as different people while he was under cover over the last few years. Most importantly there were pictures and information about his current mission. Somehow Secretary of Defense John Andrews got into the bank and placed all of this classified documentation for him to clear himself incase anything ever happened. Braden was ecstatic, and as he left the bank he tipped his attendant with three one hundred dollar bills.

"Thank you sir," the attended happily said as he stuffed the money into his pants pocket.

Outside the bank, Braden informed General Rachlav that they needed to go to Washington D.C. to see the President of the United States. Rachlav felt as though the idea that Braden had was a bad one, but in their short time together he had come to trust the American Colonel.

"We are fugitives from your Country's military," Rachlav informed Braden. "We cannot just walk into the White House and have tea with your Country's leader without raising some sort of awareness."

"Relax my Russian friend." Braden playfully slapped Rachlav on the back. "I was planning on it."

"What? Raise suspicion?" Rachlav looked worried, as Braden laughed out loud.

In Washington, Braden decided that he and Rachlav should walk right up to the front door of the White House and knock. They did not even make it through the front gate when armed U.S. soldiers swarmed both men. Colonel Braden demanded an audience with President Mason, but all they got were handcuffs and shackles. The newly imprisoned duo waited for an opening to devise a plan of escape, when General Nathan Fox and his group of loyal followers joined them.

"Well, well, if it isn't the plane thieves. The only men to ever escape from Area 51, and to almost live to tell about it." The smug Fox took a sip of his steaming hot coffee. "You two almost ended it for me, but I knew that you would come here. You had to come here."

"General Nathan Fox…your reputation for being a real dick doesn't quite cover it." Braden would have killed the traitor on the spot if he could have. "How did you know that we would come here?" Braden asked suspiciously.

"To kill the President of the United States of course." Fox sat down on a light brown metal fold up chair and scooted closer to his soon to be famed prisoners. "As I see it, the two of you conglomerated in an attempt to tear the United States apart. First you bombed New York, and then you laid low. When the time was right, you put a team of rouge pilots together and took out most of the West Coast. Finally, to cover your tracks and to finish what you started…you killed President Mason." Nathan Fox sat up, folded his arms across his chest, and laughed. "Too bad you boys didn't consider me in your little equation."

"No worries…right Colonel?" Rachlav looked at Braden and smiled.

The conceded notion maddened the U.S. General. "What's he talking about?" Fox grabbed Braden by the shirt as Fox's shaken finger pointed to Rachlav.

Braden smiled, "My foreign friend was just saying that this was going a lot easier than we had expected. Who knew that the biggest pussy of them all would be interrogating us?"

General Fox composed himself, and turned his back to his smiling prisoners. "Too bad that you killed the President before I personally killed you in a massive fire fight right inside the White House itself. The country will mourn, and under Martial Law, I will lead this broken country into a time of reunification. The North, the South, the East, and the West will be once again whole, and I will be its fearless President."

"Sorry President Dick…less, but that isn't going to happen." Braden tried to adjust his tight handcuffs. As I see it, I killed you for being a traitor to our Nation, broken or not. Your death was not glorified, nobody knew your name, and you died a pathetic death; just like you lived your pathetic life." Braden spoke confidently to his capture.

General Fox was pleased that the two individuals who could destroy his career, and possibly his life were finally caught. Fox decided that torture first, and questions later was the best thing for Colonel Braden and General Rachlav. Ten minutes or so into the beating by Fox's men; President Mason entered General Fox's private mobile command center. Immediately he ordered the abuse to cease, and to have the prisoners escorted into the White House.

"General Fox, what is the meaning of this?" The President ordered.

Fox rose to his feet to face his Commander in Chief. "Well sir, these two men were caught in a foiled attempt to assassinate your life. You may recognize the one on the left as Russian General Rachlav who had been caught and held in Gitmo Bay before his escape earlier this month."

"And the other one?" President Mason asked.

"That sir is a traitor to our country. In fact I had planned to hang him for treason a while back, but John Andrews kept me from doing so. We believe that he was the brains behind General Rachlav's escape and the original bombing on New York City." Nathan Fox spoke as he looked at the two prisoners.

"His name?" The President asked in a stern voice.

"Jack Braden. Former Colonel within our ranks." Fox looked at Mason with a questioned looked on his face.

"Have the two prisoners taken to the Oval Office. I have an idea that doesn't concern you," president Mason demanded.

General Fox waived for his guards to follow the President's command. "Is there anything else, sir?"

As the male soldiers left to take the prisoners away, Mason stayed behind to have a few words with the heated American General. "Yes Nathan, there is."

Back in the White House, President Mason told the guards to remove the restraints from the prisoners, and then to leave. He needed to talk to them privately, without any of his words getting back to his famous General Fox. Colonel Braden told the President where to send one of his men to go pick up the evidence that Braden needed to prove his innocents and how he worked solely for John Andrews.

"It's okay Private," President Mason spoke to one of the young Marines that stood guard over the brave prison escapees. "I don't think that they'll be going anywhere for the moment." The president winked at Jack, and then turned his attention back towards the Marines. "Why don't you men leave us a lone for a little bit?"

"Sir," one of the Marines stated to say to the President, "General Fox instructed us not to let these fugitives out of our sight."

"I understand Private, but I think that we'll be okay." President Mason waved the armed guards out of the Oval Office.

"Yes sir." The two Marines un-cuffed the prisoners, left the famed room, and shut the door behind them.

The President refocused his attention on Colonel Braden and Russian General Rachlav. "You boys seem to be in a heap of trouble." Mason shook his head in disbelief. "Now why would you come here?"

"To prove my innocents Mr. President," Braden looked the Leader of the Free World dead in the eye as he spoke.

The president walked across the room and ran his hand atop of the *Resolute Desk.* "Did you know that this desk dates way back? It was a gift from *Queen Victoria* to *President Hayes* in 1880."

"Yes sir," Braden answered what may have been a rhetorical question. "The *H.M.S. Resolute* was made into a fine piece of furniture," Braden snickered at his own sense of humor.

President Mason smiled at Braden's carefree way. "Not every President has used it though. Did you that it was altered twice? Once for *F.D.R.*, and once for *Ronald Reagan.*" President Mason picked up a file from the top of his desk and handed it Jack. "I only mention the *Resolute Desk* because of its strong historical connection to our Nation's past. A completely different historical connection then that of one of our Nation's most famed leaders…*President Abraham Lincoln.* He and I both have declared Martial Law. The difference is that they built *Lincoln* a statue, which you will see in those surveillance photos." President Mason pointed to the folder in Jack's lap.

Braden and Rachlav flipped through the file folder. "Yep...you have us on camera," Jack handed the file back to the President.

"Colonel, the question is why?" Mason leaned against the corner of his desk. "Why would you go to a public place before you made your way here? You had to know that you would be tracked?"

Braden liked the history lesson that the President gave them about his desk, and so Jack gave a similarly based answer. "Did you know that the plans for the *Lincoln Memorial* were first proposed in 1867? Of course the idea was put on the back burner, until 1910. In 1914, *Daniel Chester French* and the *Piccirilli* brothers started their masterpiece to the late President, and in 1922 the *Lincoln Memorial* opened for the world to enjoy. A little known fact," Colonel Braden continued as he glanced back and forth between the other two men in the room, "was that although the original 1867 idea was pretty much scrapped, the underbelly of the design stayed in tact. There is a room, a very large room, under the statue of our late great President. It was to be used to hide runaway slaves as they made their way to freedom. Not many people know about the room, and so I figured it would be a great place to hide the evidence that would free me."

457

President Mason smiled and shook his right index finger at Colonel Braden. "I like your answer. You would be a fool to bring the evidence with you, because it may not have seen the light. So you hid it right under our noses. If it's okay with you, I would like to send one of my most trusted men to go and get the evidence?" The President held up his right hand as if he were swearing on *The Bible* itself.

"That is why we are here Mr. President." Jack shifted uneasily in his soft seat.

President Mason brought in one of his most highly trusted agents from the *Secret Service* and filled him in on what he needed to do. The agent left without a word, and so the President walked over and sat behind his desk.

While the three waited in the Oval Office, President Mason told his two visitors that he had been expecting them both for some time. Secretary of Defense Andrews had explained to the President about the mission, and that Braden would come to the White House after he found his safety deposit box. The Secretary of Defense also informed the President that Braden would be bringing the Russian General with him if he had succeeded in his mission.

"You know Colonel Braden, John Andrews was a close and trusted friend? So close in fact, I knew about the two of you coming here before you did." Mason leaned forward towards his old wood desk and propped himself up on his elbows. "And that is why I believe everything that you said as the truth."

After the top-secret documents were in the hands of the President of the United States, did Colonel Braden sit back and sigh a sign of relief. The President excused himself so that he could go over the documents himself without any interruptions. When the President had left the room, Rachlav got up and walked around and admired one of the free worlds most recognized landmarks.

"So this is the most famous office in the entire world?" General Rachlav sarcastically asked no one. "I do not see the connection to greatness. Like this old desk…it is nice yes, but still just an old desk." Rachlav ran his fingers lightly over the top of the dust free *Resolute Desk*.

The President went over the documents that Colonel Braden had brought with him from New York, and the ones that his friend John Andrews had given him before he died. Mason went back to meet with his guests that he had in the Oval Office to inform them that he had issued complete pardons for the both of them. This meant that Colonel Braden was to retain his rank, and was able to move on with his life. General Rachlav on the other hand was a different story. No charges of being a war criminal would come against him, but he was to be deported from the United States immediately. Braden thanked the President, but proposed an alternate idea before the plan was finalized. Russian President Ubiikobyla was in the United States, and he was willing to listen to peace talks with the United States government.

"I have issued Presidential Pardons for both of you based on the overwhelming evidence that supported your claim." President Mason shook both of the free men's hands in a gratified manner.

"And what of General Fox?" Colonel Braden asked the Commander in Chief.

"He is being dealt with. I would not worry too much about him at this time. We have bigger fish to fry, if you get my meaning?" The President motioned the two men to retake their seats.

Thank you sir," Braden said as he sat down.

"Unfortunately for you General Rachlav, we'll have to ask you to leave our war ridden country immediately." The president of the United States looked almost apologetic to his Russian guest.

"Sir, if I may," Braden interrupted the President before he could say another word. "I...we...have a plan."

"Yes, Mr. President," Rachlav entered the conversation. "My country's President is outside of Denver, Colorado and is willing to speak realistically about the hopes of peace between our two nations."

President Mason stood up. "So am I gentlemen. It is said that war creates men. I say that war creates monsters."

CHAPTER 37

Peace talks between the United States and the Russian Federation were held in Berlin, Germany. Germany was a friendly and neutral country to both opposing parties. Russia answered questions on the actual reason war was declared, and their tactics concerning the United States maximum-security prison system. The United States also answered questions about the Geneva Convention, Russian technology, and Martial Law. The three-day peace negotiations went well, with neither side holding any real grudges; President Mason and President Ubiikobyla even congratulated each other on their use of unique wartime strategies.

"Mr. President...my ally," Russian President Ubiikobyla hugged President Mason as he greeted him after the final verdict. "I liked the cunning way that you used Russian planes to attack your own country to gain support back from your own nation, but also from around the globe. However, I do not like the way that you got those planes, but it is...how you say...water under the road."

"Bridge," Mason corrected Ubiikobyla. "It's water under the bridge."

"Of course…bridge. What was I thinking?" The Russian President laughed.

"President Ubiikobyla, was this war between our two great nations worth it?" Mason asked with the most sincere look on his face.

"What war is ever worth the high price tag of human life?" Ubiikobyla answered the American President's question with his own question. "How hard would you fight, or how far would you take it for the love of a woman?"

"Any woman?" The U.S. leader smiled"

"The woman?" Ubiikobyla put a single finger in the air to symbolize the number one.

"To Hell and back," Rich Mason answered his newfound friend.

"That is what I like to hear, for this war was in all actuality…a love story. Maybe not like in the fairy tales, but a love story never the doubt." The Russian leader threw his arm around President Mason's shoulder, as the two men walked out together. "Let us celebrate with a drink. I feel that Russia's finest *Vodka* is in order."

Back in the United States, Martial Law was once again revoked. People were free to do as they pleased, as long as it was in the confines of the law. Due process was also reinstated, making the *Bill of*

Attainder and *ex post facto* laws that were in affect, once again illegal and against the Constitution. The United States of America still stood for freedom, and the American people once again came together to aid friends, family, and strangers. It would be a long time before the ruins of the West Coast of the United States were as they once were, and in many instances they would never be the same. Nobody would forget, and nobody felt, as they should. Other countries came to the aid of the United States, including Russia. Groups from all over the globe came to help the country that had helped so many other countries over the last century.

As the rebuilding of America started to take form, trials in Washington D.C. also started. There were questions that the American people needed answers to for the heeling to start. Why did so many Americans have to die to prove a point? Martial Law was supposed to be used to protect the innocent from the aggressors, not persecute, kill and injure them.

There was talk of impeachment for President Mason, and even having him stand trial as a war criminal against the people of the United States. The Death Penalty was a punishment that had never been handed down to any of the previous Presidents in the entire history of the United States. Democracy does not work under the guidelines of

Martial Law, and the power of a nation under the control of one individual is rarely good for it's people. There was no bright side to the outcome of the war. Sure there could have been more Americans and Russians killed in the name of revenge, but the strategies used were evil in nature.

President Mason never had to stand the trials of a war criminal, and he was never impeached as the President of the United States. The Death Penalty and the impeachment charges were taken off the bargaining table in lieu of a bigger bargaining chip. President Mason would have to step down willingly as the President of the United States of America, and serve a sentence of no less than five years in a heavily protected minimum-security prison; plus he would have to give up his co-conspirators, and testify against General Nathan Fox for his crimes against the American people. General Fox was the scapegoat that Congress needed to somewhat satisfy the need for payment for what had happened to their nation during the reign of Martial Law.

General Fox was convicted in Seattle, Washington on all counts four months after the trials had started.

The most highly publicized, viewed, and world wide televised execution happened when General Nathan Fox was hanged in centrally located Yakima, Washington for his crimes against humanity.

CHAPTER 38

Major Eric Striker, who was believed to be killed after his plane was shot down during the Seattle bombings, was given, along with all of the other American pilots who piloted the Russian fighters, a postmortem dishonorable discharge, and was not allowed to be buried with other dead American soldiers. However, Striker's body was never found, which would always give his friends hope. Like the story of an unknown male who was never located by local police after leaving a small area hospital for injuries related to being shot in the chest with a shotgun after an attempted car-jacking incident in a remote area a few days after Striker's plane went down.

"That had to have been Eric. I tell you that they located his plane somewhere in that general area." Emma Watson informed her cousin, Adrian Bachmeier, as the two of them sat and watched the World News on television in a pub in downtown London, England.

"How would a small town folk lore make its way all the way from the United States to the World News? And how do you know Eric again?" Adrian took a large swig of his amber colored beer.

"Don't you follow the news?" Emma scowled at her visiting cousin. "Eric Striker was the illegitimate son of General Nathan Fox who was hanged for his part in the U.S. Martial Law thing. Eric's body was never discovered, and so the whole thing created this buzz about him. It's like an old fashion mystery."

"Where is Eric Striker? Is he dead, or is he a real life zombie?" Adrian almost fell off of his bar stool laughing hysterically as he mocked his journalist younger cousin.

The offended Emma turned and actually pushed Adrian as he laughed, which resulted in him loosing his balance for a second time and landing forcefully on the hardwood floor with a thud.

Adrian looked up unfazed, "What was that for cousin?"

"For mocking me." Emma stood up, and put her hands out, "Come here you big baby." Adrian took her hands, as Emma helped him stagger to his feet.

"Thank you," Adrian said as he bowed. "How do you know Eric again?"

"I met him before the war. He e-mailed me a couple of times, and said that he was a friend of yours back when you were kids. He sent me this picture of me that you had given him of me, and so we talked, and became pretty good friends," Emma happily explained.

"How did you know that the picture was from me?" Adrian asked offensively.

Emma shook her head in disbelief of Adrian's attitude.

"Because the back of the picture said, 'Here is a picture of my beautiful cousin Emma in England. Good luck!' Signed by you...you big dumb ox."

"I remember that," Adrian laughed. "I can't believe that you guys hooked up, and that Eric might still be alive." The two drunken family members turned their attention back to the TV and their beers.

Back in the United States, Colonel Braden was fully exonerated, and was given another medal that he could not show anyone. The life that he had worked for Secretary of Defense John Andrews was no more, but his dedication to his country demanded a promotion. Braden changed careers within his ranks to become a speaker of peace for the United States in foreign war ridden nations. The newly appointed General Braden had seen enough killing, but more importantly he had done enough killing, and so he promoted alternative strategies other than war. The new President of the United States and Secretary of Defense held out hope that General Braden would resume his previous role if and when his country needed him. That time came sooner than anticipated for Braden, but before he decided to go back to that old way of life or not, he chose to take on the most important mission of his life…he chose to go home…he chose Beth.

"General Braden, China has developed a biochemical weapon that has us very concerned," the President informed Braden.

"President Blevins, there is always something, and I'm willing to do my part to maintain world peace, but I have to do something far more important first. I hope that you understand." Jack stood up, and walked out the meeting.

A day later, Jack sat down in front of Beth's grave and asked her how her day was, and then he proceeded to tell her all about his life, and how he had been scared to come home; scared of the memories and the feelings that they would produce.

"Beth I love you! It wasn't fair what happened to you…to us. We were perfect; we were the ones that people would see holding hands in our eighties. That night…the night that you died…we never got to finish the ceremony. You died before I could place the ring on your finger."

Braden took the two platinum rings out of his pocket and placed one of them on his left ring finger. He then dug up a bit of the grass from atop of the burial plot and placed the other ring in the ground.

As Braden covered the ring with the sod and dirt, the wind came up, and through the trees he heard the words, "I do!"

"Beth...I'm sorry...I should never have left you. Please forgive me? Will you save a place for me...a place in eternity? I swear, I'll never leave you alone like that again."

Braden sat there the entire afternoon talking as if he could see and hear Beth, and he kept his promise. Jack Braden went home as often as he could.

General Rachlav went back to Russia with a new view of the world. He was able to morn the life and death of his wife, Nikolaevna. Somewhere, somehow; Rachlav found a new respect for women, and their rights as equals to all men. General Rachlav converted his upscale home into a woman's shelter for raped and abused women. The shelter, which he named *Nika's Safe Haven for Women*, was opened and running in no time. The shelter took in women, trained women to work outside of the home, trained women to think for themselves; it also taught women techniques for self-defense, and it did so much more for thousands of women across Russia. The only person that Rachlav would even consider running the facility for him was Ekaterina's sister. Since Nika did not have any sisters, and a man could not run that program efficiently; Rachlav turned to the family of his wife's friend who was killed in the attack by those American swimmers.

"Ekaterina's memory should also be remembered, and honored for being a strong Russian woman who wanted more out of life." Rachlav sat with Ekaterina's family as he told him of his ideas for the future of Russia and the world.

That new and very popular Rachlav became world renowned for his work for peace and equality. That was what led General Rachlav to become President Rachlav of Russia.

Rachlav stated the oath of the Presidential Office just as his friend and mentor Ubiikobyla once had, *"I vow, in the performance of my powers as the President of the Russian Federation to respect and protect the rights and freedoms of man and citizen, to observe and protect the Constitution of the Russian Federation, to protect the sovereignty and independence, security and integrity of the state and to serve the people faithfully."*

Both General Jack Braden and President Dmitrievich Rachlav were recognized for their efforts and accomplishments towards a better future and became joint *Nobel Peace Prize* winners.

"We look back at the first *Nobel Peace Prize* in 1901 when *Frédéric Passy* shared the award with the founder of the *Red Cross*,

Henry Dunant. Those were the men that made this world great, and those are the type of men and qualities that we look for when we choose our candidates. General Jack Braden of the United States and President Dmitrievich Rachlav of Russia have those same ideals about the future. What separates these two men from any of the other winners is that they both came from war and hate. They both lead their nations through turmoil and tribulation, before they found the passage of peace within their own hearts. Enemies…to collogues…to friends. Please put your hands together for this years *Nobel Peace Prize* winners General Braden and President Rachlav."

Both men took the stage together, but only the Russian President spoke, "Change can start with one."

The applause from the crowd rang out, as President Rachlav raised his hand to silence the spectators. Rachlav and Braden looked at each other, and then at the group of people in front of them.

"As we come together today in Oslo, Norway in the beautiful *Oslo City Hall*," President Rachlav scanned the walls of the room as he spoke, "it is many who changed my life and the life of my close friend General Jack Braden. However, it was one man who helped change both of our ways of thinking. A man that neither of us knew, but we're touched by his mark on society. Charles Jenkins was a man among men. It could be said that he died honorably, if there was ever any honor in death. He became the face of America during the war, and the face of the world after it." President Rachlav glanced over at his friend as both men raised their checks into the air. "General Braden and myself would like to donate our prize money to the Charles Jenkins Foundation. So please join us as we link up via satellite to the Charles Jenkins Memorial Park in Los Angeles, California where U.S. President Blevins is awaiting us."

"Welcome to today's celebration here in beautiful California," President Blevins spoke as the entire world watched. "I would like to thank U.S. General Jack Braden and Russian President Dmitrievich Rachlav for their efforts to make our world a better place. Charles Jenkins was an inspiration to us all, and it saddens me to think that his death was the only way for us to realize that now known fact about one of history's most profound heroes." President Blevins looked around at the enormous mass of spectators around him. "People have come from all over the globe to pay respect to a man that most have never met, but whose legacy will carry on for generations to come. We have a few speakers today, and our first guest has a truly unique and fascinating story on life and why he is here today, but I'll let him tell you all about it. So please welcome Michael Farmer and his family to the stage."

www.ingramcontent.com/pod-product-compliance
Lightning Source LLC
Chambersburg PA
CBHW030029030726
47500CB00001B/24